Death Of An Angel

bins, empty and scorched, their bases burned away by fire, so that anyone who was civic minded enough to dump rubbish into them was wasting their time, as the crisp packets, newspapers and detritus blowing freely around the square attested.

"There was supposed to be more," he muttered to himself, as another gust – straight from the Baltic, he figured – swept across the square and caught at him, making his eyes water.

Eddie had only wanted another drink, but after some stupid kid had made that comment about his hearing the voices, and laughed at him, he'd gotten upset, and – although he knew he was supposed to stay calm – he'd shouted at the little bastard, telling him that he wasn't mental.

"I'm sick!" He'd said, and the little fucker had laughed in his face.

"Sick in the head, grandad," he'd jeered back.

Which was when Eddie had tried to swing for the little bleeder, and the barman – despite having watched the entire exchange with a smirk – stepped in, said "You've had enough, Eddie," and kicked him out.

"I take my medicine," Eddie muttered to himself. "I got a right to be there. I got a right," he repeated, louder, then caught himself just in time, and stifled the shout that had been bubbling up, though he failed to stifle the anger that washed – mixed with embarrassment and shame – over him.

"I'm not mental," he muttered again, seeming to sink even further into his coat as he crossed the deserted square. "I'm just not well. But I'm getting better. And I take my medicine. I do," he stated emphatically, nodding his head affirmatively.

But he knew he shouldn't have been drinking. His doctor told him every time: "One or two won't kill you Eddie, but even a couple of small ones will interfere with the medicine. They'll do you no favours. So best you just try to leave the booze, yeah? Have a diet coke, something like that. Yeah?"

She always finished her sentences with that "Yeah?" As though she were uncertain if he'd heard or understood her.

But he'd heard. And he understood.

But he'd just wanted a couple of drinks. Not even a couple of drinks, to be honest; a bit of company. He'd been sat in that flat all afternoon listening to that bastard banging on next door for ages, then listening to Cathy's telly when she got home. She always put it on loud, and he didn't usually mind it – Cathy was a nice lady, and at least there was no arguing tonight.

But the bastard who had been banging on her door all afternoon, shouting through her letterbox had unsettled him, and he'd wanted to be amongst people who played a bit of dominoes, chatted, laughed a little.

Just... company.

He passed the alcove on the corner of his street.

At one stage, there'd always be young couples – summer or winter – snuggled in it canoodling. The word made him smile. He remembered his grandmother saying it, and remembered thinking it sounded like some sort of outward bound hobby. Like canoeing mixed with doodling.

But there was a railing around it now, the result of the drug dealers who had at one point annexed the space.

At Christmas, some local church had put a nativity scene behind the railing, but the vandals had already had a go at that, attempting to nick the plaster sculpture of the virgin, and – finding that it was chained solidly to the ground – settling instead for smashing the head off it.

A couple of forlorn cows stared up at a naked bulb that, he was sure, had been sat in front of a triumphant angel, last time he'd looked.

The angel, he surmised, turning the corner, had clearly not been chained as solidly as the virgin mother. Still, they'd be taking the whole thing away soon, what with Christmas being over and the new year a week in, he figured, the question – why this new year felt no different to the old one – flitting across his mind.

A flurry of something fell as he crossed the courtyard outside Henley Court. Snow, he thought at first, then,

Paddy shook his head. "Look: all's I'm saying is: he's got opportunity. Most people meet their partners – or their next partners – at work."

"OK," I acceded. "So, the opportunity I get, and the means, I suppose, is the fact that he gets to pick up women in the cab and could easily have met one 'at work,' so to speak and struck up a friendship. What about motive?"

"He's a man," Maz snapped. "There's your motive.

"Jesus, Maz," I rolled my eyes, "This is dad."

My sister had the good grace to look unsettled at the realisation she'd just slandered the man who'd carried her on his shoulders as a child and paid her rent for the past six months.

"I think what Maz means," Tash offered, by way of getting my now blushing sister off the hook, "Is that he's a man of a certain age."

"And mum is a woman of a certain age," I said.

"Exactly!" Paddy answered, his eyes fiery. "What a bastard!"

"But wait," I said, remembering something that had been said earlier in the conversation, "That doesn't make sense. I mean, why would he be crying, if he's the guilty party?"

"Cos he's ashamed," Maz offered.

"Or cos he's not the guilty party," Val – always the most taciturn of my siblings – murmured.

All eyes turned to her. "Well, it's not just men of a certain age who play away from home," she said, and both Paddy and I leapt to defend our sainted mother.

"She's flesh and blood, boys," Val said before we'd got more than a few spluttered objections out. "And dad's not the young man he once was. Maybe she's met someone at that new job of hers. Or maybe she's met nobody," she finished darkly. "Maybe she's just decided she wants out."

The facts were this: Paddy had keys to my parent's place and often popped around if he was in the neighbourhood. A few weeks ago, he'd popped in to what he'd at first assumed was an empty flat, only to hear the sound of stifled sobs coming from the bathroom.

Paddy had busied himself noisily making tea and had been surprised some minutes later when my father – a bright smile and breezy air failing to hide the red rimmed eyes and shaking hands – had entered the kitchen and struck up a conversation about football.

Paddy, of course – being a bloke – had said nothing about the sound of sobbing, and it was another week or so before Maz had called us all asking what was going on with our parents.

"Mum's really tearful of late," she'd said, and Paddy had finally mentioned his dad story, at which point even Tasha had admitted that she'd found mum tearing up looking at school pictures of us kids a few weeks back.

Then Val had said that she'd been worried for a while. "Lots of conversations – whispered, urgent-sounding conversations – between the two of them that stop whenever I walk in the room. They've definitely been arguing about something."

But what?

So, we'd convened here in the kitchen of the pub I nominally ran in Southwark (I had a bar manager with more pub experience than I had knowledge of the oeuvre of Miss Kylie Minogue under her belt, so all I really did was make sure that the chicken chasseur went out of the kitchen on time, the mince pies had enough mince to stave off complaints from our increasingly sophisticated clientele, and the condom machines were kept topped up).

And the general consensus had quickly settled on some form of marital difficulty that was in danger of splitting my parents up, and now I was sorry we'd started the whole conversation.

"So, what are we going to do?" I asked

"Well, I dunno," Paddy muttered, "You're – whatsername – Jessica Fletcher, innit."

Paddy was referring to the fact that – due to a streak of bad luck which I was entirely hopeful had come to an end –

the afore mentioned pub (The Marquess of Queensbury public house, affectionately known as The Marq) had been the site of several unfortunate events (or, as my aforementioned bar manager had once put it "People get murdered here so often, it's a miracle we got any regulars left").

In most cases to date, it had fallen to me to find the guilty parties and so my family had started referring to me – though not always to my face – as Jessica.

I was – secretly – not displeased by the nickname. It was certainly more complimentary than some of the sobriquets I'd suffered in my time.

My best friend in the whole wide world - the woman who had spurred me to levels of achievement I'd thought impossible, and cradled me, so to speak, when life had kicked the "To Do" out of me - lowered the copy of Vogue she'd been listlessly perusing (a teenaged model on the cover wearing two grands worth of makeup and fifty grands worth of couture alongside the headline "Cheap is the new Chic"), inhaled in the annunciative way that only a RADA trained actor or a member of the aristocracy can effortlessly achieve, and added, to the conversation "Angela Lansbury had better hair."

My hand jerked, without thinking, to the buzzcut on my head.

"Yeah," Maz said, refocussing for a minute, "What's that," she nodded at my closely cropped head, "All about."

I smiled as though to dismiss the question and waved listlessly at my head. "It's," I flailed, "Complicated."

"It looks pretty simple to me," Val announced definitively.

"Oh. No," Lady Caroline Genevieve Victoria de Montfort – the aforementioned Best Friend Forever – announced, as she unravelled herself like a statuesque and stylishly coiffured Gollum from her place in the leather club armchair by the hob, and fixed me with a challenging smirk, "It's all sorts of complicated. Isn't it, Daniel."

My mother doesn't even call me Daniel, but that "Daniel" was Caz's way of making me aware that we had reached the edge of truth.

I had a friend. I liked to call him a boyfriend, and I often did, despite the fact that he had a wife, and it was – thus – all sorts of complicated. So, I had begun to call him a friend with benefits.

To which, of course, Caz had responded "Benefits? Like BUPA? Luncheon vouchers? Free gym membership?" And I had been forced to admit that – on top of the wife (who was a wife in name only) the object of my interest had – due to his current attempts to gain promotion in his workplace – been somewhat distant of late, and so I'd decided to refresh my aesthetic, as it were.

And so – for reasons I can only attribute to a combination of jealousy, ego and desperation – I had ended up with a haircut that, as my dear sister Valerie noted, "Makes you look like a trainee copper."

Caz, nodding her confirmation, scooped her discarded Vogue from the floor.

"They could, of course, be simply bankrupt."

"They could what?" Paddy frowned.

"Well there's another reason why couples stress to that level: One – or more – of you is in trouble, and they're having issues making ends meet. Or there's addiction, debt, gambling, drink. Speaking of which," Caz nodded at the countertop where a bottle of gin, one of vodka and a half-emptied bottle of Jameson Irish Whisky sat alongside an ice bucket and a bowl of sliced lemons. "Anyone for a top-up?"

Various hands held out empty glasses, and Caz commenced pouring, chucking ice cubes into glasses, squeezing slices of lemon, and handing the glasses back to the original owners.

"Then, of course, there's concerns about you. Any of you lot in trouble?" She asked. "Illness. Business problems – you said your mum has a new job. Maybe it's too stressful. Maybe your dad wants to give up his job, follow his dream, and your mum won't let him."

"Fuck me," Val muttered, downing her vodka in one gulp and holding the glass out for another refill "You got any more?"

Caz smiled. "I have a family who have had their share of, shall we say, woes. Sometimes it's the most simple thing. Maybe it's an affair. Stranger things happen. But there are so many other potential causes of discord and the sort of upset you've been describing."

"She's not wrong," Paddy admitted. "Which is why you need to investigate for us," he finished, turning to me.

"Me?" I goggled. "Investigate? What?"

"Darling boy," Caz placed my G&T – her usual mixture where the T was present in little more than homeopathic quantities – before me and patted me on the head. "Always left holding the penny long after everyone else's has dropped.

"I'm not poking around in our parents' lives," I spluttered.

"You have to," Val announced, nodding her head definitively. "We've all already tried and got nowhere."

"They clammed up," Maz confirmed.

"She told me to mind my own business," Tash said darkly. "Like I wasn't a real part of the family."

"She didn't mean it," Paddy put a hand over hers. "You know she didn't. She's just," he searched for the word, "Upset."

"Exactly," Tash sniffed away a tear, and fixed her gaze on me. "We can all see that they're upset. We all know there's something not right. But they won't tell us."

"So, we've decided we need a detective," Maz clarified.

There was a knock at the door.

"Absolutely not," I said. I'm not a detective. I'm a barman."

"Who detects," Val responded. "Stop arguing. Go find out what's going on."

"But if they won't talk to you," I whined, not wanting

anything to do with this situation, "They surely won't talk to me."

"You're mum's favourite," Val said, and Paddy nodded in agreement.

"What's that got to do with anything?" I asked, quickly adding – lest I be considered conceited for not challenging the statement "Anyway, I'm not."

"You're the baby boy," Maz said, "Of course you're her favourite. And she could never keep secrets from you."

"And he can never deny you anything either," Paddy added, "So, if you go poking around they're less likely to shut you out."

"Danny," Ali Carter, her crew cut hairdo, I now realised, an almost perfect replica of my own, stood in the doorway, a strange look on her face.

"So, we're sorted," Val said to me, as though we'd agreed that I was going to interrogate my own parents and identify the source of their obvious distress.

"What's up Ali?" I asked the bar manager, turning back to my sister to say "We are not in any way shape or form sorted, Val. I don't know what you all think of me, but I am not some sort of gumshoe for hire, and I am not poking around in someone else's private business for sport."

"First time for everything," Caz muttered, topping up her gin.

"Danny," Ali raised her voice, clearly trying to attract my attention. "The police are here."

"Oh shit." I felt the blood drain from my face. "You been watering the gin again?"

A shake of the head.

"More back-of-a-lorry pork scratchings?"

"Danny," Ali looked shocked. She does a good injured innocence, does Ali.

"V.A.T?" I asked, slowly working upwards in seriousness of offense.

"It's not the pub," she said, and I groaned.

"Please tell me nobody has been murdered, committed

picture was in colour, but something had been done to it – the contrast turned up, the colour adjusted – to show, in ink, six letters handwritten on the back of the hand.

The letters were DANNYB, and they were written, like some playground tattoo, in red ink. There was more red in the photo – a splash of it all across her splayed fingers, and a deeper pool visible just at the very edge of the photo.

"I don't understand," I said, as another photo was selected and slid across the desk to me.

"Someone's been running up their printing costs tonight," Dot murmured, glancing across at Nick. "This what they have you doing now, PC Fisher?"

This photo was of an Apple iPhone. Not one of the newer models – this one was a few back, I reckoned. The phone was on, and opened to the contacts section, displaying the entry for THE MARQ – DANNY – and the phone number for my own hostelry beneath it.

"What's going on?" I asked, addressing Nick, who looked, in turn, at Frank Reid.

"That," Reid said sombrely, all his usual jocular menace momentarily gone, "Is what I was hoping you could tell me. At approximately ten P.M. last night," he continued, "Mrs Cathy Byrne, resident at-"

"Flat 9C Henley Court SE1," Dot finished for him. "Get to the point, Frank."

"Jumped," he finished, "From her ninth-floor balcony. And was pronounced dead – if not on arrival, shortly after she hit the pavement beneath her."

I shuddered, my stomach juddering slightly.

"And on the back of her hand, Danny, was written what you've just seen. Which," he continued, holding up a finger to stave off Dot Frost's predictable objection, "Might mean nothing in and of itself. But when we got her phone opened this morning, well, you can imagine our surprise." Here, he gestured at Nick, who looked back at me with questioning eyes, "When we discovered that the only Danny referenced in her admittedly sparse contacts book was your good self.

So: Once again, Danny, what's your relationship to Cathy Byrne?"

"She jumped?" Dot asked, preventing my repeated assertion that I had never met the woman.

Reid turned a quizzical frown on her.

"You said she jumped," Dot expounded. "Since when do you drag people into this place for suicides?"

"Dot, every time this charming young man's name crosses my desk," Reid announced, the sarcasm coming back with reinforcements, "There's a dead body attached to it. So, of course I'm going to ask him to pop in for a little chat." He smiled at me like a vulture offering cordial greetings to a half-dead caribou.

"She didn't leave a note, did she?" Dot asked.

Reid glanced at Nick, whose lips curled slightly, but who managed to suppress the smile and shook his head.

"No," Nick admitted. "No note, no suggestion that she was suicidal, nothing to explain why she ended up-"

"Spattered all over Henley Court," Reid finished for him, his previous display of respect for the dead discarded in favour of a cheap dig.

Nick frowned at him, but Reid ignored the look.

"Now I'm not saying you shoved her off the balcony yourself, Danny. Or, in fact that anyone shoved her off the balcony: Forensics have been all over the place, and there's nothing to suggest at this stage that it was anything other than what it looks like. But – like I say – your name came up, and when it comes up, there's usually a story attached to it."

"Could it have been an accident?" I asked and winced as Reid smirked triumphantly.

"Ah, Daniel. Danny. Dan. It could have been a visitation by the Santa and his elves. Fact is, the result is the same either way: I have a dead woman, no explanation, and your name on the back of her hand and in her phone. So, once again: Cathy? Byrne? Bells ringing yet?"

"I think we're done here," Dot Frost said, patting me on the shoulder.

"Done?" Reid frowned theatrically. "But we were getting on so well. I was gonna send Nick here out for some French Fancies. Maybe make a night of it."

"Frank," Dot responded, "We – Mr Bird and I – would obviously love to stay and chat but I think you'd be better popping down to the burns unit at Saint Thomas's, cos that," she gestured at his face, "Is not looking comfortable. Now my client has told you – repeatedly, and with more believability than I suspect you are used to – that he has never met, spoken with, heard of, or been familiar with this poor woman. So, unless you have anything else that you need from him at this stage, we are –as I believe I have already said – done here."

Go Dot, I thought, but chose to say nothing.

"Look," Reid held his hands out in an admission of fault, "Maybe we were a bit heavy handed, but I'm stumped here." He addressed me, the arrogance, once more, vanished. "The woman's dead, Danny," he said, "And her kids have no idea why."

"What about the husband?" I asked, despite myself, wondering where Mister Byrne was when his wife went over the balcony.

"Long gone," Nick answered. "Twenty years past. She was a divorcee, and he lives in Brazil with his partner Luis."

"Takes all sorts," Reid said, visibly uncomfortable at the idea of a man who had married and produced kids having a partner called Luis. "Which is why – whatever you had going with Mrs Byrne – there'll be no judgement here. I just want to know whether she had called you yesterday. And, if so, what she said."

"You've got her phone," I answered, frowning at Nick. Why did I think there was more to this story than I'd been lead to believe so far?

"Yeah," Reid nodded, "We do. And from it I can see that she telephoned you on Wednesday night, and again on the morning she died. So, again," he demanded, a steely glint in his eyes, "What is your connection to the woman?"

I shook my head, gesturing at the folder on the desk. "Let me see that shot of the phone again," I said, and Reid extracted the picture and slid it across to me.

"There," I jabbed the number on the phone display, and looked around three pairs of puzzled eyes. "That's not my mobile number; that's the general number for the pub. If she called that, she could have spoken to anyone of my team. But I'm telling you; She didn't talk to me."

Reid sighed. "So, you're saying I've got to drag that motley crew you call a team in here?" He asked.

"Not unless you want a string of law suits for wrongful arrest," Dot snapped back, patting me, once again, on the shoulder. "Look," she added, "Danny will talk to his employees. Right?" I nodded. "And if any of them has had anything to do with Cathy Byrne, he will let you know. But right now," she stood, slipping her handbag over her shoulder and picking up her mackintosh – beige, obviously – from where it had fallen on the floor, "It's late, and Mr Bird has a pub to run."

Reid shrugged, looked at me and frowned. "Danny," he said, a genuine air of conciliation in his tone, "If you or any of your lot know anything about this, please – no matter what it is – let us know. I don't like suicides, and I especially don't like them when they're unexplained."

And I had to admit, as Dot Frost hustled me out of the room, that neither did I.

"It looks a bit past it," I said, and she turned, furiously on me.

"Past it?"

"Well," I gestured at the item, cradled now in her arms, "it looks more pot than plant, to be honest."

"Oh, does it? To be honest," she answered, replacing the outrage with sarcasm and placing the pot gently back on the window ledge, then stroking the pot softly and staring out the window at the city skyline for a few seconds while she calmed herself down.

"Well they come back," she finally said, turning to me. "Not all the time, but this one has nine lives and it hasn't used them all up yet. And he's got no right binning it without my say so."

"Okay," I said, as the anger flared up again then died.

"Where were we?" She asked, tearing herself away from the orchid and pouring water into the mugs.

"Nick," I said, and she glanced again – for a moment – at the orchid.

"Oh yeah. He still married?" Mum asked, slapping my hand away from the pot whose lid I was about to lift. "That needs to simmer untouched," she warned.

I rolled my eyes. "Yes, mum; he's still married. But it's not like it looks."

She raised an eyebrow, pursed her lips, exuded judgemental concern, put a mug of tea in front of me, and said "I didn't say anything."

She lifted another packet of ceramic tiles from her chair, looked around the chaotic kitchen, as though wondering where to put them, spotted my arms reaching out to take them, handed them to me, and turned back to get her tea from the cluttered counter top as I placed the tiles on the chair next to me.

"You didn't need to," I answered, adding milk. "Anyway," I though, jumping straight to the point, "I didn't come round here to discuss my love life."

"Oh, you have a love life, then?" She asked, settling

herself opposite me at the tiny kitchen table.

"Nick," I reminded her.

She added milk to her mug, lifted it, and – before drinking – surveyed me over the rim. "Life doesn't wait for you, Danny. It just goes on, runs off somewhere, and if you spend too long waiting for someone to sort their own life out, you might find yours is over. I worry."

"That'll go on your gravestone," I smiled, and she smiled back briefly, before sipping her tea and wincing.

"Too hot. Seriously: How long is this situation with Nick going to go on. I mean you can get married now. They do gay weddings. You could have a nice solid relationship."

I shook my head in wonder at how my mum could make her needs so totally clear. "I have a nice solid relationship, mum. It's just," I searched for the word, "Unconventional."

"Is that what they call it these days?" She asked as I heard the front door slam, and my dad came down the hallway and into the kitchen.

"Evening stranger," He said, clapping me on the shoulder, pecking my mum on the lips, and heading over to the kettle. "How's tricks?" He asked, stopping en route to the kettle to peer rather disappointedly at the ceramic plant pot and the dry brown stick therein.

My mum's eyes caught his, went pointedly to the orchid and back to his, the unspoken threat clear even to me. "Unconventional, apparently," she said dryly, before I could get a word out.

Something in her tone made my dad, reaching now for a mug, frown. "You getting grief, Danny?" He asked, and – before he could suggest having the boys help sort out my problem – I rushed to assure him that unconventional was how I wanted things.

For now.

My dad patted the orchid pot, as though to reassure my mum that his binning her precious was a complete accident.

"How's your twin?" He asked, referring to Caz. "She not here?"

CHAPTER FIVE

"So, to summarise," Caz said, as her phone buzzed, "Both your parents insist that everything is rosy in the Garden of Eden, Dot Frost thinks you can help figure out what, exactly, her mysterious client was trying to tell her before he shuffled off this mortal, and you still have no idea why the suicidal Mrs – what was her name again?"

"Byrne," I said. "Cathy Byrne."

"Mrs Byrne would have your name tattooed on her hand and in her phone?"

"Pretty much," I said, "Though I don't think it was actually tattooed on her."

"Details," Caz waved a hand dismissively as her phone buzzed again.

"You gonna get that?" I nodded at the device.

Caz lifted the phone from the bar and glanced at the screen. "How big's a Pomeranian?" She asked, shifting on her bar stool.

"A Pomeranian?" I frowned.

"The dogs," she clarified, scrolling through whatever message she'd just received.

"Well I didn't think you were referring to a resident of the mythical land of Pomerania."

"Sarcasm," she announced, lifting a martini glass and sipping from it as she continued to scroll, "Is the lowest form of wit, you know. Anyway, it's not a mythical land. It's somewhere in Eastern Europe. Like Narnia."

I shook my head. "Bigger than a breadbin," I answered,

wondering what on earth the dimensions of a Pomeranian had to do with anything, "Smaller than a packing case.

"Helpful," Caz responded, in a tone that suggested my answer had been anything but.

"I don't know," I finally said. "About yay big?" I held my hands apart in a rough approximation of the size of what I assumed a Pomeranian would grow to.

I was basing my estimate on pictures I'd seen. There weren't many pedigree Poms on the Chaplin estate.

"And god help me for this," I added, "But why?"

"I'm buying a dog," she said, glancing from my still extended hands to the capacious Gladstone bag at her feet.

"A dog? What for?"

"For the eggs," she answered in a tone as dry as the cocktail she now drained. "Let's call that a 'maybe,' she said, typing something into the phone, lifting a stainless-steel art deco cocktail shaker from the bar and topping up her drink before turning her attention back to me.

"So: tattooed or not, the late Mrs Byrne remains a delicious little mystery."

"She's dead, Caz," I said, somewhat shocked at how easily the demise of a fellow human had been turned, by my best friend, into a fun puzzle to pass the time with.

"Well that tends to happen when one plunges head first from the ninth floor. And everyone dies, Danny. The question, as they always say in books, is: did she fall, or was she pissed?"

"I think you mean 'pushed'," I said, sipping from my own martini. "And I don't know, and I guess that's really the whole point. And why on earth are you buying a dog?"

"More to the point," Caz said, "What are we going to do about Mrs Byrne?"

"Nothing," I said. "We're going to do nothing, Caz, because there is nothing to be done. I don't know who she is. I don't know where she got my number. And I don't know why she had my name on her hand – tattooed or otherwise. And I have some more pressing issues to deal with."

"Your solicitor and her mysterious pack of newspaper clippings."

"Well, there's that," I admitted, "But I was thinking more of my parents."

"Oh darling, that's the worst thing about a happy family life; your siblings and you are completely unable to deal with the fact that nothing is happy all the time."

"My parents are," I answered. "Or were."

"And will be again. Leave it, Mr Bird. No good ever comes of lifting the lid on this sort of thing. Your parents are lovely. And as the latest in a line of disfunction that stretches back to The Conqueror, let me tell you: They – and you – will be fine. Ali, dearest," she lifted the cocktail shaker, and waved it towards where my bar manager – almost unnaturally efficient, but perpetually dour of manner – stood resembling a living embodiment of the phrase *Abandon Hope all Ye who Enter Here*, "Any chance of a top up?"

Ali didn't even look up from the glass she was polishing. "Not your skivvy," she said clearly, "And happy hour ended twenty minutes ago"

"Meaning, I suppose, that we're now into unhappy twenty-three hours," Caz sighed, put the shaker back on the counter, dipped into her handbag and extracted a large bottle of Tanqueray and a Tupperware box.

"Pig on a stick?" She asked, topping up both our glasses, and unpeeling the lid from the Tupperware. "Cheesy balls?"

"We do sell snacks, you know," Ali snarled, polishing the glass with a fury that suggested that any moment it might be ground back into the sand and silica from which it was formed.

"Knockoff Bulgarian Hula Hoops and sausage rolls that whinny when poked," Caz responded dryly. "I'll pass."

"Since when are you packing picnics?" I asked lifting a cheesy ball – some form of ricotta whipped with what smelled like neat brandy, chilli flakes, rolled into a ball and coated in powdered almond – on to my tongue, and sighing in ecstasy.

"Well I was at a launch party last night," she explained. "Ellie Nosh's new cookbook, and I got rather friendly with one of the waiters."

"Well you're nothing," I muttered, shovelling another cheese ball into my face, "If not congenial."

Caz ignored my sarcasm. "So, one thing led to another," she explained, "And…" she trailed off.

"And he let you take his cheesy balls home," I finished for her, lifting a skewered cold cocktail sausage – a cocktail stick piercing the spicy-sweet maple-chilli glaze that transformed it into a gourmet feast – and consuming it in two bites. "So, why," I persisted, "The dog?"

"For protection," she muttered, sipping from her glass of neat gin.

"Protection?"

"That tone," she said, "is unnecessary Mr Bird, and diminishes you as well as me. The city's getting more dangerous. I live in a part of town that's attracting some ne'er-do-wells, and I want some protection. What's wrong with that?"

"Wrong? Oh, where to start, Caz. Firstly, nobody has used the phrase Ne'er-do-well since Queen Victoria popped her clogs. Secondly, said ne'er-do-wells would probably need only that glance you're giving me now – yes, that one that looks like Medusa with a squint – to have them running, shitty-breeched into the night."

"Charming," she muttered dryly, the furious glare strengthening.

"And thirdly," I said, "A Pomeranian is decoration, not protection."

She opened her mouth to speak, and her eyes focussed somewhere over my shoulder. "Well, well, well," she murmured. "Don't look now, Daniel, but an unsuspecting – one assumes – heterosexual male has just walked into your den of iniquity."

I turned and walking across the bar towards us was a tall,

broad shouldered man somewhere in his late twenties to early thirties, his sandy brown hair already flecked with some gray, an angry set to his jaw, as his eyes flicked around the room as though searching for something.

"Remind me," I asked, "How you can tell he's straight."

"The shoes, dear heart. Hetero footwear. A classic giveaway."

I glanced down and saw that she was indeed right. Mr tall dark(ish) and handsome was wearing a pair of generic chain store trainers that looked like he'd marched through the Somme in them.

"You Bird?" He asked, arriving before us, and receiving a friendly smile from Caz.

"Me Jane," she said, and he frowned, nodding at her.

"Alright, Jane," he said, confusing her Tarzan reference for an actual introduction. "You Bird?" He asked again.

I nodded, went to say, "Yes, I'm Danny Bird. And who might you be," but got no further than the opening word before he'd telegraphed a right hook.

I just had time – as his shoulder rotated in what seemed like slow-motion – to turn my body so that the blow, when it came, punched me square in the shoulder rather than the face, but still managed to knock me off my bar stool.

Caz, as I fell from the floor and attempted to right myself, reached across, moved both my glass and hers out of harm's way, and dived into her handbag, extracting a slim black canister, which she proceeded to spray into the face of my attacker.

The man shrieked in pain, threw his hands over his eyes, and fell to the floor alongside me.

"Jesus," he shrieked. "I'm blind."

Ali peered over the bar. "You want I should get the Taser, Dan?" She asked loudly enough for him to hear her, as I staggered to my feet.

We didn't have a taser, and I knew that Ali was just enjoying the threat, so I shook my head.

"What the fuck," I asked, attaining my upright position

and yanking the man - no longer shrieking, but still writhing in agony, "Was that?" I nodded at the canister, discarded now on the bar.

"Black pepper body spray," Caz said. "Molton Brown. New line. It's organic," she added, emptying her glass and sliding mine towards her. "More to the point; What is that?" And she nodded at my now tearful assailant.

I turned to him as he sniffed and gulped, his eyes red and swollen, and stared furiously back at me.

"Oh it smells nice," I said to Caz, who nodded.

"Spicy," she said, "but fresh."

"I'm going to tear you apart," he growled.

"Mate," Ali, her glass-polishing forgotten now that a more interesting distraction had presented itself, growled, "You just got floored by a posh bird with a can of deodorant. I don't think anyone's stressing."

She ducked down, filled a pint glass from the tap and slid it across the bar along with a wad of kitchen towel. "Dab your eyes," she instructed, as bigger tears – these ones not, I felt, generated by the spray, rolled down his cheeks, "And tell us that the fuck that was all about."

"That's for Evan Blythe," my assailant said sulkily as he reached out, dunked the wadded kitchen towel into the water and dabbed at his eyes, "Or whoever the fuck else it was that put you up to it."

"Firstly," I said, "Who's Evan Blythe? And secondly: Put me up to what?"

"My mum," he said. "I know it was no accident. And it wasn't a suicide neither. So, if it wasn't Blythe that got you to do it, who was it?"

"Ah," Caz gestured at Ali, who poured a large Brandy and slid it towards the now openly sobbing man, "The late Mrs Byrne, I presume."

"I just want to know why," he said, looking at me with confusion and anger.

I looked at Caz. "We haven't finished with the Pomeranian," I said, as I slid off the bar stool. "Let's take this somewhere less public," I said, lifting the brandy and indicating that both Caz and the attacker should follow me.

We headed back to the kitchen.

"You've got me at a disadvantage," I said as Caz, poured slugs of the Brandy into some tumblers and put them before her and me. "You know who I am, but who are you?"

He looked sullen but lifted his brandy glass as Caz and I did ours, swigged from it, winced, sniffed, and said "I'm Callum. Callum Byrne. And I wanna know what you were doing with my mum?"

"Nice to meet you, Callum," I answered, "And nothing is the answer. I never met her. Never spoke to her. As far as I know, I know nobody called Cathy Byrne."

Callum Byrne nodded. "Yeah," he snarled distrustingly, "he said you'd say that."

"He?"

He clammed up. "My source. Said you'd deny any knowledge."

"Dear boy," Caz said, topping her glass up, "this is not Watergate. Source? What on earth are you on about?"

"I got a friend," Callum explained, "Knows someone in the plod. Someone in the local nick. Said you're always in trouble, that the police had you in after she died, but that you'd deny you had anything to do with my mum's death."

"Bloody Reid," I muttered, exchanging a look with Caz. I was fairly sure that handing out the names and addresses of interviewees in cases was against rules, if not actually against the law, and especially when said names and addresses were being handed out to unstable young men with little obvious self-control.

"I dunno his name," Byrne answered, "But he said you're always in trouble and that it would do you good to have to face some consequences for once."

"Nice," I muttered, "so, he sends you to beat the living daylights out of me." I frowned, wondering just what would have happened if it hadn't been for my teenage years at a local boxing gym and Caz's assault-grade underarm deodorant.

"Well, Callum," I said, "I can tell you I've faced consequences many times before, and – I repeat – I do not know your mum. Or this – what was his name? Eddy Blight?"

"Blythe," Callum Byrne replied, fury flaring up in him again at the mention of the name, "Evan Blythe. The bastard."

"And who," I asked, "Is Evan Blythe – the bastard?"

Byrne looked at me as though I had just asked what Oxygen was.

"Blythe," he said, "Local Councillor. Been trying to get my mum to lay off him about The Races for ages."

"Wait," I said, "You think your mother's death was racially motivated?"

"Racial? Who said anything about racial?"

"You did," I answered, nodding at him.

"Me? I never mentioned racists."

"Yes, you did," I glanced at Caz, who was watching the exchange with an amused twinkle in her eyes.

"Racial?" His puzzlement increased until finally, clarity dawned, and he shook his head. "I said The Races. It's the three tower blocks on the Molesworth Estate. Henley Court, Putney Place and Richmond Tower. They're named after boat races, so everyone just calls them The Races."

"I see," I said, having seen. Though I didn't. "And what has this homicidal civil servant got to do with The Races? Or with the death of your mum?"

He clammed up. "He's got a vendetta out on my family," he muttered. "I just know he had something to do with mum dying. There's no way she would have just jumped from that balcony."

"A vendetta?" Caz murmured. "How fabulously Sicilian."

I shot her a look.

"Well just to be clear, Callum: I've never met this Evan Blythe either," I said, and Byrne's shoulders drooped.

"I knew he'd cover his tracks. He's been doing it for

"You believe me, right?" I addressed the boy. "That I genuinely had nothing to do with your mother's death?"

He frowned, shrugged, said "I s'pose," in a tone which wasn't exactly unequivocal, "but I know that something funny happened. This wasn't an accident."

"Okay," I slapped the bar again.

"Sweetest," Caz murmured, "this place is riddled with woodworm; do that once more and we may be sitting in a pile of matchsticks."

"We're going to find out what happened to your mother," I said to Callum.

"How?" He asked dejectedly. "I mean, if even the plod have no idea."

"The plod?" Caz waved his protestations aside. "The plod – as you so poetically put it – are wonderful for missing cats or insurance reports, but they lack one vital resource, and it's a resource, dear boy, that you now have at your disposal."

She meant me, of course. Or maybe she meant her, I realised, my inflating pride going down faster than a fire-breathing conference on a Zeppelin.

Either way, the game was afoot.

I only prayed it wasn't the sort of foot that Hopalong Cassidy had.

CHAPTER SIX

"So, about this dog," I said, as Caz changed gear and put her foot down on the gas.

"Perhaps you could wear a hat," she said, casting a jaundiced eye at my haircut which – despite having had another day to grow – was still looking somewhat severe.

In the same way that Stalin, say, looked a bit severe.

"It'll grow out," I protested, reactively running a hand through it.

"Not before we get to the widow Aksoy, it won't," she announced, swerving left and overtaking a Porsche that was already doing at least ninety.

"You do know how she was widowed," I said dryly, forcing myself not to glance at the speedometer.

"Speed only kills if you lose control," she responded, swerving back into the middle lane, checking the rear-view mirror, frowning and taking one hand off the wheel to scrabble around in the glovebox for a Chanel lipstick.

"And I never lose control." She applied the bright red colour, recapped the lipstick all with one hand, threw it back in the glovebox, and indicated left to leave the motorway.

"Anyway," I said, "There's nothing wrong with my hair."

She remained silent as we whooshed along a series of country roads, finally slowing as we pulled up outside a pair of large ornately scrolled cast iron gates with an intercom mounted on a plinth beside them.

Caz reached over and pressed the button.

Moments passed, then the lens on the built-in camera opened, closed, focussed on us, and a voice, adenoidal and imperious, demanded to know who we were.

Caz gave our names, and there was a buzzing noise as the gates slowly slid open.

We drove up a tree-lined drive, then, turning a corner, came within sight of a huge Gothic place.

"Jesus," I breathed, "It's like Frankenstein's holiday home."

"Oddly," Caz admitted, "I was just wondering where she keeps the Batmobile."

The drive circled around a fountain, the centrepiece a one-third life-size Saint George having a go at a one-third life-size Dragon - well, either that or a life-size dwarf attacking a lizard with a kitchen knife - and Caz swept round the space, killed the engine, took another glance in the rear-view mirror, and turned to me.

"You're sure about this?" She asked.

I shook my head. "I have no bloody idea what we're going to do; but we never do, do we?"

She smiled. "Addaboy," and she undid her seatbelt, flung the door of the Ferrari open, and swung her legs around, exiting the car in a fluid movement without so much as hitching up the knee-length latte coloured calfskin skirt she was wearing.

"So, remind me," I said as she reached back into the car to extract a long green cashmere overcoat, the colour complimenting the tight cashmere sweater she was wearing, "Whose car this is?"

"It's our car today, darling."

"Yes, but whose car is it normally?" I zipped up my jacket as a gust of wind swept across the driveway.

"Normally? A dear friend of mine," she said, still not naming names, "Who currently has no use for it. Owing to the fact that he's in a coma."

"A coma?"

"It's Paolo," she said, as though the utterance of an Italian first name explained anything. "It's his fortieth birthday."

"And he's spending it in a coma."

"Obviously." We began walking towards the house.

"Electively?" I was bemused.

"Well what other way is there?" She asked, her turn now to be puzzled. "It's the latest thing. You get yourself put in a coma, they feed you intravenously on nothing but vitamins and saline, and apparently the body repairs itself as you remain hovering between life and death. Gets rid of crow's feet, wrinkles, puffiness, excess weight and the rest of the eight signs of ageing."

"And what," I asked, as the door before us swung slowly open, "Is wrong with oil of Olay?"

A butler – his tall, Patrician stature immediately making me feel like the living embodiment of the lumpen proletariat – stood in the doorway, looking down his nose as though uncertain whether to greet us or to release the hounds, then suddenly – as though operated remotely - his demeanour switched from disdain to delight, a welcoming smile that made him look as though he'd been at the Master's supply of MDMA, lending him a somewhat demented air.

"You must be Lady Caroline," he said, leering at Caz, before turning the crazy on me, "And Mister Bird."

I confirmed that we were definitely as advertised and he stepped to one side, ushering us into the house and closing the door silently behind us.

"Mrs Aksoy is waiting for you in the conservatory," he said, holding out an arm to usher us across an entry hall roughly the size of Saint Paul's Cathedral, down a gallery hung, on one side, with a selection of large canvasses filled with Renaissance beauties, half naked muscle Mary's either doing battle with Angels, tearing down temples or – in one study framed in more Gilt than was seemly – an Abraham who appeared to have decided, prior to sacrificing Isaac, that he'd Bench Press an Ox and then rend his garments in such a way as to expose a highly unlikely set of muscular pecs and a septuagenarian six-pack.

left hand at the computer monitor screen and waving the toy around as he smiled a gap-toothed smile, creating perfectly symmetrical dimples on opposite cheeks.

"Lovely, Finn," the woman said, turning to face Caz and I as we walked into the room.

"So, you come searching for Jo," she said, accusatorially, "And leave me hanging?"

I opened my mouth to speak, to clarify that I was not, in fact, the local constabulary, but was unable to get a word out before the woman – her slight frame, blonde curls and sparkly demeanour contrasting with the anger on her face – continued her diatribe.

"You lot think he's just done a runner, but I'm telling you he hasn't. I know George, and there's no way he'd abandon us."

Her face flushed, and she pointed at the child "He'd never have left Finn. Never."

"Look, Mrs-" I broke off, as she continued to talk.

"Wright," she said, her words tumbling over themselves as though she were afraid to speak and let me disabuse her of her ideas. "I'm Lindsey Wright. And it's Miss, not Mrs cos George and me aren't married, cos he doesn't believe in paperwork, but we have a mortgage on this place and that ties us together more solidly than any old wedding certificate, and I'm, telling you there's no way he ran away. No way. But none of you bastards are even looking for him, and I just know that something's happened."

"Miss Wright," I tried again, but once more, she just continued to talk over me.

"I've tried the hospitals; no sign of him. So, don't tell me he might have had an accident, either, cos I know that no matter how sick he was he'd have found some way to get a message through to us."

I held my hands up, and at long last, she paused.

"Look," I said, but this time, before I could get any further, it was Caz who stepped in.

"George," she said, stepping past me and smiling at the

small child. "Last name?"

"Osman," Lindsey Wright answered, surveying Caz and seemingly deciding that this smartly dressed woman was the senior officer. "George Osman."

"And – let me see if I have this right – George Osman is your – what? Boyfriend?"

"Partner," Lindsey answered, her interest in me vanishing. "George and I are three years together. Finn's two and a bit now. We – well, I – bought the flat when I fell pregnant and the council were looking to sell them off or rehouse us. George reckoned that this way Finn'd always have a roof over his head."

"Interesting," Caz noted, strolling around the room as I watched her and wondered what the hell she was actually up to.

"And what does George – Osman, right?" Lindsey nodded her head, "What does George do. For a living?"

"He's a plumber on the rigs," Lindsey responded, "Normally two weeks on then a week off. And last week was his week off, only he was here Sunday and Monday night, then went out to a plumbing job, and never came back. He should be back on the rig this week, but he's not answering his phone. And I know that something's happened." She trailed off and stood staring at Caz as she continued to prowl around the tiny but neat living room, picking up and putting down framed photos and small nick knacks.

"You've called the police?" She asked, and this one got a frown from Lindsey.

"You know I have," she answered, and Caz glanced my way momentarily.

"The thing is," I admitted, wondering why I felt guilty for the woman's misconception. "We're not the police."

"Well who the hell are you then?" She demanded, her face clouding over.

"Just some people who were looking for Jo," I answered, and she clutched the neck of her powder blue towelling leisure suit.

agencies."

"I know," she agreed, as we reached the blue painted door of 11F, the flat that Lindsey Wright had directed us to.

I searched for a knocker or doorbell and, finding neither, used my open palm to bang on the door.

A change in the light levels beyond the frosted glass said that somewhere in the flat a door had been opened.

We waited a little longer, and just as I was lifting my hand to knock again, a shadow appeared behind the glass, and we heard the sound of the lock being turned.

Then, another lock was opened.

We heard the sound of a chain being rattled, and the unmistakeable slide of a bolt being drawn.

I looked at Caz, who raised an eyebrow.

And at that point, the door was opened by a teenager.

"Is Steve in?" I asked, wondering whether this was a younger brother or a son from a previous relationship.

The boy nodded. "Yeah," he said. "You Danny?"

I was thrown.

"Depends who's asking," I answered, realising, as I did so, that who I was was a pretty empirical fact: I either was Danny, or I was not.

"It's me," he said, as though disclosing the most obvious fact ever. "Steve."

"You're Steve Haines?" I asked, unable to keep the incredulity from my voice.

"Well I'm not the Dalai fucking Lama," he answered, nodding a greeting at Caz and then turning back to me. "Callum told me I'd probably get a call."

"Did he?" I asked, as he stepped to one side and ushered us into the hallway. "Shame Callum didn't think to tell us that you existed for the calling in on."

I didn't need to be directed to the living room this time; all the flats seemed to have the same basic layout.

We walked down a fairly spartan hallway and into the living room, this one with a giant flat screen TV hanging on what would, at one point, have been a fire-breast. The fire was long gone, replaced by a radiator along the opposite wall, and in its place was a high-tech unit – all smoked glass and polished chrome. On top of the unit, a selection of boxes – Sky, DVD player, Xbox gaming unit and what looked like a VHS recorder – sat, each one square with the bevelled edge of the unit, with not a speck of dust visible, and with all the cables tied back as though the entirety were a shop display, or a sculpture in a gallery.

The TV was on and tuned to the BBC 24-hour news channel, the sound turned down to a low murmur.

On screen, a reporter's head filled one half of the screen while a photo of Mehmet Aksoy's missing banker – Vincent Armstrong – filled the other half, the words MAN HUNT running along the bottom of the screen.

"You want tea?" Haines asked, gesturing towards the kitchen.

Caz visibly shuddered. "Or coffee?" he added. "I think I have some coffee."

I shook my head, murmuring my thanks, and saying how sorry we were for his loss.

"Loss?" He froze, even his breathing seeming to pause for a moment, and then his face sort of collapsed, the brow shrinking, and the mouth gaping silently before, a blink later, he'd reset himself, summoned up the strength to repress the emotions that had briefly surfaced, and he sighed deeply.

"Things were going good for us," he shook his head. "I should have known it couldn't last," he finished, the bitterness in his voice battling with self-pity.

"Cathy," he paused, breathing deeply, "Was the most genuine, loving, brilliant person I ever met. She never had a bad word about anyone, you know? An' if anyone was sad, she'd bake 'em a cake. Brilliant cakes, she made. 'Cos all she ever wanted was for everyone to be happy."

"And yet," Caz murmured as though talking to herself, "We hear there were regular screaming matches."

Haines sighed. "Him next door, I suppose. Not right in the head, him."

"But not deaf either," I observed.

Steve Haines stared across at the doors to his own balcony and blinked back tears. "That was partly linked to her wanting everyone happy all the time. It did my head in," he added when we remained silent. "All these people taking advantage of her; taking the piss."

"People?" I prompted.

"Her kids. Callum's not a bad kid, but a bigger fuckup you couldn't find. And instead of making him own his shit, Cathy would run around trying to sort his problems out for him, so he never had to realise just how much he owed her. And d'you think he so much as thanked her? The daughter's a mess too. Both of 'em, it was take take. Even her so-called best mate, that Jo from downstairs; they had a cleaning job, and half the time Cathy did the whole thing, but did Jo ever offer her a few quid back? I wanted her to stand up for herself more, and we'd have arguments. Then I'd have arguments with Callum or Lou – Cathy's daughter."

"So, what do you think happened on that night?" I asked.

"Happened?" He looked at me as though I'd asked who the resident of Buckingham Palace was. "I'll show you what didn't happen, he said, with something like fury, walked across the room to the doorway out on to his balcony, and flung it open, the temperature in the room dropping instantly as the heat fled.

Steve Haines pointed at the small balcony space.

"Take a look," he said. I peered over his shoulder, and he stepped to one side, allowing me and Caz to squeeze through the door and out on to the balcony.

To the right a line of orange plastic-coated clothes line lead from a hook in the wall to a pole sticking up by the edge of the balcony, the string bare, now that winter was here, of any laundry. Along the wall on both sides of the door were small terra cotta pots most of which – apart from a small evergreen plant – were filled with dead plants, the skeletal twigs reaching like fingers from the dark packed earth in them.

Unlike my mum's orchid, I had little faith that any of these would revive next spring.

To the left, a small round table and a couple of collapsible chairs – only one actually opened, the other leaning against the outer wall of the balcony – sat with a butt-filled ashtray, the ashes having turned to soup thanks to a recent downpour.

I walked to the edge of the balcony. It took me three steps – this was not the balcony at Buck House, after all – and peered over.

The wall was a little over waist high, say three feet or so.

The drop on the other side – all eleven floors of it – was dizzying, the grey concrete forecourt seeming harsher, and even more bereft of features from this height, the dirty scrubland of grass which I guessed, at some point, had been considered a communal boon, resembling an abandoned quagmire. I imagined the moment that Cathy Byrne went over, the sudden tilting of sky and ground, the flailing as she tried to right herself, to stop her descent.

"So, what d'you think?" Haines asked, snapping me back to the here and now.

"Mrs Byrne's flat was under this one?" I asked.

"Yeah," he smiled sadly. "That's how we met. When I moved in, I was shifting stuff. Dragging me bits of furniture around. Only I didn't know she worked nights, so, there I was scraping me sofa back and forth when the doorbell goes, and it's this little fury in a bright red housecoat.

"'You got the Coldstream guards up here, love?' She asks, 'Only if you do, could you get 'em to play us a tune instead of just practicing the drums?' And she was gone as fast."

He smiled. "I went down later with some flowers. To apologise. I needed," he paused, as though unsure just how much to tell me, then, reaching out a hand to the back of the chair, he shook his head as though deciding nothing really mattered anymore, "I needed a friend. Couldn't afford to piss off the neighbours, you know?"

"How long ago was this?" I asked.

"About four years ago. I'd just got out after four years."

"What were you when you went in?" Caz asked, unable to restrain herself any longer, "Twelve?"

This brought a chuckle. "I've always had that younger than he looks thing," Haines admitted. "Did me OK when I went to court. Up till the last time. Mind you," he mused, coming over to stand beside us, "Even then I think it might have got me a few years off. Butter wouldn't melt, innit. Only it didn't do me that much good inside."

His smile faded. "No," he inhaled again, pushing down whatever emotion had been about to bubble up, "in my case, that last time, prison did the trick. By the time I got out I wanted nothing to do with any of it ever again. No more drugs, no more mates who aren't really mates. No more favours for mates who aren't really mates."

He gestured back over his shoulder at the tiny flat. "I just wanted to live somewhere I could get on with the neighbours, watch my telly, keep out of trouble."

"So, what," I asked as gently as I could, "Do you think happened to Cathy?"

He set his face so it looked, for a moment, twenty years older than it had when we'd first entered his life, and pointed at the wall before us. "Kathy was five foot two. All I know," he said, "And all I'm pretty sure even the filth have to have figured out, is that she didn't fall over that. It's too high. Which leaves us with two options. And like I said, things were going good for us. She had some worries with her kids, and there's always money worries – not a soul on this estate doesn't have them."

"Someone said you argued, the night before she died," I pressed again.

"Eddie James," he said, then shrugged, as though realising that denial was futile. "We had words, but nothing serious," he expanded. "Callum was in trouble, needed money. More money than any of us was ever likely to be able to get. And Cathy made some joke.

"I know it was a joke now. I sort of knew it was, even

then, but I saw red. She made some crack about how if only I was still dealing we wouldn't be short of money."

His voice cracked on the last word, and he stared off into the distance for a while, a sudden break in the clouds allowing a strand of weak sunshine to illuminate his watery eyes as he, once again, regained his composure. "I work hard," he finally said. "Every fucking job I can get – I've collected shopping trolleys, I've wiped arses in care homes, shovelled shit for the council, driven a fucking mini-cab, and I work hard, not just at the jobs, but at my life.

"I'm never going back inside. Never again. First couple of times I was a kid, and it was all a lark, and they were for a few months at a stretch. By the time I was getting used to how everything worked, it was time to go again. But that last time," he shook his head.

"I work hard at staying clean and staying legal and staying out of trouble. And Cath made some stupid fucking joke about me going back to dealing, and I snapped. Told her, if she needed money that bad, to go get it from King Fucking Solomon."

"King Solomon?" I glanced at Caz, who shivered, and suggested we step back inside.

"This place used to be a good area to live," Steve said as he closed the door behind us, turning the key in the lock and rattling the handle to make sure it was secure. "Good people. No trouble, but now it's full of villains and junkies and dealers and the likes of Solomon Masters."

I had thought that Eddie James' reference to King Solomon was linked to his delusions. "Who's King Solomon," I asked, "And what's his part in all this?"

"You ain't hearing this from me, right?" Steve sighed, running his hands over his face as his shoulders slumped in exhaustion.

"We were never even here," I said quietly.

"Solomon doesn't do drugs. Not so far as I know, though I wouldn't be surprised if he wasn't in business with the fucking dealers. Solomon deals in cash. He's an angry fucker, known to carry a machete. Lends money when nobody else will, or to buy things that not even Nat West will finance, only you never stop paying."

"And if you do?" I asked, dread creeping up my spine.

Haines drew a finger across his throat. "Warnings first. Someone you love has an accident. Then – if you still don't pay – you get the chop. Literally."

"Could Cathy have tried to borrow some money from King Solomon?" I asked, and Steve shook his head.

"Nah. Callum's up to his eyeballs with the nasty bastard. Solomon had made it known that until that debt was settled, the lines of credit to his family were withdrawn."

Caz coughed discretely. "Eddie says that Solomon or one of his goons was banging on Cathy's door the day she died."

"Doesn't surprise me," Steve sighed. "Probably looking for Callum. Silly fucker's in it deep."

"And if he was having trouble paying," I said, knowing, as I said it, that this thought exactly, had already crossed Steve Haines mind, "Then might a warning have been issued?"

"Callum's convinced this was Evan Blythe's doing."

"The local councillor?"

Haines nodded. "Yeah. Louise – Cal's sister – has some sort of conspiracy theory going about him. Reckons he destroyed her life. And I reckon Cal's caught the bug, cos when we spoke about Cathy's death, Callum swore that his issues with King Solomon couldn't be the cause. Said he was sorting things out there, and Solomon wouldn't have had any need to issue a warning. Swore this had to be Blythe.

"Only I said between Sol and the fucking Council I know which one would be more likely to," he broke off, swallowed, "to do what happened to Cathy."

Haines shrugged. "I'm still not convinced that King Solomon had nothing to do with this. But if he had, we're fucked. No-one here will touch King Solomon. You don't snitch on him. He'd kill you in your sleep."

"Where's Callum now?" I asked as Haines picked up a small framed photo.

I glanced at it, the couple – a closely cropped younger Haines shirtless, his skin deeply tanned, sat at the table outside, a middle-aged woman, her hair dark, shoulder-length and coiled in soft curls, her eyes large and brown and sparkling with humour, as an unlit cigarette hung from the side of her lip in an approximation of some sexy smouldering siren look.

The picture was a selfie, taken, I guessed, the previous summer, at the end of a long week of night shifts and day shifts and mini-cabbing and shit-shovelling, and the two of them looked, as Steve Haines had said, as though things were going good for them.

Haines seemed not to have heard me. "She wouldn't smoke in doors," he said, smiling softly. Hated the smell in the room, so she'd always go out on the balcony. Wouldn't drink beer out of a bottle neither. Always a glass, and preferably a chilled one. She was a lady, you know?" He looked up, tears in his eyes. "Not some fucking airs and graces type, but just someone who had standards. She might not have had much, but she wasn't going to give up, you know? Not ever." He turned back to the photo, and I had to repeat my question.

"He'll be at the pub. He works behind the bar at the Seven Stars," he added, mentioning what street the pub was on.

"We should go," I turned to Caz, who sighed deeply, no doubt at the thought of having to walk back down the stairs.

Haines frowned. "D'you think he's in trouble?"

"I don't know," I said, "But if King Solomon had anything to do with Cathy's death – and if it didn't kickstart repayments from Callum – then the next step – like you said – would be an attack on the debtor himself."

Haines lifted a denim jacket from the sofa in the corner and, throwing it on, said, "I'll come with you," and we set off.

CHAPTER ELEVEN

Haines slammed the door behind him, pulled a set of keys from his pocket and double locked it, then turned and walked along the landing.

"You know Cathy had my name on her hand?" I asked him, and he shrugged.

"Callum said you were lifted by the local law; that one of them gave your name to a mate of his to pass on."

"Reid," I concurred. "A nasty little toe rag, looking to cause trouble. Callum threw a punch at me."

"Not too bright, our boy," Haines said.

"Well not exactly a way to win friends and influence people," I admitted. "Do you have any ideas why my name was on Cathy's hand? Why my number was in her phone?"

Caz and I slowed as we drew level with the stairwell, but Haines walked right past it, and stopped beside the lift, pressing the call button.

"Oh, the lift's out of order," Caz announced as, from behind the scarred and pitted metal doors, we heard the distinct sound of the motor kicking in to life. "There was a sign downstairs," she finished lamely.

Haines smiled apologetically. "They leave that sign on the doors three hundred and sixty-five days of the year," he admitted. "Makes it easier, I suppose, than having to put it up every time the lifts are actually bust. Which is at least half the year. But we know to always press the button. Just in case."

Caz looked at me, then down at her shoes. "You mean I've just hiked eleven floors in these heels because some handy man doesn't want to have to put a sign up and take it down?" She demanded in tones which made me fear for the life of said caretaker if she ever got her hands on him.

"Tones the calves," I said in an attempt to lighten the mood, at which point there was a loud 'ding,' and the lift doors opened.

"My calves," Caz responded in tones that were, at the least, sub-Arctic, "Were perfectly toned to begin with, thank you very much."

We stepped in and, even before the doors closed, the scent of stale urine, chip grease and BO seemed to swell up from the floor.

"Perhaps," Caz added bitterly, "I should have walked down. Would have done wonders for my flabby thighs too," and she shot me the look that said 'We will never talk of this again.'

The lift juddered and jerked its descent, the overhead lights – one completely dead, the other blinking in a pattern that turned everything to a dim and grimy palette.

"This wasn't like this," Haines said, indicating the lift and, I suspected, the world beyond it, with a nod of his head. "Fucking council don't care no more. It's all austerity and fuck the chavs."

He looked at Caz, who had the good grace to blush. "Not from me," she responded dryly, patting me affectionately, "I have a lot of time for the chavs. But surely something can be done. I mean," she tip toed around what she needed to say, then came, eventually, out with it, "The place does look like it could do with a wash and brush up."

"That's what Cathy was trying to get done," Haines said as the lift arrived on the ground floor, the doors opening in a jerky will-they-wont-they motion and leaving all three of us to stagger out of the pee and kebab scented box to gasp lungfuls of the pine bleach scented air that the lobby was filled with.

He nodded at the notice board, and the Save The Races sign. "She'd lived here all her life, as had her kids. Couldn't bear to see the state that the council was letting this get in to. I mean, there was always a bit of dodginess – someone who could get you a telly for less than cost price, the girls what worked at Marks & Sparks up West maybe having a few frozen lasagnes that were going cheap.

"But the past few years, the drugs came in, and after that they moved a bunch of scumbags in every time some other family got rehoused, and the place feels sometimes like they've just left it to rot."

"So, what was Cathy doing?" I asked.

"She was trying to get the resident's association to sort it's shit out. Mostly, it's in the hands of the council. But between the long-timers and anyone who was dumb enough to buy their flat when the council were still selling them off, there's a lot of people who are just really pissed off with the situation."

"Can't the police do anything?" Caz asked as we set off across the forecourt and headed out on to the main road.

He shrugged. "They tried, but every time they sweep the bastards out, another load of 'em sweep in like cockroaches. I suppose, after a while, they just got tired and gave up. Or else they'd end up hassling the wrong people: Someone would ring about a gang of dealers congregating on the green, and the police would turn up and arrest a bunch of kids who were skateboarding." He shook his head.

"Hard to keep the support of the community when you're hassling their kids and leaving the local dealers to trade in peace."

"So, Cathy was going to get a residents group together," I prompted.

He indicated we should turn left off the main road and we found ourselves walking down a thin, poorly lit alleyway, the puddles we stepped over (or, in one case, into, as the deep sigh and tut from Caz attested to) containing some dubious looking and smelling liquids.

"She wanted to get something done. And when Cathy wanted to get something done, it got done. She was like a bloody Terminator." He smiled fondly.

"I needed that. Addicts do. Too many people say they'll do something, be somewhere, and they flake. But with Cathy, her word was her bond. If she said she was gonna do something, she did it."

"So, what was she going to do about this?" I asked.

"Make noise," he said. "Get enough people making enough noise – then the press would have to pay attention to the state of the place. She reckoned, if the press paid attention, it might encourage the politicians to pay attention."

"And then she fell," I said quietly.

Steve stopped. "I told you," he said firmly, "She didn't fall."

At the end of the alley, we turned to our left again. Ahead, a squat cinderblock building stood, a small crowd outside it.

The presence of pint pots in several hands suggested we'd found The Seven Stars.

"Bram Stoker," I noted, "Wrote a book once 'The jewel of the seven stars,' all about the curse of an Ancient Egyptian princess. Beautiful but murderous. And the havoc she causes."

"So, not about a shithole boozer down a backstreet?" Haines asked dryly, as we approached the crowd.

"Now Daniel," Caz murmured, "You know how we always say The Marq is the grimiest boozer in South London?"

"It's not any more, is it?" I asked, and she shook her head ruefully.

"Darling, it's The Bar at Blakes in comparison."

The crowd outside seemed tense – well, tenser than I. The general hum of conversation that one might expect from a group of fifteen or so people outside a pub on a cold winter's day was absent, and the crowd seemed only too happy to part as we made our way forward.

The pub door was closed, but from within I could hear raised voices and the sound of smashing glass.

I looked behind me. Caz finished applying a slick of vibrant red lipstick to her lower lip, pressed her lips together to blot, dropped the stick into her handbag, withdrew a small bottle of Annick Goutal and spritzed her neck and pulse, then dropped that, too, into the bag.

"Well if one is about to be butchered by South London's version of Reggie Kray," she said quietly, "One should at least look one's best."

I turned my eyes to Steve Haines. "You O.K.?"

"Are we going in?" He asked, his tone suggesting that he was fervently hoping I'd say 'No; we're going to go to Haagen Daz's for ice-cream."

Instead, "Well, if Callum's in there…" I answered, and he nodded, seeming to find some reserves of strength, and, pushing his shoulders back and his chest out, nodded at the pub door.

"Well, let's go, then," he said.

And I opened the door.

CHAPTER TWELVE

The room was L-shaped, and we were looking down the length of the long leg of the L. Down the right side of the room, a bar ran, the pitted and scarred wood still holding some swiftly abandoned glasses.

Almost directly before us was a three feet tall ceramic Labrador, a slot in his chest into which people could poke money for, the sign on the base said, "The Guide Dogs."

Except this guide dog wouldn't be leading anyone anywhere again. Someone had smashed the head off it, the decapitated noggin laying on the floor a few feet away and staring ghoulishly at us.

Along the left-hand side of the room, a series of small round tables stood, several of them – along with their hastily discarded contents – tipped over, the discarded gin and oranges and pints of Stella slowly oozing into a carpet which looked as though it had last had a hoover and shampoo sometime around the turn of the nineteenth century.

A blackboard on one wall advertised a Fish special as "Catch of the day," the day in question, I suspected, being VE day.

From somewhere, a tinny version of Girls Alouds' rendition of "I wish it could be Christmas Every Day" was playing, but it was drowned out, at times, by the sound of two people – one furious, one in agony – screaming loudly.

The screaming was coming from the far end of the room, around the bend in the L.

We stepped into the pub as quietly as we could, letting the door close quietly behind us.

"I want," a deep, almost baritone, voice yelled loudly, "My fucking money, you klaat."

"I'll get it, I'll get it, I'll get it. Oh God, stop!" That voice, I recognised, even from my brief meeting with him, as Callum Byrne's. He stopped begging as a loud thump resounded around the space, and he shrieked in pain.

"Too. Fuckin. Late." The baritone shrieked, as we approached the bend. "you had your fuckin' time, and I still ain't got my fuckin' money."

As we moved slowly down the room, I somehow ended up in front, with the other two behind me, in classic backing singer position. I reached the bend first, and, in the second before I was spotted, could see that at the end of the room were the doors – left and right of a jukebox on the wall – to the ladies and gents loos.

And on the floor, under the jukebox, a huddled heap – roughly the shape and dimensions of Callum Phillips – was being kicked in the head, stomach, buttocks and anywhere else that were left unprotected, by a giant red-headed thug.

Two more goons, one holding a kitchen knife that would have made sense only if the kitchen in question belonged to Jeff Dahmer, the other what looked like a hatchet, only twice as big, and five times as menacing.

In front of them, his back to us, and still cursing the man on the floor, stood what I at first assumed was a massively overdeveloped child.

Then he turned side on, and I decided he was, perhaps, a dwarf who'd discovered steroids and weight lifting at too early an age.

He spotted us and turned, a sneer on his face, and I decided that he was neither a child nor a dwarf, but a short man, who was almost as wide as he was tall.

I'd say about four foot seven, and weighing at least twenty stone, all of it – from what I could gather – tightly knotted muscle.

He – despite the fact that it wasn't far off freezing outside – was wearing a string vest and a pair of baggy camouflage trousers, tucked into highly polished eighteen-hole Doc Marten boots.

And in his hand – despite what I'd been told by Steve Haines – was, not a Machete, but a Scimitar.

A fucking scimitar.

I mean, if the local Am Dram had been doing a Gritty remake of Aladdin for Panto this year – you know the version where the Genie's a midget Sierra Leonean Warlord with a passion for exotic weaponry – they'd found their man.

And whilst I guessed the combination of his bizarre physical bulk and the frankly fucking huge scimitar was, essentially menacing, I had to suppress a giggle at the ridiculous contrast.

I failed.

I giggled. Out loud. In his face.

"The fuck are you?" He demanded, turning to face us full on, the scimitar gripped in his right hand, the sharp, deadly point of the blade a good two feet above his head.

"You must be Solomon," I said, attempting to stay calm, stop sniggering, and keep my voice level. "We're friends of his." I nodded at the bundle on the floor.

"That's King fucking Solomon to you, faggot," the angry sword-wielding midget before me responded, before nodding in the direction we'd just entered and adding "Fuck off outside with the rest of them. We got grown ups business here."

Something – possibly the utterance of the words 'grown-ups' by someone who looked like their dad had dragged them up as Arnold Schwarzenegger for Hallowe'en – clicked, and I giggled again. Aloud.

"Is something funny?" He demanded, a glint of true fury in his eyes.

"Look," I held my hands up in obeisance, "I'm sure we can work this out."

"Are you fucking laughing at me?" He demanded, the

scimitar swooping down to point menacingly at my stomach. "Only I've fucking gutted cunts for less."

"Look," I kept my hands up, trying to calm the atmosphere – which seemed, to be honest, as likely as getting a musicologist to write a thesis on the oeuvre of nineties boy band 5ive – and took a step forward.

The scimitar glinted dully as a beam of thin winter sunlight broke into the room.

I tried not to dwell on the thought of what my disembowelment would do to the carpet underfoot, though I figured they'd need more than a hoover and a tub of shake and vac to handle it.

"I'm not laughing at you." I said. "Why would I laugh at someone with a fucking sword pointed at me."

"It's a scimitar, bitch," he sneered back.

"It's a rather large scimitar," Caz announced, in cut glass received pronunciation, as though it were the year 1935 and she were about to announce the BBC Light program, "For such a short man."

I stopped. The world stopped.

I'm fairly sure I heard people in Shanghai gasp.

The giant redhead stopped kicking poor Callum Byrne and began to turn.

"Harry," the now furious King Solomon said, his voice as cold as the steel that was inches from my stomach, "Shoot that fucker."

Which was when I noticed the gun in the red-head's hand.

"Oh hello Henry," Caz suddenly announced in tones as bright and pleasant as though she were addressing the vicar, whose presence at an orgy was a not entirely unpleasant surprise. "Fancy seeing you here. How's your mother."

The red head – a rather startling resemblance, now he'd turned, to his royal namesake, evident in both his facial features and his height – gawped.

"Holloway? What the fuck are you doing here?"

"Well I might ask you the same thing." Caz responded, adding "Though with fewer profanities, obviously. How's your sister? Still in rehab?"

Solomon wavered, the scimitar dipping slightly. "You know this bitch?" He demanded of his goon.

"Passingly," Prince Harry responded.

"By which," Caz explained to the still rage-quivering mini-gangster before us, a she dipped into her handbag once more "He means he made a pass at me. Once. And I hospitalised him."

She smiled sweetly at the now blushing Harry.

"Not for making the pass, of course; I mean I like having passes made at me. I like being attractive, and I like being told I am. But when I decline the offer of – what was it, Henry? – 'A blow job and a fingering' and the offeror then becomes somewhat overly forceful, well that, I'm afraid, I simply can not have. So, I shot him," she explained, extracting from her capacious Vuitton Gladstone bag, a tiny, but still rather deadly looking pistol.

"With a gun rather similar to this one."

She smiled sweetly.

"Now Henry, I really don't think your dear mama would appreciate another scene, do you? I mean 'Deb Slays Cheap Thugs in Grotty Boozer' might seem sweet as a headline, but I'm not entirely sure it would do any of our reputations – yours, admittedly, post-mortem- any good at all."

"Harry," Solomon snarled, "What the fuck is this bitch on about?" His eyes didn't leave the pistol which Caz, without a tremor of nerves, still kept pointing at him

"Long story," Prince Harry snarled, slamming his foot one more time into the prone figure on the floor, "But I think this one's got the message."

King Solomon's eyes flashed angrily.

"We done here?" He asked, then, catching himself, repeated the words as a statement rather than a question, and stepped forward, the scimitar still held out towards me, as the foursome slowly made a circle around the three of us, each of us, at the same time, turning slowly so that the pistol in Caz's hand was pointing at them at all times.

"Tomorrow, Callum," Solomon snarled. "I want my fucking money tomorrow." And then they were gone, out of the pub, the door slowly closing behind them as Steve Haines and I turned, in slack jawed amazement towards Caz, who nodded at the figure on the floor, now struggling to get to his feet, slipped the gun back into her bag, said "You should probably help him up" to Steve Haines, and – to me – "Gin. Large. No ice."

CHAPTER THIRTEEN

"You shot him?" I was still shell-shocked.

"I shot his foot, Daniel. It was hardly the Saint Valentine's Day Massacre, though from the amount of blood and squealing he issued, it might as well have been."

"Jesus. So, what did you do?" I asked, swallowing my own gin in one mouthful.

"I shot him," Caz answered, sipping her third calmly. "Again."

"Wait. What?" You shot him twice?"

"Henry Wakefield – Harry to people who like to consider themselves his friend – is a psychopath. My brother made the mistake of befriending him at school, and Henry decided – because my brother was stupid enough to fall for his charms – that I'd also be easy meat.

"So, when I shot him the first time, he threatened, in between crying and shrieking, to find me, when he was better, and 'Gut you,' I think he said, 'Like a fucking sow.' So, I took my grandfather's old service pistol back out of the drawer I'd just put it in, pointed it at his other foot, told him if he ever so much as looked at me I'd aim higher, and pulled the trigger again.

"Then I went in search of someone to call an ambulance and went to the cinema in town with the chauffeur, whose name was Arnold."

"And now," Callum Byrne groaned agonisingly, "You've pissed him and King Solomon off again."

"We saw Notting Hill," Caz continued as though Callum hadn't spoken, "I didn't rate it. And the Bonsai Baddie with the Blade," she added, addressing Callum and Steve, who were sitting facing us as the pub rather quickly returned to normality, someone having thrown a handful of sawdust and a quick squirt of pine-fresh Dettol over the bloodied carpet beneath the jukebox, "Is not the person you should be worrying about."

"How'd you make that out?" Callum asked sullenly.

"Because he," I deduced, "Might have looked like the leader, but it was Henry Wakefield who decided when they should go."

"Exactly," Caz nodded. "That's Wakefield's thing: Find someone who can carry the can when it all goes wrong; let them think they're in charge, while he manipulates them, then use them as cover to have his fun."

"Fun?" Callum swallowed uncomfortably.

"I suspect," Caz admitted, "That if we hadn't turned up, he might have shot you. Oh maybe not to death," she said, holding up a hand to calm the hysteria that flared up in Callum's eyes. "But he had a gun. And his type hate to have a toy and not get to use it."

"Jesus," Callum stared saucer-eyed at the two of us.

"So, how much do you owe him?" I asked.

Callum named the amount, and this time, it was my turn to stare saucer-eyed at him. "What the fuck did you do?" I asked, "Buy Belgium?"

"It wasn't that much, to begin with," he said. "I was going to be able to win it back, only I couldn't and-"

"Wait," I stopped him. Win it back?"

"It was the machines," he admitted, shame suffusing his face. "At the bookies."

"The fixed odds machines?" I asked, incredulously. "You ran up a debt that would buy a small country on a fucking slot machine."

"I could have won," he shot back, his shame transforming instantly into anger. "I should have won." He stared me down for a few seconds, then looked at the table top. "Only them things are fucking fixes, and I didn't win, and the interest just mounted."

"As it tends to," I said, "When you borrow from the fucking mafia."

"Daniel, dear," Caz put a hand over mine, slid Callum's Scotch towards him, and smiled apologetically at Steve Haines. "We've met the mafia. Remember? And that man is not the mafia. He's a thug with a ludicrous sword and a psychotic puppet master."

"Jesus," Callum sobbed, dropping his head into his hands, and issuing a low moan, "what have I done?"

I shook my head, realising that there was almost nothing I knew about this situation except for the fact that Cathy Byrne was dead, and Callum Byrne was likely to follow her soon if he didn't get the money for King Solomon.

Only, of course, there was no way he was going to be getting that sort of money any time soon.

"Look," I finally said, "You need to get away. At least for a while until this can be sorted – or until someone sorts out your debt with Solomon."

Steve Haines laughed humourlessly. "Yeah," he grunted, "Or until you win the postcode lottery, mate."

"I got nowhere to go," Callum said, a note of panic in his voice. "I got nowhere to go."

Caz sighed this time. "Everyone has somewhere they can go," she said. "There must be a distant relative you could stay with."

"There isn't." Callum shook his head. "There was only my mum and now there's just me and my sister. And she's mental. I can't stay with her. And if I have to tell her that my fucking stupidity might have got mum killed, she'll murder me." He rubbed his hands over his face, failing to quell the terror.

"Shit," he gasped, "I'm trapped."

Caz rolled her eyes. "My family have got a place. It's in the middle of nowhere in a village in Wales. It's a three mile walk from the nearest train station, and there's a gatekeeper's cottage that's probably empty. You could stay there," she finished.

Callum turned towards her. "You'd do that for me?" He asked, and Caz shrugged as though to suggest that what she was doing was nothing, really.

"I've seen Wakefield in action," she said, "And I don't really want that on my conscience. So,you go to the Brecons, you stay there till we send for you, and you stay, for God's sake, away from slot machines, card games, or whist drives. Agreed?"

Callum agreed, vigorously, and gratefully, and Caz dipped into her bag, extracting, this time, her phone. "I'll call the old man and ask him to set it up," she said, "And you need to pack a small bag and get the hell out of Dodge before Solomon can stop you."

And so, twenty minutes later, Callum Caz and I – Steve Haines having absented himself to go see if there was any work going at a nearby building site - found ourselves stepping out of the lift at Henley Court and walking along the balcony to the still taped-off door of flat 9C.

Callum dug into his jeans pocket and pulled out his door key, waving a hand at the tape. "Do not enter," he said. "Like they're coming back. The filth've already moved on. Three suicides in this block the past year."

"You think your mum's death was a suicide?" I asked, and he shot me a venomous look.

"Course I fucking don't."

He unlocked the door, pushing it open with his toe, and we stepped into the flat.

This was a similar layout to the other flats we'd been in, except that this time, because it was a three-bedroomed home, the front door opened, rather than at the end of a hallway, in the middle, with the same long hallway leading to the left towards a bedroom, a living room, and – to the right of the living room – a kitchen, and extended in the other direction, to two more bedrooms and a bathroom.

Behind the door a trio of hooks held coats, jackets, a tangle of backpacks and handbags.

The hall flooring was wood laminate, with an Oriental style runner going almost the whole length, a track with halogen spots ran the length of the ceiling, casting diffused light downwards sometimes, and – more often – on to the framed photos on the wall, each in an identical black minimalist frame and a cream card mount, and each showing a happy family scene – a day at the beach, a birthday party, a Christmas morning with a pre-teen Callum and, I supposed, his sister in dressing gowns surrounded by piles of wrapping paper and opened toys, looks of pure joy on their faces.

To the left, just after the door, was a small lavatory, the space immaculate and smelling of lavender, a small magazine rack holding a Sunday newspaper from a couple of weeks previously.

"That's my bedroom, at the end," Callum said, gesturing towards the room next to the living room, and heading towards it as we followed.

"Only a small bag," Caz warned him. "You want nothing that'll slow you down."

We followed him and peered into the kitchen-diner.

It was a compact space but, like the rest of the flat we'd seen so far, immaculate. The work tops were clean and tidy, a small fold-out table opened out to allow one chair to sit by it beneath an oversized print of Monet's Waterlilies, surrounded by the same plain black frame as the photographs in the hallway.

In the corner of the living/dining area, a plastic Christmas tree stood, the fairy on the top staring sightlessly outwards. Below her, the tree lights had already been removed and were in a box marked "Tree lights." Another box was filled with baubles that had been taken from the top half of the tree before time stopped in this room.

The lower branches on the tree still sparkled hopefully.

"Well he's right," I muttered, nodding in the direction Callum had gone. "She definitely didn't top herself." I gestured at the tree. "Who goes to the hassle of half undressing the tree if they plan to throw themselves over the balcony. And she was planning to make a cake once she's finished.

I pointed at the kitchen table, where a dozen eggs, a jar of sugar and flower, and various packets of ground nuts sat alongside a back of oranges and an already set up food mixer.

"Why didn't anyone tidy up?" I called to Callum, who could be heard opening and slamming drawers from his room.

"Tidy up?" He emerged briefly, ran his hands absent mindedly through his hair, shook his head, and dived back into the room. "The rozzers came round, photographed everything, kicked me out, taped the place up, and told me they'd be in touch."

"So, what had your mum been up to that day?"

"Up to?" He re-emerged, a small holdall slung over his shoulder. "She was at work."

"What time did she get in?" I asked, strolling into the living room.

"I dunno," Callum followed me in, a frown on his face. "I was..." he paused, "Out."

"Avoiding Solomon," I guessed, and Callum's shamefaced nod confirmed my guess. "So, you didn't see your mum all day?" I asked.

He dropped the bag at his feet. "I saw her in the morning," he sighed. "Literally got up, got dressed, ran into the kitchen to grab a bit of toast, and she was there. Giving me grief about everything – Solomon, my life, the fact that the estate was going to shit and nobody seemed bothered apart from her."

He stopped dead, as though a boulder had dropped on him. "I ran away. Couldn't take no more, so I said I'd see her later, and did a runner."

I frowned again. There was something…

"Wait," I said, trying to remember what had been in the

paperwork that Nick had helpfully left scattered around the desk in that dingy interview room. "The cops didn't take a handbag or purse out of here. Did your mum carry a bag? Maybe the killer took it," I peered around the kitchen. "Where would she have kept it?"

"Rucksack," Callum said, gesturing – and then heading – back down to the hooks in the hallway.

"This one, I think," he said, walking back into the room with a small black leather rucksack.

He unzipped the bag and tipped the contents out on the table: A small coin purse, a Boots lipstick, a hairbrush, half a packet of wine gums and a roll of mints, a bright green BIC lighter, a packet of fags with no fags left in the packet, and a bulky manila envelope with her name – Cathy – written on it in block capitals.

Eyebrow raised, I glanced at the other two, who also stared down at the envelope.

"Recognise the writing?" I asked, and Callum shook his head.

"Nobody I know."

I lifted the envelope up and used an index fingernail to lift the flap at the back.

And a blizzard of fifties tumbled on to the table.

"What the fuck?" Callum breathed.

"What indeed," I replied, lifting the envelope to peer inside as Caz quickly counted the cash.

There was nothing else in the envelope, and – Caz quickly confirmed – just over three grand in fifties on the table.

"Where the hell did that come from?" Callum stared wide-eyed at the stack of notes.

"Savings?" I asked, and he gave me a withering glance.

"The night before she died, I begged my mum to try to think of someone who could lend me enough to keep Solomon at bay. There was nobody I – or she – hadn't already borrowed off." He shook his head. "If she'd had cash like this, she'd have let me have it."

"So maybe she found someone else to lend it to her?" I

asked.

"Fuck," Callum ran a trembling hand through his hair. "What if whoever leant her the money killed her?"

"Why would they leave the cash?" Caz asked, and I pointed a finger at the bag.

"He might have a point, you know. What if the money wasn't leant? What if it was stolen? Or," I paused, an idea coming to me, "What if it was blackmail pay-out. And the victim comes here, there's an argument, Cathy goes over the balcony and only at that point does our killer realise they don't know where the cash is? Well they're not gonna hang around: By then, they'll already be hearing sirens. And the fact that the handbag was behind her coat on a hook in the hallway would make it tricky to locate if you were in a hurry."

"My mum was the most honest person you ever met," Callum said flatly, his puzzled gaze still fixed on the cash. "There's no way she'd have pinched money. And blackmail?"

"Her only son is under real threat," I said. "Are you sure that she'd retain her usual high standards?"

"Fuck," Callum breathed again, slipping a hand into his jeans pockets. "I need a smoke."

He crossed to the balcony and tested the handle. It opened, and he stepped out, Caz and I following.

"Mum hated smoking in the flat. Always made me come out here." A sad smile flickered across his face. "Suppose I could smoke what I want to in there now. But it still feels wrong." He lit the cigarette, Caz and I having declined his offer of one for each of us, and stood to one side, smoking as though it were an important task he had to complete, and staring out across the cityscape below.

I looked around. This space was the same size as Steve Haines' balcony had been, but seemed, somehow, even neater. There was another small table (an alabaster ashtray this time) and a couple of chairs set up at one end, and an oversized terracotta box at the other end with a selection of now leaf-free plants in it.

I stepped over to the balcony and frowned.

Caz, noting what I had noted, stepped up beside me, looking from the balcony wall to my thigh. "This one's lower," she murmured, and I nodded.

"They're offset," I said, surmising that the original architects had clearly decided that from outside, and below, the balconies, if all a standard height, would look bland and standardised.

"They wanted to make it feel differentiated, so every second one is shorter than the one before. Which means that the balconies look like waves. In keeping, I guess, with the river theme of the buildings."

"And which also means," Caz murmured, peering over the edge and shuddering.

"That Solomon himself – as short as he is - could have pushed her," I finished, deciding not to look over the edge, and turning, instead, to walk back in to the living room.

I strolled idly around the living room, stopping in front of a large side unit that contained the history of Cathy Byrne and her kids: more framed photos, a certificate for swimming proficiency, Callum's City & Guilds certificate in Construction skills, a newspaper article clipped and framed in the same black wood frame, and with Louise Byrne as the by-line, and some trophies displayed as though they were Oscars and Golden Globes.

And then my heart stopped.

My blood ran cold.

The world stopped turning, and all the shit that usually happens when you realise that you've been seeing things completely wrong, as Caz, seeing my Lady of Shallot look, followed my gaze to the gold-framed picture of Cathy receiving a trophy and a cheque from a smiling woman in a navy-blue suit.

And as Caz registered the picture, her face, too, moved through confusion, concern and finally dismay.

"Oh dear," she said, turning to look at me. "That's not

good. That's not good at all.

CHAPTER FOURTEEN

"So, what are you going to do?" Caz asked me for maybe the fifth time – I'd honestly stopped counting.

"I'm going to deal with it," I said through gritted teeth. "I'll talk to her."

"And yet," she said gesturing around her, "Here we are. Still," she paused, reading a set of signs hung at the crossroads of two corridors, and moued in concentration, "At least you have some idea, now, of what might have been upsetting your parents."

"Caz," I turned to face her. "Can we not do this now?"

"Sweetie, we can not do this forever, but it won't change the fact that in Cathy Byrne's flat there is a picture of her shaking hands with your mother, said picture having been taken mere weeks before Mrs P did a nosedive from her balcony. Something's going on."

I sighed. "I know. I know," I repeated, trying to placate my friend. "But first, I want to talk to this Joanna," I looked at the slip of paper where Steve Haines had written the name Joanna Trztrzelewska, and mumbled something that sounded, I guessed, like the proper pronunciation of the surname.

"We were on our way here already," I said, as though justifying our presence. "It's only procrastination if it's something you weren't planning to do. Otherwise, surely, it's," I reached, "Whatever the opposite of procrastination is. Surely."

Caz raised any eyebrow. "We've been here before," she grumbled, pointing at a machine filled with chocolate bars and crisps, the lone 'Healthy option' being a bag of anaemic almonds that looked like they'd been boiled rather than blanched. "I recognise that flicker."

As if to prove her point, the light inside the machine began to spasm alarmingly and I cast a somewhat concerned eye around in case any nearby epileptics went rigid.

"I mean who," she continued, gesturing at the signs above us, "Asked Esher to design a hospital, and Kafka to do the bloody signage? 'Virology, Oncology, Psychology and OP'. It's like a bloody pet shop boys rap. And what in God's name is a Men's Health Clinic?"

"Bollocks, innit," I sniffed.

"Oh," she sighed, crestfallen. "I'd hoped it would be full of overly buff shirtless men advising other men how to lose ten pounds in six weeks whilst figuring out where the G-spot was and learning to Kayak in Snowdonia. Once again, the NHS disappoints me. Seriously, Daniel: We've been here half an hour and are walking around in circles. At least, if you're going to insist on doing this to avoid the more pressing issue of your mother being implicated in a possible murder, ask someone so we can find this woman – and, by the way I do not for a second think her name is pronounced like that. That sounds like a Hillman Imp starting on a cold morning."

She held up a hand to stave off my next question. "I just know, okay."

"We just need the Paediatric ward," I said, squinting around at signs. "And yes," I added, "I know. And also, yes: You can stop whining right now."

"But you know my views on children," Caz whined regardless. "Individually, they can be charming. But en masse, Daniel. En masse and poorly?"

I shook my head at her. "We're just trying to find the woman who cleans the ward," I said, "not minister to the patients."

Caz, spotting a sign I'd missed, pointed to the right, and began stalking purposefully in that direction. "Well that's just as well, Daniel, because I am warning you: More than two of the little tykes at any one time and I am in danger of rediscovering my Herodian side. So, just keep that in mind."

"Can I help you?" A booming woman's voice, with tones that suggested 'Help' was the last thing she wanted to do to us, stopped us both in our tracks.

We looked in the direction of the sound blast and realised it was coming from a large woman sat behind a reception desk, the seams on her pale blue nurses' outfit fighting the good fight against a bosom that looked as though it were determined, by hook or by crook, to best the polyester casing that was being reinforced only by the small plastic plate bearing the name Precious Nkomo.

Above her head, in letters that the naked eye would have missed, if the naked eye hadn't had the assistance of a microscope, were the words "Paediatrics Reception."

"Yes," I said, flustered by the accusatory glare, "We're looking for children."

Nurse Precious Nkomo pursed her lips, and squinted her eyes, a look of pure 'I thought you might be' suffusing her face, and, before I could say another word, Caz stepped forward and shoved me to one side.

"What my slow and, frankly, idiotic friend is trying to say," she said to Nurse Nkomo, her bright 'we're all in this together' smile plastered on her face, "Is that we're looking for someone who works on the Paediatric ward. Or who, we believe, is working here now. A Miss Joanna Trztrzelewska, she said, pronouncing the name Che-Che-Levska,"

"Jo?" Precious's scowl deepened. "What for?"

"We just wanted a quick chat," Caz, the smile dimming several watts in the face of Nurse Nkomo's suspicion.

"That's what they all say," Precious responded, her glare raking me up and down before repeating the optical strip-search on Caz. "Who're you?"

The look on her face continued to suggest that she found

us both highly objectionable.

"We're friends," I said, stepping forwards again.

"Friends who want to chat to her while she's at work?" Nurse Nkomo said. "Pull the other one. You Home Office?"

I shook my head, unsure whether being confused for an Immigration narc was a step up from being confused for an undercover cop.

"Mystery patients?" She asked, and Caz snorted like a prize pony.

"Sweetie," she said, gesturing at her ensemble, "Don't mystery patients try to blend in? This is couture."

"Couture? Fancy dress?" The nurse shrugged as though to suggest that whatever she was looking at was supranormal. Then, finally, "Fair point," Precious acceded. "Wait there."

She pointed at a trio of chairs lined up against the wall opposite her, and we sat ourselves down, Caz having firstly removed a pristine handkerchief from her bag, unfolded it, and placed it on the seat.

"I can't sit directly on plastic cushioning," she explained to my confused glance. "Sweats, sweets."

Across the corridor, Precious Nkomo lifted a telephone receiver, and – her eyes never leaving us, pushed some buttons, covered the receiver with her hand – lest, I supposed, we lipread her conversation (as you do) – and spoke into the receiver a few moments.

When she hung up, she pointed back at us, and said simply "Wait," in a tone that suggested any attempt to, say, bum rush the kids ward, would be met with ultimate force.

So, we waited, Caz fidgeting uncomfortably on the vinyl seating as Precious, from time to time, broke away from her work to scowl threateningly at us every time we stared, hopefully, at a passing teal-uniformed cleaner.

"I was trying to decide how to approach the elusive, if not unpronounceable Joanna Trztrzelewska when Caz dug me in the ribs, jolting me back to the present.

"Here's your opportunity," she said, nodding at another vending machine further along the corridor.

This one had clearly been set not to flicker at a seizure-inducing frequency, but was, instead, blinking on, for a minute, then switching itself off – plunging the merchandise within into a less than attractive gloom – for another sixty seconds.

Anyone bothering to peer into the machine and select product was clearly either a Jonesing sugar addict or an aficionado of shit merchandising.

Either way, the man bent over the machine at the moment, his full attention on the goods within had clearly failed to spot either Caz or me.

"Ask why your mother's shaking hands with the deceased," Caz stage-whispered as she shoved me from my seat towards him.

"Dad?" I asked, as my dad, his grey hair curling over the collar of his overcoat, straightened, a look of surprise swiftly replaced by a smile.

"What you doing here?" He asked. "You OK?"

"Fine," I said as a bag of Maltesers dropped, with a soft clunk into the drawer of the machine, and my dad's change was issued with all the grace and subtlety of a Gatling gun. "I was going to ask you the same thing."

"Me?" He dipped down, recovering the cash and the confectionary, and smiled at me in response. "Just dropped off a fare. Elderly man. Think he was going to have his feet done. Fancied a bag of sweets," he shook the bag before me. "What about you?"

"Just visiting a friend," I lied, waving my hand over my shoulder.

"In Paediatrics?" My dad asked, and I nodded, then swiftly shook my head.

"No; I mean yes. My friend's not a patient. She works there. In Paediatrics," I finished lamely, as my dad frowned at me.

"Good," he finally said, nodding.

"Is mum at home?" I asked, and he frowned.

"Mum?" He asked. "No. She's out, I think. Working.

Why?"

"I was gonna pop round," I said. "Something to ask her."

"Well she's not there," he said, pocketing his change.

"Well I can pop round tonight," I said, and my dad blanched. "I don't know if she'll be in," he stammered. "I think she's going straight out with some friends. Some girls night out."

"Mum?" I asked, incredulously. "On a girl's night out?"

"That's what she said," he answered. "What do you need to speak to her about?"
"Oh," I paused, uncertain how much to tell him, "I just want to ask her something."

"Well I can ask her if you like," he answered, and it was, now, my turn to frown.

"When are you going to see her?" I asked. "I mean: If she's going straight out from work."

"Well she'll come home," he snapped, in a way that made me wonder if she would.

My siblings were right: Something was going on with my parents, and the combination of my father's behaviour and the presence of that picture in Cathy Byrne's flat, made me worry that whatever it was, was – as Caz had expressed it – not good at all.

"It's OK, I smiled, "I'll give her a shout tomorrow."

"Yeah, well not too early, alright Danny? She's going to need a rest if she has a late night tonight."

I'd never known my mum drink more than a few glasses of sherry at Christmas, so the idea of her hungover was baffling, but I nodded my understanding as my dad hefted the Maltesers and nodded back up the hall.

"Well I'll let you get back to your friend in Paediatrics. Look after yourself," he said, and we hugged briefly before he turned and headed slowly along the corridor and I, looking after him for a moment, a degree of confusion and concern welling up in me, finally sighed, and turned back to the vinyl seats where Caz sat, her face set in the one that Aristos have been using for centuries every time they've had to interact with the natives and not let their utter bafflement show.

"So?" She asked when I re-joined her.

"He's dropping someone off," I answered, eyeing a two-year-old copy of GQ on a low table to one side of me.

"Fascinating. And is your mother involved in a murder?"

"Caz!" I looked at her in shock.

"Well?" Caz persisted.

"I don't know," I said. "I didn't ask. She's going out tonight, so I'll go round tomorrow and ask her, shall I?" I finished, ladling the sarcasm on.

"Out? Sweetheart your mother's less likely to go out voluntarily than Kevin Spacey. The woman's so homely she makes Martha Stewart look like Mata Hari. What the hell is going on chez Bird?"

"I don't know," I admitted, "but I am beginning to get worried."

"So: That was your opportunity to put your mind to rest, and you blew it."

"I can't ask my dad about this," I replied. "I don't know what he knows. If there are questions to be answered, I'll ask them of my mum. It's fair."

"Fair." Caz muttered the word in the same way that a normal person might say 'Gonorrhoea,' and was doubtless about to launch into an explanation of why my desire to be 'Fair' at all times was an affectation caused by my guilt and having once moved – even if only for a time from the working class to the middle class.

The fact that I'd slid back down to the not-working-but-running-a-shitty-boozer class would, I was sure, not feature in her amateur dissection of my psyche.

I was spared, momentarily, her Cecily Freud impersonation by the appearance of a petite woman dressed in teal blue overalls, who approached Precious, exchanged a few murmured words, during which each of them studiously avoided looking anywhere near Caz and I and went away again, returning a few minutes later, just as Caz had launched into her explanation of why my inability to challenge people I loved was rooted in my fear of rejection, to address us both.

"Why do you want to see me?" The woman demanded plainly, her naked suspicion reflected in the eyes – brown and almond-shaped – that regarded us keenly.

"Are you Joanna Trztrzlewska?" I asked, standing, and realising that – even at average height – I towered over the woman, her pale blonde hair tied in a simple pony tail as she fiddled with a hairnet in her hands.

"Well I'm not Marie Curie," she responded. "Listen, I'm on break, so whatever you want, can you get to it while I eat my dinner?" She smiled briefly, the movement dimpling the rose-coloured cheeks of her heart-shaped face.

"We can do better than that," I answered. "We can buy you dinner."

"Is there a bistro nearby?" Caz asked, as Joanna, having considered my offer for a millisecond, nodded her agreement.

"There's a cafeteria," Joanna said, heading towards the lifts.

"A cafeteria?" Caz repeated, savouring the word as though it were a novelty. Then, realising what she had actually just said, she fixed me with a displeased frown. "They'd better have a decent wine list," she muttered as the lift pinged, the doors opened, and Joanna Trztrzelewska stepped in, waving us impatiently on.

"I haven't got all night, folks."

"Call me Jo," Joanna Trztrzelewska said as she tore a crusty bread roll in two over her plate, allowing the crust flakes to descend on the beef stew beneath like snow onto an almost black lake. "Everyone else does. Mostly 'cos they can't pronounce Mrs Trztrzelewska,"

She smiled and nodded at Caz's tray. "You sure that's gonna be enough for you?" She asked, and Caz smiled, tore open the packet of water biscuits and lifted a slice of stilton on to one and smiled back.

"A feast," she said, eyeing the stew as though it were something from a lab. "Albeit one that might have been improved if this establishment had had a bar of any description."

"It would have," Jo answered, "If it was a Hilton, not a hospital. But I'm not sure anyone would want a surgeon doing little Johnny's appendix if they spotted a decent Burgundy on the menu."

"Fair point," Caz acceded, emptying the glass of water she'd – to my surprise- insisted on pouring from the communal font – into a giant ceramic pot containing a rubber plant – without, seemingly, noting that the plant was made of genuine plastic, and the 'soil' was some sort of resin – and removing a small bottle of port from her handbag.

"You're carrying a bottle of Port around?" Jo asked, in amazement.

"Since Christmas," Caz answered, as though it were the most natural behaviour in the world. "One should always be prepared." She waved the bottle at me, my polite refusal eliciting a displeased moue from her.

Jo watched as a decent slug of port was added to the empty glass, then turned to me.

"What's this all about?"

"It's about Cathy Byrne," I said, and her demeanour changed instantly.

"Newspaper?" She asked suspiciously.

"Jo, sweetest," Caz replied before I could get a word in, "How many local journos wear Balenciaga? And before you ask, we're not national either. My friend here is an esteemed detective and barman, who – apart from turning teetotal on me," she pouted, "Is looking into Mrs Byrne's death."

"I'm Danny Bird," I said, and, realising how conceited the announcement sounded, clarified it by explaining "Cathy had my name in her phone when she died. Any idea why she would have?"

"Were you looking for a cleaner?" She shot back,

delicately forking a chunk of beef into her mouth?

I shook my head. "We've been there. Nobody seems to know why she would have had my name, or why she went over the balcony."

"Well I can tell you why she didn't go over the balcony," Jo answered, two slices of carrot and a chunk of potato following the beef.

I waited as she chewed, swallowed, then took a sip of water.

"She did not go over because she was depressed, distressed, despairing or suicidal. Cathy Byrne was a fighter, and if there was something bothering her she faced it head on. She worked, and she raised her kids, and she never once gave me any reason to think that this," she shook her head, seemingly unable to articulate the words, "that this would happen."

"Her son Callum mentioned you might be able to tell us what her last movements were."

Jo sighed. "Well her last movement is common knowledge," she said, dunking the bread roll into her gravy and making an ascending and suddenly descending arc with her other hand. "But before that, we were at work all day in the sugar house. We got home about seven. I left her in the lift and went to make dinner. I don't know what she did between then and when it happened."

"The sugar house?" I glanced at Caz who added another slice of stilton to another water biscuit and turned towards Jo.

"The. Sugar. House," Jo said. "All capitalised, like it's not 'A' sugar house, but the only one that ever there was. It's an apartment block down by the river. Used to be some sort of warehouse back in the olden days, and now it's all – what was the phrase – 'Loft Living in The Heart of The City.' Only it's not – in the heart of the city. It's on the side of the river that faces the city, but it backs on to South London in all of its" she searched for the phrase "Variety. The flats cost at least a couple of million each.

"Cath and me cleaned the Sugar House, when we weren't here cleaning this place. She did the flats, and I did the public spaces."

"The public spaces?" I asked, imagining a lobby and some corridors, "Wasn't that a bit one-sided?"

"It worked for us," Jo squinted her displeasure at my suggestion she'd been getting the easy job, and I remembered Steve Haines' comment. *Cathy wanted everyone to be happy*. "There's a lobby, there's lifts, landings, the residents lounge – which no bastard ever uses but I still need to dust and polish – a gym, a swimming pool, changing areas, sauna, the underground garage and the panic room."

So maybe she wasn't on such a cushy number after all.

"Wait," Caz paused, water biscuit halfway to her mouth. "Did you say panic room."

Jo nodded, even this minor motion oozing disgust at the excesses of the inhabitants of The Sugar House. "It's," she added, quoting, I assumed, from a brochure she'd seen, "a hermetically sealable, atmospheric controlled residents lounge where they can be comfortable and safe in times of unrest or strife for up to three days. In case," she added, slipping out of the sales-speak, "the residents are home when the revolution comes, I suppose. Which is unlikely cos half of them have never even seen the bloody flats. All bought off plan and owned by billionaires who just want to own a bit of property in London. With a gym and a panic room."

"So, did anything odd happen that day?" I asked, getting us back to the topic in hand.

"Odd?" She considered the question. "Not really. We wiped down surfaces nobody ever used. We picked up knickers that cost more per pair than Cathy and me were earning in a month." She eyed Caz's Balenciaga the way I imagine Lenin might have eyed the Tsarina's jewel-encrusted evening gown.

"It was," she shrugged, "a normal day."

"Listen," I leaned in, "We found some money in Cathy's bag. A lot of money."

"Money?" Joanna shook her head, puzzlement obvious on her face. "Cathy never had any money. She was skint, always."

And yet there it had been, fluttering from the envelope like giant pink confetti.

"So, you've no idea where the money could have come from? Why she had it?"

"You got to be mistaken," she shook her head again. "Cathy with money? It doesn't make sense."

I decided to leave that line for now. "Okay," I prompted, "tell me about Cathy." Joanna shrugged.

"What's to tell: She was a grafter. And she always did what she said she would. The only annoying thing about her was that she would never cut corners, and she'd give me grief if I tried to not do a room this week, or skip hoovering an unused spare room, you know? But she had a heart of gold, and her family were everything to her. She fretted about her kids, she worked three jobs to make ends meet."

"Three?"

"Yeah, she worked here too, cleaned The Sugar House and she did some work at the local primary school – The Nye Bevan.

"She was a dinner lady, only they laid her off a couple of months ago. Cuts," she said venomously, "While half the council can still afford dinner at The Ivy on expenses."

"And how did getting laid off impact her?"

"Well it didn't make her throw herself from the roof," Joanna insisted. There was a pause, and she shrugged. "It upset her. Obviously. She needed the money. But it was just another thing to fret about. She was talking to our boss at House Angels – they're the ones with the contract for The Sugar House and a few of the other developments around. Cathy wanted to get another few jobs out of them. Even if rich people don't wanna pay taxes to keep dinner ladies in the schools, they're usually happy enough to pay dinner ladies to clean their toilets."

"So, she was okay that day?"

"She was worried. To begin with. Her son was in trouble. Her daughter had been in some trouble or other. She was worried it might cost her a job."

"How?"

Joanna shrugged. "Mister, I'll be honest with you: I got my own problems, you know? I listen to Cathy, but I don't always hear her. Anyway, she'd forgotten it by the time we left, cos by then she was fed up cos she had to come back."

"Come back? To the Sugar House?"

Joanna nodded. "Yeah," she said. "Cathy was not happy that day cos she didn't get to do all the flats. She got held up by one of the residents. They're not supposed to be there; well, it's better if they're not. But one of them was and wanted to chat. There is nothing," she fixed us with a beady stare, "Worse than a Chatty resident." She said 'Chatty' like you or I might have said 'Homicidal.' "Yes, so anyway, she said that she'd have to go back in tomorrow to clean the other flat in case."

"In case of what?"
Joanna shook her head. "She didn't say. And I didn't ask. Cathy was one of those people who did every job she did as though she was doing it for herself. She kept her own flat like a showroom, and she cleaned other people's places – rich people, half of who were never even in the bloody flats – as though she was cleaning her own. She was so bloody – what's the word? - conscientious. And she was one of the best friends I ever had.

"If I was short – of milk, of something for the kid's dinner, of the rent money – she'd give me whatever she had. And she was always making food – cakes, pies, sometimes a big pot of stew. So, when she said she was going to have to go back the next day, I told her fuck them. You got your own stuff to do, you know? But I didn't ask her why she needed to go back."

Jo paused, the bread roll still in her hand. "Does that matter?"

CHAPTER FIFTEEN

My mobile rang as I was turning the corner into my parent's street.

Glancing at the screen, I saw that it was my sister Maz calling, and I answered it, saying "I'm on my way there," before she had a chance to speak.

"Well have you found out anything?" She asked impatiently. "I was calling them all last night and they weren't answering the phone. Finally got hold of dad on his mobile, and he said he was out in the cab. But there were background noises like he was in a pub or a restaurant – voices, clinking glasses, cutlery on plates. What the hell is going on?"

"Mum went out last night," I said plainly, "With her girlfriends."

"Out?" The incredulity couldn't have been greater if I'd said our mother had gone on a one woman killing spree with a chainsaw. "Mum doesn't go out. And she's not got any friends that do."

"Well she seems to have some now," I said.

"Jesus," Maz breathed down the phone, "This is worse than we thought, isn't it?"

"I'm here," I said, stopping outside their block and pressing the button for their flat. "I'll call you back when I've spoken to her."

My mum's voice – tinny and weak – issued from the speaker over the buttons, and I announced myself, hearing the click and buzz as she unlocked the door for me.

Pulling the door open I stepped into the lobby and crossed to the lift, pressing the button to call it.

In my thirty-five years, I had never seen my mother with a hangover, and the shock, when I'd ascended to the fourth floor, let myself into the flat, and found her in the living room, was almost indescribable.

Not to put too fine a point on it, she looked terrible.

"Jesus," I said, "What happened to you?"

"Tequila," she almost wept, pulling the blanket she was wrapped in tighter around her. "And a very late night."

My dad appeared from the kitchen, concern etched on his face. "What are you doing here?" He demanded as he placed a steaming cup of lemon and ginger tea into my mum's hands.

"Lovely to see you too," I said, nodding at my mum. "I came to see mum. Wanted to ask her something."

"Can't it wait?" He asked, gesturing at my mum, who sipped the tea, winced, asked if I drank ginger and lemon tea, offered me the cup and asked my dad to make her a decent cup of proper tea.

Dad shook his head at me, nodded at my mum again, shot me a look of pure annoyance, and pottered into the kitchen to make another cup of tea.

I took the proffered lemon and ginger and sat on the sofa next to my mum.

"Of course," she said, as I sipped the drink, "You know why Marxists only ever drink fruit teas, don't you?"

I did. It was an old joke, and one which almost everyone in our family knew and recited regularly. "Because," I said as we both chorused the punchline, "All proper tea is theft."

She chuckled. "I taught you well."

"Mum," I dragged a coaster across the coffee table and set the mug down on it. "What's going on?"

"I told you," she said a sheen of sweat on her forehead, "Tequila. And – I think – a few glasses of prosecco."

"Prosecco?" I did not for a second believe her. "You were

drinking prosecco?"

"Well it was a special night," she said, "House Angels got a new contract. We're going to be cleaning in six new developments and it's all under my franchise, so I took a few of the girls out for cocktails up in Soho."

"You?" I was almost speechless. "Went drinking in Soho?"

"Oh," her hand covered her mouth, "I've just realised, I probably should have spent the cash at The Marq. Family business and all that. But I just thought the girls would enjoy a trip up West."

I waved aside her concern over venues and tackled the real reason for my visit.

I had been awake most of the night, worrying whether the personal problems that had clearly been bothering my parents were linked to the situation with Cathy Byrne. My mum's mention of House Angels, and of contracts to clean new housing developments suddenly made sense of the picture of Cathy Byrne and her, but still left me with the fear that whatever was going on it had Cathy's death bound up, somehow, in it.

"Mum," I asked, "How did you know Cathy Byrne?"

"Cathy?" My mum frowned. "She's one of my girls. Cleans a few days a week for me. Why?"

And I realised, at that moment, that my mum was still talking of Cathy in the present tense. "She's dead," I said, and my mum gasped as my dad entered the room with her PG Tips and a plate of chocolate digestives.

"You alright, babe?" He asked, frowning.

My mum smiled weakly and shook her head. "What happened?" She asked me.

And I told her.

"The thing is," I finished, "She had my number in her phone, and I'd really like to know why she had it."

"Well, she had it because I gave it to her," my mum answered, her cup of tea untouched on the coffee table. "She said she wanted to book your pub for a party."

"A party?" I said, somewhat unconvinced. "How did she even know about The Marq?"

"She'd seen it in the papers. But I don't think it was a party she wanted you for. Cathy was asking about those murders you'd solved. Wanted to know if you could be hired. 'What would you want to hire him for?' I asked her, and she went all coy. 'I might not,' she said, 'Only there might be someone I know who could use him'."

My dad coughed. "Listen Dan. I know this is important, but couldn't you do it later? Or tomorrow? You can see she needs to rest," he smiled at my mum, and I wondered, for a second, whether there was a trace of guilt in his smile. Had my mum gone drinking because of something my dad had done?

Mum sighed, waving away my dad's protests. "I put the number into her phone myself. Cathy was a smart girl, but she had some sort of number dyslexia. If you told her a number, she'd mix the digits up every time. So, I typed the number in."

"So, did she give you any explanation on who this 'someone' who might need me was?" I asked, ignoring my dad's request.

"No," mum shook her head.

"Danny," my dad said, his tone containing a warning.

"I'm nearly done, dad; I promise."

"It was at the awards ceremony," my mum mused, and an image of the photo in Cathy Byrne's flat my mum in a smart blue business suit shaking hands with Cathy, who was holding an envelope aloft in the other hand.

"Cathy had received a glowing commendation from one of her customers, and House Angels likes us to do recognition nights, so we had a bit of a 'do.' She got a certificate. She was due a bonus in this month's money."

"She was," my mum paused and smiled fondly, "A good woman. Always wanted a bit more work – needed the money, I think – but always did a top job. And kept herself to herself. Wasn't one for sharing her woes – not like some of the girls – or for washing her laundry in public. Yeah," my mum nodded, "I liked her, so when she asked about you," She paused, frowned, "I gave her your number."

"But you never asked why?"

She shook her head. "I never asked, and she, apart from saying she might want to book The Marq for a party - which even I could see was unlikely - never told. But maybe," she said, thinking back to the day in question, "Whatever she wanted you for had something to do with The Sugar House."

"In what way?"

"I don't know," my mum shook her head sadly, "She just – well, she went on about the place a bit. She did a couple of other places for me, and when I said that we might have some new contracts coming up, she got a bit concerned. Wanted to know if we'd be moving out of The Sugar House. Seemed a bit worried that she'd not be cleaning there any more.

"Which is a bit odd, cos most cleaners couldn't give a monkey where they're cleaning, so far as they're getting paid." My mum stared into the middle distance for a moment. "I wonder why she was determined to keep doing that place?"

"Why indeed?" I asked, as an idea formed in my head.

CHAPTER SIXTEEN

"I am not happy," Joanna Trztrzelewska said, her displeasure clear in every syllable. "Not happy at all. This job I need, you see? I can't afford for fuck ups. And this," she indicated Caz, who appeared to be dragged up as Heidi, "This is taking the piss."

"What?" Caz, her face a mask of injured innocence beneath a high-piled bun that seemed to consist of more plaits than should have been feasible with her hair, gestured at her outfit. "This," she announced of the cheesecloth blouse, dirndl skirt and chunky, cork soled, Birkenstocks on her feet, "Is serviceable."

"This," Joanna responded, nodding furiously at the ensemble, "Looks like a Sex-Heidi Cross-dresser. This," she indicated her own outfit – a pale blue smock with the House Angels logo stitched on to the left breast pocket, a pair of jeans poking out the bottom of the smock and a pair of trainers on her feet, "Is what cleaners wear. I thought you wanted to blend in?"

This last was addressed to me, and I had to admit that Joanna was right. It had taken some persuasion last night to get my mum to agree to let Caz and I come visit The Sugar House undercover as cleaners.

"This is my work," she'd protested in similar tones to those Joanna was now using to describe Caz's attempts to dress as a cleaner. "It's not just some pin money thing, Danny; it really matters to me."

"I know, mum," I'd replied, and I really did – I really did understand how important this was to her, especially if she and my dad were going to split. She'd want an independent source of income. "But I need to know what Cathy Byrne did on her last day, and since most of it seems to have been spent at The Sugar House, I want to see inside, see who she met, get a sense for what was going on there that day."

"But why?" My mum persevered. "I mean, why you? Surely the police are looking into all this?"

"I don't know," I shrugged. "They don't seem entirely convinced there's anything fishy about it, but I'm not sure they've actually got much to go on. And as far as some of them are concerned, she was a woman of a certain age who had money and family troubles."

"No love," mum shook her head definitively, "there's no way Cathy Byrne jumped off that building."

"I know," I said. "And that means that if whatever – or whoever - sent her over the edge is linked to the Sugar House, then the only way to find out is to get in there and take a look around."

"And that's what worries me," my mum had said.

"It's not so much that you look like this that upsets me," Joanna continued, still glaring furiously at Caz's Drag-Oktoberfest costume, "But that you actually think I might turn up to work dressed like this."

"Well my cleaner Inge wears similar," Caz (who I happened to know hadn't had a cleaner in the fifteen years I'd known her – as the state of her apartment testified) deadpanned.

"Darling," Jo replied flatly, "If this is what she is wearing, you do not have a cleaner: You have an off duty Alpine Hooker who polishes surfaces for kicks. And I'm not going in there with you dressed like that."

We were sitting in a small café around the corner from the luxury development. This place was called "Cilla's" and seemed to specialise in bacon. I swear even the bowl of cornflakes were served with optional streaky slices on top.

Joanna Trztrzelewska now dipped down to the carrier bag at her feet and extracted, with a deal more rustling than I suspect was entirely necessary – a couple of duplicate pale blue smocks for us.

Caz, her bacon and eggs untouched before her, blanched.

"I'd rather die," she announced, and Joanna shrugged her disinterest.

"Die," she said, nodding at Caz's current outfit, "Stay here like that. I really don't care. But you're not coming in to my job dressed like that."

"She has a point," I said, accepting my own smock. "If we stand out, that will become the topic of conversation, rather than what Cathy was doing here on her last day."

"But they're," Caz swallowed, as though the word she was about to be forced to say was already creating a foul taste in her mouth, "Nylon, Danny. I can't wear nylon. It brings me out in blotches. I'll look like a leper by the time we leave."

I sighed. "I'll spring for a facial," I attempted bribery.

"At a spa of my choice?" She asked, her poker face sipping in to place.

"So long as it's in the home counties," I answered, hoping I wouldn't have to also pay for transport.

"But it's not my face that'll be irritated," she countered. "My whole body is about to be encased in powder blue nylon. And not even ironically," she complained, and though I wanted to point out that it was – at best – her torso, and that we were talking about a loose-fitting tabard, not an iron lung, I figured that the time for haggling had passed.

"Okay," I conceded, "A body wrap. But seaweed, not collagen. I'm not made of money."

Caz still regarded the smock – folded now and placed on the table as Joanna tucked into her poached eggs on toast (with a side of crispy speck) – as though it were nuclear waste, and, after heaving a sigh of such depth that it suggested a tragedy unknown since the sinking of The Lusitania was about to unfold, finally snatched the item up, muttered "I want lunch paid for too," and stalked off to the single loo at the back of the café to repair and reconfigure her char-lady disguise.

I turned to Joanna. "So, what's the plan?"

"Plan?" She speared a corner of the toasted white slice on her fork and wiped it through the yellow sloshing around her plate. "You think I should have a plan? I'm not the Hart to Hart of South London. *You*, I thought, would have a plan."

She had a point.

"We'll do the flats in the order Cathy did them. So: Top to bottom or Bottom up?"

Joanna considered this and nodded. "Bottom to top. Yes. While I always start with the residents' lounge on the very top floor and work my way down to the basements."

"The basements plural?"

She nodded. "They have an underground carpark down there. Once a quarter a man comes with a pressure washer to do the floors and walls. But on a weekly basis, but I do the office and the lifts and the lobby in front of them. Then there's the Swimming pool, gym, sauna, changing rooms and the panic room."

"Cathy had the hardest job with the flats, to be honest. I covered for her once or twice, and I'd much rather be on my own in the garage – even if it is a bit creepy – than dealing with some of the residents. It's better when they're out, but sometimes they're not, and you have to interact," she said in tones that suggested she considered interacting with the residents a practice akin to human sacrifice with a side order of necrophilia attached.

"Mind you," she added, "half the places – like I said – are empty. Foreign investors," she said, in a way that left me in no doubt whatsoever of her thoughts on people who buy flats as investments and never live in them. "They really ought to do something about those people," she said bitterly. "I have friends on waiting lists. Friends with kids. Little kids. Stuck in shitty Bed and Breakfast places that you wouldn't put a dog in, and here are flats – big, spacious, clean flats – fully furnished with all the latest gadgets - just sitting there empty."

She came out of her reverie. "Usually, I'm done on mine fairly quickly, so I go and help Cathy to finish hers. Or I used to," she finished, as the fact that she wouldn't be helping Cathy any more hit her. "Oh, and while I think of it," she added, "Don't use bleach."

"No bleach?" I asked, intrigued.

"It's absolutely verboten. The rich," Joanna announced po-faced, "Like the world to gleam with an antibacterial sheen but hate the smell of anything cheap. So, it's all Neroli-scented this, and Magnolia-scented that. I found that out when I helped Cathy out once. She got complaints from some poncey French guy cos I'd shoved a load of Domestos down his toilet. Well, it was either that or sandblast the thing."

"Did you help her that day?" I asked, and she shook her head, a look of disgust settling over her face.

"No. The garage was a mess. There'd been a car accident the night before, and the police had used the office to take statements, which meant I had more coffee rings and pen marks on the worktops than you'd believe; plus, well, I hadn't done much with the residents' lounge over Christmas, so I had to give that a deep clean and then I knocked the bloody Christmas tree with the hoover and it fell over so I ended up having to set the sodding thing up again. I fucking hate Christmas trees," she added, venomously.

"Well quite. So," I said, moving the conversation on, "you didn't see Cathy that day at all?"

"No," she said, "But like I said, she was busy too cos she ended up getting back to the lobby around the same time as me and she'd been delayed in one of her apartments – we're not allowed to call them flats. And also, that," she nodded at my piece of paper, "If it has names or alarm codes, you must never let them see it.

"This lot are all about their security and their privacy. The idea that you might have a bit of paper with their names and their alarm codes on it will send them all off the deep end."

I glanced at the paper in front of me. It contained the apartment numbers, names and alarm codes for the six flats Caz and I were going to be cleaning (and I use the term very loosely) today.

It looked like this:

1A/ Raffles Fund (666555)
1B/ Constable Investments (990991)
2A/Mrs Xiu (450996)
2B/ M. Foucault (330122)
3A/ Mr Stepanov (605411)
3B/ Dinnertime Limited (190566)
4A /Dreyfus Intl. (999666)
4B/ Mr Soong (326692)
5A/ Mr Fyne (000001)
5B/ Mr Makhtoum (246335)

"Well I'd better make sure they don't see it then," I said, folding the list, and slipping it into my pocket, as Caz returned from the loo.

"You next," Joanna said, chucking another smock at me. "And you need to take that off."

I followed her gaze to where Caz had pinned what looked like a platinum, diamond and emerald panther-shaped brooch over the words House Angels.

"Never," Caz said coldly.

"Be realistic, Caz," I said. "How many cleaners do you know who turn up for work with a chunk of Asprey on their pinny?"

"I think," Caz deadpanned, "We've already covered this: I don't know any cleaners. But if I did, they'd wear their dear old granny's brooch to work as a way of keeping her close. And as a final two fingers to a world of uniforms and," she retched slightly, "Nylon."

"Fuck it," Joanna waved a hand in exasperation. "I tell them she's my cousin Magda. Magda," she confirmed to me in a stage whisper clearly intended to reach Caz, "is not all there. In the head, you know?"

"Oh, I know," I smirked, glancing at Caz, who glowered furiously before shrugging her bag over her shoulder.

"Can we get on with it, please?" She demanded. "Only I'm rather keen to get this over before I have any further indignities piled on me."

I looked questioningly at Joanna, who shrugged. "As good a time as any," she admitted, emptying her mug of tea in one mouthful, and standing.

CHAPTER SEVENTEEN

"We go in around the back," Joanna eyed the double-width minimalist front door with undisguised loathing. "By the bins. We are never," she eyed Caz, "To enter by the front door. That," she switched to an impersonation of a toff, "Is for residents h-and their guests h-alone."

"I don't think I've ever gone in anywhere by the tradesman's entrance," I muttered, receiving, for my thoughts, a discrete cough from Caz and a raised eyebrow that said 'I am not going to rise to that unashamed double entendre, and for that you will recognise me as the good friend that I am.'

We were standing in front of The Sugar House, a huge Late Georgian Warehouse that had been built, as a repository for incoming sugar and associated imports from colonies, and as a place to store goods en route back to the same colonies and plantations. See: I'd done my homework.

The warehouse, along with the neighbourhood around it – and, let's be honest, most of the inner city around that – had, over the years, gone through its ups and downs. Mostly, it seemed, downs. Even I could remember when this part of the city – on the opposite bank of the Thames from the vast temples to Mammon, the palaces of the Royals and the Rich, and all the glamour that was London with a capital 'L' all – was, well, for want of a better phrase, a bit shit.

Not feral dogs and hunger games levels of shit; just dead, derelict, uneasy shit.

Like going to the house of an ancient relative you haven't seen for decades and realising that they've become decrepit and unwashed, and feeling guilty yet hating them for making you feel guilty shit.

And now, once again, The Sugar House had a function. The sandstone front had been sandblasted so that it looked as though it had been built last year, and the double-width door had security locks on it so that neither the depraved the deranged, the lost, the lonely nor – God forbid – the locals could wander in unannounced and check out what else the designers and architects had done to the place.

I stepped back to the edge of the pavement and craned my neck back.

From the street, it was impossible to see into any of the apartments. All I could see was a shining monolith towering overhead, with minimal signage, no obvious inhabitants and no visible access points.

It was as though an alien spaceship had assumed what it thought was a passible form as a London building, and simply landed in the space, the blast blowing all trash, refuse, detritus far away and leaving the strange sense that I was looking at a movie set rather than a home.

As I gazed up, a whirring began from somewhere to my left. I glanced that way and a sheet of matt black metal – the sort of thing that looked like it might be used to make stealth bombers or anti-terrorist barricades – slid slowly upwards, revealing a sloping entrance that seemed to lead under the building itself.

A car – something hulking and gunmetal grey – rolled slowly up the ramp, paused at the top, the indicators suggesting that it was about to turn left, then, the engine purring in a discrete fashion that belied the sheer bulk of the automobile itself, slid into the street and went on its way.

The blast-proof door began to automatically descend, and something on the opposite side of the street caught my eye.

I glanced across to where another building, similar to The Sugar House but clearly still under renovation stood, a number of doorways creating shadowy nooks into which, I was sure, someone had just dipped.

I squinted, and sure enough, three doors along, could see a small figure that seemed to be fiddling with a camera. Whoever they were, they were so intent on the camera that they failed to spot the man who ducked under the garage door as it descended and stalked across the road towards their hiding space.

This new arrival was tall and muscular, his hair styled in the sort of military crewcut with a flat top that used to be fashionable in the US Marines and certain Leather Bars. His black suit was fitted in a way that suggested Italian tailoring, but the width of his shoulders implied a smartened-up bouncer, and his body language openly stated that he had whatever the Italian for "The Raging Hump" was.

"Oi!" He shouted, causing the figure to look up startled. "I've warned you," he said, pointing a finger.

The figure stepped out of the doorway, and beside me I heard Joanna gasp.

I squinted across and a flicker of recognition ignited somewhere in the back of my brain.

"Piss of now," the man said, his finger continuing to jab at the woman who was now standing on the pavement opposite staring him down with an undisguised contempt that seemed only to further enrage him, "Or I'll have the Rozzers on you again."

"You don't own the bloody streets yet," the small woman responded, throwing her head back in a show of resistance, that made the man pause.

"Is that Louise Byrne?" I wondered aloud, seeing some similarity between the woman – the way she held her head, the line of her nose – and the pictures I'd seen in Cathy's living room.

Joanna nodded. "What's she doing here?" She whispered, as the tall man loomed menacingly over Louise Byrne, words were exchanged, and he stalked back to The Sugar House, entering, this time, by the front door, which he opened with some sort of electronic fob on a chain attached to his uniform.

Caz, Joanna and I watched as the woman opposite, now that the threat from the doorman had passed, deflated slightly, fiddled once again with the camera in her hand, then turned as though to leave.

"Wait," I called, and, with Caz and Joanna in tow, ran across the street to the opposite pavement.

She'd turned and blinked in puzzlement at us.

Louise Byrne was wearing a full length black puffer coat. The sort of thing that looks like you've basically borrowed a duvet and turned it into a garment, and on the top of her head a beret perched – seeming to be more about style than warmth.

"What do you want?" She asked me, then, focussing over my shoulder, smiled in recognition at Joanna.

"Lou," Joanna smiled back. "What's going on?"

"Sorry, Jo," she said, "Forgot it was your day. I don't want to get you into any trouble, so I'll pop round the block a bit and you won't even know where I am when you get out."

"What's going on?" Joanna asked again, her frown deepening.

"I've got him," Louise said, a blaze of triumph – the triumph of the evangelist convinced they've just had irrefutable proof of the existence of God – flashing in her eyes and illuminating her face.

"I got proof the bastard's on the take. Proof he helped Constable break my estate. They killed Alex as good as if they put the needle in his hand, and now I'm going to prove it."

"Shit, Lou," Joanna's frown was a look of real concern now. "You've got to drop this. It's not helping you."

But Louise Byrne was already rambling on about a series of connections she'd made, and how all she needed was access to a few bank statements and she'd be able to prove completely, and then she stopped, focussed on me and Caz for a moment, then frowned at Joanna Trztrzelewska and said, “Where’s my mum? I’ve got to tell her.”

And I looked at Caz, who looked at me, and we both looked at Joanna.

Who stepped forward, put an arm around the young woman’s shoulder, and said “Let’s go for a coffee, Lou. Get out of the cold, eh?

“You two coming?” She asked over her shoulder, as she lead the bemused woman away.

CHAPTER EIGHTEEN

"She's never been what you'd call entirely stable," Joanna muttered to me, casting a worried eye at the figure huddled behind a table in the corner of the café.

Louise had taken the news of her mother's death in silence, staring fixedly at the sugar dispenser on the table, before reaching out to rearrange the plastic squeezy bottles of ketchup and brown sauce so that they stood on either side of the sugar, and it was only when she looked up that I realised she had tears streaking her cheeks.

"He got her," she whispered, as I moved to put an arm around her. "No," she mumbled, shrugging out of my reach. "He got her, and it's my fault."

I glanced at Caz, who raised an eyebrow and said nothing.

Joanna moved, her chair squeaking against the floor tiles. "Who got her, Louise?" she asked, reaching a hand out and putting it over Louise's so that the young woman's hand was enveloped.

"Blythe," Louise said, seeming to focus in on Joanna. "Evan Blythe." She swallowed a sob. "What am I going to do?" She asked.

"Well first," Caz said, "You're going to have a cup of tea. Strong, and with sugar," she said, heading to the counter.

Knowing Caz's thoughts on tea, I figured there'd be a brandy dropped into it. Joanna squeezed Louise's hand before joining me and following Caz to the counter where my friend was already in the process of topping up a mug of tea with the contents of a large metal container – not so much a hipflask as a side-arm – to the bemusement of the woman behind the counter.

"Another coffee for me," Caz instructed, before turning to me. "And eggs, bacon, a fried slice and half a tomato. I'm going to sit with her," she nodded back across the room, and he," she pointed at me, "Is paying."

"Who's Alex?" I asked Joanna in response to the comment about Louise's stability – or lack thereof, "and what's this about him being killed?"

"Lou's boyfriend," Joanna responded, ordering her own breakfast, and pointing at me when it came to payment. "They lived together on an estate a down Dulwich way. Nice little flat, only Alex got into drugs. Heroin," she added, the disgust plain in her voice. "The estate went from pretty and safe to a warzone overnight, and Alex was, I suppose, a casualty. He died," she sighed, "and, well, it sent her a little – how is it? – doo-daddy?"

"Doolally," I corrected, asking for a slice of toast and a poached egg. "So what's Evan Blythe got to do with that?"

"She blames him. And no," Joanna added before I could ask another question, "I don't know why; you'll have to ask her. But I do know that Cathy was worried. Like I say, Louise was always artistic. Fragile. Whatever happened with her man pushed her close to the edge." She glanced over her shoulder at the table where Caz and Louise sat, my friend attempting to make small talk. "I don't know what will happen now."

Having ordered, we headed back to the table. Louise looked up at me as I sat down, and jerked her head at Caz. "She says you can help me. Help get that bastard for this."

"Help you?" I shot a look at Caz. "I want to know what happened to your mum, but I'm not sure if it will help."

Louise laid a hand on the table. I noticed the shake as she did so – like her whole body was under control but the turmoil of emotions she was feeling had to come out somewhere and were channelled to her left hand, which almost vibrated with fury.

She closed her eyes, steadied herself again. "He gets away with it," she whispered. "Every. Fucking. Time. And I've made so many mistakes – shown my hand too early and given him the chance to worm away every time. Nobody believes me anymore."

She opened her eyes and looked straight at me, the fury in her gaze no longer controlled.

"If you can't help me get this bastard – get justice for my mum, for Alex, then I'll do it myself."

She moved as though to leave the table, and I stopped her. "Look," I said, "I can't promise anything. But I want to know what happened to your mum; and I promise you, if it had anything to do with Evan Blythe I will make sure he pays."

She hesitated, the look in her eyes like a dog that expects, always, to be kicked, but still can't help wanting to trust. "Talk to me," I said as she sat herself back down. "Tell me the whole story."

"Blythe heads up the planning committee on the local council," she began, in a tone that suggested she had told this tale before, many times. "He owns the planning committee," she clarified.

"And Constable Construction owns Blythe. And they've been getting him to pass through redevelopment plans; to convert commercial properties into residential, to level buildings of historical value – or places that mean something to the people who actually live where Constable wants to develop."

I had a flashback to the posters that Cathy Byrne had put up in the lobby of her flats. "And they were looking at The Races?" I asked.

"Looking?" She snorted. "I – when I was a kid – I had a blog. Used to go out every night to clubs, pubs, loved going to museums. London," she said, her monologue becoming, now, a stream of conscious one, "Greatest city in the world. Art and culture and nightlife and design and architecture and fashion. I had a reputation. If I said something was good, people went to see it. If I said it was a bit naff, they stayed away. I was believed."

She sipped her liquor-infused tea as the other breakfasts hit the table. "It – the blog – was called "The Cityist." She smiled fondly at the memory.

"And The Cityist, when I left college, got me a job on The Chronicle. They wanted me to do the same: report on nightlife, theatre reviews, you know? I was grown up. Proper job, and a little flat I'd moved into with my boyfriend Alex."

His name made her smile, then she clenched her jaw hard, breathed in deeply as though, again, making a supreme effort to control her emotions, and carried on, "And we were living in a nice little flat on a nice little estate. Good neighbours. A community hall that was clean and welcoming. All the basic shops you'd need: A doctors, dentists, D.I.Y., chip shop and a little grocers."

"I'd move in tomorrow," Caz murmured, slicing her tomato into quarters.

"Not now you wouldn't," Louise snapped. "First, the rents on the shops went up. They left. Then the council started moving in people who'd been evicted from other estates – violent tenants, mentally ill, drug dealers and junkies, alkies, all the usual neighbours from hell. Someone burned the community centre down.

"And that was when I discovered that Constable Construction had been doing land registry searches on the place. So, I asked some questions. Put two and two together. Of course, at that point, I came up with five, but I was still in the general area of right on my guesses."

"What happened?" I asked.

"Nothing." She chuckled bitterly. "The Chronicle wasn't really interested in it, to be honest. Turned out they weren't really interested in much beyond puff pieces on local restaurants and four hundred words in praise of the latest redevelopment project by Constable or their ilk."

"In other words, the very people you'd discovered were

corrupting the planning process."

She nodded. "The people who live in places like the one I lived in – or who live in The Races - don't buy advertising space, you see. Constable and all their mates in the five-star restaurants and poncey wine bars set up to service the people who buy their flats do. 'Cept, of course, half the time there's nobody living in the bloody flats."

"So, what did you do?"

She laughed again, the sound anything but happy. "Nothing. I needed the job. We can't all be Lou Lou Byrne: Girl reporter. Or we can't if we want a roof over our heads and food on the table. And then Alex died."

"Drugs," she said simply, her face setting in a solid mask, as though even letting a frown out would bring her whole well-constructed façade crashing down.

"Drugs he didn't do before someone started flooding our estate with them," she said simply. "And I moved out, and the last I heard, the whole estate had been written off as a crime-infested urban planning mistake. The residents – what's left of them, the ones who couldn't or wouldn't leave their homes – have been rehoused out in bloody Norfolk, and the whole thing has been sold off cheap and is now a multi-billion-pound construction site for Constable Construction.

"Who were researching main sewer lines, electrical cabling, ownership and zoning on it years before they could have believed they had any chance of acquiring it."

"Jesus," I sighed. "So, what's going on round the corner?"

"The Sugar House," Louise explained, pushing a piece of toast around her plate, "Is a Constable development. Typical too: Take something that could be put to local use, gut it, leave a façade that you sandblast to fuck, put in super luxury flats and flog 'em off to people who never actually live in the bloody things, and make a fortune in the process. Those flats cost millions to buy. And Evan Blythe is living in one of them."

I frowned. "How?"

"How d'you bloody think?" She demanded. "It's payback for all the help he's given Constable.

"So how did you get on to him?" I asked.

"My mum," Louise answered. "She saw him here, realised he was living in the building, and once we figured out how much the cost of one of these places was, it became obvious he had money coming in from somewhere other than his council salary. I mean, this isn't even registered as an address for him. He supposedly lives in an estate over Bermondsey way. But he's here four nights a week. And I proved that. I wrote a series of articles. Showed the connections between the council and Constable and the deliberate destruction of my estate. Tried to warn people that if they got away with it once before, they'd try it again. But The Chronicle wouldn't print it. Then I wasn't working there anymore."

"They fired you?"

She shook her head. "They knew I'd have had them at a tribunal if they just fired me. Nah, they said if I was interested in news as opposed to culture, they'd let me do a few smaller stories – said they'd dig deeper into my Constable series, but meantime I should have a look around for some – how did they phrase it? – less contentious local news stories.

"So, I did, and I got on to a few stories, which I ran with, they picked up, they published. Then one of the nationals – one of the ones with friends in Constable – picked up one of my stories – a council health officer taking kickbacks from one of the fast food chains to pass the food from their filthy kitchens as acceptable for human consumption - and ran it too.

"At which point it turned out to be fake. I'd had my doubts, but management convinced me it was solid enough."

"Ouch," Caz said.

Louise lifted the toast, but a corner of it. "Ouch," she repeated. "Do you know what happens to a local journalist who writes a story that embarrasses not just the Southwark Chronicle, but a National Bloody Paper? One that defames a multi-national chain of burger and chicken nugget restaurants?"

"Law suits," Caz murmured, as though reciting from memory, "Hate mail. Disciplinary panels." She trailed away, staring morosely into the lake of yoke swimming around her greasy plate.

"I'm guessing it's career suicide?" I offered.

Louise laughed. "Career homicide more like."

"They set you up?"

"I can't prove it. Nobody can. But, you see, anything I say or do or write about Constable from here on in is coming from 'The discredited and clearly unhinged Louise Byrne.' So, a few days ago, I had bumped into a mate who does some freelancing for a broadsheet. Turns out he'd had a meeting with some of the leads at Constable. And they were actually crowing about how there was nothing to stop them regenerating the rest of this neighbourhood now.

"Regenerating, AKA crushing the people who live in The Towers. So, I went round to The Sugar House. I didn't quite know what I intended to do. Then it hit me: I'd had my blog, and I still had it. If the mainstream media wouldn't print the story, I could still research it, write it, get it out there."

"So, you've been hanging round The Sugar House, hence the concierge kicking off.

"Oh, the hanging around mightn't have been such an issue, if I hadn't seen Blythe that first night and attacked him."

"You did what?"

"I saw Blythe and his girlfriend – some skinny old posh bird - coming out of the building, in his car – a car he couldn't possibly afford on his council salary - and something snapped. I mean, Jesus, these people aren't even hiding in plain sight. They're living in millionaire's row and driving top of the range cars, and everyone just pretends he's good with money."

"And you attacked him?"

"Well, the car. I was frustrated. Furious. They'd destroyed

my career. Destroyed the place I called home. Killed my boyfriend, and now my mum was calling and saying that the shops around The Races had all been told their council tax and rent was going up. I knew what was happening, and I told her to start gathering the troops; only most of the other residents didn't believe it would ever happen."

"But you knew different?"

Louise nodded. "Yeah. So, I walked over to the car – they were slowing down to turn right – and I knocked on the window, and he winds it down, all smiles. And I punched him in the fucking face. Told him that if he went near The Races – or let his mates from Constable go anywhere near the place – I'd tear him apart. Told him my mum was watching, and if I heard of so much as a short circuit at the community centre I'd crucify him."

"Your mum?" I said, a shiver running down my spine. "Did you tell him who you were?"

"I didn't need to," she laughed dryly. "He already knew. Once the punch in the face came, he remembered me from the last time I'd dug into Constable. 'You're Louise Byrne,' he said. Then he told me to stay the fuck away from him or he'd have me arrested. Then the stupid bastard went mental, lost control of the car and totalled half the parked cars on the street," she finished with a wry smile.

"So, what are you doing now?" I asked.

"Well what I am not doing," Louise replied, "is staying the fuck away from him. I'm watching. He'll slip up eventually and when he does…"

I wondered if he already had. Maybe the close to disgraced Blythe had gone to Henley Tower attempting to find and silence Louise and, coming across her mum instead, had taken action to silence her source.

CHAPTER NINETEEN

"Where's the normal pair?" The flat-topped concierge demanded, suspicion coming off him in waves alongside the cheap cologne he appeared to have bathed in.

I looked at Caz, who looked back at me. We were destined, it seemed, to announce Cathy Byrne's fate to all we met today.

"Jesus," flat-top whispered when we'd brought him up to date and he'd called House Angels to confirm what he called our "Bona Fidelis". "That's fucking twisted. What made her jump?"

"Who," Caz asked, "said she jumped?"

"You're kidding, right?" The concierge – his uniform, now we were up close, looking less Giorgio Armani and more George at Asda – gasped. "She was pushed?"

"Nobody said she was pushed, either," I said, shooting daggers at Caz. "Fact is the police are still investigating."

"And thus," Caz said, holding her arms out and curtseying in a way that said she'd clearly been trained at some point to curtsey, "You have us."

"Silver lining in everything," Flat-top grinned, his eyes raking Caz up and down. "But what about the other one?"

We'd left Joanna at the café with Louise Byrne, who was really not safe to be left alone.

"She's not well," I said, a little too quickly perhaps, but the concierge was too busy perving on my best friend to ask what exactly was wrong with Joanna.

"My name's Caroline," Caz said in her best Gypsy impersonation. "What's yours?" She stuck her hand out.

The concierge licked his lips, reached out, took her hand and – without shaking it – held it firmly, whilst looking unwaveringly into her eyes. "It's a pleasure, Caroline," he growled. "I'm Roy Bell."

"Pleasure to meet you Roy," Caz simpered, as he smiled at her again, and leaned forward to kiss the back of her hand.

Caz exerted every fibre of her being not to recoil from the kiss. And failed, though the lecherous doorman was so engrossed in his act that he didn't notice the look of outright horror that crossed her face as his lips brushed against the back of her hand.

"Well, Roy," she said, the dizzy blonde act packed away and the smiling, but deliberately distant Patrician stepping to centre stage, "It's a pleasure to meet you. This," she gestured at me, "Is Danny. He's going to be helping me today."

Which made me, I felt, sound like a magician's assistant, and not the only one of us who would know the business end of a Vacuum cleaner from a Henry Moore sculpture.

I shot her the look.

You know the look: It's the thing every pair of friends have. Oh, it varies from pair to pair, but it's a signal that basically says 'You'll be doing the bathrooms, love,' and the look – and the unspoken threat it contained – got her full attention.

Which was more than I got of Mr Roy Bell. He barely glanced at me.

"So, listen," I said, leaning on the countertop, "where do we go from here? Is there a service lift? Do they have Hoovers and stuff in each flat or do we drag them around with us?"

These questions finally got his attention, and he pulled himself away from Caz, replacing the sort of look that a famished wolf might give to a lamb – albeit a lamb which, unbeknownst to said wolf, could flay him, fillet him and serve him with mange tout and a coulis of wild berries, if she chose to do so – with the sort of look that a pedigree Persian might give to a scabby street moggy.

"Didn't House Angels tell you how it works?" He demanded, as though expecting him to direct us to the starting point was an outrage so far beneath his dignity as to be offensive.

"Sorry," I shrugged, "The whole thing was a bit of a rush, to be honest. Due to the, you know, *unfortunate circumstances.*"

He stared me down a little longer, then suddenly jerked his shoulders as though shrugging out some tension knots.

I knew that tension knots were not the purpose of the movement. This was a display of his size and power – a way to show me that he was the Alpha here. But it put a picture in my mind, of this man – this big, ripped meathead - on a balcony with a smaller woman. How easy it would have been for him to lift Cathy Byrne up and throw her – as though she were a sandbag – over the balcony.

"Alright," he jerked his head, his neck putting the sort of strain on his collar that every nuclear test puts on Pyongyang's relations with the rest of the world. "I better give you the scoop, then. Listen up."

He crooked a finger, and both Caz and I leaned in to hear what he had to say.

"This place runs on discretion and on absolute perfection. Here, nothing ever goes wrong."

"Wasn't there a scene the other night?" I asked, unable to resist the impulse to wipe the smug off the gorilla's face.

"Scene?" He hesitated, a flicker of confusion crossing his face and swiftly being replaced by a look of fury. "Oh that. Some fucking loon attacked one of the residents."

"Really?" Caz leaned in, making sure the neckline of her tabard dipped enough to show a whisper of cleavage. "What happened?"

"One of them – man in 1B – has a stalker. Mental case. She'd been waiting for him to leave and attacked his car. Y'know: Beating on the bonnet, screaming how he murdered some bloke and she's gonna get him. Only he's driving one of them new space-age cars. You know the ones what run on petrol or electric or – I dunno – fucking unicorn farts. And they have that thing where the cars'll drive themselves, like Buck Rogers in the Twenty-first century or something."

I didn't like to point out that we were already in the Twenty-first century, and that the reference to Buck Rogers aged him dreadfully. So, I kept quiet and listened as he continued.

"You're not supposed to be able to engage the robot driver or whatever the fuck it is, but this geezer out of 1B panics, pushes some escape mode button and the fucking car goes mental. Shoots across the road smashing into a Deliveroo parked on the opposite side of the road, then does a reverse u-ey and takes out the corner of someone's Bentley. Nearly flattened the silly bitch who was still running after him banging on the windows.

"1B finally gets the bloody thing under control and the stalker vanishes just in time for the Law to arrive. Place was crawling with them for two days. They're still driving past every hour. Well," he puffed himself up again, "We've got some very VIP's here, you know."

"*Very* VIPs? Caz asked, unable to keep the disdain out of her voice.

"Foreign royalty," Bell said, leaning in and trying, briefly, to steal a peak down her tabard before looking into her eyes, "T.V." He added, seemingly expecting Caz to be more impressed than she was.

"And them people," he explained bluntly to me, "expect the job – whatever the job is - to be done with maximum efficiency and minimum fuss. There's two lifts." Here, he gestured across the marble lined lobby, "They go from the basement carpark directly to the flats. The left one to the A flat on each floor, and the right to the B flat.

"They open up directly into the flat in question, so you'll need the entry code for each."

I unconsciously patted my jeans pocket, where the folded bit of paper with the scribbled codes currently resided. "Got them, I said."

"Oh, you won't be using them lifts," he sneered. "You'll be using this one." For the first time, I became aware of the narrow lift door behind him. "It goes to the service lobby on each floor. You'll need to enter the flats via the service doors. You'll still need them codes, mind, for the alarms. You haven't written them down, have you? Only this lot go mental if they find out you've compromised security."

"No," I shook my head, giving a good facsimile of outrage that he'd even think I might compromise security by writing down the apartment numbers, resident names and security alarm codes on a scrap of paper and shove them in my Tesco Jeans. "God, no."

"Good." He nodded, his steely blue eyes still boring into mine, as though waiting for me to cave and admit that I had not only compromised security, but that at present a Pickford's van full of hippies was waiting round the corner to occupy and squat in these luxurious apartments once I'd disabled the alarms. "I'll take your phones," he held his hand out.

"My what?" I balked.

"Your phones," he repeated. "That bit about confidentiality, security, all that stuff? None of the residents want pictures of their bathrooms all over the web. So: Phones. Now, please."

I sighed, shaking my head and casting a glance at Caz, whose jaw was clenched in what I can only describe as an unhappy set.

We put our phones on the counter, and Bell picked them up, turned around and opened a cupboard that seemed to contain door-keys for each of the flats, put the phones in it, and – considering he then proceeded to put the key back on top of the box – somewhat pointlessly re-locked the cupboard.

"Cleaning shit's in there," he nodded at a cupboard to the right of the service lift. "Let me know if you need any help," he said, this last addressed to Caz with a smile that approached harassment, whilst I was – once again – dismissed.

"I think we'll manage," Caz smiled frostily back, as though she were Princess Margaret and he a waiter who'd had the audacity to ask whether she'd need help cracking her Lobster. "Danny?" She gestured towards the service cupboard, and – with the sort of trepidation normally reserved for proctology exams – we entered within.

CHAPTER TWENTY

"Well," Caz and I regarded each other as though we were a couple of chorines on opening night, and our gaze drifted to the service door of apartment 1A.

It felt odd that we were standing in front of what, to me, was a front door, whilst – because the residents had lifts that went straight from the underground carpark to their apartments – it was probably never used for any access other than the cleaners.

"Raffles fund," I said, glancing at the paper in my hand and eyeing the keypad to the right of the door.

"Well this should be a quick one," Caz murmured. "I mean," she added, catching my puzzled glance, "Uninhabited flats don't get dirty enough to need much more than a quick dust and a hoover, do they?"

"How d'you know it's uninhabited?"

"Lord, Danny. Where've you been? It's a concrete money box, isn't it? Someone who has a lot of money they'd rather not leave in a bank account needs to acquire an asset, and an apartment in glamorous London Town is a good asset to acquire: Low risk, decent appreciation, and fairly liquid as long as you can find another tax dodger or sanctioned despot to sell it to when you need the cash back."

"Tax dodger?"

"Well obviously. If you bought a flat, would you register it to an offshore fund if you were happy for the world to know you owned the asset? This'll be someone who shouldn't really have the money, would rather avoid paying tax on it or explaining its origin to various authorities, but needs to do something with it. So: A concrete money box. What's the code?"

I told her and she pressed the numbers on the key pad.

There was a soft click, a whoosh as of an airlock releasing, and, at a light touch from Caz, the door swung open.

"Remind me," She said, lifting a plastic basket full of cleaning products and pushing the door wide, "Why, exactly, we're about to 'do' for Bashir Al-Assad?"

"Because by my reckoning Cathy wasn't that long home from this place when she was pushed over her balcony."

"But I thought we'd settled on the mighty King Solomon for any wrongdoing in that case," she said, as I hoiked the vacuum up and followed her into the hallway.

"Maybe it was Solomon," I said. "Maybe your mate Harry did it. Maybe someone else from The Races shoved her over. But we'd be – what's the word – remiss? We'd be remiss if we didn't take a look at the last place she was before she went over."

"Indeed," Caz said, finding the light switch and illuminating the entrance hall.

The square footage of the hallway was probably twice the size of Lindsey Wright's living room at Henley Court, and the first thought across my mind was "Bland," followed by "Caramel," which, in turn, was replaced, once again, by "Bland," and finished on "What is that amazing smell?"

"What," I said to Caz, "Is that smell?"

"Money," she said, dropping her basket of wet wipes and Mr Sheen on the polished hardwood floor. "And Jo Malone. It masks the stink of corruption."

I closed the door behind me. "Only us," I called out loud, making Caz jump. Cleaners!"

"Cleaners?" Caz turned to me with disdain. "What bit of 'The residents demand discretion did you not get?"

"Sorry," I whispered, lifting the Dyson up and tip-toeing down the hall.

"Oh, don't worry," Caz replied at a normal volume. "I'll bet you there's nobody here. Like I told you."

"Concrete money box," I said as she dived into the basket of cleaning supplies, extracted a can of furniture polish and a duster, spotted her reflection in a vast rosewood framed mirror on the wall, hissed like a vampire spotting a six-foot-tall crucifix and stalked off muttering, once again, about nylon.

The hallway stretched out into the distance. The first room to our left was a living room, the space in deep darkness due to the ceiling-to-floor curtains pulled over what I discovered on pulling one back were ceiling-to-floor windows that ran the whole length of one wall. The furniture was a selection of oversized sofas and chairs in a chocolate brown velvet, the floor was highly polished wood covered, here and there, with Oriental carpets in shades of coffee caramel and pale pink. In front of one of the vast sofas stood a low coffee table made almost entirely of three-inch-thick green glass, and on the walls a selection of – once again – oversized art prints, consisting mostly of what looked like Renaissance architectural drawings for a Palladian mansion, all framed in the same rosewood as the mirror outside. The whole proclaimed the understated taste and unlimited budget of the interior designer who'd bagged the gig to dress the place.

"Well." Caz stood, hands on hips, and surveyed the scene. "Dignitas Chic springs to mind. We're not going to find anything here other than a bag of receipts from some tasteful Mayfair galleries, and a few delivery notes from some furniture places in Belgravia."

And, so saying, she lifted the can of Mr Sheen in her right hand and let loose a firm and constant spray of the contents into the air, waving it from side to side for a few seconds before, like the dwarf in Poltergeist, announcing "This room is now clean," and beginning to search through the drawers in a beautiful marquetry covered sideboard.

"We can't just do that," I said, shocked.

Caz tutted as the first drawer proved to contain nothing more than a brochure for 'Lady Lissie Lennox, Interiors and Styling'.

"Styling," Caz said, as though the very word offended her. "Do what?" She asked, zoning back in to my comment.

"Well," I gestured at the middle of the room where light creeping through a tiny chink in the curtain was showing the last of the polish falling like dust motes, "That. Not clean."

"Not clean?" Caz opened the second drawer, pulled out a David Linley catalogue, flicked through it, and, realising I was still standing in something between concern and outrage, dropped it back into the drawer, and shoved the drawer closed.

"Oh, you can't be serious," she said. "You're upset because I'm not cleaning? But that, Daniel, is because I'm not a bloody cleaner. I don't have the char gene. And be honest: When James Bond goes undercover as a horse doctor, do you think he expects to ever have to conduct an appendectomy on a Shetland bloody pony?"

She had a point, but I still felt concerned. "This is my mum's gig," I reminded her.

"And we are short notice replacements. If anyone calls House Angels and complains that the two of us didn't do a robust enough polishing for their likings, your mother can explain the situation, offer to send the lovely Jo and a selection of genuine cleaners around to do a free tidy up, and all will be well.

"But I remind you, Daniel, that it was your idea to come here today to look for anything that might suggest a link between the late Mrs Byrne and this place. If you'd said we were going to be bleaching the sinks and doing the skirting boards while we were at it, I might have remembered an alternative appointment."

I sighed. "Okay," I said, peering around and realising that there was nothing – not so much as a magazine – on display in the room.

"You're still worried about your parents, aren't you?" She

asked, getting - as Caz so often does – right to the source of my discomfort.

"I hate admitting that Paddy Maz and Val are right," I admitted, "But something doesn't feel right."

"And yet both of your parents have told you either that all is well or that you should butt out of their affairs and mind your own business."

"Please don't say 'affairs,'" I pleaded as we left the sitting room, satisfied that there was nothing of any interest there, and headed into the first of three bedrooms with en-suite bathrooms.

"And yes, I know they say all's well. But they're saying it too belligerently. Like, if they can convince me, they'll be able to convince themselves."

"Families," Caz muttered opening the doors on an entirely empty wardrobe as I peered dubiously under the unmade bed, "Run on secrets, Danny. Even when you love each other, it's the disfunctions that make the seas ebb and flow, give the entire enterprise something approaching life."

"My family," I said as I poked my nose into the en-suite, discovering a gleaming space of chrome and polished enamel, devoid, once again, of any suggestion that anyone had ever lived in the space, "Are not dysfunctional."

"Says the man," Caz responded, giving another spritz of Mr Sheen to the bedroom whilst simultaneously spritzing the air in the en-suite with CIF Bathroom cleaner, "Who's currently using his mother's business as a cover for hunting a suspected murderer."

"Well," I said, "Your family are even more dysfunctional than mine."

"Of course we are, dear heart," she guffawed as though I'd just stated the most bleedingly obvious fact ever. "We're titled. Lord, imagine what a state the country'd be in if the ruling class had all been well adjusted logicians for the past thousand years. We'd be bloody Norway."

I considered whether this was a concept worth debating with her as we made our way fruitlessly through the other bedrooms and bathrooms and found ourselves in a dining room with a dining table and eight chairs constructed of more of that green glass from the coffee table.

"Lord," Caz sighed, nodding at the monstrous chandelier – more green glass, this time cut in irregular chunks and slivers, and looking as though someone had repurposed the ship that Superman was sent to earth in. "It's like Game of Thrones meets come Dine with me. This," she said, gesturing at the scene before us, "Is why nobody with a title should be allowed to design anything more than a coat of arms."

"You'd get piles," I mused, "Sitting on them chairs."

"Exactly," Caz announced triumphantly. "We need the levelling sanity of real people to prevent the craziness going overboard."

"Real people?" I asked incredulously. "Did you really just refer to my family as real people? Am I 'real people'?"

"Hmmm?" Caz looked up from the – as always – empty sideboard she'd just searched and smiled. "Oh no, dear heart. You're not real. You, I'm often convinced, are a figment of my fevered brain. There's nothing here. Now are you going to start searching with me, or are we going to continue debating the social inequality that lets Loony Lady Lissie Lennox loose on a flat like this while you get to B and Q your bedroom at the Marq?"

"Kitchen," I said, dragging the still unused Dyson out of the dining room and off to the final door at the very end of the hall.

I pushed it open and stood gaping for a moment before the door reached the extent of its apex, the spring mechanism kicked in and, like the kitchen doors in most restaurants, it swung back slamming into my face and rousing me from my trance.

This was the most exquisite space I had ever seen.

The flat was arranged as a squared-off 'U' shape, with the upright legs containing the living, sleeping and dining spaces, and the kitchen, occupying the base of the 'U' was thus the entire width of the apartment, and almost as deep, the space split into various distinct zones.

Directly facing the doorway, I was standing in were the polished steel doors of what I assumed was the private lift. The space before these was set up as a typical country kitchen – all solid pine table and chairs, pendant lighting and cosy chesterfield with a horse blanket slung casually over it (for, I assumed, the horse you'd just ridden across town on to get here).

On the far-right side of the room another polished steel door, we discovered, led to a walk-in freezer the size of my bedroom, and arranged around this space was a zinc and chrome wonderland of kitchenry – an island large enough to double up as a coroner's slab, a sink you could drown a teenager in (if drowning teenagers was your thing) and worktops housing mixers blenders juicers and other equipment the cost of which would have paid the rent on a flat in The Races for a year.

And all of it untouched and unused, and likely to stay so for as long as the flat was nothing more than an investment vehicle.

The left-hand side of the room contained more cupboards and drawers with crockery and cutlery aplenty, but not so much as a hint that Cathy Byrne had ever been in this flat, let alone that anything here could have contributed to her demise.

"This place feels like a ghost town," I said, and Caz, spraying her polish once again, sighed something about how it felt like her entire childhood, then suggested we go next door.

CHAPTER TWENTY-ONE

Apartment 1B was where we hit something approaching interesting.

The flat, which was shown on my list as belonging to Constable Investments, and which had an entry code of 990991, was configured differently to the first one.

In this flat, the living room occupied the space which had been given over to the kitchen in 1A.

This one was clearly occupied, as evidenced by the piles of discarded newspapers, coffee cups, a pair of socks dropped beside the recliner opposite the vast flat-screened TV and the small army of cigarettes – at least three with a bright red lipstick ring around them – sitting in a vast marble ashtray on the finger-smeared coffee table.

A metal and glass shelving unit held a collection of trophies and awards – certificates thanking Evan Blythe for his work with charities for sick kids, lame donkeys and lonely pensioners; a photo of him surrounded by smiling infants at what looked like some inner city school; a selection of tombstones celebrating business deals that Blythe had been involved in, a photo of him shaking hands with the Prime Minister (with, behind it, a photo of him shaking hands with the previous PM), a medal recording his completion of a marathon on behalf of a hospice charity, a cup commemorating his success in a golf tournament and, I felt sure, if I dug any further, his driving theory pass certificate and the badge he got for diving for a brick wearing only his pyjamas when he was in the cubs.

Caz surveyed the mess strewn around the room and

shuddered.

"You okay?" I asked, afraid she might be about to throw up, burst into tears, flee the room, or all three. At once.

"Okay?" She turned a frosty glare on me. "If you weren't my best friend, we would never be speaking again. It's only by reminding myself that my ancestors went into battle, onto the gallows and – in one case – to a posting in Kuala bloody Lumpur with stoic detachment and studied bravery that I'm managing to deal with this. So, no, Daniel, I am not 'Okay.' But I shall be. Now: You pick up the detritus, and I'll get to work on whatever the hell this one has been spattering all over the coffee table."

Half an hour later, we were in the kitchen, which – somewhat obviously, perhaps - occupied the space that had been, in flat 1A, the living room. This time, the floor-to-ceiling windows had been replaced by a constant line of pale blue coloured glass that stretched the whole length of the space above polished steel workbenches and an industrial sized hob.

This one had clearly been used – there were grease spots all over the stainless steel and an unwashed pan that looked like someone had made scrambled eggs in it.

A knife block containing a full set of Sabatier cooks knives stood to one side, the chopping knife abandoned in the Belfast sink.

Caz nodded at the egg-encrusted pan. "I'm not touching that," she said before I could open my mouth.

"It'll need soaking," I muttered, grabbing the pan and stalking to the sink.

"New manicure, sweetest," Caz justified as I ran instantly scalding water from the tap into the pan and dipped into the cupboard under the sink to find some washing-up liquid and a pan scourer.

Behind me, Caz sprayed something onto the hob and began to clean the grease splashes away.

"What sort of dirty, lazy bastard leaves a manky old pan on the hob?" I growled, putting some effort into chiselling baked on egg from the Teflon.

"The same type of person," Caz announced, several minutes later as we stood in the doorway of a bedroom and stared in horror at the pile of clearly used pants that had been discarded willy-nilly across the moss green shag pile carpet, "That flings his pants on the floor when," she nodded in the opposite corner of the room, where a lidded wicker basket stood, "There's a bloody laundry basket in the corner of the room."

I turned my back, dipped into the panier of cleaning products, and came out with a pair of disposable plastic gloves and a surgical mask.

"Here," I held them out to her, and Caz favoured me with the sort of look that one imagines Queen Mary might have bestowed on anyone who suggested having that nice Wally Simpson round for petits fours.

"I will not," she said, her voice so cold I felt ice forming in the room, "Stoop to vulgarities, but if you think I'm touching," Caz tilted her head a millimetre in the general direction of the floor and it's unexpected covering "Those, you have clearly lost your mind."

"Well someone's got to do it," I said, "And I'll be too busy rooting," I nodded at a rosewood chest of drawers against the wall, "through his drawers looking for info."

"Sweetie, this is not a Le Carre. You are not a super-secret spy. And I – I repeat – am not touching those. Gloves or no gloves."

I sighed. "Why's it always me that gets the dirty jobs?"

"Because," Caz smirked, as I struggled my hands into the marigolds, "You're so good at them. I just hope," she added, pulling open the first drawer, "that whoever lives here is a little tidier with their clothing post laundry."

I stooped to lift the first pair of pants and took the moment to glance under the bed. Bare, save for an overlay of dust on top of the carpet.

"Anything?" I asked, a bundle of discarded pants in my hands, as Caz shoved the first drawer closed.

"Well, apart from the fact that whilst Blythe lives in this multi-million-pound apartment he's too cheap to buy new underwear when his whiteys get grey, and that he buys his white towelling socks," (this last said with a hard swallow that suggested Caz had just brought a little sick up in her mouth) "at Primark, no. Nothing. How are you getting along with the laundry?"

I lifted the lid on the wicker basket and dropped the pants inside, then stepped over to the wardrobe, flinging it open.

"Keep looking," I said, "I'll check here."

I checked.

I discovered that Evan Blythe liked blue sportscoats (there were six, ranging from a heavy-weight dark navy wool blazer to a pale cornflower linen one) and that he purchased his shirts at Next and put them straight on hangers with the tags still on. Other than that – nothing.

It was in the next room, which was set out as a study with a tall filing cupboard, a large rosewood desk, and a huge leather chair – the sort that reclines, goes up and down and is on castors so that it resembles more a fairground ride than a place to rest yourself whilst you deal with your correspondence – that we struck on something interesting.

The computer on the desktop was switched off, and I knew that it would be password protected. I switched it on and tried the same code that I'd used on the alarm – 990991 – to no avail. I tried all the zeroes, the Constable – with and without a capital letter – and, when it looked like the machine might be about to lock itself out, abandoned the P.C. and took a look at the polished steel filing cupboard.

Which, of course, was locked, and which I opened in all of fifty seconds with one of the Sabatier knives from the kitchen.

Inside was the registration documents for a new Asimov hybrid sports car (registered to Haywain Llc) and a bank statement, in the name of one Mr E Blythe.

"So, Louise wasn't mistaken," I said, opening the letter and goggling at the balance shown. "And how, I wonder, does a local councillor end up with a bank account with that many zeroes before the decimal point?"

"Mergers and Acquisitions," Caz replied absent-mindedly, clarifying, in response to my puzzled glance, "Pre politics, Mister B was a banker in Mergers for Windsor & Right," she gestured at the framed certificates on the walls announcing various promotions and business deals – a privatisation of the national utilities in an Asian country that, nowadays, was a by-word for corruption, the purchase of the people who made the car he had the deeds for by a much larger multinational motor firm, and a letter of thanks from the self-described King of Social media thanking Blythe for his part in helping smooth the acquisition of a potential competitor.

"Blythe probably made millions in M&A before deciding that he wanted to give something back to society by entering local politics," Caz mused, inspecting her nails and tutting, I assumed, at the damage already done to them. "Either that or he figured that international takeovers weren't corrupt enough and local politics was a better way to guarantee decent money."

"So, he's got a Swiss account," I tapped the letterhead, missing, momentarily, the sarcasm which Caz had ladled over her last comment. "with," I added, scanning the last page of the statement, "seven and a half million in it, a day job and still wants to be a Civil Servant?"

"Maybe he's all about doing things for the little man," Caz said, in a tone that suggested she didn't believe for a second that anyone, since the death of Jesus Henry Christ, had ever been all about doing things for the little man (and wasn't, to be frank, entirely convinced by Jesus Henry's PR either).

"Or maybe he's all about doing over the little man for his mates at," I nodded at the statement "Constable investments. Haywain Llc. They've got to be linked. Jesus," I sighed at her blank stare. "The artist. Constable. Didn't they teach you anything at that Swiss Finishing school?"

"Only that art ceased to have any validity after about fifteen ninety," she shot back.

"Constable's most famous painting is called The Haywain. Constable are the developers making a fortune out of this place. They appear to have given Blythe a free million pound flat."

"On the lower floors," Caz noted, "which shows how highly they value his contribution."

"Yeah, well," I said, "maybe there's a hierarchy of corruption: The more dodgy you get, the higher up your accommodation. Whatever: Constable and Haywain between them appear to have provided Mr Blythe with millions in cash, property and a car. He's only a cuddly toy and a trip to Hawaii short of the full gameshow experience. I wonder what his constituents – not to mention the authorities - would think of him having this much money in a *Swiss* Bank Account?"

"I'd be more worried about the fact he's got a hybrid car. I mean: what sort of maniac killer drives a hybrid?"

"But this isn't any basic hybrid," I said, having researched the car since meeting with Selene. "This is an Asimov. Next generation of cars. Hybrid, self-drive capacity (for when governments make self-drive cars finally legal), limited editions, walnut dashboards. These are the Rolls Royce Phantoms of the twenty-first century. They go for close to two hundred grand a pop."

"You know you lost at least twenty gay points during that, right?" my friend deadpanned, pulling an emery board from her tabard and buffing the edges of the thumb on her left hand.

"What?" I asked, "It's forbidden for the likes of me to know about cars?"

"Yay, verily," Caz replied, finishing the buffing, blowing on the nail and squinting suspiciously at the nails on the other hand, "For it is written in the book of Barbra that to love both Kylie and the Carburettor is an abomination and ye shall not suffer such a queen."

"That's offensive," I said, as she stepped back to admire her work, and pointed, first, at the hoover in the corner, the floor, then me.

"I'll tell you what's offensive," she answered. "You failing to be a stereotype. Is this what Oscar Wilde died for? So, you could know about cars? You ought, my dear boy, to be ashamed of yourself."

"Do one, Caz," I said as I plugged the vacuum cleaner in and my best friend left the room to begin ransacking the next one.

"A. Shamed," she shouted from the hallway. "And don't forget to relock that cupboard."

"Wait," I said, and either this, or the fact that I hadn't switched on the hoover, brought her back into the room.

"Wait what?" Caz asked.

"If Cathy Byrne discovered this," I held up the bank statement, "then Evan Blythe might have had grounds to want to shut her up."

"If she discovered it," Caz nodded, "and if the source of the funds is less than entirely kosher."

"But how would Cathy have found it?" I asked. "I mean, we had to take a knife to the cupboard to open it."

Caz nodded. "Maybe it would have been enough that Cathy saw Blythe. Or saw him doing something she shouldn't have. I'm not entirely sure the bank balance is evidence of sufficient wrongdoing for murder. Having money – if, indeed, it did come from a reputable source – isn't illegal. And if living in a home that's legally owned by a trust or investment fund was declared to be against the law, most of South Kensington would be emptied out by Sunday. No," she shook her head, "I'm not sure you can prove that Cathy Byrne finding out about the money would be grounds for much more than her dismissal."

"But what if he realised who Cathy was: The mother of the woman who had sworn to bring him down, and who had actually attacked him the day before? What if he thought Cathy was a spy, and wondered what she's already discovered?"

"What? The old 'Murdered because she might know

something' trick? You really have strayed into Le Carre land." Caz remained unconvinced. "I repeat: We still can't explain how Cathy would ever have even found out about any of the contents of that drawer."

Which was when we heard the ding of the lift doors from the living room.

"Shit," I hissed, stuffing the paperwork back into the filing cabinet and attempting to use the thin bladed knife to re-engage the locking mechanism.

"What do we do?" Caz demanded in a whimper, my panic infecting her.

"Keep," I waved in the direction of the living room "Them busy. Go. Go!" And Caz fluttered out of the room.

I heard her voice drifting back down the hallway. "Oh hello. We didn't know you'd be here." She was doing what I suspect she was convinced was a believable cockney accent.

She sounded, in reality, like Edith Evans giving her best Dot Cotton.

"Shitshitshit!" I hissed as the drawer closed but the lock failed to engage.

A man's voice – rumbling and distant – said something.

"Well we won't be long no in any way."

Again, the low drone, sounding even from where I was desperately attacking the lock, supremely disinterested.

"Well, that'll be nice, I suppose. Yes, there's two of us today," Caz intoned, every syllable sounding more like a central casting East End villain who'd had a stroke recently, "'Oooh no, dearie. Just me and Danny."

'Don't give out my real name,' I wanted to shout, as she took a shovel and dug deeper into the pit she was digging. The fucking lock stuck, the blade straining to shove the catch forward, and I was almost convinced the knife blade was about to snap off on me, but I kept on jiggling, sweat pooling under my arms.

"Oh no, love," Caz extemporised, and I feared that at any minute, the accent, which was sliding further west, would go full Lady Bracknell and we'd be, as The Divine Oscar might have put it, rumbled, "Cathy's not 'ere today. Ain't you 'eard?"

The voice barked something.

Interested now, I thought.

"Oh, didn't you hear dearie?" Caz answered, grabbing the accent by the scruff of the neck and hauling it back towards Albert Square, "Cathy died. Awful, it was,"

Dearie? I thought, and knew I had to get out of this room before my best friend went into two choruses of 'My old man said follow the van,' 'It's a Jolly 'oliday with Mary,' and offered to tell whoever the fuck was in the living room his fortune for a half a tanner.

I jiggled the knife, and there was a quiet thunk as the lock finally re-engaged.

"Thank you," I mouthed to heaven, and raced out of the room, realising only when I was halfway down the hall, that I was still gripping the Sabatier and probably looked like a deranged, Tabard-loving serial killer.

I paused, slipped the knife into my back pocket, recomposed myself and entered the living room where Caz was regaling a tall, broad man with a description of Cathy Byrne's death.

"And so 'ere we are, as what you might call temp'ree replacements, as it were. Such as it is," she trailed off, as I entered the room.

"Well I won't keep you," Blythe shuffled through the pile of newspapers and magazines – the pile I had not that long ago tidied into a neat single block – pulled out a manila folder, rifled through the contents, and dropped the newspapers – scattering them all over the floor again – "I just popped back to grab this for a meeting this afternoon. Oh, hello," he registered me, "A male cleaner, How, um, equal. Make him work hard, hey?" He leered at Caz, and, if I hadn't already been convinced he was what Caz's alter-ego might have called 'a wrong 'un', I most certainly was now.

CHAPTER TWENTY-TWO

I stood outside 2B, juggling the hoover whilst trying to slip the verboten paper from my back pocket, the attempt making a racket something akin to a school orchestra percussion band tuning up.

"Dearest," Caz murmured. "Might I just remind you that Lurch downstairs stressed that the residents demand tranquillity and an absolute absence of stress?" she said, making the place sound less like a block of flats and more like a rest home.

"You're doing the loo in this one," I growled back, typing the code into the pad.

"When hell freezes," she smiled back, as the door to 2B opened. "You want to arm wrestle me for it?"

"Maybe later," I said, stepping into the flat and dragging the vacuum cleaner behind me.

Monsieur Francois Foucault appeared almost as soon as we entered the hallway, his finger to his lips and a furious 'Ssssh' issuing from him.

"I am writing," he announced, in an accent somewhere north of Inspector Clouseau, and in a tone that suggested even our breathing might be enough to have his muse calling an Uber. "I must have total silence. Total."

"Shall we come back later?" I asked, hoping against all hope that he'd tell us to sling our 'ooks so that I could take a quick look around his flat when he wasn't present.

"Mais non," he said, a look that said 'Quelle horreur' "Just," he gestured at the space around him, looking for all the world like a man being attacked by invisible wasps, "Do it quietly, s'il vous plait." and he vanished back into his office, closing the door behind him.

"Well you won't be doing any digging around in there," Caz observed in a whisper.

This flat, we quickly discovered, was laid out similarly to the first one we'd entered, with a huge open plan kitchen / dining living space occupying the room that the lift opened on to. In this flat, however what had been a walk-in freezer was a temperature-controlled wine cellar, with row upon row of unopened bottles of what I assumed was not Le Piat D'Or laid on angled shelves.

In fact, the whole space was oddly neat, as though nobody had been living in it since the last time it was cleaned, and dusting (well, waving a duster a few inches from the surface while Caz squirted furniture polish into the air) took little time.

The living room featured a wall of leather bound tomes on French literature and philosophy, and a mirrored bar that seemed to have every spirit known to man including, as Caz confirmed once she'd downed a sizeable glass of it, a very passable Armagnac.

The bathroom, too, immaculate, though it did contain a bottle of cologne shaped like a Zeppelin and called Eau Du Humanité.

It was only when I put the vacuum cleaner on that Foucault reappeared with another furious round of Shusshing and exhortations to make no noise.

"Monsieur," Caz said as I scrambled to switch the unit off at the mains, "il n'est pas possible d'aspirer une pièce en silence."

"Well," Foucault suddenly switched into confused English as quickly as Caz had turned on the perfectly accented French. "I need silence. I must have silence."

"Well I repeat," Caz said, as though talking to an unrealistically demanding child, "We can not vacuum the space without making some noise. Ce n'est pas possible."

"Then go," he said, throwing his hands up in despair, as

though our inability to figure out how to silently vacuum (vacuuming, perhaps, in a vacuum?) was a frustrating disappointment for someone who was used to the world failing to come to their high standards. "Go."

Caz looked at me.

I looked at Caz.

At the moment where the scenario was about to turn into a French movie, she shrugged, Said "D'accord, comme to veux, monsieur. Au revoir," nodded at me, the hoover, stuffed her dusters and polish cans into her basket and, head held high, stalked the hallway like a catwalk model.

"Wait!" Foucault called after her.

Caz paused.

"You intrigue me," Foucault said, as she turned slowly to face him. "I like your spunk," he said, though to be frank, it came out more as "Ah Laaak ewer spawnk".

I hovered with the hoover, unsure whether we were still dismissed, or about to be asked to get going on his back bedroom.

"I'm having," Foucault said without even acknowledging my continued presence, "A soiree, this weekend."

"A soiree?" Caz asked, an eyebrow that had been worked to perfection raising only slightly. "What sort of soiree?"

"Some friends," the writer expanded slightly. "Some like minded, grown up friends. Some grown up friends with benefits."

Still Caz waited.

"Some very important people," he went on, seemingly oblivious to her studied disinterest, "who are friends of mine, and who would, I think, enjoy meeting you."

"Oh," Caz pressed an immaculately manicured hand to her throat, miming overawe at being of interest to this puffed up ball of ego. "You want me to meet your friends and your friends to meet me."

He wiggled his eyebrows - they were huge and black and thick, like a couple of undergroomed Dachshunds glued above his eyes – and smirked at her. "I think my friends would get a lot out of you."

"And put a lot in," Caz muttered. "So: This soiree," she carried on, before her aside could register with Foucault, "It's an orgy, really, isn't it?"

The Frenchman winced. "I find that word so… so…" he searched for the word.

"Sordid?" Caz offered. "Creepy? Squalid? Debauched? Degenerate? Do stop me if I hit the bullseye," she finished, smiling sweetly.

"Ma petite," the short man smiled up at her, still unaware that what he had assumed was some sort of superiority – social, economic, cultural – over her had already evaporated beyond the vanishing point, "for a girl like you, spending some time with these men could be very useful."

And that, basically, did it. "Monsieur," Caz drew herself up to her full height, "For a girl like me – for any girl, anywhere on the face of this dirty little planet – spending time with these men – or, in point of fact, with you alone – would be useful for one party in the transaction, and one party alone. I'm not sure how often you try this, or how successful it usually is, but I would rather starve than spend time with you or your very important friends with benefits. Now, I'm going to carry on with my job, and I suggest you pop back into your living room," here she nodded her head towards the space, "Mix yourself a large gin and tonic, and finger your leather-bound Balzac. Grab the Dyson, Danny; we're off."

And so saying, she exited the apartment like a countess, me struggling behind her with the uncooperative vacuum cleaner.

CHAPTER TWENTY-THREE

By the time we exited Flat 2B and let ourselves into Flat 2A, Caz was still fuming.

"Nasty little pipsqueak," she raged as the door closed behind us and the hall lights, triggered no doubt, by some motion sensors, switched on. "How dare he talk to me – to anyone- like that? Like I'm – what? – a toy? A piece of meat? How," she raged on, "dare he?"

"He dares, Caz," I said sadly, "because he can. Cos you're a cleaner. A nobody. Someone who could be impressed by that shit; and because – if you weren't – there'd be not a thing you could do about it."

Caz deflated before my eyes. "The question, Daniel, was rhetorical. I," she seethed, her fists clenching and unclenching, "I fucking loathe that type of man."

Caroline – my dearest friend in the whole wide world – has been around me for many years. And whilst she has witnessed me uttering a veritably panoply of profanity, I have rarely, if ever, heard her swear.

So that 'fuck' was a big deal.

"He's just a sleaze ball, Caz," I said, attempting to mollify her. "They exist."

"Yes, well," she inhaled deeply, stood straight, squaring her shoulders, and resuming her air of unflappability, "one hopes they don't exist for much longer. Now," she hoiked up her basket, "Shall we press on?"

This flat was configured in an identical way to the first

one we'd entered, and the results of our investigation was similar: Lady Lissie Lennox was the Botticelli of beige and brown décor, and Mrs Xiu – if, in fact, Mrs Xiu even existed – hadn't been in the flat for a very, very long time.

We ran through this flat in short order, headed on to the third floor, and discovered that 3A – occupied by a Mr Stepanov, and accessed once I'd typed 605411 into the keypad beside the door – was more obviously occupied, but – beyond encouraging me to wonder which was worse – Lady Lissie's bland approach, or Mr Stepanov's, which seemed to consist of day-glo colours, walls-full of gallery-framed modern art and stylized crowns at every turn – of little obvious interest.

A wall of the living room was filled with white bookcases which seemed to contain nothing but coffee table books of black and white photography, the subjects of which were – almost without exception – lithe young men in progressive stages of undress and varying unlikely environments (you know the thing: Late night burger bar; Greek donkey sanctuary).

A flier on a bedside table suggested that Mr Stepanov had either recently attended London's "Premier Gentlemen's Sauna," to enjoy the festivities at their "Christmas & New Year Big Bang-a-thon," which – I have to admit – pleased me: I didn't want to think that this building – home to a rather large number of unpleasant but to date homogenously heterosexual crooks, tax-dodgers and lowlifes – was without at least one rainbow flag waving inhabitant.

I felt, momentarily, like the presence of this clearly gay Oligarch was one in the eye for the patriarchy.

I was wrong.

"Total closet case," Caz sniffed, gesturing at a Warhol-esque portrait of a wide-eyed pouting youth hanging above a corner sofa covered in violet velvet and festooned with fuchsia throw cushions.

"You know him?" I asked, as she turned her back on me and began decanting half his Louis XIII Cognac into an empty bottle before slipping it amongst her cleaning products as I demanded to know just what the fuck she thought she was doing.

"I'm liberating France," she said, "from the Russians. Or this one at least. What? You've never met Olly Stepanov?"

"Caz," I gestured around the living room, the pictures on the wall having cost, by my reckoning, more than me, my parents, Paddy, Val and Maz had earned – or would ever earn – in our lifetimes. "Unless I served him a happy hour shot of Stolichnono at The Marq of an evening…"

Caz sighed. "Daddy –Igor. Igor Stepanov?" She shook her head at my failure to immediately recognize the name. "Well, Dad owns the oil. All the oil. And now he owns all the oil, and has all the money, he's embarked on a little crusade to make Russia Holy again."

"Wholly what?" I asked, envisioning a Russia that was wholly Tchaikovsky, Pushkin and Catherine The Great (without the block-and-tackle and the somewhat perturbed thoroughbred).

"Holy," Caz clarified. "Sanctified. Though 'Wholly' works too. Wholly Orthodox. Wholly white. Wholly Russian. Wholly straight. He's a fan of the Tsar. Any of them, but mostly Ivan the terrible. He's known in certain circles as Igor the atrocious."

I pushed all thoughts of Catherine the Great and her (I'm sure) entirely fictitious amorously equine demise from my mind.

"And poor old Oleg is stuck here in London acting as an 'agent' for various of Pappa Stepanov's less unacceptable enterprises, whilst supposedly dealing in art, and dreading every day that daddy will discover he loves a bit of what they made Tchaikovsky take arsenic for."

"Wait," I waved the extension of the hoover around, "how d'you know this? I mean: how do you know any of this?"

"Because," Caz busied herself, suddenly, in polishing every single glass on the marble topped bar, "I dated him.

Once or twice."

"Who?" I frowned, "Oleg? Igor? Oh my God," I steadied myself on a plinth, upon which a partial sculpture of a Satyr was doing something to a Maenad that I suspected Oleg's sainted daddy would have objected – in public – to, "Both of them."

"It's not like it sounds," Caz murmured, opening the Louis XIII and swigging directly from the bottle.

"Okay," she raised her free hand, "It's exactly like it sounds. I was introduced to Igor by some friends. He was older – okay, old – but he was charming, and we dated a couple of times. I met Olly – his son Oleg - saw a boy who was sweet and charming and fun, and that was that.

"Igor and I fizzled out and a few months later I get a random call from Stepanov asking if I'd like to accompany him to The Fine Arts Ball."

She shrugged. "So, I went."

I shook my head.

"He was lovely," she said. "Smart, witty, attentive, and – unlike his dear but deadly dull papa - genuinely interested in me and in what I had to say."

"So, what made you think he was gay?" I asked, receiving, a withering stare in return.

"Danny. The men I meet – in the circles I'm doomed to frequent – have been indoctrinated since birth to view women as necessary evils or enjoyable vehicles. They don't normally care what I think or say or feel. Unless," she pointed a perfectly manicured fingernail at my head and traced it down to my feet.

"Doesn't stop me trying," she said, "but I knew in half an hour that dear old Oleg would be nothing but a friend and wanted me to be nothing but a beard. And I haven't seen him since."

"So, do we rule him out? I asked, and Caz shrugged.

"He's tall. Goes to the gym. A lot."

"You don't say," I muttered, struggling – and failing – to keep the bitterness from my voice.

"By which I mean he's strong enough to throw Cathy over the balcony."

"And if she'd threatened to disclose him to his dad," I conjectured.

Caz's lips formed a wordless 'O.'

"The money," I said.

"But why would he pay her off then follow her home and kill her?"

"Because killing her here would have left him with a body to dispose of?" Caz offered, then

shook her head. "Nope. Olly was the most gentle and sweet boy. A bit like you," she added, "only richer, and," she glanced around the room, "Less sophisticated. But I'll check it out. See where he was, figure out if he could have worked the stairs – let alone the lift – at Henley Court."

"You sure?" I asked, and she shook her head.

"No. This place, Danny. This place feels like some moneyed Tower of Babel: Every time you think you've got it nailed down to filth with finance, one stumbles across an Olly Stepanov and suddenly it's people again. But Olly doesn't strike me as the type."

CHAPTER TWENTY-FOUR

"Won't be a minute, Cath," a voice sang from deep within the bowels of apartment 3B.

Caz and I froze momentarily, then I dragged the vacuum cleaner a little further along the hallway and left it leaning against the wall before heading into the vast kitchen space. This one was less country kitchen and more industrial tech.

Between me and the lift doors an island unit – the whole thing constructed of the same brushed steel that the lift doors were made of – hulked. A series of metal shelves against the wall beside me were packed with seemingly every kitchen gadget known to man – mixers, blenders, juicers, slow cookers, pressure cookers, a fish kettle big enough to take a small shark, and a lemon reamer that looked like a H.G. Wells Martian.

The floor here was some form of rubberized tiling, into which some reflecting chips had been mixed so it had the effect of shiny granite without the slip hazard, and the huge industrial lights suspended from the ceiling reflected in twinkling flares as we moved a little further into the kitchen.

Whist the kitchens we'd been in today had all had the feeling of film-sets – somewhere where an espresso might be made, but a Sunday dinner never roasted – this felt like the real deal.

From what had, in previous flats, been the pantry, chiller or wine cellar, a woman emerged.

She was small but solid, and seemed to be wearing a black

rubber overcoat, the thing buttoned up to the neck, and extending down as far as midcalf. From under it, the ends of a pair of black jeans poked, and her feet shod in a pair of fluorescent pink Crocs were the only colour present.

The reason for the overcoat might have been the fact that, draped over her left shoulder like a fat-encrusted bloody stole, she had what looked like a headless pig.

Which, on closer inspection, turned out to be a headless pig.

"You're not Cathy," she – the woman, not the headless pig – said (though to be honest, the scene was already surreal enough that if the porcine tippet had started speaking I would not have been entirely surprised.)

"No," I said, stepping forward and preparing to go into an explanation for my presence.

"Gimme a minute, lovely," the woman said, halting any attempt at an update, as she walked in three steps to the island, bent her knees, tilted slightly, and slid the carcass from her shoulder onto the metal worktop of the island – transformed, now, from a kitchen prep space to some sort of autopsy set.

"Be right back," she winked, turned, and headed back into the fridge.

Which was when it hit me.

"Caz," I turned, whispering urgently, to my friend, "That's…"

"Ellie Nosh," Caz said, namechecking one of the nation's favourite T.V. Chefs. "I know," she added in tones that suggested she was not entirely impressed.

"But weren't you at her book launch?" I gasped, wondering, suddenly, how we were going to get Caz out of here without her being seen by the chef.

"Along with about five hundred of London's most sociable or desperate liggers," she responded. "In fact, the only cook, blogger, celebrity, PR or journo who wasn't at La Nosh's book launch – and I know this as my friend Jocasta was the publicist who got stuck with the job of not only organising the bloody thing but of explaining her absence – was Ellie herself. Oh, don't worry, dear heart," Caz said, patting me on the shoulder, "even if she had been present she'd never remember me."

"Right," Ellie Nosh re-emerged from the freezer, the Rubber butchers coat replaced by a black apron, her hair pulled back into a pony tail, the well-known jet-black mane streaked, today, with silver that twinkled, like her flooring in the kitchen light.

"So," she smiled, crossed to the island and, after bending slightly at the waist and fiddling around in a drawer, stood erect holding a large saw, and smiled again. "Is Cathy alright?"

"Oh," I jerked myself awake as she commenced sawing a leg off the pig. "I'm afraid I've got some bad news."

The sawing stopped. "How bad?" She asked. "Only I have some chicken soup in the fridge. You can take it round to her, tell her I send my best."

"Look, I'm sorry about this," I said walking across the kitchen to stand beside her, "But Cathy's dead."

"Dead?" She stopped cold, whatever she'd been about to say dying, itself, on her tongue. "What do you mean dead?"

"She," I paused, uncertain how much detail to provide, "She died."

Ellie Nosh put down the saw and frowned. "Well, yes, being dead would suggest that she died, but she was only here a week ago. And she was right as rain. What happened to her?"

She instantly held a hand up to stop me answering, an air of shock and confusion seeming to settle over her. "D'you want a coffee? Tea?"

She barreled over to a Belfast sink big enough to bathe a small pony in and filled a jug with water.

"No thanks, I said."

Ellie poured the water into an industrial sized espresso machine, fiddled about with the coffee holder, pushed a tiny cup under the spout, and pressed the button.

"Dead," she said aloud., her shoulders slumping as the jet plane noise of the espresso machine began whooshing coffee into the cup.

I glanced at Caz, who raised an eyebrow, dipped into her basket and – to maintain, I assumed, the impression of a cleaner – extracted a bottle of cleaning fluid and a cloth.

Then I glanced back at Ellie Nosh and realized she hadn't taken the coffee cup, and that the drooped shoulders were shuddering, as emotion overwhelmed her.

"Are you okay?" I stepped forward, reaching a hand out towards her.

"Me?" Still with her back towards me, Ellie's voice came out bright and breezy – her trademark Always-happy-always-fun-always-stick-another-slab-of-butter-in-it breeziness. "I'm fine," she sniffed loudly, wiping a hand across her face, lifted the espresso and downed it in one, then turned to face me.

She seemed, in the seconds that had passed, to have aged a decade. Her eyes were red-rimmed, her face sagging, the skin grey, and a look of real sorrow settling on her.

"So that's why she didn't come back. What happened to her?"

I gestured to the country kitchen table on the opposite side of the room, and lead Ellie to it, while Caz, hovering nearby, began squirting something that smelled of the sea on the closest worktop and began polishing it.

"You were expecting her to come back before now?"

Ellie lowered herself into a chair, her eyes darting around the room. "Do you have a cigarette?" She asked. "I had some cigarettes, but I can't seem to remember where I left them. I don't suppose you have any. Nobody smokes these days." She laughed dryly.

Caz suddenly appeared, a pack of Sobranie already opened and extended in offering. Ellie reached out, a wistful smile crossing her face, and selected a cigarette, putting it between her lips and leaning forward as Caz held out a rose gold Zippo lighter and torched the thing.

"I didn't know you smoke," I said to Caz, knowing full

well that there wasn't a vice on the planet she was averse to.

"I don't," she replied, slipping both the cigarettes and the lighter back into the pockets of her pinny, "but I know people who do, and it always pays to be prepared." She turned back to the worktop and continued polishing it.

I turned back to Ellie Nosh. "You said 'That's why she didn't come'," I prompted. "What did you mean by that?"

Ellie blew a long thin stream of smoke into the air, used her thumb and forefinger to pinch an errant flake of tobacco from her tongue, and – the glamour puss mask back firmly in place – fixed me with a forensic look.

"What happened to her?" She asked, ignoring my second attempt to address the assignation she seemed to have set up with Cathy.

"She fell," I said at last. "From her balcony."

"Jesus," Ellie gasped, put the cigarette – in hands shaking so badly that the ash fell from the tip and landed on her pinny – to her lips, and sucked once again. "From the ninth floor. Fuck."

"You know where she lived?" I asked. "Have you been there?"

At this, she laughed. The laugh felt hard and bitter – not quite a performance, but nothing like a real laugh. Again, I got the sense of a woman who wanted to scream and sob but who had chosen, instead to make this barking half-laugh.

"Darling, I'm on the telly. I'm the number one bestselling cookery writer in the country. Okay," she shrugged, "number two in the years when that fat cockney puts one of his books out, but I'm famous and glamorous and live a charmed and shiny life. Popping round Henley Court for a cuppa was never on the agenda."

And at that moment, a tear appeared in her right eye spilled over the lower lid and rolled slowly down her cheek.

"But you know where she lived. How she lived."

"Cathy." Ellie Nosh sighed, glanced over my shoulder, frowned, wiped the tear away, sniffing loudly, and refocused on me.

She smiled, manner brittle, and tried again. "Cathy was my friend. My only friend, if you can believe it. We talked, about her life, about mine. She was brilliant at putting things into perspective. After," she waved her hand in the air, the cigarette leaving a trail where it went, "all that shit last year…" she trailed off.

She didn't need to say any more. A year or so ago, Ms Nosh had been entering her fifth year married to Mark Goss.

Goss had been described as a modern Svengali, and his start with a few ropey boy bands had quickly developed into his managing the most successful bands and artistes in Britain. Then he'd gone to Hollywood, pitched a bunch of formats to American TV, ended up acquiring a bunch of hot actors and actresses in his stable, and – by the time he returned to blighty – had basically owned the media, on both sides of the Atlantic.

And then the rumours had started. La Nosh failed to turn up to a shoot for her new TV show. Mark Goss began to sport a well-disguised but still noticeable black eye. Her drinking – previously limited to a glass or two of her trademark prosecco – was rumored to be on the increase.

And then one of the Sunday newspapers ran an exclusive of Britain's Favourite Home Chef snorting what looked like a pound of baking soda up each nostril in her elegantly appointed Berkshire mansion.

"Mark," Ellie said sadly, "Made sure I lost all my friends. He wanted a divorce. Wanted to trade in my tired old carcass – his words, lovely, not mine – for one of those tighter brighter whiter L.A. types. Only I," she dragged on the cigarette, "would not go gently into that good night. So, he told me, plain and simple, that if I didn't give him the divorce he wanted, he'd ruin my career. Him and his mates at the News on Sunday."

She dragged on the cigarette again and blew the smoke into the air.

"Well he won," she said. "The last shot – the drugs – was nearly the end of me. I had to call in a shitload of favours, and my public approval rating took a hell of a kicking."

"Public approval rating?"

"I know," she shook her head in bemusement, "like I'm some sort of politician instead of a woman who bakes fucking cakes. Or," she gestured at the abandoned pig carcass, "figures out the all-time best roast pork recipe.

"So: He got what he wanted. I got out, and as soon as he got what he wanted, he let a few nice stories about me into the press. So, I might still have a career, even if the Berkshire mansion has become this rather pokey gilded cage."

I glanced around the kitchen.

"Yes," Ellie held a hand up, "I know. I know. Pokey is, perhaps, subjective. I hate it here." Her eyes blazed furiously. "I hate the constant reminder that he won, that I lost. I can't even go out without the whispering. My friends – my so-called friends – all abandoned me lest Mark get upset with them and paint them as violent drug-addicted drunks. The only bright moment of the week was when Cathy turned up. She'd clean, we'd chat, I'd make coffee, and then she'd be about her way. She fell? Are you sure she fell?"

I glanced at Caz, cleared my throat. "As opposed to what?"

"As opposed to being pushed."

"Why would she be pushed?"

"I don't know," Ellie sighed, then: "Look, are you police, or what?"

"Police?" I coughed, locked eyes with Caz.

Busted.

"What makes you think that?" I asked, trying – and failing – to keep the tremble out of my voice.

"It's the hair, isn't it?" Caz asked. "I told him it looked like a probationary PCSO."

"It was not the hair," I hissed back at her. "What was it?" I asked, turning back to La Nosh. "Was it the hair?"

"No," she finally smiled, "it wasn't the hair. It was the fact that you," she pointed the knife at me, "Ask too many questions. Most cleaners – even the chatty ones like Cathy –

clean as they chat. They need to get in and get on to the next flat. Plus, the fact that your glamorous assistant over there with the forty quid fags has just used floor polish on my hob and is about to use stainless steel cleaner on the glass door of the oven."

I shrugged. "We're not police," I said.

"Private?" She frowned. "Neither of you seems the type."

"We're friends – sort of – of Cathy's," I said at last.

Ellie Nosh studied us in silence for a moment, then nodded. "So, she was pushed, then."

"We don't know," I admitted. "The police can't tell either way at this stage, but It just didn't feel right."

"She was supposed to come back," Ellie said. "We made plans."

"Plans?" I prompted.

"She was here," Ellie said, dropping the dead cigarette into the espresso cup, "On the day, Cleaning. It was the day of my book launch, and I was terrified. I hadn't faced people since the disaster of last year. My publishers assured me that everyone loved me. But I was terrified.

"Finally, while she was doing the bathroom, I decided I wasn't going to go. 'But it's your party,' Cathy said. 'You can't not go.' She seemed shocked at the profligacy of it all.

"'Look,' I said, 'Nobody – after the first few minutes – will even miss me. No,'" Ellie Nosh shook her head, remembering the day in question, "'I'm just not going to go.'

"'So, what are you going to do?' Cathy asked. 'Stay here,' I said. 'Keep the lights out, the phone off the hook, and have a night in. I might make some banana bread.'"

"So, what happened?"

Ellie, snapping out of her reverie, focused back on me. "A few hours later, she called me. Said she was going to have to come back – that she didn't get to finish her work here. She was so good at pointing out my bullshit, you know? Said she couldn't stand the thought of me being here on my own on the night of my party, and – if I was making banana bread – she had a great custard recipe, and did I want company after she'd finished the few flats she had left."

"So, she was coming back?"

Ellie Nosh nodded, the sadness back in her face. "Which sort of begs the question: Why would someone call me, arrange to bring the makings of their family custard recipe, then throw themselves off their ninth-floor balcony?"

I had to agree.

CHAPTER TWENTY-FIVE

Flat 4B was another unoccupied space, this one seeming even more Spartan than the others, the low humming of an electrical generator running faintly through the bleach-scented air.

In the living room, a huge u-shaped arrangement of sofa unit sat on bleached bare floor boards, the cityscape slowly beginning to light up outside the windows, the place feeling cold and empty and dead.

A quick run around disclosed nothing of interest in the space, and so we – having stood in each room and sprayed Mr Sheen – headed to 4A, where we discovered that Mr Von Oldenwald was still in residence.

"I don't give a fuck what Franklin said," a voice echoed down the hallway as we stepped into the flat, "The balance sheet is sound. That little bastard will not be bringing this bank down. Yeah, well if fucking Interpol were doing their fucking job, the piece of shit would be sitting in a fucking gulag by now. Yes, I'm going back in to the office. About an hour or so. Well, those bastards at the FCC want a conference call, and I want Waldorf and Kent on the fucking hook alongside me. Hang on a minute, Christine, there's someone here."

A head popped out of a doorway halfway down the hall, glanced at us, stopped, frowned, withdrew, "I'll call you back Chris," the voice said, and I heard the phone being hung up.

"Oh no," I heard Caz breathe behind me.

And then the head reappeared, this time attached to a

neck shoulders chest – such a chest – torso and legs.

If a Renaissance master had decided to do Jesus in a designer-frayed Polo shirt and baggy jeans, to trim the beard to a smart goatee and to replace the agony of Gethsemane with a somewhat stressed look, he would have ended up with the tall, rangy man who stood, barefoot, before us.

"Caroline?" he asked, the stressed look breaking into a gap-toothed smile. "What are you doing here?"

And now Caz's gasp made sense.

"Well," Caz's voice, came from behind me, the bright tone clearly forced, and when I turned, the glance she shot me – half-plea, half-fury – spoke volumes, "Andy. I didn't know you'd be here."

"Well I live here, silly," the man she'd called Andy smiled, opening his arms wide and advancing down the hallway in search of a hug.

"Daniel," Caz introduced me, deftly sidestepping the proposed embrace, "This is Andy – Prince Andreas Von Oldenwald, Saxe und Wurttemberg und – what else was it Andy?"

"Knicker elastic und Old Biddies," Andy Von Oldenwald smiled, embracing her tightly. "Who cares?"

Over his shoulder, Caz continued to plead with me to, it seemed, figure out how to build a time machine and never have entered this flat.

But it was too late. Von Oldenwald eventually released her from his grip, held her at arm's length, sighed, "Christ, I'm glad to see you. I've not seen a single friendly face since this whole fucking Armstrong debacle began. Jesus, Caz, is that the Countess's panther?"

Caz squirmed, seemed to realise that he was focussing on the brooch and not on the Nylon tabard it was pinned to, and smiled her best Landed Gentry smile. "Well obviously. I wasn't going to wear anything paste to come visit you, dear heart."

At which point Andy frowned. "And such an unusual ensemble."

"Andy?" A voice sounded from the other end of the hall. "Everything OK?"

I turned, and actually caught my breath. The woman at the end of the hall was as tall and muscular as Von Oldenwald, her hair a blonde bob cut so sharply that the edges could, I was sure, give you a papercut. Her cheekbones and almond shaped eyes gave her the air of an Uma Thurman, but her lips were fuller, and her shoulders broader.

"Caroline," Von Oldenwald put an arm around Caz's shoulder, ushering her past me and extending an arm out towards the other woman, "Let me introduce Rachel Fiennes. My rock."

Rachel Fiennes was wearing a loose cream silk blouse over diaphanous black wide-legged trousers, a pair of patent leather beige court shoes on her feet and a chunky amber bracelet around her right wrist.

"Ditch the hoover, love," Caz, who was still wearing a nylon tabard and a pair of Birkenstocks, hissed out of the side of her mouth as she was swept down the hallway.

"Rachel, this is Caroline, one of my oldest and dearest friends. And actually," he said as though suddenly realising, "my first girlfriend."

"Who's now a house cleaner," Rachel – suddenly diminished in my view for the obvious pleasure with which she made the pronouncement – smirked.

"Of course," Von Oldenwald stopped, withdrew his arm from around Caz and gestured at the tabard. "I knew I recognised the outfit. What on earth is that all about? Oh Caz," he was suddenly filled with what sounded like genuine concern, "you're not in money troubles are you? Only, if you are, well I'm afraid I'm not exactly in a place to help out."

Caz glanced at me.

Well, I say glanced, but actually, it was more like filleted me with her eyes, held my still beating heart in her hands and dumped it into a bucket of Maldon sea salt.

'This,' her eyes said, 'ultimate humiliation is your fault.'

All of that took seconds, and then she was laughing a

laugh so fake even Helen Keller would have spotted it.

"This?" Caz gestured at the tabard, undoing the bow that kept it tied and slipping it off, "This is – what is this Danny?" She asked, and for what seemed the first time, the other two seemed to see me.

"Undercover," I said, a voice in my head shouting that the first rule of going undercover is not to tell the subjects you're investigating that you're investigating them. "This is," I gave in, "Undercover."

"Yes, well, you've said 'undercover' twice," Rachel Fiennes twisted her lips in something that I felt sure she'd intended to look like a smile, "but still not explained what 'undercover' means."

"I'm Danny," I said, extending a hand. "Danny Bird."

"Charmed, I'm sure," Fiennes replied dryly, her arms crossed, her left toe – the beige patent leather reflecting the recessed spotlights all along the hallway – tapping impatiently "But none of that explains what you're doing in our flat, or what, indeed, 'undercover' looks like."

"Well I think a drink might help ease explanations," Von Oldenwald said, ushering both women into the living room, Caz happily, Rachel somewhat more reluctantly.

I trailed along, into a room furnished in what I now realised was a style: Early twenty-first century money. Low lighting from hidden lamps illuminated the space. Oversized sofas were dotted around a huge Turkish carpet, a chunky coffee table on which were set – as though with mathematical precision – a lacquered box, a coffee table book on early racing cars, a catalogue for a recent exhibition at the V&A, and a selection of the days newspapers, the Financial Times folded on top.

Music – light jazz with a trip-hop beat over the top – was playing on hidden speakers, and a five-wicked candle was blazing away in a corner, filling the room with the scent of Basil and Mandarin.

"Gin?" Von Oldenwald asked, "Vodka? Anything else?"

"Gin," Caz said, dropping herself into one of the

oversized sofas and giving me a look that suggested I should join her. "Wave the vermouth at it, and throw a twist of lemon in, thanks. Well, now," Caz, who had rediscovered her equilibrium, turned a dazzling smile on the other woman, "Isn't this a lovely room? So," she sought for the word, "Cosy. Not like the old Andy I knew."

The subject of her observation chuckled, busying himself with glasses ice cubes and booze at a mirrored bar on the opposite side of the room. "A futon, a cd player and bag of ice was my limit back in those days," he said, handing a drink to Rachel, who smiled beatifically at him. "But this," he gestured around the room, "Is what the love of a good woman will do.

"Well, that and an investment bankers salary."

"Of course," I said, remembering the overheard conversation, "Armstrong. He's the missing banker, isn't he?"

"Weasley little bastard," Von Oldenwald – his face setting in a mask of fury – muttered.

"Andy's one of the directors at Fenchurch Brookes," Rachel said, sipping her drink. "So, as you can imagine, the past few days have been simply horrific."

"How much has Armstrong done a runner with?" I asked, wondering once again why Mehmet Aksoy had had a newspaper article about him in his possession.

"Millions," Rachel said morosely. "Maybe as much as a hundred million. What?" She suddenly seemed to notice the glare that Von Oldenwald was giving her.

"We're not supposed to discuss it," the banker explained to me. "It was electronically transferred. We might – should – get most of it back. Even if we can't get him back. But once the moneys back with us the little bastard will have nowhere to hide. Wait," he suddenly turned his attention to Caz. "Is that why you're here? Didn't you used to work for a magazine? Are you after a story? Only, if you are, everything that you've heard in this room is firmly off the record."

"Darling, I did fashion and beauty, so unless your errant

investment banker is running around South America slathered in Crème de la mer and dressed head-to-toe in Pucci, it would have been little use to me. Besides which, the magazine and I are no longer an item."

Rachel Fiennes necked her drink and waved her empty glass at him. Von Oldenwald resolutely ignored the request for a refill. "So, what are you doing now?" He asked Caz– transparently to turn the subject away from any further discussions about Vince Armstrong.

"Now?" Caz had the good grace to blush. "Well, apart from running through the trust fund faster than either I or the trustees would like, I assist Mr Bird here in his investigative endeavours."

"Investigative?" Von Oldenwald frowned at me. "You said 'Undercover,' but I assumed that was some sort of slang. You're a private investigator?"

"Amongst other things," I murmured as Rachel Fiennes rose from her seat, went to the bar and started making herself another martini.

"Anyone else want a top up?" She asked, and Caz moved to help her.

"So, what are you investigating now?" Von Oldenwald asked as his phone vibrated on the coffee table.

"Your cleaner," I said, "Cathy Byrne, fell to her death a week ago."

"Really? Wasn't she your friend, Boobear?" He asked Rachel Fiennes as his phone vibrated again "Oh Christ," he picked it up, glanced at the screen and winced.

"Christ all fucking mighty. Sorry," he smiled at me, "This is important. Boobear, I'm gonna have to go in."

Rachel turned, a martini halfway to her lips, and frowned, firstly at him then at Caz and I.

"Caz, sweetie, what a joy to see you. We must meet up again soon. Let Rachel have your details and we'll set up dinner or something, yeah? Love you Boobear," he pecked Rachel on the cheek, pointing at the glass in her hand, "And not too much of that, yeah?"

Then, winking at me, he added "Good luck. With the cleaner. I'm sure Rachel will be fascinated," and left the room.

A moment later, we heard the 'Bing' of the private lift arriving in his flat.

"Well," I sighed, smiling around in a way that I knew probably made me look a little simple, "Exciting times."

Rachel snorted. "Armstrong's a million miles away by now," she said, "And a part of me hopes they never find him."

"Has anyone ever mentioned a man named Mehmet Aksoy in connection with Armstrong?" I asked, and she tilted her head thoughtfully.

"Aksoy?" No. She shook her head. "Not in my hearing. Why?"

"He died," I said, "A few days ago, in somewhat mysterious circumstances, and left some paperwork that suggested a connection."

"But I thought you weren't investigating Armstrong," she smiled, easing herself back down onto the sofa.

"We're not," I said, "But seeing as we're here..."

"Well I," Rachel said sipping her martini, "hear little more than you Danny. Since I left Funchurch-Brookes, I'm an outsider."

"You worked there?"

Rachel smiled. "Till about a year ago. Andy and I were – well, Andy was my boss. Though we actually met at Uni. He was doing politics and I was doing engineering, and we loathed each other at first sight, so it was funny when we ended up working together a few years later, and then," she paused, "Well, one thing led to another. I ended up as his assistant. To be honest, I think he still thinks I am, hence the expectation that I'd take your contact details," she smiled at Caz, "And entertain you both when he had to leave for the office. Old habits die hard, I guess."

"So, did you know this Vincent Armstrong?" I asked, and she shook her head.

"After my time, I'm afraid. Never even met him at the Christmas do; I stopped going when it became rather too unpleasant to be around some of the senior management. So," she asked Caz, the old iciness thawing quickly as the second martini settled in" how did *you* meet Andy?"

"Me?" Caz frowned, trying to remember. "At a party. "Friends of friends, that sort of thing. Of course, it could never have lasted. He needed a nanny-cum-housekeeper; I needed a - well," she gulped her drink, clearly realising that whatever she needed Von Oldenwald had still not become it, and thus Rachel Fiennes was, basically, the nanny-cum-housewife Caz had avoided becoming. "Well, I needed something more than he could give."

Rachel laughed brightly. "You had a lucky escape. Oh, don't get me wrong: I love Andy, and I'm with him because I choose to be; but Christ, the world he's part of. You know they made me resign?"

"The bank?"

"Mhmm." She sipped her drink again. "Soon as they found out he and I were in a relationship, I was informed that we could no longer go on working in the same department."

"Is that legal?" I asked. "I mean, can they just get rid of you like that?"
"Oh they didn't get rid of me. They offered me an 'equivalent role.' In the Back Office." She said the words 'Back office' as though they were, say, 'Leprosy colony.' "Nobody in the back office will ever make the bonuses I was making – or stood to make. So, when I declined their offer and stalemated them, they paid me off. Said they were reducing the number of desk personnel and I was offered a very nice package to leave.

"I think that they were secretly surprised that I'd simply refused to take the hint. But then, a month after I left, they decided – surprise surprise – that business was going so well they could afford to expand the desk again, and lo and behold, Vince Armstrong."

I shook my head. "Sounds just wrong."

"Danny, life is just wrong. Whatever," she shrugged, "I'm just super glad I'm not caught up in the shitshow at Fenchurch."

"A shitshow," Caz observed, "that they wouldn't have had if you had been retained, surely?"

Rachel shrugged, "you might say that…" She smiled, suddenly. "I like you, you know. I wasn't sure at first, but I do."

"So how well did you know Cathy Byrne?" I asked.

"Cathy?" her face went into does-not-compute mode as she trawled her memory banks trying – and clearly failing – to put a face to the name.

"Your cleaner?" I prompted, and she jerked as the record was retrieved.

"Oh," she said, waving the association aside, "Barely. I'm usually here, but I tend to go out when she comes round, so as not to get under her feet, you know? Why? What's happened to her?"

"She's died," I said simply. "Were you home last Thursday."

"Thursday?" She blanked again, as though recalling her whereabouts a week ago was an ask too much.

"Day before Friday," Caz murmured low enough that the blonde, still leaning against the bar, hadn't (I hoped) heard.

"Thursday?" Rachel Fiennes drawled the word again, as though slowing it right down might help her remember what she was doing on the day. "Oh!" She snapped her fingers. "Got it! I was at a shoot – a photo shoot," she clarified, in case, I assumed, she thought I might have thought it was a Grouse shoot. "In Islington. One of Pablo's. Do you know Pablo?" She asked Caz, having clearly decided that there was no way I'd know Pablo.

Caz shook her head noncommittally.

I pressed in. "So, you didn't see her?"

"The cleaner?" She shook her head. "Not that day. I mean, she was here, because the place was cleaned when I got back, but she'd been and gone before I got home."

"What time was that?" I asked, and she laughed.

"You do look like a policeman." she said, to which Caz made some entirely predictable comment about my hairstyle and I swore never to visit the Cut to the Corps in Peckham High Road ever again.

Rachel ignored her, and carried on, "But you ask questions like what's-his-name?"

"Morse?" I offered.

"Dick Van Dyke in Operation Murder?" Caz suggested.

"Columbo!" Rachel finally ejaculated, her clearly booze soaked memory function taking it's time to come up with a TV Tec she recognised. "Yeah," she nodded, glassy-eyed and smiled. "Cute."

I smiled back, a smile which I suspected, if given free travel and unlimited time to do so, would have struggled to reach my eyes. "Time?" I prompted.

"I dunno," she shrugged, "Well it's not like I clock in and out is it? I suppose I was home for the end of the Channel four news, so: Just before eight. Thereabouts. Why?"

"Just trying to get a handle on what time she was here, who she might have seen, all that sort of stuff."

She nodded, her brow knotted and a serious pout on her lips, as though she were considering the passing of time and the absence of justice in the world, then refocussed on me briefly.

"They should bring that back, you know: Columbo. Except instead of a grubby raincoat, he could dress like you. Be fun. I might mention it to my friend Jonty. He works in Telly."

CHAPTER TWENTY-SIX

"Sorry," Nick said, putting his arm into his shirt, throwing the other arm behind him and frowning. "I don't know what he wants, but when he's like this, it's usually best to just answer the call and get round the station.

"It's okay," I smiled languorously, stretched from the sofa where – until a few minutes ago – we'd been spooning, crap T.V. playing unattended in the background, and reacquainting ourselves with each other after a few days apart. "Here," I stood as he continued to frown and jab his left arm around behind him, "It's inside out," I smiled, catching the shirt and righting the sleeve he'd been searching vainly for.

"You had it off me so quick," he smiled sheepishly, and my heart – at the mixture of embarrassment and delight in his green brown eyes, the half—smile on his full lips and the mussed hair he was totally unaware of – soared.

"Well you shouldn't be so bloody cute," I smiled back, pecking him on the cheek.

"Maybe," he joked back, searching around for his left shoe, "If I wasn't so cute, Reid wouldn't want me reporting back in this long after my shift."

"Jesus," I glanced at my watch as, from beneath us, the jukebox in The Marq pumped out a medley of Girls Aloud hits and the punters sang loudly along, "It's not even ten. You're such a fucking civil servant: 'I've done me hours."

He smiled back, threw a mock punch, spotted his shoe on

the opposite side of the room, and dived for it, as though it were likely to scuttle away once it knew it had been spotted. "Listen," he said, dropping back on to the sofa and bending to lace the shoe, "I've been fighting crime since early this morning. All I wanted was a bit of me – and you – time."

"I'll be here," I perched on the coffee table so I could face him, "when you're done. Come back."

"I might take you up on that. Oh," he snapped his fingers, "Before I forget: I asked around about your missing man: George. What was it?"

"Osman," I said, the smile fading somewhat. "His name was George Osman."

"Or would have been," Nick said, finishing with the shoes and standing up, "If he'd ever existed."

"Come again?" I asked, and he wiggled his eyebrows suggestively.

"Any time, darling."

"No," I swatted him, "I'm serious. What do you mean, 'If he'd ever existed'?"

"Well the woman turned up – Linda Wright?"

"Lindsey," I corrected him quietly.

"Yeah, well, when she turned up at the station – this kid in tow – she was close to hysterical. Babbling about how her husband had gone missing, and how she was worried and we needed to find him. So, I spoke to the duty officer who dealt with her, and she reckoned that this Lindsey suddenly seemed – when asked for anything to help identify this husband – to get all vague.

"No id. No photos we could take."

"He doesn't like having his photo taken," I whispered, parroting her words.

"Baby, none of us do, but this is the twenty-first century. Mobile phones have cameras, everyone takes snaps of everything, and she didn't have a single photo of him. Then it turned out there was no marriage license, because they were never married."

"What about the mortgage?" I asked. "She bought the

flat."

"Yup," he nodded, "She did. Only thing that made us sit up. Nicely priced ex council place, right-to-buy, and she only needed a thirty per cent mortgage. Reckoned the mysterious George Osman put up the rest of the money, only it seems to have hit her bank account in cash. That, need I say, made the money laundering gang prick their ears up."

"So, you're saying she's involved in something dodgy?"

Nick shook his head. "They poked around. No sign of anything iffy. But also, no sign of a man. Some of her neighbours remembered a bloke coming and going, but they couldn't be sure it was the same bloke every time, and they never really got a good look at him."

"She claimed he worked on the rigs," I said, "Spent lots of time away from home."

Nick shrugged into his coat. "Well, if he did, we haven't had any missing people reports from any of those either – they checked the PNC. So, the only person who seems ever to have met this George Osman is your Lindsey Wright. And the only person who claims he's missing is your Lindsey Wright. And Danny: It wouldn't be the first time someone claimed their breadwinner had done a runner."

"But why would she?"

He shrugged again, leaned down to peck me on the lips. "Maybe she wanted your sympathy. Maybe she's scamming the building society. Who knows?"

I stared into space. "She seemed so genuine," I said quietly.

"Well, I'm not saying she doesn't completely believe everything she told you – and us. But believing it don't necessarily make it true. I've got to go."

I snapped out of my reverie. "Okay," I stood, walked him to the door and accepted a hug.

"Listen," Nick said, releasing the hug but holding me at arm's length so that he could look into my eyes, "the whole of the Met is on the lookout for this banker that's done a runner. We've got some computer programmer who's been found knifed in his flat, a business man who was kidnapped from outside his house in broad daylight, and half the journalists in London trying to make out that the police are losing control of the streets, so searching for a man who doesn't seem to exist is not top of anyone's list, baby. You're not responsible for this woman and whatever her problems are. You tried, okay?"

"I know." I smiled weakly then, sensing that he remained unsatisfied, redoubled my efforts. "I do know. Now go. And remember: give me a call if you want to pop round later on, after your shift."

Behind me, my telephone began to ring.

Nick pulled me close for one last smooch. "I should get that," I said, gesturing vaguely back into the room.

You should," he said. "And I will call later. If I can get back here, I will," he said, finally letting me go. "And promise me you won't dwell on this."

And then he was gone.

I dashed back and picked up the phone just as it was about to go to voicemail.

"Hello," I shouted over my own voice telling the caller to leave a message. "Hold on; it'll switch off in a second. Hello?"

"Dan," my brother's voice came down the line.

"Paddy?" I frowned. I couldn't remember the last time Paddy had telephoned me. "What's up?"

"You spoken to mum and dad yet?" He asked, skipping any preamble.

I sat down on the edge of the coffee table again, running a hand through my hair. "Yeah," I said carefully. "Why?"

"What's going on Dan?"

"Nothing," I answered. "Or so they claim."

"Well I've just left there. She's locked in her room and won't come out. He's claiming she's got a jippy tummy, but he's clearly been crying. What the fuck is happening, Dan?"

"She went drinking with her mates," I said, my voice coming out as a whisper.

"She hasn't got any mates. She's our mum," Paddy shot back.

I sighed. "Paddy, she has friends. Notwithstanding the fact that you think her life revolves around us. She does have mates. And she ended up hungover as fuck when she went out with them."

"She drank?" He asked, in the same tone he might have used if I'd said she masterminded the importation of sixty kilos of grade A Heroin. "She went out on the piss? My mum?"

"Our mum," I corrected him. Paddy was the oldest, the first-born, and he had always had a somewhat proprietorial view of our mother. "Yeah, I was round there and she looked like shit."

"Dan, she doesn't drink. Okay, maybe the odd Christmas sherry, or birthday fizz. But – whatever - how did we get from her hitting the bottle with some mates to being locked in her room and him crying his eyes out?"

I shook my head, stared at the empty sofa, where a few minutes earlier I had felt safe and secure and protected from the world. "I don't know, Paddy."

"You think she's got a drinking problem?"

"Jesus, Pads; that's a bit California. She got pissed. Half the country is permanently wasted. I run a fucking pub, remember? A wild night out hardly makes her William Holden."

"Well I dunno who this Bill Holdman bloke is, but the only thing we know for sure is that she's drinking, and things aren't looking good. Jesus, at least dad's not having an affair."

"As far as we know," I said, and could have bitten my tongue off.

"What's that mean?" Paddy leapt on the words. "D'you know something?"

"Only that people don't usually just start drinking like that."

"So, you think he started it? It's his fault?"

"No," I stood, started pacing the room, "I don't think it's anyone's fault, Paddy. I'm just saying."

"Well I thought you were going to find out," he said, a note of petulance mixing with his frustration and fear. "They tell you everything," he said. "If they're not talking to you, then what are we going to do?"

"Nothing," I said. "I'll give it another go tomorrow. But please, Paddy, don't push this; you might just make it worse."

"Worse? Jesus, Dan," he sighed "Okay, let me know tomorrow. You alright?" he asked, suddenly switching into the niceties he'd skipped at the front of the conversation.

"I don't know," I sighed. "It feels a bit like nothing makes sense at the moment." I wanted to tell him about Cathy Byrne, Mehmet Aksoy, The Sugar House and Lindsey Wright, but instead, I forced a smile. "Look," I said, "I've got to go somewhere tomorrow, so I'll ask dad to give me a lift. That'll give me a chance to ask him what's happening. And I'll call you afterwards, okay?"

"Okay," he said. "And Dan: thanks. I know we put a lot on you, but you really are the only one of us who can get them to open up."

"I'll try," I said, and my brother rang off.

I dropped back down in the sofa, staring sightlessly at the flashing images on the TV screen.

After Caz and I had left Rachel Fiennes earlier, the rest of The Sugar House had been uneventful.

The top two floors were filled with two seemingly unoccupied flats – registered to Mr's Makem-Brown (with an alarm code of 000001) and a Mr Makhtoum (246335). The floor above that was the glass surrounded residents lounge, a team of professional window dressers carefully dismantling the giant Christmas tree.

In the very basement, several floors below the street, and with a huge door that looked more like a vault door was what at first appeared to be another private lounge – all leather seats, a bar, empty buffet table and cinema screen. It was, of course, the Panic Room, and its presence – eerily quiet, and deserted whilst set up to provide the residents of The Sugar House with a luxurious place to hide out riots and civil unrest gave me, quite frankly, the shivers.

Just below it, the indoor swimming pool was dimly lit and eerily empty when we arrived, the scent of chlorine masked by a hundred weight of expensively scented candles burning all over the space.

The basement garage space featured a selection of expensive looking cars and nothing of note, and eventually we had made our way back to the street outside where I telephoned Joanna.

"Jesus," I said, as she answered the phone, "How do you do that every week?"

"Because I need the money," she said, "And because there is nothing I love more than cleaning up the filth that lazy good for nothings are too bone idle to clear up for themselves. But mostly because I need the money. Did you find anything?"

I sighed. "I don't know," I admitted. "That's not normally how it works. I needed to see where she'd been. Now I need to let it stew and see what comes up. How's Louise."

"Not good," Joanna's voice lowered. "She's still here. She seems a bit – what is the word – itchy? Twitchy? Twitchy," she decided. "Yes, and I'm not sure how long she'll stay, but she can stay as long as she wants."

I continued to stare at the screen, imagining Joanna, her kids, her husband – had she even mentioned a man on the scene? I couldn't remember – and Louise Byrne all sharing the tiny flat, whilst not that far away the vast empty spaces in The Sugar House remained unoccupied, and my mind – despite Nick's entreaties – rambled back to Lindsey Wright and her little olive-skinned curly-haired boy, sitting on a sofa in that flat waiting for some news – any news – about George Osman.

But what was Lindsey Wright: A crook? A liar? Or delusional? And why had her story seemed so realistic?

I guessed, eventually, that there was only one way to find out.

Pushing myself up from the sofa, I grabbed my coat from a hook in the corner and jogged down the stairs, through the bar and out into the dark damp night.

CHAPTER TWENTY-SEVEN

I shrugged, turtle-like into my jacket and cursed the fact I'd forgotten to wear a hat, as I turned the corner past a bizarre nativity scene – the plaster statue of the virgin had, it seemed, been beheaded at some point and someone had decided to replace the head with a papier mache one onto which the face of Theresa May had been added – and crossed the wind-blasted square, passing the wasteland that – I assumed – had once been a village green, and approaching the front door of Henley Tower which, as I reached it, opened, two figures exiting.

I shrunk back into the shadows, recognising the duo as the two minions that King Solomon had had at The Seven Stars – Mr Huge Knife and Mr Hatchet.

Tonight, instead of the implements they'd wielded when last we'd met, each of them was juggling two well-filled black plastic bin bags, their progress impeded by the fact that the bags were clearly heavy.

I froze, holding even my breath lest an exhalation draw their attention to the damp-smelling corner I'd squeezed myself into, and listened as they paused in the doorway, the shorter of the two giggled at something his mate muttered.

"Yeah, well, he's fucking heartless, innee," shorter said when he'd finished giggling, and his mate – a deeper voice than I'd expected – said something about how commenting on what 'He" was or was not mightn't be a wise thing to do.

Short giggly one stuttered some apologies and

explanations and the two hefted the bags and walked away from me towards the car park on the far side of the building.

I reached out and stopped the door closing, then waited until they'd gone from sight before pulling it open and entering the lobby.

The lift, tonight, appeared to be definitely broken down. I pressed the button and nothing happened. I pressed it again, and still nothing happened, so I turned and headed for the stairs, making my way up to the seventh floor.

I was breathing heavily when I arrived and paused at the top of the stairways to calm my breathing, which was when I heard, from somewhere on the landing, a door open.

"We'll talk soon," a voice I recognised said, "And if you need me, you know where I am."

I looked around desperately, for some more shadows to sink into, as footsteps approached, then realised that the only way to avoid being seen would be to run up another flight of stairs and hope that King Solomon – for it was he – was heading down, not up.

I got lucky, peering over the banisters at the top of his head as he swaggered around the turning and began to jog down the stairs, pausing just before he turned the stairwell, as though aware he was being watched, and glancing upwards just as I jerked myself from sight.

I didn't think he'd seen me, but I still waited a few minutes to be sure he was gone before descending the stairs and making my way to the door of flat 7B.

I knocked, and a few minutes passed with no response, so I knocked again, and this time a chink of light was visible behind the glass as – somewhere in the flat – a door opened.

Lindsey Wright looked pale and shaken, and it took her a few seconds to realise who I was.

"You?" She said, a wash of relief running over her features. "What are you doing here?"

"I came to see you," I said. "Can I come in?"

She glanced over her shoulder. "I've only just got Finn off to sleep, so you'll have to be quiet," she said, stepping to one side and letting me in. "Go on down to the living room," she whispered, and I made my way towards the chink of light at the end of the hallway.

"Listen," I said, when she'd joined me in the room having checked on her son, "I'm not sure where to begin with this, but-"

"Have you found him?" She asked, hope making her face light up, the light extinguishing almost as immediately, when I failed, instantly, to say that yes, George Osman had been found.

I shook my head, and her whole body seemed to slump.

"No," she breathed, staring at a patch on the carpet, "I didn't expect you would. He's gone, and that's that."

"Lindsey," I said, glancing around the room, "Was King Solomon here just now."

She blushed, her glance rising from the carpet and moving from resigned sadness to almost animosity, as she fixed her eyes on mine. "What's that to you?" She asked.

"What did he want?" I asked and waited as her emotions danced across her face.

"He just popped round," she said, "But what's that got to do with you?"

"Lindsey, he's not good news," I said. "You really don't want to be getting too involved with the likes of him."

She laughed then, a sound that had more frustration and fear in it than humour. "You reckon? Look," she shook her head, "you don't know me, and you don't know my life, and if you actually did do anything to find George, well, thanks. But it didn't work, and you're done now, so you should probably go."

She nodded towards the door but made no move to throw me out.

"Look," I said, "I'd like to help, but you really need to take care around him."

I got no further. "I've got no fucking money," she hissed. "Nothing for Finn's dinner, nothing for the mortgage. The account is empty, and the bank laughed when I asked them for a loan."

"So, you're borrowing off Solomon," I said simply.

"What the fuck would you do?" Lindsey demanded, then threw her hands in the air. "Oh, you'd probably sub off a mate, or pop along to that posh bird you had last time and get a few quid to tide you over. I've got no mates, Mr fucking don't-borrow-off-Solomon. I'm not stupid, you know: I know what he is, and I know what a fucking mess this is. And everyone I know is back in Rochdale, and most of them were glad to be rid of me. And when I moved down here and got this flat I had a job, only then George came and he said he didn't want me working, cos he'd take care of me. Only now George is gone, and I've got nothing, and what would you do?"

"What did you do?" I asked, more to stop the torrent of words, "before you met George?"

She paused. "I had a little café. Just breakfasts and sandwiches, but it was nice That's how I met George."

"Couldn't you do that again?"

Lindsey sighed. "Can you just go? Please."

"Why not?" I persisted.

"Because I've got no money. What am I gonna get stock with? Rent for a café?"

"Maybe you could waitress," I offered desperately, and she laughed out loud. "Just to get some money together."

"Yeah," she snapped, "right! And what do I do with Finn? Tie him to my back while I take orders? 'egg and chips twice and your baby needs changing, love'? I've been down the council applied for benefits, and they'll take weeks – if I get them – and in the meantime I've got a baby and no way of getting any money except selling George's clothes to that fucking louse Solomon."

"Look," she said, all her energy seemingly having been expended on the explosion, "I need money now. Not at some point in the future. Not something that has me doing a couple of lunchtime shifts for pin money. I don't see the fucking Halifax hanging around while I figure this out. And unless you're about to deliver George Osman, then all I have is King Solomon and his deep pockets."

"I'm having – the police are having – difficulty," I finally admitted, "Getting a fix on George."

"What are you on about?" She asked, the old belligerence bubbling back up. "I gave them a description, told them where he worked, detailed his last known whereabouts. What else do they need? What else do you need?"

There was no other way for it: "Proof he existed," I said at last, and she stopped, her lips formed in an 'O' shape.

"Proof?" Lindsey said at last. "Of what?"

"Look," I held my hands out in a placatory fashion, "There's no photos of George. None of your neighbours seem to have ever really met him. And none of the rigs you mentioned have ever heard of him or reported him missing. It's like he didn't exist."

"Didn't," she paused, swallowed, a look of confusion sweeping across her face, "didn't exist? Didn't exist? Well if George didn't exist," she said, the anger building as she pointed at the wall between the living room and the bedroom, "What the fuck is that in there?"

"Look," I reached out to her, and she backed away from me.

"Didn't exist?" She shook her head, an almost crazed light in her eyes. "Just go. Go away."

I reached out again, and she swiped my hand away. "Get the fuck out," she finally screamed, and from the other side of the wall, a cry came. "Fuck, she snapped, "see what you done now? Just fucking… Wait!" She ran towards the door as a full-throated crying came from the bedroom.

I followed as she entered the room, switching on the overhead light which further startled the tiny boy who had been sleeping on the double bed, and causing an increase in volume and anxiety of his crying.

"Didn't exist," Lindsey flung open the wardrobe door, froze, a cry coming from her now. "He was here," she said, gesturing at the empty space, the hangers swinging crazily, a single sock lying on the floor.

"Solomon took them," she said, turning her attention to me as Finn's cries – catching her confusion and terror - became hysterical. I reached out to him, tried to shush him, calm him, and Lindsey, swiped my hand away.

"Don't touch him," she said, the tears beginning, now, to flow silently from her. "Solomon took them. Said he'd give me a good price. They were good clothes. Armani. Gucci. George loved nice things. That's how I met him. I, that caff over on Marsham way," I knew it; it was the one that I'd taken Louise Byrne to to tell her that her mother was dead.

"And George started coming in, every morning, regular as clockwork. Two poached eggs, whole-wheat toast, no beans, coffee, black, and always," she smiled through her tears, "Always really stressing no sugar. 'No sugar, beautiful,' he'd say, and I'd say 'Them designer togs ain't gonna fit you if you put on weight, and he'd smile."

I looked around the sparsely decorated room, no sign of an obsession with expensive designer clothes evident now and wondered if Osman had been living beyond his means.

He wouldn't be the first man in history who'd run up debts then done a runner.

But then I'd have expected bailiffs to be crawling out of the woodwork.

"And then, after a couple of weeks, he asked me out," she went on, as though retelling their story out loud would make it real, and a couple of months later I fell pregnant," she stroked the boys hair, leant down to plant a kiss on the top of his head, "and George was over the moon. He made me buy this place, cos I had right to buy as a sitting tenant, gave me the deposit, said he wanted his son to have a roof over his head, and he moved in with me. With us," she held the child tighter.

I glanced at her clothes. George hadn't spent money on upgrading Lindsey's chain store wardrobe; she was head-to-toe Primarni; but then she was a mum with a toddler. Prada would have been somewhat pointless when plastered with crayons snot and toddler puke.

"And he was always so well dressed," she trailed off, seeing my eyes raking the empty wardrobe, the bare drawers. "Solomon took them," she said, the colour draining from her voice, as though the reality of her situation were finally hitting home, as though she was realising that a mistake had been made, but was unable to decide which of her actions, which of her decisions had been the worst mistake. "But they were here. I needed the money. The mortgage is due next week, and I have nothing. He gave me a good price," she repeated and an image of the two henchmen, giggling as they struggled away with bin bags full of George Osman's clothing, came to my mind.

Her tears seemed to trigger a shaking that made her whole-body tremble, till a triumphant light came on in her eyes and – leaving me shocked and Finn now silent and watching his mother with saucer-sized eyes – she left the room.

I heard some clanging and shuffling, and a moment later, Lindsey re-entered the bedroom, a grey Emporio Armani polo shirt clutched in her hands, and threw it on the bed before me.

"From the washing. I haven't done much since he vanished. But he was here," she said, pointing a trembling finger at the garment. "Don't you dare tell me he wasn't. It still smells of him," she said, pulling Finn closer and fighting back tears.

CHAPTER TWENTY-EIGHT

My dad has – as long as I've known him – viewed punctuality as being next to – if not actually – Godliness. If he says he'll be with you at 0930, then there's little point putting your coat on at 0920, cos you'll only be standing around for ten minutes. Equally, if you're still struggling to get your coat on and get down the stairs at 0932, the horn of his taxi cab will be honked. Loudly.

"Thought you'd overslept," he said – only half-jokingly – when I finally dragged myself into the back of the car. What? No Lady C today?"

"You do know she doesn't actually live with me, right?" I asked, not even deigning to address his accusations of tardiness on my part.

"Pity," he responded, "you might actually be on time if she did."

"I am on time," I replied, kicking myself for rising to the bait.

He chuckled, slipping the taxi into gear and sliding away from The Marq.

"So," he said, "Where are we off to?"

"My solicitors," I said, giving him the address of Dot Frost's offices.

He eyed me in the rear-view mirror. "You in trouble with the law again?" He asked.

I smiled, shaking my head. "No, and that 'again' needs clearing up. I've not been in trouble with them before. I've,"

I searched for – and found – the phrase "Been helping them with their enquiries."

"Fairly regularly," he added dryly. "So, what's this? A social call?"

"Sort of," I admitted. "Dot asked me to look into something for her, so I'm popping round with an update."

And it wasn't much of an update. When I'd finally returned from Lindsey Wright's the night before, the pub had been kicking out, and Ali, having made some pointed comment about how smoothly it seemed to run when I was too busy to get too involved with the place, had told Ray and Dash they could finish up and head into the kitchen with me.

"They've stuff to tell you," she added gnomically, "But make sure the kettle's on. I'll be in in twenty minutes. Three sugars, and one of those chocolate shortbreads if you lot haven't scarfed them all by then. Off you go," she nodded to the twins, who'd been standing to attention like Pavlov's dogs.

They headed to the kitchen, and by the time I'd put away my coat, the kettle was bubbling away, a laptop was opened on the table, and the boys had decanted about a kilo of biscuits onto a serving platter.

"So," Ray gestured at the laptop, "You asked us to look in to the names that Mehmet Aksoy had in this mysterious package he left with Dorothy Frost.

I sat. On screen was an image of the newspaper cuttings that had been stuffed into the envelope. "And have you found anything?" I asked.

Ray tapped a key and the image changed to what looked like a modern art sculpture: All twisted red metal and strange angles jutting out like broken limbs. I stared at it in horror. "Is that the car?"

Dash nodded. "It's a miracle there was still enough of your man left to identify. The car, according to police reports, picked up speed as it headed into the curve."

"Seems a dangerous way to drive," I said, and Dash gave

me his most pitying look. "Not if you're Steve McQueen in Bullitt. Unfortunately, this was Mehmet Aksoy in Sussex. They reckon it was doing about a hundred and seventy when it hit the ground."

"Didn't explode, though." Ray added, "Cos it didn't spark."

"But it should" Dash added, "By rights have gone kablooey."

"Kablooey?" I asked. "Is kablooey even a word these days?"

"Mate, do you want the story or not?" Dash asked.

I held my hands up in supplication as Ray plonked three mugs of tea on the table and flung a teabag into the fourth cup which he left by the kettle.

"So, the autopsy report."

"Which you have how, exactly?" I interjected.

The two looked at each other, reached as one for the plate of chocolate biscuits and, in synch, dunked their cookies into their tea, counted – aloud - to two, withdrew them and shoved the melted biscuits right into their mouths.

"From a friend." Ray said through a mouthful of McVities.

"Called Harry The Hack," Dash expanded, for which he received a stern glare from his brother.

"You've hacked the coroners?"

"No," Ray mimed shocked. "Someone else hacked it; we just found the report in our emails."

I sighed. "One day you two are going to get in trouble."

"Only if you keep asking them to do you favours," Ali snarked, shuffling into the kitchen as Dash jumped up to reboil the kettle and pour water over her teabag. "Cheers, love," Ali smiled at him, sat herself down and snatched a chocolate biscuit from the plate.

"The missing girl is a non-starter," Ray began, tapping at the 'Where are they now' article. "Her name was Katie Jewel and she'd been bullied by one of her schoolmates for years. Then Katie's mum died, and the bullying was redoubled until eventually she snapped and went for the schoolmate with a pen knife. There's a scuffle and the schoolmate gets stabbed, the ambulance takes an age to get to them and the schoolmate ends up nearly dying.

"By this stage young Katie's done a runner and to this day hasn't been seen."

"Interesting," I mused. "Could Aksoy have seen her?"

"Unlikely," Dash said. "She's in Greece running a bed and breakfast on Skiathos. Took us less than an hour to track her down."

"And the law haven't traced her yet?" I asked incredulously.

"I'm not sure the law have been that bothered about tracing her, to be honest," Ray said. "The schoolmate – Jasmin Hill – turns out to have been a right piece of work. On top of which, she didn't die. They found enough dope in her locker to – once she was out of hospital – charge her and a bunch of her mates with supplying."

"Hunting down a bullied schoolgirl who'd actually helped them uncover a drugs ring just so they could charge her with wounding was probably not on the top of their list."

"So why the news story?" I asked, and Ali chuckled.

"Space filler, innit," she said.

"Okay," I sighed, "so there's no obvious reason why Aksoy would have this article in the envelope. What about the front page: Vince Armstrong?"

"Well everyone knows everything there is to know about this guy, really," Ray said. "He's a local lad done well – he started working at Fenchurch a year ago. Trading assistant on the," he checked his notes, "Currency desk. Did okay, ended up as assistant to one of the senior guys, and then didn't come in to work after the Christmas break."

"Management didn't worry too much till mid-morning, when they got a phone call from one of their finance team asking about a series of huge payments that had left the bank overnight," Dash filled in, "Only the payments had pushed them close to the limit in their accounts, or something, so they took a look and lo-and-behold, the payments were instructed by the missing Vince Armstrong, who still hasn't shown up for work."

"At which point they did worry," Ray took the story back up. "Someone – at that point – called his mobile and got no answer. Someone else went round to his flat – oddly enough, he was still living with his mum – and she claims he'd not been there all over Christmas. Sent her a text to say he was going to Asia on a business trip and would be a few weeks. Only the bank know nothing about any business trip, and that's when they realised that Mr A has done a runner.

"They try recalling the money he sent out of the bank, only ten minutes after it hit the first bank accounts, it was split into a couple of hundred smaller amounts and transferred to other accounts all over the world, so the money is well and truly gone, as is Vince Armstrong."

"His boss reckons they'll get most of it back," I muttered, remembering Von Oldenwald's insistence on the point.

"Well his boss is either delusional or stupid," Ray answered. "I've seen some of the transfers and the splits and I'd say within an hour of the money going out it had been split and shuffled so well that finding it – let alone proving that any money found was the money that came from Fenchurch Brookes – ain't gonna be easy at all."

"And what are the chances of finding Armstrong?" I wondered aloud.

"The police have been searching for him since, but there's no sign of him, and no evidence of him leaving the country under his own name."

"So maybe he's still in the country," I said. "And maybe Aksoy spotted him."

"But if that's the case," Ali said, thoughtfully dunking her biscuit into her mug for a count of two, "why not just call the rozzers. Or leave a note saying 'I saw Vince Armstrong at number 22 Crooked Banker street'? Why all this?" she gestured at the newsprint on screen.

I had to admit, I didn't have an answer. "Plus," I said,

"Why would Armstrong then kill him? And how would he kill him? I mean, the reports I've seen say he was going too fast, took a corner, lost control and totalled the car, so unless he was being chased by Armstrong, how is that anything but an accident?"

"Unless the car was tampered with," Dash mused.

"Tampered with?" I frowned. "Was it?"

Ray shook his head. "No sign of it in the reports. Brakes – when tested – worked; there was nothing to suggest that the speed was the result of a jammed accelerator."

I stared at the screen. "And yet, not a week before the accident, he gives Dot Frost an envelope with 'In the event of my death' on it. Like he knew what was coming."

"He couldn't have," Ray said, shaking his head. "Not without a crystal ball."

"Unless it was suicide," Dash said.

He had a point. Then I thought again. "But if it was, why not leave a suicide note? I mean," I gestured, again, at the random clippings, "none of this screams 'Goodbye cruel world.'"

"Maybe, then, it genuinely was an accident," Dash mused, and three heads turned to him. "Well," he blushed, "we're all assuming a deliberate action of some sort, and that this," he gestured at the computer, "was something to do with it. But what if it was a genuine accident?"

I considered this. "Okay," I said slowly, "But that still leaves us – as you say – with this. And the mystery, in that case, isn't so much why and how did Mehmet Aksoy die as it is what was he trying to tell us in these pages of random junk?"

We all considered this for a moment, and then: "What about the other story?" Ali asked, pointing at the screen. "This Bill Duffy geezer?"

Ray perked up. "Now this," Dash jumped in before his brother, "Is interesting. Businessman. Runs a string of garages. Goes out one morning for his daily jog and is seen by a witness being surrounded by masked men and bundled into a white van. Wife doesn't even report him missing till that evening when she gets back from work, and by that time the trail is stone cold."

"Kidnapping?" I wondered aloud.

"Looked like it, only so far there's no suggestion of any ransom demands."

"So, are we sure he's been abducted?" I asked. "I mean, he hasn't just done a runner? There's a lot of it about," I added, thinking of Lindsey Wright.

"Right," I said, "what's been going on in Bill Duffy's life? What could his link with Mehmet Aksoy be?"

"Cars," Ray said, his eyes lighting up as a realisation dawned.

"Go on," I said, "I'm listening."

"Well Duffy runs a few garages, but they've been trying to go upmarket lately, so they've closed a few of the service shops round here."

"Layoffs?" I asked, musing whether disgruntled ex-employees might have nabbed their old boss for revenge.

"Nah," Ray shook his head, "Most of the engineers moved to the newer places up Mayfair. I mean, it's a commute, but I'm not sure it's cause to kidnap the boss."

"And did they service Aksoy's motor?" I asked.

The light in Ray's eyes began to dim. "Nah," he said again, "that one was a specialist motor. Only ever went to the Asimov garage in West Drayton."

"So, Duffy's going upmarket, and Aksoy ends up interested in his kidnapping, only it doesn't really look like a kidnapping now, because there's no sign of any attempt to ransom him." I sighed.

"All these missing men: George Osman, Vince Armstrong, Bill Duffy. Why do I get the feeling there's a connection?"

"Because you can never just accept that things are as they are," Ali said, hoiking herself out of her chair and rinsing her mug in the sink. "That sometimes shit happens and there's no connection to anything."

"Thank you, Miss Chaos Theory 1979." I sighed, receiving, for my attempt at brevity, a slap on the back of the head.

"No, you said it yourself, Nero Woofter: the contents of that envelope are a load of random tat. What if the whole thing was just a joke on his part. He's got no plans to die, so handing that envelope in is just some stupid joke on his part."

"A joke?" I considered the proposal. "But it's not funny. I mean-"

"Oh, love," Ali interrupted me, "What people find funny is as unpredictable as wind. I knew a bloke once who would wet himself laughing at videos of operations. Every time there was a documentary on telly – 24 hours in A&E, Extreme Chiropody, you name it – or a decent episode of "Casualty" with a nice appendectomy being acted out, Norman Jones'd be shrieking with laughter. Claimed it was a nervous reaction, but I think he was just a sick fucker. Most people are," she sniffed, before finishing with the Bar Maid's mantra: "Now: have you lot not got homes to go to."

I leaned forward, pulled the jump seat down, and scooted over on to it so that I could be nearer to the back of my dad's head. "Dad," I said, my mouth already going dry as I broached the subject, "Is mum okay?"

My dad was silent for a moment, then said "How many times? She's fine. You're such a worrier," he shook his head. "She's fine."

I tried another tack: "It's not unusual for partners to deny a problem, you know," I said sympathetically – I hoped. "Because the problem has become normality for them. Dad, are you okay?"

"Dan," we stopped at a pedestrian crossing and a coachload of Chinese tourists, all muffled up in overcoats that made them look like Polar explorers, began shuffling over the crossing, pausing every so often to photograph each other, the cab I was sitting in, or the orange flashing beacons on either side.

My dad half-turned to face me, a somewhat stressed half-smile hanging vaguely around his face. "What are you going on about?"

"You," I answered. "I'm asking if you're okay?"

He shrugged. "I'm fine. I hate these dark mornings and dark nights. I hate that I'm still driving a cab at my age when I always thought I'd be retired to Portugal by now, and I hate everyone poking around in my business. There's been a lot of it lately – you, the girls, Paddy."

"'Cos we're worried about you," I confessed. "We really are, dad. We're not blind, and we know something's going on."

"Oh, you do, do you," he said with a look close to the one he'd given me when I'd sat him down to discuss the results of my investigation, at age six, into the whereabouts, in July, of a Mister Santa Claus. "Well there's nothing going on. And I don't know why everyone's so determined to make out that there is."

"Mum's drinking," I finally said, as two tourists, each wearing a foam hat shaped like a red telephone box stood, their backs to the cab, giving peace signs to a third, who photographed them while he, in turn, wore a foam hat shaped like Big Ben.

"Mum's what?" My dad asked, his face clouding.

"She's drinking," I said, the tension knot at my father's looming disapproval already tightening in the pit of my stomach. "And it's serious enough to leave her with hangovers, days in bed. Val reckons she spent a day last month throwing her guts up. That's not right, dad. Not normal."

"Normal?" My dad punched the horn on the cab, the resultant noise causing the tourists to jump and shriek. "Come on!" He yelled, "It's not a fucking photo studio! Normal?" he turned to me. "You want to talk to me about what's normal?"

My heart sunk. "Dad-"

"You had a job and a nice house, and a future, and now you're – what? Running that shithole pub, hanging out with that pisshead mate of yours – and how fucking dare you talk about your mum having a few drinks when you and that Caz are on the gin at breakfast – and what have you got, Danny? What have you got to show for it all? Your mother thinks the sun shines out of your arse, thinks one day you'll make good, and here you sit, talking to me – to *me* – about normality?"

"Dad," I tried again, "We're worried. We really are. We need to know what's going on. We need to know," I repeated, a note of desperation audible even to me.

"No," he turned from me, released the handbrake as the tourists finally crossed the road, and the cab rolled forward. "No, you don't. What you need to do is give your mother the respect she's entitled to. Is leave her and me the fuck alone to sort this out. Look, I'm sorry Danny, but this is grown-up business, and you just need to leave us to it."

"So, you admit there is business of some sort to be dealt with," I said, and the cab stopped.

"Look," my dad turned again to me, and I recoiled from the look on his face, "I've had enough. I've got to make some money this morning, so I'm going to let you out here."

I was stunned. "You're chucking me out of your cab?"

"There's a tube station two streets over," he pointed to the right. "Five minutes' walk. I need to be somewhere else."

"Dad," I reached a hand out to him, caught his eyes in the rear-view mirror. "I'm sorry," I finally said, a feeling of total deflation sweeping over me. "I didn't mean to upset you. I'm really, really sorry."

"I know," he said, still with his back to me.

I opened the taxi door and stepped out.

"Danny," he said, winding down his window, "I'm sorry too. You're a good kid. A great kid. And you've never made us anything but proud. But I can't talk about this, okay? I promised. Sorry," he said again, and then he drove away, leaving me standing on the pavement, remembering that pause right at the start of the conversation, as though – in response to my opening question – he'd had a momentary debate, as though he'd been trying to decide – in that split second of hesitation – between telling me a lie or the truth?

But what worried me most was the fact that - when he'd looked back at me in the rear-view mirror – I'd seen fear – real naked fear - in his eyes.

CHAPTER TWENTY-NINE

I was late getting to Dot Frost's office, and the lady herself pointedly glanced at her watch as I was lead – a bit sweaty and out of breath – in to her.

"Been running?" She asked, gesturing at a sofa on the far side of the room and joining me on it. I put the envelope on the coffee table before us.

"Long story," I answered, "suffice it to say that the tube never seems to get you anywhere as fast as the website says it should.

"I thought you had a cab on tap?" she smiled, ordering tea for us.

"Not as on tap as it used to be," I answered, deciding I wanted to move this conversation on. "So, I'm not getting very far on your Mr Aksoy," I admitted, gesturing at the envelope.

"Nothing from Selene?" She asked. "No sixth sense of yours telling you to worry?"

I shook my head. "I mean, she's his wife. If anyone has a motive for murder, it's usually the wife. But in this case, I can't see anything that suddenly made a motive appear; I can't see how she would have made it happen; and more to the point: I can't see what any of it would have to do with the cuttings in that envelope."

She sighed, nodding slowly. "I see." She sounded almost disappointed, then, as tea was served and her secretary left the room, she perked up a little.

"Well, at least I can let Selene know that it was just nonsense," she said, adjusting a pen so that it lay straight. "I don't mind telling you I was really worried, Danny; Mehmet was always a bit of a dreamer. We used to call him and Selene Venus and Adonis, except the genders were totally mixed: Selene was always hunting, always moving up and on and out, and Mehmet was love – pure and unadulterated fun and idealism and craziness."

I looked around the room, still somewhat phased by the fact that Dot and I weren't having a conversation in an interview room at Southwark nick. "The thing is, Dot, I still can't understand why."

"Why?"

"Why'd he send you the envelope? Why'd he write 'in case of my death' on it? Why?"

Dot smiled sadly. "Maybe he was planning something."

"Planning something? What, like suicide?"

She shook her head. "I doubt it. Mehmet wasn't the type. So," she sipped her tea, "One time Mr Frost and I turned up to dinner and Selene and Mehmet's. It was not long after our twenty-fifth wedding anniversary. So, two, three courses in, Mehmet sidles over to me.

"'How'd you like them onions?' he asks, and I smiled, nodded over my champagne, and wondering what on earth he was going on about. Then it hit me. You want some cookies with this, Danny?"

I shook my head, still unsure what silver wedding anniversaries, onions and dinner parties had to do with the envelope on her desk. "I'm good, thanks," I said.

Dorothy Frost lifted her cup, sipped the tea again, placed it perfectly back down on a porcelain saucer and returned to the point: "A few days earlier, I'd received a box here. I have some odd clients," she gestured at me. "Well, being friend of the Mediterranean gent we both know, odd is – to be frank – putting it mildly. Well, I open the box, and inside is what, at first, I assume, is a pile of dead daffodils – ripped out of the earth, bulb and all, and just shoved in a box, with a note

saying 'out of tears comes shining beauty.'"
"Very poetic," I said.
"Yes," Dot drained her cup, "I thought so too. Then I binned them. "I mean, don't get me wrong: I love a bit of whimsy," and again, she indicated me, "but in my business it's a fine line between whimsy and, well, crazy. So, in the bin they went. Only, thank god they didn't go off to landfill, cos as Mehmet was waggling his eyebrows and smiling that dimpled grin I remembered my wedding day, when I stood stolidly while Mr Frost and Mehmet Aksoy cried their eyes out. Seriously: It's usually the bride and her bridesmaids that bawl through the whole thing, but at my wedding it was the groom and his best man.
"I wondered, momentarily, if they'd had something going on. Don't look at me like that," she shook her head reproachfully at me. It was the eighties, Danny. Everybody slept with everybody. And then I realised: Mehmet knew that Mr frost and I were marrying for Love, and he and Selene had married because," Dot frowned, "Well, to be honest, they married because Mehmet's family could help Selene, could move her up.
"So," she frowned. "'How'd you like them onions,' he asked, and I came straight back here that night, remembered the tears he cried at my wedding, and got the box out of the bins downstairs, and discovered that what I thought were manky daffs were flowering onions. And he'd hollowed out two of the bulbs and inserted platinum Tiffany salt and pepper shakers into them, each," she smiled sadly at the coffee cup, "Engraved with 'How'd you like them onions?'"
"So, this," I gestured at the envelope, even as Dot Frost gazed fondly at the ring on the second finger of her right hand, "Is – what? – A game? A joke?
"Well," Dorothy shrugged, "I can't explain it otherwise. Especially if there's no suggestion that Selene – or anyone else – had a hand in his death. Can you?"
I shook my head.
"Life," Dorothy Frost breathed out, "Never ends when

you think it should. Maybe he had plans. Some joke, something that would make sense when he made it make sense. Only he took a corner too fast…"

I left Dot's office, the envelope now back in her safe, and left her to her day. But the conversation we'd had would not stop playing in my head.

There was something wrong with it; something about how quickly Dot had been willing to accept that the whole thing was a bust, file it under "Mehmet's sense of humour," and move on.

I wondered if our Maltese friend – or one of Dot's other shady clients – had persuaded her to stop looking into a connection between her friend, a missing banker and an abducted businessman, and I was still pondering the chances – Dot had not struck me as someone who would ever be pressured into doing anything she didn't want to – when I unzipped my jacket, loosened the scarf from around my neck, and turned the key in the lock of the door at The Marq and pushed the door open.

It had barely moved when something walloped me on the back of the head, a shove sent me sprawling forward, and only the door stopped me pitching headfirst on to the carpet.

"Where is he?" A voice growled, and I recognised Caz's 'old friend' Henry Wakefield's voice.

I righted myself and turned as Wakefield, Solomon and the two rent-a-goons, each holding a snarling staffie on a lead piled into the bar.

I wanted to look at me watch. It wasn't long till lunchtime; when would Ali or the twins be in to set up? Were they here already?

I scanned the bar quickly, but there was no sight or sound of them.

The strangled breathing of the dogs, their throaty growls and the sound of the door lock thunking loudly as Solomon firmly shut the exit echoed round space.

"He asked you a question," Solomon said, stepping

forward and pulling, from his waistband, a huge gun.

At this point I should note that the gun in question was just average size, but that any gun – when you're unused to being around guns, and when the gun in question is being solidly pointed in your face – can appear huge.

So, a huge gun was pointed in my face, and Solomon, a look of almost pleasure on his face, repeated the question that Prince Harry had asked as he'd shoved me into the door.

"Where is he?"

I knew who they wanted: Callum Byrne, the prize they'd been enjoying tormenting, had been spirited from their reach, and they were not happy about this turn of events. Someone would have to pay, and it was going – clearly – to be me, as Wakefield would never go near Caz again, and not just because she'd already shown she was more than capable of standing up for herself, but because he'd know that any damage to her would be taken seriously by the type of authorities he preferred to avoid.

Whereas I was a nobody and thus fair game.

But I wasn't going to give them the satisfaction they wanted quite so easily. "Where's who?" I asked, and Solomon's thumb came up, cocking the gun, as one of the Bull terriers barked loudly, and Prince Harry shoved a table – mercifully free of glasses – over.

"Don't fuck around with me," Solomon growled, the gun holding steady as Wakefield began violently stamping on one of the table legs until it snapped. "Oh, don't worry: I won't shoot you," Solomon sneered in answer, I supposed, to the look of fear that must have gone through my eyes. "Not right away. No, first," he nodded at the splintered table leg, jerked his head at Wakefield, whose eyes were sparkling with something that looked almost like sexual pleasure, "I'll have my mate here do to your left leg what he's just done to that table leg.

"Then I'll have him do the same to your right leg. Then I'll have the boys here set the fucking hounds on you till – by the time they're finished – you'll be fucking begging me to pop a cap in you."

I laughed.

I couldn't help it, and I knew even as I was doing it that I was most probably somewhere near the edge of hysteria. I stopped the laughter, but it was too late.

"Are you – Did you – Did he just fucking laugh at me?" He demanded of the goons who now looked even more scared than I'd felt a moment ago.

"Sorry," I said. "Rude. But 'pop a cap in you'? I mean Solomon, we're closer to Compton Street than to East Compton. I was – I admit – genuinely worried till then. But that sort of popped the bubble a bit. Hard – even with that," I nodded at the Gatling he was still pointing at me "to be terrified when the dialogue goes all HBO."

Solomon stared at me, the joy he'd been suffused with a few moments earlier turning before my eyes into a building fury. "Harry," he said, wiggling the gun at me, "Fuck this Chichi Bwoy up. Fellahs," the goons snapped to attention, even their dogs quietening, "Make a fucking mess in here."

They looked at each other, dropped the leashes and, one having pulled a claw-hammer from the back of his trousers while the other removed a Stanley knife from his pocket.

"Oh, not the fucking upholstery," I groaned. "We've only just had it redone." At which point – out of the corner of my eye – I saw Wakefield move, the broken table leg firmly in his grip as he swung it at my head.

To this day, I still have no idea what made me do what I did next.

I should have ducked down.

Or jumped back.

Or stood still and taken a length of hand-turned (and probably wood-wormed) Victorian table leg smack in the right ear.

But I didn't.

Instead, I shifted my weight fully onto my left foot, lifted my right leg behind me and swung it with as much power as

I could muster up, in an arc, and into what Solomon's grannie, I'm sure, would have referred to as his 'private parts,' the force of the blow having a number of almost simultaneous effects.

The force of the impact unbalanced me, and I staggered backwards, so that Wakefield's table-leg attack – rather than smashing my right ear and probably concussing me – slashed across my scarf – a particularly voluminous one that I'd been wearing to de-butch the copper haircut I'd inflicted on myself – becoming tangled in the fabric and, in turn, destabilising him, so that he toppled forward into Solomon, who was already bent double.

The trajectory of the large aristocratic redhead onto the diminutive would-be Yardie resulted in Wakefield almost somersaulting over Solomon at exactly at the moment that an enraged Solomon, still grabbing his balls with his right hand, yanked himself upwards, the gun pointed squarely at my chest.

And as Solomon pulled the trigger, Prince Harry barrelled into him, so that the explosion from the gun resulted in a bullet missing me by a miraculously safe margin and slamming instead into a bottle of bathtub gin, shattering it, and sending slivers of green glass ricocheting around the room.

Prince Harry, the force of the gun's discharge having flung Solomon backwards and slightly upwards at the exact moment that his own direction of travel was towards and down on to the short-arsed gangster, was thus the recipient of a headbutt that created both a cracking sound audible even over the ringing of my ears and a firework-like explosion of claret that spattered outwards across the bar.

Which was the exact moment that one of the dogs finally snapped, began barking like a deranged beast, and threw itself at the source of the noise that had upset it.

Which was how one of Solomon's own attack dogs ended up attached to his left arm.

Chaos ensued, with one of the goons yelling "Fuck's sake

Duke, stop that, it's Solomon," which – as said goon had a pronounced lisp – made the chaos of a shrieking Solomon, a Prince Henry who looked like he'd been had at with a claw hammer and the other goon who had decided to set the other dog on to poor deranged Duke, only to have the animal misunderstand the order and attack, rather than his canine colleague, the target of said canine colleague's wrath, so that Solomon was set upon by both dogs, the result being that he dropped the gun.

At my feet.

I'm not a fan of guns. Which, now it's out there, seems like the most fucking obvious thing to say – like "I'm not fond of death," or "Little Mix are the Spice Girls with more budget and fewer tunes," but, in light of what happened next, I feel it necessary.

I picked up the gun.

I mean, what did you think I was going to say? I left it lying there and let the hounds finish savaging Solomon before turning on me?

Anyway, they were no longer savaging Solomon, having been removed from the sleeve and hem of his coat, kicked once or twice by their handers, yanked to a seated position, and pointed my way as though the goons were waiting for order to release them at me.

Which – as I was now holding a gun on the group, while Solomon let loose with a chain of profanities some of which even I hadn't heard before, Wakefield bled copiously down the front of his doubtless very expensive jacket, and the dogs, kicked to submission, whined piteously – didn't come.

"I'm gonna gut you like a fucking fish, you filthy shit stabber," Solomon shrieked.

"That's Mr Fucking Shitstabber to you," I said coldly, pointing the gun in roughly the same area I'd aimed my kick. "And unless you want the damage I've just inflicted to be permanent, I'd get one of those two remedials to open that door you made such a show of locking and get them, your dogs, your poncey posh mate and your tragic incompetent arse out of my fucking pub before I decide to do the public a service."

I almost missed it, but Caz had prepared me to look out for it: Solomon's eyes flicked to Wakefield – in exactly the way that she'd predicted they always would; the way that a junior partner in anything looks to the boss for approval – and Wakefield twitched almost imperceptibly.

"I want him back," Solomon shouted, pointing his finger at me as though I hadn't just witnessed him taking orders from Prince Harry, "and I want him back tomorrow. He owes me money."

And he turned on his Cuban heels, the two goons turning at the same time so that a minor pile-up occurred at the still locked pub door, with snarling from Solomon, shocked silence from the dogs and mutterings of menace from the goons before the door was yanked open and they began piling out of the pub.

Only Wakefield remained, his coat glistening with the spray from his nose, his chin and cheeks caked in drying gore like a newly-blooded teenaged fox hunter, a sardonic smile on his lips.

"I can see why she likes you," he said. "Why she's made you her little pet project."

"Jog on, wanker," I snarled, wiggling the gun at him. Yes, I know it was hardly Wildean; but I'd like to see Saint Oscar come up with anything better after what I'd just been through.

"Nice place," he said, casting an eye around the bar. "Victorian? Solid." He cast an eye on the shattered table, the two seats that the goons had managed to slash and smash. "But not very fire retardant."

"We've been burned before," I snarled back, remembering an earlier arson attack, "and we're still here."

"Ah," he smiled, turning towards the door, "but I'll bet you weren't burned by professionals," he said in a tone that made me wonder where one might purchase asbestos pyjamas. "Nice to meet you, Mr Bird. I suspect we'll be meeting again," he said, and he smiled at me, and let himself out of the pub.

CHAPTER THIRTY

"Okay," Caz tutted, lifted a leg and, in the dim illumination cast from the distant street lights, inspected her leg. "That's a pair of Wolford's you owe me."

Even in the half light, I could see the ladder working its way up her right calf. "Do you want to call this off before I start figuring out the damage to the shoes?" She added darkly.

I looked around me. From somewhere distant, the city symphony of traffic rumbled on, honking of horns and percussive grip-release of air breaks adding tonality to the hum. The torch on my phone was waning fast, our breathing was coming out of us in visible clouds, my feet were damp and my head felt as though I were wearing a nettle cap, so heavy was the fast encroaching fog. I wasn't entirely sure what I was hoping to find here, but I had a horrible feeling that we were not on a wild goose chase.

"Seriously," Caz – exasperation crumbling as outrage loomed – stopped dead and threw her hands up.

I turned, following her outraged stare downwards where her left foot had landed in a puddle so deep she was now up to the ankle in muddy water.

"Christian. Louboutins," she said, pronouncing each of the words as though they were a sacrament. "You have me crawling around an empty pitch-dark building site in Louboutins. I must be out of my mind."

"Well you should have changed," I replied, extending an

arm to help extract her from the puddle, "put on something more workday."

"These," she glared, "*Are* my workday shoes. Because Daniel, my average work day does not involve following mysterious tipoffs on derelict construction sites in the middle of the night."

After Solomon, Wakefield, Duke, his doggy mate and the two goons had absented themselves, I'd helped myself to a huge vodka, placed the gun carefully on the bar, and had still been sitting there shaking slightly when Ali had turned up.

"I take it this wasn't an unexpected visit from the V.A.T man," she said, casting an eye around the semi-ruined bar.

"Don't ask," I said, as she righted a turned over bar stool, found a mop behind the bar and began sweeping up the shards of glass.

"You going to need that again," she said, nodding at the gun which – to be honest – I'd almost forgotten was there.

I shook my head and she lifted the piece from the bar, emptied the cartridge, confirmed the chamber was empty, used a beer towel to clean the items down, dropped both into a bin bag, and dropped the bin bag into the trash can behind the counter.

"We got Turkey soup for lunch today," she said, jolting me out of my shock, and I staggered back into the kitchen to warm the soup up and put the bread rolls into the oven.

By the time I returned half an hour later, the bar looked not much more dishevelled than usual. True, one or two of the seats were now sporting Duct tape bandages to stop their stuffing spilling out, and the table with the smashed leg was leaning against a wall, a stool filling in for the missing leg.

I called Caz, leaving a short message on her voice mail, and the serving of soup to a busy lunch time crowd had filled the next couple of hours, after which I'd gone round to see my brother, who had listened to a recounting of my conversation with my dad in shocked silence before assuring me that I had done the right thing, then calling my sisters to tell them that my dad and I had had an argument.

They, of course, had come rushing round to gloat at the golden boy brought low, though their gloating faded once they saw how genuinely upset I was.

"Something's going on," Val said darkly, "And him reacting like that tells you how serious whatever it is that's going on is: He adores you. They both do."

"Yeah, but suggesting that my life isn't normal," I tailed off, afraid to voice the concern that he'd been talking of more, perhaps, than my job and friendships.

"Well it sort of isn't entirely normal, is it?" Maz said. "Oh, don't jump on me, Dan," she held up a hand placatorily, "I'm just saying: I don't know anyone else who runs around town sorting out murders. I mean, I'm nosy – we're all nosy," she looked around the room, and my other siblings nodded as though nosiness was something taken for granted. "It's genetic, to be honest, in this family. But you take it to a whole new level. You just can't see something odd and not dissect and explain it. And they worry, you know."

"Worry?"

"Danny, if there's murders, then there's murderers, and you do have a habit of messing around in things that don't really concern you."

If only you knew, I thought, whilst aloud, "But I was only poking around in this mess because you lot asked me to," I protested, and they had to shrug their general acknowledgement of the truth of my statement.

"Yeah," Val acknowledged, "But maybe we should leave it for now. I don't want daddy upset any more than he is. Maybe I'll pop round tomorrow, let you know if the coast is clear or not."

And so saying, the meeting had broken up, I'd headed back to The Marq and – on arrival – had been greeted by Dash.

"Here," he'd said, "You just missed some bird. Telephoned and said that you needed to get yourself over to Marsham Way right now and check out the building site. Said it had to be you, cos nobody else would believe her.

"I think she was trying to disguise her voice, cos she was doing it all whispery, like 'it's coming from the house' style, you know what I mean?"

"Nobody else would believe her?" I suddenly felt exhausted. "What the hell does that mean?"

"Search me," he answered, "But it's what she said.

"This woman have a name?" I asked, and Dash shrugged.

"Probably. But she didn't give it to me."

So, I'd gone out back to the kitchen to make myself something to eat, and – as the water for my pasta boiled – it had come to me.

"Nobody else would believe me."

Louise.

I'd telephoned Joanna Trztrzelewska, who hadn't seen Louise since that lunchtime, and who'd given me Louise's phone number.

I'd called that number and listened to the phone ring and ring and ring, and eventually I'd called Caz, explained that I needed her help, and arranged to meet outside the hoardings advertising Constable Developments new twelve super-luxe apartment building on Marsham Way.

Of Louise, when we arrived, there was no sight, and in fact the whole site seemed deserted, the absence of even a night watchman testimony to both Constable Developments' misplaced faith in the efficacy of their security, and to their general cheapness.

I filled Caz in quickly on my meeting with Solomon and Harry, and she listened with an air of grim resignation as though the story did not entirely surprise her.

"We'll sort them tomorrow," she said as we stood before the padlock on the gate. "After we deal with whatever's brought us here. The lock was huge and solid, but Caz took one look and nodded. "I should be able to get in to that."

"Really." I was impressed.

"Yeah," she nodded again, "If I only had a hairpin. Oh, and a bolt cutters."

My excitement faded.

"Maybe an oxy acetylene torch," she finished, fixing me with her beadiest eye. "Daniel, that's an industrial lock; I was being sarcastic."

I looked around.

The hoarding ran the entire length of the block, and at the corner they turned right, as did we.

This wall, still plastered with the Constable logo and a series of artists drawings of a traditional stone-fronted building and text advertising high spec luxury homes for modern city dwellers (as opposed, I assumed, to late Georgian city dwellers, who – owing to the fact most of them had been dead for two hundred years – would never have gotten a mortgage on these flats). But in this wall, there were no breaks, no doors, no gates.

It wasn't until we turned right again on to St Giles lane, which ran parallel with Marsham Way, that we got lucky.

Here, a smaller gateway – more, I presumed for individual visitors than for the giant trucks that would have entered at the front of the site – had also been fixed with a padlock, though this one was smaller and infinitely less challenging to us, due to the fact that – whilst it was hooked into the chains holding the gate closed – it wasn't in actual fact, locked.

"Can you promise me something, Danny?" Caz asked as she pushed the gate slightly open and we squeezed into the site.

"For you, Caz, anything."

"When we get arrested, can you have the lovely DC Fisher sort out the lighting on my mugshot. I mean: The camera adds ten pounds, and I really don't want my mug shot making me look fat."

"We're not going to get arrested."

"I think this is fairly straight forward trespass," she'd muttered, as I'd switched on the torch on my phone and led her further away from the street.

"The gate was open," I said, "And we heard a crying cat."

"A cat?"

"A cat," I repeated.

“Are you deluded? This is London. People can’t hear murder going on and you’re going to suggest we committed breaking and entering cos you have hearing like a bat and were concerned for the wellbeing of little Tabby?”

I shook my head at her. “You have a heart of stone. And besides, I’m not sure it’s breaking and entering when the padlock wasn’t actually locked.”

“I have a heart of precious stone,” she corrected me, then having considered my proposal, decreed. “We heard a woman scream. Much more likely round here.”

We looked around us as the gate closed silently behind us.

We were standing on a layer of mosaic tiles, the tiny squares a plain cream colour, with the words “Porters Entrance” spelled out in a darker green tile across the space. This, from an immediate glance, seemed to be almost all that was left of whatever building had been here once.

I could see why Constable had spent little to no money on security here: Whatever building had once occupied the block was almost completely gone. The wrecking ball had clearly done its job, and the rubble had already been removed to whatever landfill had space for the remains of an unwanted mid twentieth-century building.

Only one wall remained partially present at the opposite end of the site, the jagged edges silhouetted against the orange halon glow cast by the distant street lights. The rest of the site was unlit and devoid of machinery man or any other reason for trespassers to enter.

So why had Louise Byrne asked me to come here?

A thin mist hung in the air, soaking through my jacket and jeans, and adding to the melancholy air of the place, which – with its cratered earth, random lumps of rubble and that hulking, almost floating wall at the far end of the site – felt like a battle field after everyone had packed up and gone home.

Or, at least, after all the survivors had packed up and gone home.

We stepped gingerly off the tiled entryway and

immediately the earth beneath us – soaked by the mist and recent rains – felt spongier.

"What now?" Caz whispered, and I shouted out Louise's name, causing Caz to emit a short shriek and grab at me.

"Louise!" I called again and waited. "You there?"

Back came a reproving glare from Caz and the rumble of the traffic.

"Can you never do that again without warning me first?" She demanded.

"I don't understand," I replied, "She definitely wanted to meet here."

"But she didn't give a name," Caz responded, "So how can you know that the call came from her?'

"I said I trusted her, that I believed her. She said nobody else did – that she'd been made to feel crazy – and the woman who made that call said the same thing to Dash: 'He's the only one who'll believe me.' I know it was her."

"So, where is she?"

I sighed, looking around the vast space. "Right," I said at length, "I'll go left, you go right. Shout if you see anything."

"Not happening," Caz shot back. "If you think we're splitting up and I'm crawling around this place in the dark on my own, you clearly don't know me very well. We stick together, or I'll see you in that perfectly charming little wine bar we passed a few streets back."

"Fine!" I threw my hands up in exasperation and, Caz close on my heels, stalked off to the left, the dim light from the torch on my phone giving me some view of the razed and raddled earth around me.

And from then on, it had been a succession of rubble-heaps, puddles, and general gripes.

"I hate to be the bearer of bad news," Caz said at length, "But I don't think your Miss Byrne is here."

"I'd arrived at that conclusion myself," I grumbled back, sweeping the phone around one more time.

"So why are *we* still here?" She demanded. "What, exactly, are we looking for?" Caz asked for not the first or second time.

"I still don't know, Caz," I replied through gritted teeth, "But-"

"You'll know it when you see it; yes, I've heard that song before." She sighed theatrically and, at that moment, the clouds parted, a moonbeam illuminating the area around us momentarily before the winds blew the clouds back and blotted the light out once again.

"Stop!" Caz called, grabbing my arm, and yanking me to an immediate stop.

I'd seen what she'd seen: Directly in front of us – maybe another couple of steps ahead – was a trench. I shone the torch down on it.

"Jesus," I whispered. I'd been shining the torch ahead, not keeping my focus on the ground almost immediately beneath my feet, and I hadn't even seen this hole, which had to be six or seven feet deep.

"If we'd dropped in that, we'd have been a goner," I whispered.

"Well, something more than laddered tights, for certain," Caz whispered back, "But I think 'A Goner' is a bit dramatic, don't you?"

We approached the edge and peered down into the trench.

"Foundations?" I mused.

"That," Caz said, "Or Constable have uncovered a gateway to hell. Oh-" and she broke off. "That's odd," she said, standing stock still.

"Odd?" I asked, wondering what part of the two of us standing in a freezing cold, wet, derelict building site over a potential death trap was oddest. "Odd how?"

"Turn your torch over there," Caz said, pulling my arm so that I shone the fading light to the right of us.

I moved it around a little, and then I, too, frowned. "What's that doing there?"

My torch had landed on what looked like a roll of carpet down on the floor of the trench.

"Well I assume," Caz said dryly, "That someone put it there. The question, surely, is why someone put it there?"

I looked around – unsuccessfully - for a ladder, or even for a box; something I could step down into rather than just jumping into what looked, as I stared down into it, like a really deep hole.

"Here," I handed Caz the phone, zipped my jacket up to the top, and edged closer to the hole.

"What are you going to do?" Caz whispered, as I tested the earth at the edge with my shoe. It held firmly, confirming to me that – If I did what I planned – I wouldn't, at least, end up in a pit I couldn't claw my way out of.

"I'm going in," I whispered back, gesturing at the trench. "And why are we whispering."

"I don't know," Caz said at normal volume, the sudden increase seeming to startle even her. "What do you mean you're going in."

"I mean," I said, gesturing once again at the carpet, "That I'm going to climb down there and see what that is."

"Well we can see what it is from here," Caz responded in her no-nonsense tone – the one she'd clearly acquired from a nanny somewhere along the way. "And I'm not entirely sure that flinging one's person into a hole that deep is a wise decision. Wouldn't it be better to just call someone?"

"Who?" I asked. "The Carpet Patrol? International Rug Rescue?"

"I liked you when you were smart and funny," she deadpanned. "No; the police, obviously."

"And tell them what, Caz? That we've broken in to a building site and would like to report someone else has been fly-tipping?"

"You said it wasn't breaking and entering if the padlock was undone. And fly-tipping is a serious offence."

"There are more serious," I answered, sighing heavily as I slowly lowered myself so that I was sitting at the edge of the hole.

The damp earth immediately soaked through my jeans,

and beneath my palms I felt bits of grit and glass. "Well," I said, after a brief pause, during which my brain had sought to remind me how stupid this action was, and during which I had decided, regardless, to go down into the trench, "here goes."

"Are you sure," Caz asked, but got no further as I pushed off, and dropped into the hole, landing, with a loud splash and a squelch, up to my ankles in mud.

"Well those shoes are ruined," Caz, safe on dry land, noted, shining the torch straight in my eyes. The light, even though dim, blinded me.

"Shine it over there," I said testily, gesturing towards the other end of the trench.

The light, from where Caz stood, gave almost no illumination.

"Damn it," I heard my friend hiss, as the torch wavered then went out. A moment later, it came on again further down the trench.

"Be careful," she called as I began to slowly inch my way along the trench, the carpet now illuminated, but the ground on which I was walking in stygian night. "Don't fall over, you could break an ankle down there."

I gritted my teeth. "The thought," I said, "Had crossed my mind. But thanks for reinforcing my fear."

I moved slowly, keeping my outstretched right hand against the wall of the pit, gingerly poking the earth ahead with my toe, conscious of trip hazards, mud, and of the fact that there could be a secondary pit somewhere around here if this had been some sort of drainage system.

At length, I arrived next to the rolled-up carpet, and knelt down to inspect it.

The rainfall had already soaked it, and I could see that it was tied together with thick black duct tape. I could see, also, that it was not an empty roll – it was way too big, for starters. I pulled at the tape, and it gave a little, then held fast.

Suddenly, something thudded into the earth beside the

carpet roll. I glanced across and shook my head.

"Why am I surprised?" I asked, pulling the switch knife from where Caz had thrown it, so that he blade had embedded in the earth. "I don't suppose you've got a stepladder in your handbag?"

"Open the bloody carpet," she breathed back down. "The suspense is killing me here."

I slid the blade of the knife under the first strip of tape, and sliced hard, the tape separating and the carpet shifting slightly as something inside it began to bulge outwards.

The next strip took a few sawing motions, so tightly was it wound, but it too, eventually, gave way, the movement of the carpet putting so much stress on the third strip of duct tape that almost before I'd touched it with the knife, it had parted, and the bundle began to unroll.

"When you're ready," Caz said, the torchlight shaking slightly as I leaned forward and parted the roll of carpet, knowing, even as I did so, what I was going to find in it.

I looked down into a pair of sightless eyes, staring back up at me, as the rain began to fall harder, and I fell back onto my heels, turning my face up towards Caz.

"Well I'll be honest," I said after a momentary silence, "that is *not* what I was expecting to find."

CHAPTER THIRTY-ONE

"So," Reid gestured into the pit, "Any idea who he is?"

The rain, by now, was falling down with a vengeance, and I was caked head to toe in mud. Caz was standing by the edge of the trench, a police-supplied umbrella over her head as she stared fixedly down into the now arc-lit space.

A small army of police, crime scene technicians and photographers were crawling – despite the heavy rain – all over the site.

I'd almost assumed, by the time I'd started to undo the roll of carpet, that it would contain a dead body, and I'd expected that the body would belong to Louise Byrne. She'd called, asked me here, then been killed and dumped in the trench.

Now, of course, I realised that that string of assumptions didn't actually hang together very well, and the entire edifice had collapsed as soon as I'd pulled back the carpet and stared down into a man's face, the side-parted blonde hair sticking to the forehead and the huge, pear-shaped rain drops spattering on his cheeks as the rain began in earnest.

"Bird," Reid snapped his fingers in front of my face, breaking me from my reverie. "Who is he?"

I glanced across at Caz, who looked up from the trench, her eyes locking with me.

They'd find out soon enough. Not even Reid could fail to figure out who the man was. But for some reason I didn't want to be the one to enlighten him. I shook my head.

"No," I said, "I've no idea."

"Any idea what he's doing in a bloody hole slap bang in the middle of my patch?" Reid growled, and again I shook my head.

"You try," he barked at Nick, waving a hand towards a team of white-suited forensics inspectors. "I'm going to have a word with the Casper squad," and he stomped off as though afraid that if he hung around me much longer he'd do or say something he'd regret.

"Danny." Nick stood directly in front of him, locking his eyes with mine so that I had to look at him. "Danny," he said again, "stop this."

"This?" I asked, injured innocence slathered onto my face and tone. "What 'this'?"

"This," he repeated, waving a hand up and down my body. "Stop fucking about, Danny. This is serious."

"You don't say?"

He heaved a sigh. "Alright. Have it your way. Tell me again why you were here?"

"I got a call," I said, "At the pub."

"What time? Who from?"

"That's the thing," I shook my head, "I wasn't there, so I don't know the time, and the caller didn't leave a name, so I have no idea."

"And they said what? 'Come down here and let yourself in'?"

"Not in so many words," I answered, "But I didn't have to let myself in. I mean the padlock on the back gate wasn't actually locked."

"Obviously," he answered flatly. "Whoever dropped our mate there into the hole was clearly not bothered locking up after themselves. Probably assumed nobody would be around till well into the new year, and by then that would be four-foot-deep in rain water and mud, and Constable would either concrete over it, or scoop it off to landfill."

"Him," I whispered, glancing across at the trench, and clarifying, to Nick's puzzled look: "You said 'it.' He was a man."

I could still see the discoloured lips, purple-blue and the eyes, bulging as though, from his prone position, he could see the most mind-boggling scene going on above him. The rope he'd been strangled with – plain plasticized washing line like the sort I'd seen on Steve Haines' balcony – was still around his neck, dug tightly into the skin, and I knew I'd be seeing it for a very long time.

"Danny," Nick leaned in towards me, "does this have anything to do with your missing man who never was?"

"George Osman?" I shook my head. "No," I said, "that's not Him."

"Well help me out here," Nick pleaded. "You know more than you're letting on, I know that much."

I looked him in the eye. "I can't believe you don't know who that is," I nodded towards the trench, where the team were finally winching the body out of the hole.

"You know him?" Nick asked, wide-eyed.

"So do you," I nodded. "That's the most wanted man in Britain."

"Vincent Armstrong," Caz said, putting a hand on my arm. "Bank fraudster extraordinaire. Only all the money he stole isn't doing him much good any more."

"That's Vince Armstrong?" Nick looked amazed.

"He hasn't even dyed his hair," I said, as the gurney on which the body lay passed us by.

"What the hell is Vince Armstrong doing in a hole here," Nick asked, "And who the hell sent you to find him?"

"Those," I said, "are questions I've been wondering about myself." I glanced at Caz. "Look, do you need us anymore? Only, it's late."

Nick looked from me to Caz and back. "You're not going to tell me, are you?" He asked.

"Not here," I answered. "Not now. Can you come round to my place tomorrow? I'll tell you everything we've figured out then."

"Danny," he was exasperated. "By tomorrow, whoever

did this could be on the other side of the planet. If you know anything, you need to tell me now."

I looked behind me as the gurney was slowly and carefully transported over the uneven ground. "I really don't know anything, Nick. Only what I've told you. I have some ideas, but they're all a bit fuzzy yet, and there's no proof of anything. I promise, I'm not keeping facts from you."

He looked unconvinced. "Wait here," he said, before walking off towards Reid.

"Boss," he called, and Reid turned from his conversation with a harassed looking man in a suit – a rep, I assumed, of Constable Construction.

Reid and Nick exchanged some words, Reid looking up and narrowing his eyes as he stared over at me, then they both walked towards us.

"Vince Armstrong?" Reid called as they approached us. "You've known since you found the body whose it is, and you're only telling me now?"

I shot my angriest glare at Nick. I couldn't believe he'd dropped me in it with his boss.

"I thought you'd know who it was," I answered Reid. "I mean, he's only been all over the news this past week or so."

"We'd have recognised him," Reid sniffed back, "in better light."

Beside me, Caz muttered something under her breath, then "Well, now we all know who the man in the mat was, can we be off? Only a girl needs her beauty sleep."

Reid squinted at her. "Hang on a minute," he called to the officers who'd been tasked with wheeling the gurney across the uneven landscape. They paused, and he lumbered over to them, wrestling on a pair of disposable gloves, and unzipped the body bag.

Reid peered down into the bag, then muttered something obscene, yanked the zip back up, ripping the gloves off his huge hairy hands and stalked back over to us.

"You ever met him?" he nodded at the gurney.

"Never in my life," I answered, and he squinted at me as

though seeking the tell-tale signs of lying – I don't know, enlarged pupils, sweaty upper brow, whatever his Ladybird book of Policing had told him to look out for – then demanded the same of Caz.

"Not to the best of my knowledge," she answered.

Reid looked from each of us to the other. "What is it about you two?" He demanded in exasperation. "Every time there's a body. Every time there's a bit of bother. Any time I want a nice quiet week, there the two of you are, him," he gestured at me, "Giving it all the 'butter wouldn't melt' act, and you," he pointed at Caz, "looking down your nose like I'm heading up the Keystone cops."

"Inspector Reid," Caz smiled sweetly, "You've just wheeled out one Vince Armstrong, investment banker wanted for the theft of millions of pounds, and – up till my friend here stumbled on him in that ditch – most wanted man in Britain.

"And yet, I repeat, despite being the most wanted man in Britain, it took a barman and – well, not to put too fine a point on it – his fag hag stumbling round in the dark to locate a man that your entire force has been seeking for several days. So, you'll have to forgive me if I think you referencing the Keystone Cops is a rather risqué thing to do."

"You knew he was here," Reid said, his face darkening. "And if I find that either of you is hiding anything from me or my team, I'll have you both for obstruction. I don't care who you are, or what you are. Now, for the last time: What aren't you telling me about this? And why aren't you telling me?"

"Callum Byrne," Caz said, her jaw jutting out, as she looked down her nose at Reid, "Assaulted my friend here."

"And I should care about this because?" Reid snapped back, his face darkening.

"Firstly, because I've just reported a crime you don't seem to be that bothered about, and secondly because Callum Byrne got Danny's name – and the fact that he'd at first appeared to be involved in Cathy Byrne's death – from someone at your police station."

Reid's face moved, swiftly, from darkening to thunderous. "Says who?" He demanded.

"Says Callum Byrne," Caz snapped back triumphantly. "And that, D.I. Reid, means you have a leak in your station. And even if you're not bothered about innocent members of the public," (This accompanied by a gesture at me as I attempted to put my most innocent look on to my face) "being beaten up for nothing, I'd assume you'd care about the fact that someone in your station is leaking names of people of interest to angry relatives."

Reid nodded. "Fisher," he ordered, "get on to that tomorrow. Anything else I should know?" He asked Caz, some of his anger seeming to have diffused as the reality of what he'd just been told sank in.

"Danny got a phone call," Caz replied, "I came along to hold the torch. That's, basically, it."

"Wait: How is this linked to Callum and Cathy Byrne?" Reid suddenly demanded, and Caz and I – before we could stop ourselves – glanced at each other.

"Aha!" He jabbed his finger at us once again. "Spill it!"

"We don't know," I said. "Honestly. I thought that Armstrong might be linked to something else."

"What else?" Reid demanded, and I instantly had a flash of Dot Frost's face if I gave away a word of the secret she'd entrusted me with

"Nothing," I shook my head. "I don't see how Armstrong could be linked to Cathy Byrne. I mean, they live in different worlds."

"Armstrong grew up on The Races," Nick announced, and the three of us turned to face him, his face illuminated by the light from screen on his phone.

"He," Nick tapped the screen a couple more times, frowned, tapped again, looked directly at me, his eyes questioning, for the first time ever, whether or not he could trust me. "Armstrong went to school, sir, at the Whyte Street

Comprehensive. We'd need to check records, but his age matches."

"Matches what?" Reid snarled, his eyes never leaving me and Caz.

"I think, sir, though like I say we'd need to check the school records, but I think."

"Get on with it Fisher."

"Cathy Byrne's daughter Louise also went to the Whyte Street Comp. I think Armstrong and Louise Byrne would have been in the same year together."

"Okay," I threw my hands up. "Look, it's hearsay 'cos I didn't take the call, but we – that is, I – suspect that the call was from Louise Byrne."

Reid's eyes glowed yellow. Thinking back, I believe that they had just caught the sodium shade of the streetlights, but at the time, it made me think of a wolf who's just spotted his prey, the effect being completed by the lupine grin on his face.

"So, we've got a dead banker, and a dead cleaner, and one of them has your finger prints all over the body, while the other had your name on her hand, and yet you've told me everything there is to tell? And then suddenly, you remember this extra little nugget.

"Well, love," he glanced at Caz, "I don't know about you, but I find the presence – even via hearsay," he added, sneering at me, "of a young woman who went to school with the dead banker, and who's already known to me for being a bit – shall we say – unstable, highly interesting.

"Almost as interesting," he finished, turning his attention back to me, "as the fact that you waited so long to even mention her involvement. Fisher?"

Nick put his phone back into his pocket and shot me an angry glare.

"Get these two out of here," Reid ordered him. "And Keystone cops or not," he said, addressing Caz, "both of you should be prepared for a visit from my team tomorrow, cos – if I have to - I'll drag you back in to my nick every day till I get the whole story out of you."

Nick nodded his understanding, Caz glared her outrage at being ordered around, and I tried vainly to catch my boyfriend's eyes as he ushered us away from the scene and back out on to Marsham Place.

CHAPTER THIRTY-TWO

By the time I woke the next morning, the value of Vince Armstrong's larceny had multiplied, and Fenchurch-Brookes, incorporated in 1793 and a stalwart of the international finance world since then, was almost certainly heading into bankruptcy.

I got dressed, downed a cup of coffee, and watched a series of talking heads banging on about lax controls, the challenges of keeping money safe in a digital world, and the implications of this crime for the rest of the financial system.

At one point, on the local news, the newsreader mentioned that police had discovered the body of a man last night at a building site in Southwest London. "The body," I was informed, "Is as yet unidentified, and police are calling for witnesses who might help identify it."

Well, I mused, as I pushed my feet into my trainers, Reid appeared to have plugged that gap pretty quickly. I wondered, briefly, what game he was playing at: Why hold off announcing that Vince Armstrong was no more?

And then I realised: Because the money was still missing. And that suggested, either, that Vince had had an accomplice, hitherto unknown, or that he'd been working alone to begin with, but had now been offed by someone who'd taken control of the cash.

Either way, I figured, Reid was trying to avoid frightening the horses.

The night before, after Caz and I had finally been let go,

we'd gone to Joanna Trztrzelewska's flat via that of Steve Haines. Neither of them had been, shall we say, overjoyed to be awakened in the middle of the night, Haines letting loose with a string of profanities before realising he was standing in his doorway wearing only a t-shirt and no underpants, listening to what we were actually telling him, then running inside to dress, and coming with us up to Joanna's flat.

Jo, in turn, had answered the door wearing a red fleece dressing gown and a pair of Doc Marten boots, and had stood blinking at us in shock.

"What time is it?" She asked, her unhappiness at being awakened in the early hours not so much telegraphed as megaphoned.

"Have you heard from Louise?" I asked, repeating the question as she ran her hand through her dishevelled hair and pulled her housecoat tighter around her.

"Lou?" She asked, still struggling to fully wake up. "No," she shook her head, and stood aside to usher us into her flat. "Not since this morning – well, yesterday morning, I suppose. Why? What's going on?"

This last was addressed to Steve, who gestured helplessly at me. "I dunno, love," he grumbled. "None of this makes any sense to me."

"I'm not entirely sure," I said, following her down the hallway towards the kitchen.

"Keep it down," she whispered, consciousness kicking in, "The kids are asleep, and it's a school night."

We entered the kitchen. Joanna closed the door firmly behind us and glanced at the microwave clock.

"Jesus, it's nearly 2a.m. What's happened?" she asked, as I noticed, strung across the end of the kitchen, a line of the orange plasticized rope, devoid, right now, of drying clothes.

"Why do you think something's happened?" Caz asked, filling – unbidden – the kettle from the tap.

"Because," Joanna replied, wrestling the kettle from Caz, shoving the lid on it, and putting it to boil, "It's two in the morning. Nobody comes round anyone's place at two in the morning demanding to know if they've seen their dead friend's kid unless something's happened."

"The police," I said, "have found a body."

"Oh God," Joanna put a hand over her mouth, and sort of folded into a kitchen chair which Caz slid under her.

"Don't worry," I hastily added, "it's not Louise. But, well, we have reason to suspect that Louise knows something about the death."

"Knows something?" Joanna frowned at me. "What does 'knows something' mean? Steve? What the hell is going on here?"

"I'm as in the dark as you, Jo," Haines said, turning his face, once again, towards me.

"It means that Louise called the pub earlier tonight," Caz explained, dipping in to a cupboard and extracting four shot glasses. "And left a message for Danny here, which lead to the discovery of the body of a man who appears to have gone to school with her, before he went off to a life of riches and – ultimately – crime."

She pulled a bottle of Courvoisier from her handbag, uncorked it, and poured four slugs of the brandy into the glasses, before putting one in front of each of us.

Haines had downed the booze almost before the cap was back in the bottle.

Joanna slammed the spirit down without wincing and turned back to me.

"So, you think she killed this man?"

I shook my head. "I don't understand why she would, or what the connection – other than school – would be to him. And Louise must have left school – what? – ten years ago? So – if there is a connection – why now?"

Joanna pointed at the empty shot glass, and Caz refilled it. "I don't know," she said, having downed the brandy. I only moved in here eight years ago, and Lou was already working at the paper by then."

"The local rag," I mused, having downed my own shot. "Could she have reconnected with him there? You know:

Local boy done good story?"

"Reconnected with who?" Joanna asked, as, behind her, the kettle came to a boil.

"Vincent Armstrong," I said.

"The banker? The one who's done a runner with all that money?" Joanna was shocked.

"You know him?" I asked.

"I have a T.V." Joanna responded flatly, "though I hear from," she waved a hand airily towards the front door, "the – grape tree? Grape vine? The grapevine - that his mother still lives on the estate. Perhaps she knew Cathy?"

"Armstrong?" Steve frowned. "I don't know – not for sure – but I think she was one of the ones who wanted nothing to do with the 'Save the Races' campaign. One of those 'I'm sure the council know what they're doing' types."

"So, did Louise have any contact with her?" I asked, and Haines, having considered the question for a moment, shook his head.

"Doubtful. She's a bit of a stuck-up cow, to be honest, so unlikely - if she wouldn't deal with Cathy - that she'd have much time for a char's kid."

I nodded my understanding, then turned back to Joanna. "So, tell me about Louise. How was she after you got her back here yesterday?"

"She blames Constable and Blythe for the state of her life. And for Cathy's death. She felt, I think, guilty. Like this was linked, in some way, to her crusade against them."

"I don't suppose, after she left here, she came down to see you?" I asked Steve Haines, who shook his head.

"I've not seen her for weeks," he said sadly.

"Okay, then. Anyone got any idea what time she left? Or where she went?"

"My kids – Ewa – gets home from school about half three. Tomasz had football, so he was later, but she was gone when Ewa got here. I called her mobile, went round to the bedsit she'd moved in to, but there was no answer, and she wasn't there."

‘What about her brother?” Caz asked. “Has Callum heard from her?”

It was a good question, but as Caz had sent Callum away for his own safety, Joanna had had no way to contact him.

“He called me,” Steve said, “When he arrived to say he was safe, but hasn’t called since.

“Okay,” Caz pulled her mobile from her handbag, dialled a number, and put the phone on the table, set to speaker.

We listened to the ring tone three four five times, and – just as I was sure the call was going to voice mail – there was a click, and Callum Byrne’s voice – heavy with sleep – came on.

“Hello?” He asked, the sleep fading as a tentative tone overcame it.

“Callum,” I said, “It’s Danny. I’m here with Caz and Joanna and Steve.”

“It’s half two,” he said, “What’s up?”

‘See,’ Joanna’s look said, ‘I told you: nobody calls at two in the morning unless something’s up.’

“Callum, have you heard from Louise today?”

“Lou?” He was awake now, I could hear him struggling upright in the bed, his tone changing, instantly, to one of concern. “What’s up?” He asked again.

“Louise didn’t know about your mum,” I said, and he coughed.

“I went round her place, the day I found out. But she wasn’t there. I left a message. Asked her to call me.”

“You didn’t call her?” I asked, struggling to keep the feeling that Callum wasn’t telling me everything from my voice.

There was a silence at the end of the line.

“Lou and me had a falling out. It was all linked to Alex – her boyfriend – died. Al had money – or his family did – and he pissed it away on junk. I was so angry with him, with her. But she wanted to blame everyone except Alex. Like he didn’t choose to start on that shit. Like he didn’t choose to sell her laptop when the money ran out.

"And then she found out – I suppose my mum told her – that I was in trouble with Solomon, and – for the first time in ages – she came round to the flat and let rip at me. Called me a hypocrite; said I was more stupid than Alex, cos I'd seen how this game worked, and was still trapped in it."

"What do you think she meant by that?"

"Lou has a paranoid conspiracy idea. Everything bad that happens in The Races is the fault of Constable, and their – what she calls – agents."

"Said agents being Evan Blythe and King Solomon," I muttered. "What about Vince Armstrong?"

"Armstrong?" Callum's confusion was audible. "What's he got to do with this?"

"I don't know," I said, "But Louise was obviously devastated by the news about your mum. She was angry, and upset, and she left Joanna's flat some time yesterday afternoon without anyone knowing where she was going, or what her plans were. Then she phoned the pub last night and left a cryptic message that lead to the discovery of Vince Armstrong's dead body on a Constable building site. And then we learned that Louise and Vince went to school together."

"Vinny Armstrong? I don't think they were even in the same classes. I knew him through friends of friends, but I don't think Lou would know him if he stood in front of her."

"He grew up in The Races," I said, and Callum interrupted.

"Mate, hundreds of kids grew up on The Races. It's not like we all hung out together. As soon as he was done with school and got into a decent job, he was gone, and he never – as far as I know – looked back."

"And yet, Louise lead us tonight to his corpse."

"This doesn't make any sense," Callum said, and Caz snorted.

"Never a truer word," she muttered. "Listen, Callum, do you have any idea where Louise would be? We need to find her."

Again, the silence, as Callum considered the question. "You think she killed him?" He finally said.

"Truly," I said, "I don't know. Like you said, it's sort of come out of nowhere, but if she had anything to do with this death; or even if she only saw something and was too afraid to go to the police herself, we need to find her, and fast."

"I suppose," Callum said, "She might have seen Vince as one of the enemy. Like, maybe, he should have been one of us but he'd become one of them. Like I say: Once he had money, he never looked back. But Armstrong's been in hiding. How would she have even seen him? No," Callum said, "This makes no sense. Look," there was the sound of sudden movement at his end of the line, "I'm going to come back. I need to be there. Fuck Solomon: This is family."

"Are you sure?" Caz asked, the concern clear in her voice. "If we can't find her, I'm not sure how much value there is in you coming all the way back.":

"Well where have you looked?" He asked, as the sound of him stuffing things into a bag echoed down the line.

I glanced at Caz and Joanna. "Well, here, to be honest. Joanna checked her digs, but she hasn't been there. There's always the possibility, of course – assuming she didn't murder Armstrong," I said.

"Which, believe me," Callum answered, "she didn't."

"Well there's always the possibility that we haven't found her because whoever did kill him has also either grabbed Louise or killed her too."

There was a silence. "We need to find her," Callum said, "and I'm going to come back and help you look, no matter what Solomon or his trolls say. So," he said, "where do we begin looking?"

I thought for a moment. "Okay," I said, "She's not in any of the places of safety we'd expect her to run to, so I guess we need to start looking elsewhere."

And then it came to me.

"We need to look at places she'd go if she was looking to

nail the people she holds responsible for your mother's death. We need to go back to The Sugar House."

CHAPTER THIRTY-THREE

The street, even at 7am, was deserted.

Most residential neighbourhoods and the apartment blocks on them, I reasoned, would, at this time on a work day, be buzzing with people heading off for the day, or returning from night shifts, but not The Sugar House.

But then it was clear from my recent visit that the residents of The Sugar House were either not early risers or were not the sort of people who needed to go to work at any time of the day.

As we stood at the top of the street, scanning doorways and shadows on either side of the street, a sleek black Alfa Romeo drove slowly down the street, turned right, and entered the underground carpark beneath the apartment building.

The shutters slid down with a metallic clank, and silence reclaimed the deserted street.

"Okay," I said to Caz, "You try that side. I'll check this," and we separated, each to our own side of the street, and went about searching for any sign that Louise Byrne had been here recently.

I paused by the doorway we'd previously seen her loitering in, but there was no sign either of her or of any recent occupation.

A little further down the street, I found an empty cigarette packet discarded, but I couldn't recall whether Louise had smoked or not, finally decided not, and that the packet had simply blown here on the wind, and, squatting to check under a couple of parked cars, carried on to the end of the street where – on the opposite pavement – Caz stood, a frustrated look on her face.

"What next?" She mouthed, as though to raise one's voice in this empty and silent street would be akin to whistling in a Cathedral.

I shrugged, crossing over to her.

"Nothing?" She shook her head.

"She doesn't strike me as being an untidy stalker," she said, "But still: If she's been here lately, there is absolutely nothing to suggest so."

I took one last glance along the street and shrugged. "Well, if she has been here, there's one person who might know. If he's started his shift yet."

I nodded at the vast double-width door of The Sugar House, where Roy Bell was visible through the glass, his suit buttoned up tightly, his flat top hairdo immaculate and his attention focused on a newspaper that he had laid out on the reception desk. He looked up when I knocked and rattled the door.

A buzz and a loud *Thunk* indicated that he'd unlocked the door, and Caz and I stepped inside, the door closing and relocking behind us.

"Morning, Roy," I said, trying to make my voice as bright and breezy as I could.

"Back so soon?" He answered, suspicion gleaming in his eyes.

"We were wondering," I answered, figuring we might as well pile straight on in, "Whether Louise Byrne had been around here lately."

"Louise Byrne?" He frowned, as though trying to place the name.

"The stalker," Caz filled in. "The one who attacked Evan Blythe."

"You know her name?" He asked, suspicion levels increasing exponentially.

"Amongst other things.," I mumbled. "So: seen her lately?"

He shook his head. "She was out there yesterday afternoon, just staring as usual. I went over, told her that she'd have a long wait, 'cos Blythe had gone away on business that morning."

"And was this true?" I asked as a sonorous buzz echoed around the lobby.

Roy peered over my shoulder, then scrabbled to press the release for the door. "True?" He bristled. "'Course it's bloody true. I don't go around telling porkies just to get rid of loonies. He rang down, asked for a taxi to Heathrow, and came down with a little overnight bag. Said he'd be away till later today, and off he went. So, when madam turned up and assumed her normal position, I figured – well, she might be mental, but I don't see why she should waste her time."

The person who'd buzzed the door entered, a small woman encased from head to toe in a black burka, a cerise pink Birkin bag slung over one shoulder.

"Good morning, Mrs Makhtoum," Roy called, his tone obsequious.

The woman nodded, her eyes scanning him, then us, and hitching the bag tighter to her, as though afraid that one or more of us was moments from yanking it off her shoulder and doing a runner.

She crossed to the lifts, pressed the button, and – when the lift on the left opened immediately – stepped into the box.

She was still watching us when the lift doors closed.

"Mrs Makhtoum," Bell announced, forgetting, for a moment, his spiel about discretion. "Five B. Always goes everywhere by taxi, cos she can't drive."

I glanced at Caz, who was still staring at the lift.

"I don't suppose," she murmured, nodding at the door.

"What?" I asked, completing the question. "That that's Louise?"

Bell sniggered. "Mrs M's been coming here with and

without her husband since I started. She came back yesterday morning, straight from Heathrow. So, no, if you're thinking that your looney stalker's managed to disguise herself, get past me, get into apartment 5B and is living here disguised up as that lovely lady, you're as mental as she is. The stalker, I mean; not Mrs Makhtoum," he rushed to clarify lest, I suppose, she had super-powered hearing, and was easily offended.

"How did Louise Byrne seem?" I asked him, reverting to our earlier topic of conversation, "Yesterday."

"Are you taking the piss?" He glared at me. "She seemed insane. Like she usually does."

"Grief'll do that," I said. "So what time did she leave?"

"I dunno," he sniffed. "She wanted to know where Blythe had gone, and I told her that was none of her business. Then she started off on the usual 'He's a bad man. He's destroyed communities. He killed my boyfriend. Blah blah blah.' And maybe he did, and maybe he didn't but the thing is this is a nice little job, and I'm not required to like this lot; just to keep the lobby clean and tidy and take their deliveries, ring up their guests, and arrange their taxis. So, I told her 'Well, love, whatever he did, he ain't doing it in there today. Cos he's gone away, so you might as well go home.' Then I came back in."

"And what happened then?" I asked, and Roy shrugged.

"I got on with the day. Deliveries, guests, like I say."

"Were any of those guests a tall blonde man?" I asked, describing Vince Armstrong.

Bell fixed me with his sternest glare. "Really? You think I'm going to tell you who comes here and who they see? You think that bit about the residents paying for privacy and discretion means nothing?"

"Was worth a go," I smiled back. "So? Were they?"

"You should probably be off," he answered, his face a mask of blandness. "Unless you've got some cleaning to do."

"I don't suppose," Caz interjected, "Andy Von Oldenwald's in? Apartment 4A."

"What's it to you?" Roy turned his unfriendliness on her.

"Old friend," she smiled back. "Thought, since we're here, I'd pay a visit. Be a good boy and announce us," she said, her smile hardening.

Roy bristled. "Really?" He asked, his tone suggesting that he felt it highly unlikely Caz and Von Oldenwald would ever have met, let alone been friends. "Yesterday, you were a char lady and today you're – what? – landed gentry or something?" He guffawed.

"Not 'or something,' actually," she smiled back, the smile not reaching her eyes. "Call him. Tell him Lady Caroline Victoria Genevieve de Montfort is here, with Mr Bird. "

His mask faltered, the arrogance flickering off and then back on like a faulty bulb."

"You're shitting me, right?" He finally demanded of me, rather than Caz.

"'Fraid not," I answered. "Landed."

"Back to the conqueror," Caz added.

His hand hovering over the phone, Bell blushed, and began a stammered apology for any 'Inadvertent rudeness," which Caz waved aside.

"Don't mention it," she said, "people often treat me like shit when they think I'm just a cleaner."

This last caused him to blush to his roots, and had him calling up to 4B, into which – several moments later – we stepped.

"I thought I saw you outside," Von Oldenwald said as he closed the door behind us. "I've just come home," he clarified, and I realised that the Alfa Romeo that had swept past us as we'd hunted for signs of Louise had been Von Oldenwald returning home.

"All-nighter at the bank trying to sort this whole mess out," he explained, ushering us into the kitchen. "Wondered what the hell you were doing out on the street at this time of the morning."

"Looking," Caz explained, as we sat at the kitchen table, "For Louise Byrne."

"Byrne?" Von Oldenwald, his back to us as he fiddled with an industrial sized espresso machine, frowned over his shoulder. "Was that the cleaner you mentioned yesterday?"

"Her daughter," Caz explained.

Von Oldenwald flicked a few switches, turned a tap and the machine sprung into life, hissing and sputtering coffee into a tiny espresso cup.

"But why," he asked, putting the cup on a saucer and handing the coffee to Caz, "would you be looking for her on the street at this time of the morning?"

"It's a long story," I confessed, "but the thing you need to know is that Vince Armstrong is dead."

"I know," my coffee was put before me. "but how did you find out?"

"We," Caz said dryly, "found the body. Who told you?"

Von Oldenwald sipped his espresso. "The man is wanted for a multi-million-pound robbery. The police called the bank and they called me first thing this morning. Or rather, in the middle of the night."

"Hence," I ventured, "The all-nighter."

Von Oldenwald nodded. "None of this makes any sense. I mean, who would kill him? Why is obvious – the money is incentive enough. But was it an accomplice? And if so, who?"

"The police," I said quietly, as Caz, unseen by Von Oldenwald, discretely pushed the coffee as far away from her as she could without standing and tipping it down the drain, "Think that our Louise Byrne had something to do with it."

"The cleaner's daughter?" Vol Oldenwald dropped into the chair opposite me. "What's she got to do with this?"

I sipped my coffee. "Louise Byrne lost her boyfriend not long ago. A heroin overdose, I'm told. Shortly thereafter, she lost her job, and her home. She claims – and it's possible that she has a valid claim – that the events are connected. Either way, she's clearly struggling through grief and attempting to make sense of everything that's befallen her. And she's somewhat fixated on one of your neighbours – an

Evan Blythe."

"Blythe?" a cloud crossed Von Oldenwald's face.

"You know him?" I downed my coffee and reached over for Caz's discarded thimbleful.

"Years ago," Von Oldenwald admitted. "He was in mergers, I think. Our paths crossed at a few conferences, parties, that sort of thing. He was never my type. One of those people who took too much pleasure in making things happen to think about whether he was making the right things happen."

"Louise Byrne blames him – and some people she believes he's working for – for ruining her life."

"Okay," Von Oldenwald had the look of a man who's not certain whether he's missing the point, or whether there even is a point to the conversation, "But what would that have to do with Armstrong."

"What indeed?" I asked as a loud 'Ping' announced that the lift had arrived.

The doors opened, and Rachel Fiennes, her lithe muscular body encased in sweat-soaked Lycra entered the kitchen. From her head, she removed a lime green baseball cap featuring the Chanel logo, swept her hand through her blonde bob, pulling the hair that had been plastered to her forehead back, plonked the baseball cap back on her head, and wiped her face with a towel slung across her shoulders.

"Oh." She stopped, seeing us, and a flicker of annoyance crossed her face but was instantly banished in favour of a look of bland disinterest. "Morning, baby," she strolled over to Andy and placed a kiss on his forehead. "How'd it go?" she cast a glance at Caz and I.

"It's alright," Von Oldenwald answered, gesturing at us, "They know."

"They know?" She turned now, hands on hips. "How do you know?'

"Apparently," Von Oldenwald announced, heaving himself out of the chair and heading back over to the espresso machine, "*They* found the body. The police," Von

Oldenwald continued, "think the cleaner's daughter's gone crazy and started murdering people. But her real target is Evan bloody Blythe. Is that about the gist of it?"

"Blythe?" Rachel pulled a face before I could answer. "The gimp downstairs? What's he got to do with anything?"

I gave Caz the glance that said 'Your friend's an arsehole,' while she gave me the glance that said 'He's not my friend. Also, yes, he is an arsehole.'

"Well, that's not entirely correct," I attempted to clarify, "But Louise called my number yesterday evening, and that call lead us to Vince Armstrong's body. And yes," I answered Rachel, "Louise Byrne does seem to hold Evan Blythe responsible for the deaths of her boyfriend and her mother."

"So why would she kill Vince Armstrong" Rachel shook her head, walking over to a blender on the countertop, the jug filled with what looked like the contents of an organic vegetable box, and flicked the switch.

The room was filled with a racket like an airplane taking off, and the noise was, seconds later, joined by the clunk and hiss of the espresso machine doing its thing again, with another espresso put in front of Caz, who – almost before Von Oldenwald's back was turned – slid it towards me, where another one was placed, meaning that – by the time Rachel Fiennes had her smoothie – I was well on the way to my fourth espresso.

I need a pee," Caz suddenly announced, adding, for Von Oldenwald's benefit, "all that coffee. Where's your toilet?"

Von Oldenwald directed her out of the kitchen and to one of the doors along the hallway we'd come down.

"So," Rachel Fiennes sat down opposite me and used the towel to wipe, once more, her face, whilst seeming to have moved on from her last question. "This – what was her name? Louise? This woman murdered Armstrong? What did she do? Shoot him?"

"Strangled," Von Oldenwald said grimly, leaning against the espresso machine. "Well, at least, that's what the police said."

So much for Reid plugging those leaks. His mob seemed, with each passing moment, to resemble, more and more, a colander.

"But again: Why?" Rachel asked, swigging what looked like a mouthful of plankton. "I mean, how would she even know Armstrong?"

"They went to school together," I said, figuring I wasn't disclosing anything that Reid's mates wouldn't get around to disclosing soonish, "Or at least to the same school at the same time."

"And they think she was in on the robbery?"

That was a new slant. "Nobody's said so much yet," I admitted, "And it does seem a bit unlikely."

"Unlikely?" Von Oldenwald chuckled. "The trader's assistant and the cleaner's daughter? You really think they colluded to hack one of the most sophisticated IT systems in the world?"

"Well someone did, sweetest," Rachel shot back, the sarcasm evident in her words. "And unless you've upgraded substantially since I left, I reckon a first year IT student and a couple of twelve-year-old code-monkeys could have broken that system. I mean, darling, let's face it: Vince Armstrong was the trader's assistant. And nobody's managed to produce the computer whizz who assisted him.

"Yesterday, you were convinced it was all his doing, and you'd get the money back, and now, as of today, not only are you no closer to getting it back, but the total's gone up; your number one suspect is dead; and the number one suspect for that killing is a woman you're now disparaging because she's – what was it? 'A Cleaner's daughter'?"

"Shut up, Rachel," Von Oldenwald spoke through clenched teeth.

"Well don't be such a snob," she shot back, gulping another shot of liquified Kermit. "If this woman killed Armstrong, we have to assume she knows where the money is. So maybe, instead of dismissing her, you should be thinking about that. Before she flees the country for good."

Which was something I hadn't considered, and which might have explained our inability to locate Louise Byrne.

Caz re-entered the room. I glanced across, and something about the look on her face made me sit up.

"You Okay?" I asked, and she stood, staring across the table at Von Oldenwald.

"I'm not sure," she murmured back to me. "This whole mess just gets weirder and weirder. I'd forgotten," she said to Von Oldenwald, "How we met."

"How we met?" He frowned in recollection. "Jesus, it was back in the Bronze age, wasn't it? Some days, I can hardly remember how even we," he indicated Rachel Fiennes, "met."

"You interviewed me. For a job," Fiennes responded tersely.

"It was at a party," Caz responded. "I'd forgotten till I saw that photograph you have. The one in the bathroom."

"Oh," Von Oldenwald threw his head back and laughed, "That. Jesus," he peered closely at Caz, as though trying to recollect something from a lifetime ago, "You weren't at that party, were you?"

"Not the one in the photo," she answered. "Thankfully. Not the one in the photo where you and your chums are dressed in SS uniforms. But a lot of the same mob were at the one we met."

"Yes," Von Oldenwald nodded seriously, "Terribly bad form really. Shouldn't display it really, cos some people just don't see the humour. Nothing meant by it, of course, but it only takes one misery guts to turn it into something it wasn't."

"Something it wasn't?" Caz asked, waiting for the penny to wend its way through Von Oldenwald's cerebral cortex, roll around the helter skelter of his mind and, as the saying goes, drop. "You mean it wasn't a bunch of over privileged white boys dressed up as Nazis?"

Without even noting the tone, Von Oldenwald chuckled

and shook his head, "Well, yes, but look: We didn't mean it in a disrespectful way, it was. Aha!" He suddenly smacked the worktop, causing his Sevres espresso cup to jangle alarmingly on its saucer. "I remember. We met at that party where Lulu St Marr fell into the swimming pool wearing that stupid bloody wedding dress. Right to-do," Von Oldenwald – wired to the tits now on a combination of espresso, sleep deprivation and, I suspected, other stimulants leant forward as though confiding in me. "Turned out the dress was an antique. One of the Tzarinas had got married in it. Bloody thing was ruined. Couldn't show our faces round that house for a while, I can tell you."

"That house," Caz added, through a mask set to hide every emotion battling within her, "Being Wakefield Hall."

"Wakefield?" I frowned. The name rang a bell.

"As in Henry Wakefield," Caz responded. The current Lord Osworthy."

"Henry Wakefield who you once shot?" I asked. "And who you recently described as a psychopath?"

"The same," Caz said.

Von Oldenwald now had a somewhat bemused look on his face. "What's Wakefield got to do with any of this?" He asked.

"Possibly nothing," Caz responded, hooking her handbag from the back of the chair it was swinging from. "But if we're looking for someone who might have initiated your robbery and then murdered young Mr Armstrong, he'd be worth considering. Especially when one considers – as even you, Andreas, have to have noticed – that Henry Wakefield specialises in getting impressionable idiots to do his dirty work before discarding them just before the trail can lead back to him."

She turned to leave, and Rachel Fiennes stood to show us out, directing us not to the lift she'd entered by, but out into the hallway and towards the 'staff entrance'.

We left Von Oldenwald staring after us open-mouthed. I had to admit that I felt a bit agog at what the last few minutes had thrown out, and we were at the door before I realised Rachel Fiennes was talking to us in an urgent whisper.

"He'll go back to the bank this afternoon, once he's slept. Or tried to," she said. "Can you come back then?"

I paused, as she opened the door, my puzzled look clearly communicating the fact that I had no idea what she'd been talking about.

"I can't tell you here," she said, "But it's important. Don't, for God's sake, tell him." She nodded towards the kitchen, "or anyone else. Just – come back. Please? Say about seven?" She pleaded.

I glanced at Caz who, to be honest, seemed as shell-shocked as I, and nodded. "Okay," I said, and we were out on the landing, the door closing behind us.

"What the hell," I turned to my best friend, "Is going on?"

Caz looked back at me. "I don't know," she finally said, "but I know someone who might."

CHAPTER THIRTY-FOUR

"So, how long exactly did you go out with Andy?" I asked, as the first drops of rain began to fall on the pavement outside The Sugar House.

Caz tilted her head to one side, mentally calculating. "Not long. I had been working at the magazine for a year and I suppose it lasted three, four months or so. And we weren't really 'going out'. I mean, we went out, but... God, why am I trying to justify this?"

She stopped in the middle of the pavement and gestured behind her. "Look, Danny, he's an idiot. He's selfish and greedy and as amoral as only someone who's never had to consider morality his whole life can be. And yes, he's tasteless and vain. But he's far from the worst of what I can only, tragically, call 'my circle.' Or, at least, the circle I had back then. Nowadays it's all barmaids and petty thieves."

"At least you've never had to shoot any of us to stave off an attempted rape."

The rain started to fall heavier, the sky darkening to twilight.

Caz dipped into her ever-present handbag and extracted a packable umbrella which, at the touch of a button, blossomed open.

She held it above herself, and, with a tilt of her head, bid me join her under it.

"Well yes," she said. "There is that. And Henry Wakefield – unlike Andy, who is just generally not a very nice person –

is actually evil. It took all I had to get my brother away from him before Wakefield could use Bobby and leave him holding the can. Bugger this," she added, indicating a doorway we half huddled in.

She sighed deeply, staring out as the charcoal sky emptied itself at volume. "I didn't mean it, you know?"

"Mean what?" I snuggled closer to her.

"The disparaging remark. About barmaids and petty thieves."

I laughed. "Caz. That's not entirely disparaging. Ali is a barmaid."

"Bar Manager," Caz corrected me, almost as quickly as Ali – if she'd been present – would have.

I nodded. "And the twins, whilst they are currently good boys who love their mum, have a rather checkered past."

"I was actually thinking of you," she smiled, explaining to my outraged mugging, "I've seen you at the Salt and Vinegar Crisps. Ali watches that stock like a hawk, you know, and she'll be bound to spot that the numbers don't tally."

"I'd be more worried," I answered, "By the fact that Ali seems to have a ready supply of a snack product that's still perfectly edible despite the Best Before dates on all the packages being sometime in the nineties. I mean, there are Egyptian Mummies with less preservatives in them. They," I said, referring to the little family I'd assembled at The Marq, and not the Egyptian mummies, "like you, you know. A lot."

"That's good," she smiled gently. "But to be clear," she added after a moment's pause, "Not everyone in my circle is a nasty, self-obsessed psycho."

"Just the ones you introduce to me," I deadpanned, and she laughed, punching me in the arm.

"That's gonna bruise," I said.

"You need to toughen up, sweetheart," she shot back and, looking out at the rain, I nodded.

"Ain't that the truth."

"You could walk away from this, you know?" Caz said, though I knew that she knew I never would.

"I'm in it now," I said, "and I can't leave something unfinished. So here we are. With the narcissist up there," I jerked my head in the general direction of Von Oldenwald's apartment, "And the ginger psycho."

Caz reached a hand out, testing the rain. "Yes," she said, pensively.

"So, do we confront him?" I asked. "See if we can tie him to Armstrong's death? Or back to Cathy's? Though I don't see what the link could be between Cathy and Armstrong."

"No," Caz shook her head. "Henry Wakefield's what your dear old Dad would call a nasty little toe rag. Actually, I'd call him worse. But he has a particular modus operandi: He gets other people – more impressionable, more disposable – to do his dirty work. That way, if – or, more usually, when – the ordure hits the air conditioner, he's able to walk away with little more than the smell of another scandal hanging over him. Speaking of your dear old Dad," she said, changing the subject completely, "What's the latest with your parental concerns?"

I shook my head dejectedly. "The latest opinion amongst my idiot siblings is that my mother has become a raving alcoholic."

"A late bloomer," Caz smiled broadly. "How lovely: there's hope for us all. And you? I take it by the reference to the mental capacity of your brother and sisters, that you have an alternative opinion."

"Me? I have no opinion, and no idea what's going on. Though Paddy Maz and Val are right: something is going on. I'm just no longer sure that I want to know what it is."

"Well quite," she murmured as the rain began, momentarily, to slow then - as if calling 'ha ha! Fooled you!' Redoubled its efforts. "One's parents, one feels, should always remain an enigma. Something to be aspired towards rather than understood. As soon as you begin to unravel them, the spell is broken and, well, at that point, what's left? For any of us?"

"That's very profound," I said as rivers of rainwater ran

down the pavement. "Did you make that up?"

"I'm not sure," she said. "I may have read it in a fortune cracker. So, you're leaving well alone?"

"For now," I said.

"What happened to not leaving things unfinished?"

"Touché. I guess, with Cathy I want to know. I want to understand."

"You want to make it right?" She offered, and I inclined my head to suggest that she wasn't entirely off the mark. "And with your parents," Caz finished, "You think, perhaps, that making it right may be beyond you."

"It's hard," I said. My whole life has been those two. They worked hard so that the three of us kids could have things they never had. But not just things: We went everywhere as a family. We did things with our parents that their parents were too tired or lost or frustrated to do. You know," my turn now to change the subject for no reason at all, "I didn't even need to come out to my parents. I mean, I did. I sat them down in the kitchen. Worked myself up. Convinced myself that my life would be over; that I'd either lose them, or that I'd lose something as important. I don't know: Their love? Their respect?

"Anyway, I sat them down. Radio in the background cos they never turn that off. But turned down low. Three mugs of tea steaming away on the table. Night like this, it was. And I started. Only I couldn't say it. I was so afraid of that moment when I wouldn't be able to take it back. So, half an hour later, I'm going round in circles when my dad cuts in.

"'Son,' he says, and my mum joins in 'Is this about the gay thing?'"

"'The Gay Thing?" Caz chortled.

"Well," I smirked back, "As you might say: quite. Only there were no capitals. It wasn't The Gay Thing, like that fucking place behind us. It was lower case, and my mum says 'Is this about the gay thing,' and I stop. Dead. My jaw hanging open. Panic mode kicking in. What am I going to say?

"'Only, if it is,' my dad says, 'We already know. And we don't give a monkeys.'"

"I love your parents," Caz said quietly.

I nodded. "I think you're right: Very few kids are enigmas to their parents. But the other way round? I don't want to know what it – whatever it is - is."

"Good," Caz nodded. "And do tell your mother, if she needs a drinking buddy, my dance card is at her disposal."

I laughed. "I love you," I said. And meant it. "I used to think you were the beauty, and I was the brains. But I'm not so sure these days."

"Well dearest, only one of us has the Pre-Raphaelite bone structure that marks out true classical beauty, and I'm afraid that your proletariat genes rule you out. So, if you keep mum about me having any intelligence whatsoever, I shall ensure you never sit in any light that would expose your potato-like features. Do we have a deal?"

I kissed her.

Caz smiled fondly at me, removed her lipstick from her handbag, applied a slick, peered out at the rain, and announced that we'd wasted enough time, before stalking off, me skittering along behind her trying to keep under the brolly.

CHAPTER THIRTY-FIVE

"So, wait," I stepped aside as an elderly woman her right hand holding leads attached to an out of control trio of Husky dogs, fled past.

"Slow down you fuckers!" She shrieked at the dog pack.

The dogs, needless to say, paid no attention.

"I'm waiting," Caz, who, as always, had managed to note the approaching dog pack – like something out of Jack London transported to the tundra of New Cross Gate - prompted me.

"Okay," I took a breath, took a moment to recollect myself, and took a look around to make sure that no more pet-propelled pensioners were local. "We're not going to see Prince Harry?"

Caz chuckled. "Sweetest, not without Westminster clearance and a pageboy or two. Lord Osworthy is currently resplendent in his Ermine and no doubt three fifths full of Burgundy. The government's latest bill on Social care," she said, as though stating the words would make any sense to me at all.

She sighed. "This is why democracy is doomed. I'm fine: feudalism's genetic in my family. As," she cast a sideways glance at me, "in yours. I suspect. The government has proposed a bill that will take what I believe you would call 'a shitload' of money away from the disabled, the poor, the damaged and the lost. And they've managed to get it as far as The House of Lords. It needs their assent to proceed.

"The government have, of course, wheeled out the entire panoply of usual suspects - including (according to my father) one who's basically on life support but will be wheeled into the chamber so his nurse can press the bloody button on his behalf – to ensure the vote goes through. And Henry Wakefield, I imagine, was only too pleased to slip on the robes, pile into the Lords bar, rumble into the house and vote to crucify some poor and weak people. It's what, if I may be indiscrete and crude for a moment, gives him – I'm told – a rather insubstantial stiffy.

"So, no, there is no chance of getting hold of Henry today. But also: why would we want to, when the tool he's used sits yonder."

She nodded across the road.

It had stopped raining, but the threat of clouds hung over the scene. A parade of shops – brightly lit, plastic, many of them proudly displaying marques from a selection of internationally recognised fast food franchises lead, inexorably to the trio before us: A Bet free shop offering 'Best Odds' on the upcoming England Lithuania Football game, and a Mick Moore betting shop, again offering superlative margins on an upcoming boxing match and advertising 'Instant Win' slots on the premises.

As we watched, a young man emerged from the latter, his shoulders drooped, his whole demeanour announcing his failure to best the Mick Moore slots, before glancing to his right, shoving his hands in the pockets of his leather jacket, and entering the shop between the two bookie shops.

It was called Kashfast, meaning that King Solomon could add assault of the English language to his litany of crimes and misdemeanours, and it – thanks to a couple of calls to Steve Haines and Callum Byrne – had been described to us as the place we would find King Solomon.

Caz looked at me. "Darling. You look so disappointed. What did you want? A final showdown with the Ermine clad psycho? Or a solution to your mystery?"

I stared back across the street. "What makes someone so

twisted?" I mused.

"Solomon?" Caz asked, her eyes never leaving the doorway of Kashfast, "Or Wakefield?"

"Oh, Solomon I get," I said. "You come from nothing, and you decide for whatever reason that only the strong and the psychotic thrive, so you become stronger, and before you know it you've forgotten that this was a part you were playing. It becomes you."

"Someone's in a charitable mood," Caz murmured back.

"No," I shook my head, "I'm wondering why someone like Henry Wakefield – who has all the money, all the prestige, all the power – has to be such a total bastard about it."

Caz's eyes, still locked on the shop opposite, narrowed, and she looked for all the world like a cat contemplating the dismemberment of a small rodent. "His mother didn't love him," she said quietly. "His father was the nicest old boy you could imagine. His sister is certifiable but really, when you think about it, who wouldn't be. And none of that is an excuse or an explanation for the fact that Henry Wakefield is the nastiest piece of work I've ever come across. Some people," she smiled sadly, "As my poor mama sometimes noted, are simply trash. Shall we?"

We crossed the road, reaching the door of the shop as it opened and the young man we'd seen earlier came out sans, this time, the leather jacket he'd gone in with.

We stepped into the shop

The space was about eight feet deep, and absolutely bare. The floor we stood on was naked chipboard, and the walls – a bland magnolia once – were a grimy grey now, streaked with fingerprints and occasional spatters like someone had had a food fight, or had their brains dashed against the walls.

The ceiling above us was naked plaster with three bare bulbs hanging down, one of them dead, the other two barely kicking out twenty watts between them.

"Victorian values," Caz muttered.

Before us a counter stretched the width of the shop;

above it a wall of reinforced glass, this too streaked with fingerprints and dried fluids.

A woman sat behind the glass.

Pale, bespectacled, her ash blonde hair pulled so tightly into a pony tail that her eyes were almost unable to blink. A nameplate in front of her said "Charity," which seemed either an unlikely name or evidence that God exists and is an ironist.

"Solomon here?" I asked, figuring that niceties would be rather out of place in this situation. Desperation seemed to leech from the walls.

"Never heard of him," she answered, as from somewhere behind her Radio One tinnily played, some EDM about Miami, Champagne and how "Life is just a party."

"Solomon Masters. Nasty bit of work. Likes a machete."

"You pigs?" She asked, and from somewhere behind me Caz tried – and failed – to suppress a snigger.

"It's not growing out fast enough, is it?" She asked.

"Look," I turned to her, oblivious, for the moment, of the puzzlement on Charity's face, "My hair does not make me look like a Special. It was the language. It was, wasn't it?" I demanded, turning back to Charity, who gawped at us both in silent confusion. "It was the way I spoke to you, wasn't it?" I prompted.

"Well if that's the case," Caz said, "I'm not letting you watch any more Crime things on TV. It's strictly News night and Drag Race from here on in. So, what was it made you think he was a rozzer?" She asked of Charity. "The tone of voice?" She prompted. "Or was it the dreadful 'do'?"

Charity came slowly to her senses.

"You two should go," she said simply.

"Look," Caz gently but firmly moved me to one side and stood before the window, turning on her billion-watt smile. "Charity. My," the smile went up a couple of kilowatts, "what a lovely name."

"Are you taking the piss?" Charity's eyes, already stretched to slits, were unable to squint further, but her mouth pursed into what can only be described as a cat's arsehole of disapproval.

"I?" Caz had moved from Genial to Patrician. I knew where this escalation was heading and hoped Charity caved before we got full-on Droit de Seigneur.

Charity, however, was having none of it. "Piss off out of it," she snarled, "or I'll get the boys on you."

"Look," it was my turn now to move Caz to one side, "Solomon. We know he's here, and we need to see him. Now just pop out the back and tell him Callum Byrne's mates from the pub are out here and want a chat."

"All okay, Chazza?" One of the goons from the other day suddenly materialised somewhere behind her, the remains of a doner kebab still held in his pudgy fingers.

"It's alright, Marco," Charity – her eyes never leaving us – answered, "these two Laurel and Hardy comedy motherfuckers were just off. Weren't you?"

Marco glanced towards us and frowned. In real time, we watched as the signals from his eyes reached his brain, were processed, and recognition flickered across his face before settling into angry clouds.

"What d'you two want?" He demanded, dropping the kebab on a desk and storming up to stand behind Charity, matching her glowering demeanour.

"Solomon," I answered simply. "He in?"

"Never heard of him," Marco deadpanned.

"Ooh," Caz deadpanned back, "If you do it again, we could join in on the third chorus."

"Look," I said, trying to inject my voice with the required level of boredom, like I knew we could play this game all day but they'd eventually wheel Solomon out, "Just tell him, if he wants to know where Callum Byrne has got to – or to save himself the hassle of a squad of rozzers crawling all over this place with fine tooth combs looking for clues in a murder case – he should get his short psychotic arse out here and talk to us."

"Murder?" Marco paled. That had gotten his attention.

"What murder?"

"Marco, mate, no offense, but, y'know: monkey / organ grinder? Solomon," I said. "Now."

Marco smouldered uncertainly a moment longer, then turned on his heels, leaving only Charity to fume silently at us."

"Can I just ask," I murmured, dropping my voice and leaning in to the narrow slot at the bottom of the glass, "When you called us Laurel and Hardy: Which of us is the fat one? It's her, isn't it?" I inclined my head towards Caz.

"Fuck off, batty," Charity snarled as a loud thump echoed around the empty space and a section of the left-hand wall swung open.

"This way," Marco called.

We stepped through the door, and my eyes watered. The place stank of flowers. Lavender, I thought, with layers of Magnolia and Orange blossom over and amongst it, and cinnamon too.

"Jesus," I said, coughing as the door was closed behind us. "It smells like someone set fire to a Yankee Candle store in here."

Marco said nothing, just marched away from us, turning to the right and leading us down a long dark corridor filled with the smell of lemon lime and vanilla.

At the end of the hallway, he paused, knocked on a door, and waited till, from the other side, Solomon's voice bid him enter.

Marco stepped aside, ushering Caz and I through.

"The fuck do you want?" Solomon, his blubbery bulk overflowing the office chair he was seemingly wedged into.

I smiled down at him. "No," I said, holding my hand up as, with one sweeping movement, he swept the remains of his own doner off the desk and into a waste paper basket beside it "Don't get up. You're looking well. Have you had a haircut?"

I dropped into one of the two seats facing him, Caz, having inspected the other seat, extracted a Hermes silk square, settling it on the grimy upholstery and seating herself beside me.

"Marco," Solomon snarled, his eyes sparking malevolently, "fetch the hounds. These motherfuckers need a lesson."

"Ooh, puppies," Caz smiled. "Lovely. Although I'd hold off for a moment or two Marco."

The goon, put off by the audible absence of any fear in Caz's voice, hesitated.

"Are you hard of hearing?" Solomon snapped at the hapless Marco. "Get my fucking dogs! And bring my blade an' all!"

Marco turned to leave.

"Charles Haney," Caz intoned, dipping into her capacious handbag and extracting a photograph, which she slapped on the desk in front of the corpulent crook.

Both Solomon and I glanced at it. From where I was sitting, it was upside down, but even from here I could see that it showed a man hanging from a scaffolding, his eyes staring sightlessly at the camera.

Solomon pulled a face. "S'posed to mean something?" He demanded, as Marco, looking over my shoulder, made a noise like he had a bit of his kebab stuck in his throat.

"Larry Keenan," I intoned this time, as a picture of another dead man – this one lying flat on the ground, dark circles on his shirt front showing where he'd been shot repeatedly – left Caz's handbag and was laid on top of the hanged man. The first one might have been a suicide, but this one would have been a hard sell for anything less than deliberate homicide.

"The fuck you on about? This bitch on drugs? Solomon, a sheen of sweat on his face, demanded of, first, Caz, then me.

In response, Caz extracted another photo, a tilt of her head giving me the honour of naming the subject.

"The honourable Cyril Fearnley," I said flatly as, one more time, a black and white shot hit the desk.

This one was a young man, his fair hair swept to one side,

a look of total confusion on his face as he was half lead, half-dragged by a trio of Met Policemen, his hands handcuffed behind his back.

"He survived," Caz said, tapping the picture with a nail lacquered in a red the colour of blood. "Because not even Henry Wakefield would risk killing a member of the aristocracy. But the others – and there have been others – were all dispensable. Like you."

"Get the fuck out of my office!" Solomon waved an unworried hand at us, flicking the photos – which flew from the desk and fluttered to the floor – and turning back to his copy of The Sun.

Only the slight tremor to his hand suggested he was anything other than totally unimpressed with our little slide show.

"Marco," Caz said, the smile still in her voice and on her face, "If you're going, can you close the door behind you? And if you're staying, can you please step in and close the door behind you.

"Either way," she turned and beamed at him, "Could you close the door please? The stench of Luscious Lavender, or whatever that stink is, is giving me a migraine."

I opened my mouth to protest, but Marco had already stepped into the room and closed the door behind him, meaning that there were now four of us squashed into a tiny room, with, I had noted (though Caz had clearly overlooked) at least two scented candles burning away.

Sparkling Cinnamon and Ginger fiesta filled the room with a smell that can only be described as an explosion at a Chinese takeaway.

"You got something to say," Solomon snarled, "Then say it and fuck off. Only, as you can see, I'm busy."

I glanced around.

Immediately behind Solomon was a door, a large metal filing cabinet on each side of it. Above one of the cabinets, a framed portrait of Padre Pio hung somewhat disconcertingly; as though this place had, at some time, doubled as a meeting room for The Catholic Mothers' Guild.

Maybe it still did.

"Us?" Caz lowered her head in her patented Lady Diana Spencer does shy move. "Oh, I think it should really be you who has something to say, Solomon. I mean, it's you who'll end up dead when it all goes – what's the phrase? – Tits up?"

She lifted her head, her eyes no longer shy, but burning with a defiance that was almost deliberately confrontational.

"Girl," Solomon spoke, though he couldn't have been more than a year or two older than her, "I don't know what shit you're smoking, but you have thirty seconds to drag your skinny posh arse out of my office and take this faggot with you before I get Marco and the boys to let loose with the machetes and turn you into fucking mince."

Caz chuckled, like Solomon had just made a passible joke. "No," she shook her head, "you won't be doing that. At least not to me. Sorry Daniel," she smiled at me briefly and, my disposability apologised for, carried on. "Because – if you did – Henry Wakefield would be very upset. You see, he doesn't mind you assaulting, scaring, scarring and terrifying the residents of the various council estates around here. He – if I know him at all (and I do) – actively encourages it.

"But you see, Wakefield is at heart a coward. A sadist, certainly, but a coward really. He wants to see how low you'll go, how far down the road you'll journey. And he wants to watch you make these people suffer, knowing every time you do that it's one more nail in your – not his – coffin."

"Hear her out," I said as Solomon's eyes bulged, his mouth opening to let loose with another string of profanities. "She knows what she'd talking about. These blokes," I indicated the photos lying sprawled on the floor, "Were all in your position once. 'Cos Henry Wakefield's spotted a niche in the psycho market. He likes to find people like him – people who like a bit of power, love a bit of cruelty – only further down the ladder. People who he can help. He's helped you, hasn't he Solomon? I mean the lease on this place must have needed a few quid to get sorted."

"Place is a fucking goldmine," Solomon, his fury abated for now, snarled.

"Doubtless," I said. "But when you signed the lease, I bet you needed help. A deposit. A guarantor. Someone like Flatford Financial."

Solomon frowned, filled the gap by folding up the newspaper and putting it in the bin on top of the kebab, the scent of which was mingling with the Sparkling Cinnamon, the Ginger Fiesta and something else – something sweeter and more cloying – to give even me the start of a migraine.

"I don't know what the fuck you two are on about," he said, though his tone had become far less certain than it had been.

"Some associates of mine," I said, imagining Ray and Dash's smiles if they ever knew I was referring to them as 'associates' and not 'reprobate nephews' "Are expert at accessing IT records and they had a look at the details of the guarantor on this place.

"You signed the forms, Solomon, but you had a guarantee from a company registered in Grand Cayman. Ever been to Grand Cayman, Sol?"

He glowered at me.

"I wouldn't rush," Caz said when – after a beat or two – it became obvious that King Solomon wasn't going to say anything. "It's full of crooks. The worst sorts: The ones in sharp suits and two hundred-dollar haircuts."

"But you know what these crooks have? Or rather," I said as he continued to stare at us in something that looked like confusion but was almost imperceptibly progressing to concern. "They don't have a lot of imagination."

"I mean, we've been looking into the death of Callum Byrne's mother Cathy." I paused as Solomon continued to glare wordlessly at us, a sheen of sweat on his upper lip. "She was thrown from her balcony a few nights ago."

"And – apart from having the misfortune to be related to someone who owed you a lot of money - one of the things that Mrs Byrne had been doing quite loudly in the days before her death was protesting against a company that was trying to demolish the estate she lived on. Trying to push all these troublesome, booze-addled, crime ridden, debt crippled poor people out of the estate they've spent their lives on so it can be razed and turned into billions of pounds of prime real estate for more crooks in suits."

"Dunno what you're on about," he said, finding his voice.

"Well Mrs Byrne knew what we were on about," I said. "Because her daughter had already been through it: seen the neighbourhood she lived in turn into a drug infested hellhole, thanks to the corruption of a local councillor who's living in a luxury development that this company own. Only the flat he lives in – like the car he drives – isn't his. It's registered to a company called Haywain Investments."

"Can you guess where Haywain Investments are based?" Caz asked, like a primary schoolteacher asking a particularly slow child what one plus another one might add up to.

"Grand Cayman," I answered for Solomon.

"Land of crooks with sharp suits, expensive haircuts and legions of lawyers," Caz added.

"And do you know what else joins these two companies?" I asked, not even waiting for an answer. "Constable: John Constable. English painter."

Seventeen seventy-six to eighteen thirty-seven," Caz chucked in, explaining, to my surprised look, "I Googled him. Well I couldn't have you lording it over me with your knowledge of fine art."

"Constable," I turned back to Solomon, "Painted a picture called The Haywain. It's quite famous; you may have heard of it? Seen it somewhere?"

"Not his taste," Caz added, sotto voce.

"He painted lots of pictures, but another one – called 'Flatford Mill' is the one that might, really, be your undoing. Well, that and the fact that whatever criminal mastermind is running Constable Construction has no imagination whatsoever."

I knew that the byzantine corporate structure that Ray had

uncovered, allied with Cayman's secrecy made much of what I was now entering into hearsay, but was banking on Solomon not unpacking the detail to a level that would allow him to call Bullshit, so I pressed on.

"You see, we know that Constable Construction – multi-billion-pound corporation building palaces for people who rarely even live in the buildings they construct, is linked to Haywain Investments, and that Haywain, in turn, has a sizeable interest in Flatford Finance. The same Flatford Finance that funded you setting up as a – how are you describing yourself, Solomon? Pawnbroker? Private financier? Loan shark?"

"Businessman," he coughed Tourette-like, his voice giving way on the last syllable so it squawked like a parrot. "I'm a businessman, and none of this has anything to do with me. Or my business," he barked on.

"And your business?" I prompted, picturing Marco and his mate giggling as they'd hauled binbags full of clothes away from Lindsey Wright's flat. A move that had felt pointless and now felt almost deliberately cruel.

"Does it have anything to do with making people vanish?"

Solomon's face went grey.

"The fuck you on about?" He croaked out, coughing to clear his throat.

"Wakefield really doesn't care, you know," Caz interjected. "You probably think he's a nice guy. I mean, he helped put you in touch with Flatford, moved you up from – what were you before? A thug with ideas? A punk with potential? – made you the," she coughed gently, "Businessman you are today."

"He probably even lets you think, from time to time, that you're in charge. He did the same with someone I care deeply about," Caz added. "But there's one thing you need to know: Henry Wakefield is using you. If he used you to get rid of the troublesome Mrs Byrne; if he used you to dispose of Vince Armstrong.; if he's used you to dispose of Louise Byrne. However, he's used you, and whatever you've done under his watch – even when you're so very sure you did it of your own volition – Henry knows where the bodies are. And – like," she gestured at the photos on the floor, "Others before you, you'll end up dead or disgraced before you can bring any trouble near his door."

Solomon glared malevolently at us, his face seeming to radiate pure fury as the very walls seemed to radiate ginger, lily and vanilla scent, and after a few moments he spoke, his voice tight like he was struggling to contain himself.

"Get the fuck out of my office?" Solomon croaked.

"We want Wakefield," I said calmly – or as calmly as I could manage, "not you. Your time will come eventually, Solomon, but we want the puppet master, not Punch and Judy."

And that was when Solomon pulled another gun on me.

I mean, I don't know why I was surprised: if he'd had one, he was almost bound to have another.

Only this time, the desk between us made it unlikely that I'd be able to get to him or the gun before he did any damage.

I put my hands up. "All we want," I said again, "is for you to go to the police and tell them all you know about Wakefield. 'Cos I'm telling you, Solomon," I said indicating the trio of photos, "things are not going to end well for you when this all ends.

Which was the point at which Solomon twitched.

Not his whole body; that would have been of little note, him being a clearly twitchy psycho at the best of times.

No: for some reason, Solomon decided that this was the time to twitch his finger. His right index finger, to be precise.

The one that was hovering over the trigger.

Luckily for us, he'd been uncertain which of Caz or I he wished to threaten most, and so had been hedging his bets pointing the gun at the space between us both.

This was, however, unluckily for Marco.

He'd been leaning against the door behind us, and the

bullet shot, with – I shit you not – an audible whistle between both of us and embedded itself in the door inches from Marco's right ear.

"Fuck," Solomon breathed, as Marco, a high-pitched noise somewhere between a shriek and a fart, issuing from him, feinted dead on the floor.

I glanced at Caz as Solomon, who seemed not yet to have realised he hadn't actually shot his lieutenant in the head, stared in shock at the pistol still held in his trembling hand. Caz stared back at me.

And then we made a run for it, kicking Marco's unmoving body out of the way, wrenching the door open, fleeing the stink of Cinnamon, Ginger and Cordite in favour of Lavender and Vanilla, and running down the hallway, me, like some avenging Wicked Witch of the West, yelling "Deliver Wakefield" as we pelted out the door and onto the fresh scented streets of New Cross Gate.

CHAPTER THIRTY-SIX

"Well at what point would you call the police?" Caz demanded, emptying the Starbucks latte into a plant pot, extracting a bottle of Courvoisier from her handbag and decanting the remains of the bottle of brandy into the cup, before clicking the lid back in place and swigging from the cup.

"When one of us has been plugged by the mob, perhaps? Or would you wait till the New Cross Cosa Nostra's actually poured the concrete? Only I'm not sure about you, but I tend to think psychotic loan sharks waving around Uzis is something that should be brought to Reid's attention. Or is that just me? Hmm? Danny?"

I was lost in concentration, sinking into the soft furnishings of the Starbucks as waves of trip-hop washed over me soothing my jangled nerves.

"It was a pistol, Caz," I sighed back. "Hardly an Uzi."

"Oh well excuse me if I'm not a firearms aficionado. It went bang when he pulled the trigger and the resultant impact took a chunk out of that doorframe which – had the chunk been out of you – would have required more than a flat bloody white to fix. And yet, here you sit. Like this is just another piece in the puzzle to be solved."

"What do you think Rachel Fiennes wants to tell us?" I asked, in an attempt to change the topic, but Caz was having none of it.

"Perhaps she wants to tell us that when people start

waving firearms around one should consider cutting one's losses and calling in P.C. Plod. At the very least, someone should at least let Reid know that there's a firearm which is more than likely unlicensed on the loose in New Cross Gate."

"Caz," I sipped my coffee and put the cup down. "There's more than likely a substantial number of unlicensed firearms on the loose in that neighbourhood.

"We go near Reid, he's going to want to know what we were doing there. And what do we tell him?"

"Well," She swigged from her 'Latte,' "The truth, obviously."

"And the truth is what, exactly?"

"We went to see King Solomon to warn him off threatening you, get him to back away from Callum Byrne and get him to incriminate Henry Wakefield in-" she paused.

"What exactly were we going to get him to incriminate Wakefield in?" I asked, "Cathy's death? Armstrong's? The Fenchurch-Brookes job? The destruction of the community around The Races? Corruption of elected officials? No," I shook my head, "We still don't have a clue how any of this fits together, do we? I mean did Wakefield mastermind the Fenchurch Brooks robbery and then kill Armstrong to silence him and keep all the cash?

"Or did he murder Cathy Byrne? And – if so – why? And why did she have my name on her hand? And – if Wakefield killed Cathy - is there a connection with the Fenchurch-Brookes job?'

"And where is Louise?" Caz murmured.

I nodded. "Exactly. What do we think happened there?"

"Well I think we can be fairly clear she didn't murder Vince Armstrong," Caz said, though there was a note of uncertainty in her voice.

"Can we?" I asked. "I mean, maybe the police were right. What if this is two different strands? What if Solomon and Wakefield killed Cathy as a warning to Callum Byrne to pay up or else, and meanwhile – unaware of what was going on with her brother and her mum – Louise had met her old school mate Vince and they'd hatched a plan to embezzle millions from the bank he worked at?"

"I mean," I chuckled. "It would be a rather neat irony if Wakefield ended up being nabbed for something as pointless as a debt collection gone wrong while a multi-million-pound robbery occurred under his very nose."

Caz shook her head, swigged her brandy, and sighed. "You don't get it, do you?" She asked. "Henry Wakefield is currently sitting in the House of Lords deciding how this country will be run for the next few years; finalising and approving a scheme to take money away from disabled children and spend it, instead, on tax breaks for," she waved her hand airily at the Scandi décor and dim lighting around us, "Multi-nationals. Whatever happens, Henry Wakefield will not be nabbed. He will not 'go down'. That is not," she finished, definitively if somewhat dejectedly, "how it works."

She shook her head. "If we're lucky, there'll be enough linkage for him to be exposed to the people who matter to him. Enough scandal to mean that the invites to the right parties, the access to the right people, is disrupted. That's about the best we can hope for."

"Well then we're definitely not going to the rozzers," I said bluntly, setting my jaw in a way that I hoped made clear to her that there would be no point in arguing. "Until I have something that can put him away for some of this, I'm not ringing a bell, and allowing Wakefield to get off on this."

Caz looked at me with something like pity in her eyes.

"So, what do we do, then?" She asked.

"We find out what Rachel Fiennes wants," I said, as my phone rang.

I glanced down and saw that the call was coming from The Marq, then hit answer and lifted the phone up.

"Danny?" It was Ray, "I thought I should let you know we had another weird call."

"Weird?" I frowned. Nothing about the past few days had been anything less than bizarre. "How weird."

"Well she said 'Armstrong was a warning. Next, I will have vengeance on my enemy.'"

My jaw dropped.

"Friend of yours, was it?" Ray asked.

I looked at Caz who had clearly sensed something was wrong, as the brandy-filled cup had been placed on the table.

"Louise Byrne," I said, as much for her benefit as in response to Ray.

"Well she doesn't sound right," Ray surmised in his own inimitable style.

"You could say that," I answered, wondering what in hell it could mean.

"Revenge on her enemy," Ray muttered. "It's all a bit Inigo Montoya, innit?"

"Shit." The penny dropped. "Thanks Ray," I said, ending the call immediately and staring in horror at Caz. "Evan Blythe."

Caz shrugged as though to say 'what of it,' and I shoved the phone into my pocket, standing. "Louise Byrne just called The Marq again," I explained, and Caz shook her head.

"Really, Danny; can't you just send a text with your mobile number? I mean what is this? The nineteen seventies?"

"Caz," I said, something about either my tone of voice of the look on my face silencing her, "She's going to make a play for Blythe."

"Evan Blythe?" Caz frowned, puzzled.

"No," I answered, "Blythe Danner. Of course, Evan bloody Blythe."

"But he's away on business," she answered, scuttling after me as I headed to the door.

"Except she doesn't know that," I answered. "But it means we at least know where she'll be. This might be our chance to catch her."

I piled out of the café, Caz right behind me and stood scouring the street for a taxi.

Typically, there were none to be seen.

"Don't you think we should call Reid?" Caz asked as I waved futilely at any passing car.

I roundly ignored her. She had a point, of course, but I needed to understand what Louise was playing at first. I still didn't believe she'd killed Armstrong, but if she hadn't, why had she called my attention to the whereabouts of his body?

As a familiar black shape appeared in the distance, I flung myself into the road, looking like I was doing star jumps in an effort to attract the driver's attention.

"I've got one," I called, and I distinctly heard Caz mutter something about the entire neighbourhood spotting that before the cab pulled up beside me, I gave the address of The Sugar House, added "Quickly, please," and we piled into the back.

Five minutes later, we pulled up at the end of the street, and, having exited, paid and watched the taxi pull away, we stood on the pavement, scanning the area.

There was no obvious sign of Louise, but I knew from my previous search of the street that there were enough doorways, alleyways and shadowed corners to keep her hidden.

"Right," I said, keeping my voice low, "You try that side, and I'll try this one."

"I still think you should call Reid," Caz whispered, and I nodded.

"I will," I agreed, "As soon as we find her."

Caz tutted, crossed the road, and peered down an alleyway opposite.

I turned, scanning the doorways on my side of the road.

As before, we met at the end of the street with nothing to report.

"Armstrong was a warning," Caz intoned. "It's a bit theatrical, isn't it? Louise never struck me as the dramatic type."

I had to agree she had a point. "The bit about having 'vengeance on my enemy,' sounds like something out of the

Old Testament. "Regardless," I gestured hopelessly at the street, "There's no sign of her anywhere here, so the vengeance-" I stopped.

"You've gone quiet," Caz said after a moment. "That's always a worrying sign.

"What if she knows he's gone away?" I said.

"Knows?" How could she?

"Caz, she watches the place like a hawk."

"A deranged, obsessive hawk," Caz added in a low voice.

"What if she saw him get into his taxi and head to the airport?"

"Oh, I see," Caz said. "And you mean, what if she followed him to the airport, found out where he was going; and what if she just happened to have her passport and enough money to buy a ticket on the same plane as her favourite obsession? And what if she's currently in a Hilton somewhere waiting for Blythe to finish his conference on urban planning for the twenty-first century before she garrottes him with a length of clothes line she also happened – handily – to have in her bag? That?"

"Yes," I said, deflated, "That. You don't think?" I trailed off as Caz threw her hands up in exasperation.

"I don't know what to think, Danny. As stupid as it all sounds, it's possible. Anything's possible, in this mess. But why call you?"

"There's really only one thing for it," I said, turning and making my way back down the street to The Sugar House.

Roy was – as always – behind the desk, and once again looked up with a frown when I knocked on the glass of the door, the frown deepening as he released the door lock and allowed Caz and I to enter.

"You again," he said, somewhat redundantly. "What is it this time?"

"Roy," I said, sidling up to the desk, "Do you know where Evan Blythe's gone?"

"Know where Blythe's gone?" His frown – which had vanished when my friend had entered the lobby – returned and deepened. "What sort of question's that?"

"I think he might be in danger," I said, figuring that honesty might, this once, be the best policy.

"Okay," Roy said in a tone that suggested he was urgently fingering the button under the desk marked 'Crazy Squad.' "And you think this why?"

"Because the woman who's been stalking him is currently wanted by police for the murder of an investment banker. It's a long story," I added in response to his look – equal parts disbelief and confusion.

"Anyway, the thing is that she's sent a message saying that the banker was a warning, and she's going to kill Blythe next," Caz – cutting straight to the chase – offered.

"A warning?" Roy – spectacularly failing to grasp the most urgent clause in her sentence – stared at Caz.

"I know, right," she nodded back. "A brick through a window; a canary in a shoebox. But a dead investment banker in a ditch on a building site? Overkill, as far as warnings go."

"So?" I prompted, snapping Roy out of a reverie of – I assume – great warnings in history. "Any chance you know where Blythe is? So, we can warn him of the danger?"

"But what about the police?" He answered. "Shouldn't it be them warning him? I mean no offense your highness," I swear he almost curtsied in Caz's general direction, "But what are you two doing running around like the Famous Five?"

"Well, apart from being two people and a dog short," I answered, "There's no time to get the police here."

"But Blythe's not here," Roy interrupted. "He's gone to-"

He got no further because from somewhere within the building there was a sound, or rather, a giant absence of sound; almost like a giant gasp. My ears popped, the entire world seemed to go silent and, as I turned my eyes towards Caz the room was filled with an apocalyptic explosion, the doors of the lifts rattling as the glass around us shuddered, one pane cracking diagonally from top to bottom.

A framed print of a Warhol portrait fell from the wall, the glass smashing and scattering all over the polished granite of the floor.

"What the fuck was that?" Roy, his manners forgotten in the shock, half gasped, before his brain caught up with his mouth. "That came from downstairs," he said, already running for the door behind him, with Caz and me hot on his heels.

CHAPTER THIRTY-SEVEN

"If it's any consolation, she probably died instantly." Nick rested a mug of tea on the desk and slid it across to me, before lowering himself into the chair opposite me.

I looked down at my hands, laid, palm down on the Formica of the desk, the soot caked in every line, gathered under my nails, the knuckles of one hand and the fingertips of both scorched and bloodied.

And, even though they were lying flat on the desk, both hands were still shaking.

"You tried your best, Danny." I turned my eyes towards Nick – my Nick, who had once lied to me and experienced the full wrath of my anger, and now here we were, me having, if not lied then certainly not shared the full truth with him.

He was looking back at me with worry in his eyes.

"It isn't," I answered, my voice cracking. "A consolation, I mean." I reached for the mug, but the shaking in my hands was too much; I dropped them back to the desktop. I reeked of petrol and of scorching, and of something else, something more chemical-smelling.

The car – the same black Alfa Romeo that had passed us, panther-like in the street the day before – was ablaze, the paintwork already bubbling and blistering, the figure in the driver's seat already a charred mannequin.

The explosion had buckled the doors and roof of the car,

blown the bonnet into the air and across the garage, so that the clean lines of the vehicle were turned now, via sheer force, into a bulbous, almost cartoonish version of themselves.

We'd run forward, the three of us, towards the same spot – the driver's door – before seeming to realise that we'd better expend our energies on multiple points of access and splitting up.

I grabbed the handle of the passenger door, whipping my hand away and realising, as I did so, that the handle was almost incandescent, and that either the door was locked or the metal had buckled so badly that it was immovable.

Caz, meanwhile, was attempting to get around to the passenger side, her progress hampered by both the flames spurting from the shattered rear window and Roy's health and safety training leading to him – in a possibly misplaced bout of chivalry – throwing his arms around her and attempting to drag her, shrieking in umbrage, from the wreckage.

I threw myself against the door, the heat from within scorching my shoulder as I tried to break the glass on the driver's window.

I was shouting at the figure in the car, immobile and silent as the flames burnt away something on its head, scorched the hair beneath, and I was crying to Andy Von Oldenwald to open the door, to do something, anything, when I realised that Andy Von Oldenwald was standing next to me, his face a mask of terror.

And in the seconds I watched him, his eyes scanned the scene, registered confusion, terror, then, focussing on the figure in his seat, as the flames finished consuming the baseball cap and began to turn the hair on the already blackened head to smoke, horror.

"Rachel!" He screamed, throwing himself against the door, heaving at it, and – as the scent of his scorching flesh mixed with the stink already filling the darkened space – managing to haul it open, the change in air pressure making the flames inside the car curl up into a ball before, as though the fire was malevolently conscious, expanding back out, consuming, even as Von Oldenwald sobbed Rachel's name, the woman in the driver's seat completely and irrevocably.

"It makes no sense," I whispered, may eyes fixed on my bloodied and blackened hands as my vision tear-blurred.

"You tried," Nick repeated, resting his hand as close to mine as he dared with the impassive uniform behind him. "But she was dead before you even got there."

His thumb touched mine.

All I wanted to do, at that moment, was hold him, and cry till I finished, and never let him go ever. And yet, I couldn't stop picking at this thread.

"Why her?" I asked, looking up, and fixing my gaze on his. "Why kill Rachel?"

"She wasn't the target," he said, his voice low. "She'd asked Von Oldenwald if she could borrow the car to go to the gym. She usually jogged there, but it looked like rain," he trailed off as I shook my head in confusion. "Von Oldenwald was the intended victim," he finished.

"Whose?" My throat hurt, and my shoulder, where I'd smacked the glowing metal of the Alfa, was stinging and throbbing.

"Louise Byrne," Nick said. "We've been doing some more research, and she did know Armstrong. Dated him back in the day. And it turns out a subsidiary of Fenchurch-Brooks were the people who foreclosed on her mortgage. Reid thinks she blamed Fenchurch for ruining her life and was out to kill as many of their players as she could."

"But that makes no sense," I shook my head. "She wasn't stalking Von Oldenwald, she was outraged at Blythe's involvement with Constable."

Nick's shoulders dropped.

"And what about the money?" I pressed. "Was she involved in Armstrong's robbery?"

"About that," he said, his head suddenly jerking up as

some sixth sense told him of advancing problems. "Listen, Danny, there's something else going on. I need you to be honest."

"Honest?" I asked, as the door of the interview room opened and a procession of people entered the room.

The first to enter was Dorothy Frost, who came straight to my side, sat next to me and leaned in close.

"Are you okay?" She asked, and I almost laughed as she told me that if I needed to, I should call a time out and consult with her in confidence.

I would have told her that I needed neither a time out nor a brief, except my eyes were still fixed on the doorway where Caz walked into the room, her head held high, her fringe singed, one of her eyebrows burnt almost completely away, and her makeup giving her the air of an Alice Cooper tribute act on a bad night.

Like me, Caz's forehead was smeared with soot.

She nodded at me as she came around the desk and sat by my side.

"Loving the new maquillage, Mister Bird," she said *sotto voce*.

Behind Caz was a man who looked as though Gollum, having sorted all that Ring business, had bought a pinstripe three-piece suit and, on the way out of Jermyn street, met someone who sold law degrees and coats of arms, and had purchased one of each. You know how, when people say someone's ageless they usually mean 'eternally youthful' and not 'looks so old it seems impossible that he could still be living without the age of Necromancy'?

Well, I leave it there.

"Dorothy," he smarmed to Dot Frost, like a puma condescending to acknowledge a moggie.

"Arbuthnot," Dot Frost smiled warmly back, clearly used to receiving and ignoring his disdain. "How's the missus?"

"Ex," he settled himself next to Caz, his previous smugness dinged ever-so-slightly, and I loved Dot Frost as much as I'd ever loved her.

"Really?" She fluttered her eyes like an ingénue, everyone in the room now knowing that she'd known the answer before asking the question. "Shame. How's the secretary?"

"Fiancée," Caz's brief snapped back, before leaning in to mutter to his client.

The last person to enter the room was DI Frank Reid, his bulk making an already crowded space feel claustrophobic.

"The truth," Nick said, his eyes no longer meeting mine as his boss collapsed into the chair next to him.

"Christ," he said, shoving a desk phone to one side so his fat finger could stab at a recording machine, "We are housing a gathering of the great and the good ain't we? I suppose I should recite the Dramatical Personae. For the purposes of the tape," he added, though the machine he'd stabbed was clearly digital and as close to tape as his Marks and Sparks shirt – each button straining in ways that no button was ever expected to strain – was to the Turnbull and Asser on Caz's brief.

"The time is," he glanced at his watch, "Twenty-three fifteen, and we are in interview room six at Borough station. In the room, apart from P.C. Grant," he glanced over his shoulder at the still impassive uniform, "Are myself, Detective Inspector Frank Reid, DS Nick Fisher."

I stopped him. "D.C." Nick was a constable, though I knew he'd been trying for some time to achieve the next level in his career.

Reid fixed his full attention on me, his lips curling slightly as his eyes sparkled balefully. "Oh, Danny, how little you know of our young Nick. As of this morning, he's got through his exams, his interviews, and even the swimsuit round, and is now a fully-fledged DS."

Nick, who had begun to colour at the swimsuit dig, blushed to his roots, and stared fixedly at the desk in front of him.

"Well," Reid beamed around the room in the manner of a piranha taking in a herd of hobbled cattle that had just been dropped into its pond, "Who else do we have then?

"There's Mister Daniel Bird. Danny to his mates. Amongst whom, since we've spent so much time in each other's' company, I'd like to count myself." He bared his teeth at me. "With Mister Bird is his brief Mrs Dorothy Frost, and alongside Mister Bird is the lovely Lady – now let me see if I can get this right – Caroline Genevieve Victoria de Montfort. Did I get that right, m'lady?"

Caz nodded briefly, her tear smeared eye makeup running down to her upper lip which was caked with lipstick, soot, and snot.

"And accompanying Lady Caroline, in the red corner, as it were," Reid carried on, clearly relishing his chance to showboat, "Is Mr Arbuthnot Postlethwaite, who has never heard of the Keystone Kops," he finished, making sure he got a dig in at Caz for her earlier jibe to him.

Postlethwaite, in response, frowned as though reference to Mack Sennett's comedy constabulary might be grounds for some sort of super injunction, and he was already mentally computing his likely fees.

He said nothing.

Caz shifted her eyes to mine.

I looked intently at Nick, realising I'd been so wrapped up in everything else that I hadn't even remembered to ask how his promotion was going. What did our inability to communicate with each other mean for the future of our relationship?

Nick glanced up, his green eyes meeting mine for a moment, and Reid, in characteristic mode, broke the moment with two words.

"Solomon Masters."

I turned to look at Caz, who reflected my confusion back to me.

"What about Rachel Fiennes?" I asked.

"Louise Philips?" Caz added, and Reid waved his hand as though to say we'd get to the petits fours after the main course had been consumed.

"Solomon?" I asked, finally refocussing on him.

"Inspector," Postlethwaite declaimed, as though chastising a small boy, "This is not what we understood we were here to discuss."

"Well, Arby, as the late and well lamented Cilla Black often commented: 'surprise, surprise,'" Reid leered back. "Whilst I know you've both witnessed a difficult – not to say traumatic - event this afternoon, I'd much rather ask you why my officers - who've been staking out a known violent offender who'd become a major threat of late - witnessed you two popping in for tea with him earlier today."

"Difficult event?" Caz spoke, her voice catching at the second syllable. "Inspector," she coughed the catch away, "You're not surely referring to the immolation of an innocent woman as a 'Difficult event'?" She glanced at Postlethwaite, who lifted his hand a millimetre off the table as, I assumed, a warning to remain silent like a good girl should.

"Only," Caz (who to the best of my knowledge hasn't been 'a good girl' by the yardsticks of Postlethwaite and his ilk since the early nineties) continued "Watching someone being barbecued before your own eyes is something more, let me tell you, than difficult."

"How about finding the body of someone you've been looking for being eaten by dogs?" Reid shot back. "How does that rank in your 'difficulty' rating, love?"

"Inspector," Postlethwaite ejaculated, as though the use of the word 'love' was more disturbing than what had gone before it.

"Frank," Dot Frost said quietly, "It sounds like there's something you know that nobody on this side of the table does."

"Oh Dot," Reid snarled, "The past few days have been littered with bits and bobs that nobody on either side of this table knew about."

I glanced at Nick.

Caz dropped her head into her hands. "Whatever," she sighed. "Just say it, whatever it is. I'm tired of all of it, to be honest."

Postlethwaite rested a hand on her shoulder.

"Acting on information received," Reid said, struggling – and almost failing – to contain his temper, "this station has been monitoring the activities of one Solomon Masters, who goes by the moniker of King Solomon, and who – by all accounts – is a nasty little toe rag with a thriving loan shark business and a side-line in violence for hire. So, you can imagine our surprise, Mr Postlethwaite, when your client and her mate here," he jerked his chin at me, "turned up this morning to hang out with the aforementioned scumbag."

Postlethwaite turned an enquiring look on Caz, who nodded silently.

"Even more surprising," Reid continued, "was the nature of their departure some minutes later. My constable, who was stationed, in plain clothes, in a car parked just opposite King Solomon's place of, well work seems too polite a phrase-"

"Get on with it," Postlethwaite said tersely, adding "Please," in a more conciliatory tone.

"My constable," Reid carried on, as though there'd never been an interruption, "used the phrase 'like bats out of hell.'"

Dot leaned in to my ear. "Something you need to tell me about?" She asked. "Only I can call for a break at any time."

I shook my head. I didn't know where this was going, but I wanted to get there before I decided whether I should lawyer up or not.

"Your clients, folks, fled that place like their life was in danger. And a very short period of time later, King Solomon and his crew did the same. They locked up and they scarpered like rats who've just seen a particularly angry tiger heading their way.

"Unfortunately, they didn't bother taking Solomon's dogs with them. Although for us that was rather fortunate, because the animals, left alone, started barking, then fighting, and that was when one of the neighbours called the RSPCA who got a warrant to gain access to the property to rescue what were clearly some distressed dogs, and my boys went in with them."

"So, it sounds like we're adding animal cruelty to the list of crimes this person's guilty of," Postlethwaite responded. "But what does this have to do with my client?"

"Well, it wasn't just animal cruelty, was it?" Reid sneered back. "But then, I think your client and her mate know exactly what we found in there, 'cos I think they found it first, and that's what had them running for their lives."

"Oh, for god's sake," I snapped, "just tell us what you found."

"We found a body," Reid snapped back, folding his arms and leaning back in his seat, the better to observe the multiple looks of utter confusion that swept between the four of us on our side of the table. "Or rather, the bits of it that one of Solomon's hounds hadn't had for breakfast."

"Right. That's it," Dot Frost suddenly said, "I want a conversation with Mr Bird. You've no right to drop a bombshell like that, Frank, without giving my client and me advance notice to prepare ourselves."

"Yeah," Reid hauled himself up, "I figured you'd want to have a chat at this point. We'll be outside," he tapped Nick on the shoulder and, having advised the machine that the interview was "*temporarily* suspended," Reid, Nick and the silent P.C. Grant left the room.

"Lady Caroline," Postlethwaite addressed his client while shooting a look of pure distaste at Dot and I, "Would you rather a private space?"

Caz looked confused, then followed his glare, and rolled her eyes. "Mr Postlethwaite, Danny is my best friend, and there's nothing that can't be said in front of him or his brief. Besides, this story is so complicated, I think we'd both rather just tell it once rather than have to go over it individually with each of you."

"Very well," Postlethwaite replied, though his tone suggested he remained far from happy with the shared space.

"Right," Dot turned to me. "Body. King Solomon. Get

going."

So, we did. We told them about the results of our investigation, of wanting to warn King Solomon away from the residents of The Races, at which Postlethwaite raised an eyebrow and enquired of Caz whether she'd really intended to threaten a psychotic gangster.

"Well it's worked before," Caz answered, and as the tale continued on past Lindsey Wright and her desperate search for her missing partner, across Cathy Byrne and Vince Armstrong, me wondering aloud what connection – if any – there was between them, and on through Louise Byrne's obsession with Evan Blythe, poor Arbuthnot Postlethwaite looked like he was about to have an attack of the vapours.

"Did you say Blythe?" Dot asked at one point, an odd frown on her face as I nodded, explained who he was and – conscious of the time – went on with the story.

"And that's how we came to find Rachel Fiennes's body," Caz finished, as Postlethwaite went through every shade of green on the paint chart.

"His Lordship is not going to like this," he moaned. "Not one little bit."

"So, you know nothing of this body?" Dot asked, and I shook my head, my mind wandering back to the smoke-filled garage. "Poor Roy Bell was devastated by Rachel's death. He reckoned she was the only resident who even acknowledged his existence. Used to cover the desk for him when he needed a loo break or a crafty fag."

"Danny," Dot snapped her fingers in front of my face. "Back to Solomon Masters: I can understand why you went to see him, but what did you say to him? What made him pull the gun, and what made the whole gang pack up and leave as soon as you'd left?"

Caz and I exchanged a glance. "We were trying to ascertain if he'd been responsible for George Osman vanishing."

"You asked him," Caz reminded me, "whether his job had anything to do with making people vanish. That's when he went a bit grey, if I remember."

"You're right," I said, snapping my fingers. "And right after that, you said something about," I eyed Postlethwaite, uncertain how involved with the circles Henry Wakefield moved in, "An associate of Solomon's being the sort who knew where the bodies were buried."

"He thought we knew," she said, as a firm knock on the door advised us that Reid had given us enough time. "He thought we knew that he had a body buried there."

"Buried," Reid chuckled, catching our last exchange as he barrelled back into the room and dropped himself once again into the same chair, to the same chorus of protestation from the furniture. "If only he'd buried it. No," he shook his head. "Didn't even bother putting it in the freezer. I mean, he had one, but it appeared to be full of frozen Kebab meat. At least," he raised an eyebrow as Nick sat next to him and the impassive uniform took up his position against the wall, "We think it's kebab meat."

"The candles," I murmured, the stink of lavender and vanilla and something else, something I hadn't been able to put my finger on, filling my nose again. "He had about a million scented candles and plug-ins going."

"Probably to mask the scent of decomposition," Nick answered. "We think the victim had died some days ago, so there would have been some smell by now. No sign of foul play, mind, so we're still uncertain what Masters was up to. What gets me most is why he hadn't just got rid of it."

"Or at least got rid of the kebab meat." Reid leered.

"Frank," Dot finally stepped in, "any idea whose body it was?"

"Oh, we know that," Reid grinned back. "Victim's face has been plastered all over the place for the past week or so, ever since he was lifted off the street outside his home. Initial report from the white coat mob suggests it was a heart attack finished him off as opposed to violence. Probably the shock of getting lifted right off the street."

"Bill Duffy," I said, remembering the news story that had

been jammed into the envelope Mehmet Aksoy had given to Dot.

"Friend of yours?" Reid asked, and I shook my head.

"No," I said, "but I reckon Solomon was holding Duffy for ransom. Duffy's business had expanded quickly of late. The capital for that expansion: I bet it came from Solomon. And when Duffy couldn't repay, he was lifted off the street.

"His wife's put the family home on the market," Nick said quietly, glancing sideways at Reid.

"So, she could pay off Duffy's debt to King Solomon," I surmised. "Which she'd be less than likely to do if she discovered that her husband had died not long after being taken."

"So, Solomon's what? Waiting for the wife to sell the house and fork out the proceeds to him at which point what? He thinks he can just hand over a mouldering corpse and she'll be alright?" Reid asked incredulously.

"I'm not sure," I muttered, "that Solomon thinks that far ahead. All he knew was he had a body he couldn't just dump, and – if he could keep it a few days more – he'd have his pay-out."

"Then we blunder in," Caz finished quietly, "talking about buried bodies and making people disappear, and he panicked."

At which point the phone on the desk rang, the sudden noise causing Caz and I to jump in our seats, Dot Frost to call out for her Lord and Saviour, and Postlethwaite to knit his eyebrows together and scowl at the offending instrument in a manner that suggested he'd never agreed with the telephone since it had been invented.

Reid snatched the receiver up, pressed it to his ear, barked his name, and listened in silence, a light coming on far behind his eyes.

"Thanks," he said when the person on the other end of the phone had stopped speaking. He hung up, turned briefly to Nick to smile wolfishly and waggle his eyebrows in a way that suggested the message he'd just received was good news.

I stared at the keypad on the phone, wondering if keeping secrets from each other was something that Nick and I would have to get used to. Like my parents keeping secrets from their kids. Like George Osman seeming to be completely open with Lindsey Wright, but – when he vanished – proving to have had some secret he was hiding. Something serious enough to make him appear never to have even existed.

As I wondered on the nature of secrets and how well we can ever know anybody, the conversation went on around me.

"I'll be honest," Caz said, "I was half expecting you to say that the body was Louise Byrne."

"Louise Byrne?" Nick frowned. "Why would Solomon Masters have her body?"

I tore my eyes from the telephone keypad. "It makes more sense than the suggestion that she set a bomb in Andy Von Oldenwald's car. Was there any CCTV down there?" I asked, something forming in the back of my mind.

"Lots," Reid answered, a smirk that said he knew something I didn't, "But not in the corner where the car was parked. Blind spot, you see. Anyway, Louise Byrne didn't kill Rachel Fiennes. Or Vince Armstrong."

"She didn't?" I sat up straighter in my chair, waiting for Reid to pull the rabbit I knew very well he had stashed, out of his proverbial.

"Well her Ladyship here," he nodded at Caz, "Mentioned how scared Miss Fiennes had seemed the last time you met, and how she'd asked you to come back to see her later. And we've had some people take another look at Von Oldenwald's computer log-ins on the Fenchurch-Brookes system, and, well, long story short, it looks as though our investment banker is not necessarily the innocent victim of the crime. He's currently helping," Reid nodded at the phone, "our friends in The City with their investigations and as soon as they've finished with him, he's getting bussed over here to talk to me about two murders that seem very tightly connected to Fenchurch-Brookes recent difficulties."

I was stunned. "You think Von Oldenwald is the thief?"

"In partnership with Armstrong," Reid answered. "Only it was a partnership that Von Oldenwald decided needed to be terminated, hence the body that you claim Louise Byrne called you to confess about."

"I'm confused," Postlethwaite chipped in. "Is this Louise person also a party to the Fenchurch- Brooks robbery?"

"Nothing is being ruled out at the moment," Reid responded, "but the fact she did a runner as soon as Armstrong's body was discovered does suggest something's going on."

Something was bubbling under the surface. An idea nagging at me, but in a voice I couldn't quite hear. A woman who'd become invisible; another woman who'd had my name written on the back of her hand; a massive theft and some cryptic clues drawing me to places I wouldn't otherwise have been, as though I was being played, drawn into some game, the rules of which I did not understand.

I looked back at the telephone, then Nick flipped open the file on Armstrong, the pictures of the body, the clothes line dug into the flesh on the neck, the frame capturing the edges of the carpet it had been wrapped in, and a bell went off somewhere.

And I knew.

CHAPTER THIRTY-EIGHT

Ray and Dash ushered their bleary-eyed charges through the lobby of The Sugar House, some of the handful of Henley Court residents looking gawping at the polished marble, original artworks and immense vases of fresh flowers around the space.

"All accounted for," Ray sidled up to me.

I nodded my thanks. "Where'd you find Callum?"

"He was staying with Steve Haines," Ray answered.

"And the computer," I said, returning Lindsey's Wrights sad smile as she led her son, by the hand, through the door behind the reception desk.

"It was there," Ray dipped into a messenger bag slung over one shoulder and extracted a sheaf of papers. "Just like you predicted. Printed it for you."

I took the printouts and flicked through them, nodding in satisfaction. "Well that's nearly all of it," I turned to Caz, who had managed to remove and redo her makeup before we left the police station.

"Dear heart,' she'd said to Reid's protestations, "If you think I'm unmasking a murderer looking like this, you're clearly crazier than you look. And she'd shrugged her handbag over her shoulder and swanned out of the room.

"Are you sure about this?" She asked, a note of concern in her voice.

"Not really," I said. "But it's pretty much firming up in my head, so I suppose now's as good a time as any. Right," I turned to speak to Reid, and discovered he'd stepped outside to check on the positioning of the cohort of coppers he'd brought along.

My eye met Nick, who smiled softly at me.

"Here we are again," he said, as Caz, deep in conversation with Ray, rambled away.

I looked around the lobby. Roy Bell was standing behind his reception desk, his face a picture of conflicted emotions. Off in a corner, heads together in deep conference, stood Postlethwaite and Dot, neither of whom had been willing to let this scene unfold without their presence.

"Why didn't you tell me about the promotion?" I asked.

"I did," he said back. "End of the summer, I told you I'd done the exams. The interviews were the past week, and I only found out this morning. That's why Reid hauled me back in the other night. I haven't even officially got the letter yet."

"But you didn't tell me you were close to the decision stage," I whined, and he shrugged, embarrassed.

"To be honest, I didn't think I'd get it. But Reid put a word in."

"Reid?" I was amazed.

Nick chuckled. "I've told you before: He's old school, but he'd not as bad as you think he is."

"Are we discussing D.I. Reid?" Caz came back into our orbit.

"How'd you know?" I grumbled, and she smiled.

"I heard the words 'old school,' and 'as bad as you think.' It was either him or Genghis Khan, to be honest."

I wanted to continue this conversation with Nick, but it seemed now was not the time. Besides, he suddenly snapped his fingers and said "Oh, yeah, and you were right about that stabbing victim. How'd you know they'd be there?"

"I didn't," I smiled at the impressed look on his face.

"Please don't say you guessed," he smiled back, and my heart did a little samba.

"Well, it was a sort of educated guess," I admitted. "I figured that someone who'd already got away with murder might have gotten careless second time round. Doesn't prove anything definitive yet, but I think it'll be a wedge to crack the façade."

"Fascinating," Caz raised an eyebrow. "When you two boys have finished talking in code, I was asked to let you know that we may have a problem, by the way." She inclined her head towards the reception desk where Roy Bell was deep in conversation with my nephew Ray.

I walked over, Caz and Nick behind me.

Bell was still not sold. "This'll cost me my job," he said, shaking his head.

"Look," I said, "It'll be fine. Constable are going to be offering you a promotion and a pay rise after this." I highly doubted either of these propositions, but I needed to do something. Half the residents of Henley Court were already ensconced in the plush panic room downstairs and I needed the residents of The Sugar House added to their numbers before too much time elapsed and our killer made their escape.

"But why here?" Bell whined. "Why this way? I mean," he added, as though logic had handed him a trump card, "You can't even be sure they'll head there; they might just get in their cars and leave."

"Roy," I patted him reassuringly on the shoulder, imagining him as a skittish colt and myself as the Concierge whisperer, "I'm assuming by now that every one of them knows that a vehicle was blown up here this evening with a young woman in the driver's seat. when that thing goes off, the last thing any of them are likely to do is run for their cars."

He remained unconvinced. "But if you know who did it," he griped, "why not just send in the law and let them deal with it?"

"Because sending in the law," Caz said, laying a hand on his hand and staring into his eyes in a way that made even me blush, "Is so prosaic. This way: This is drama, darling. And besides, it's a police order, isn't it D.S Fisher," she glanced at Nick who half nodded before realising that it was actually no such thing, "So you have to comply, or you could be arrested."

Bell frowned, looking from her to me to Nick. "I'm fairly sure that's not how it works," he said as the front door opened again and Reid stomped in, the shoulders of his overcoat glistening with beads of rainwater.

"Right," he growled, the smell of the crafty fag he'd smoked whilst ostensibly massing his troops, wafting on his breath, "What's occurring? Only it's two in the morning, I've been awake for twenty hours, that turkey korma I had fourteen hours ago seems to have finally worked its way through and I'd like to get this over and done with so I can take a shit in peace."

"I take it back," Caz murmured. "Genghis was classier."

"Lock the doors," I instructed Roy as gently as I could.

He hesitated a moment, then, sighing deeply, reached under the reception desk and pressed a button.

"We're sealed," he said simply, fear painted on his face.

"Push the button," Reid ordered Roy, who looked for a moment like he might be about to demand to see the warrant that authorised this unprecedented breach of protocol, then glanced at Reid's bulldog glare – like a really pissed off Winston Churchill with piles – reached under the reception desk, firmly pressed a hidden button, then stepped back, his eyes closed tightly, a look of absolute terror on his face.

"Attention!" a voice roared out, echoing around the lobby so loudly that Postlethwaite winced, clapping his hands over his ears, "Attention, all residents of The Sugar House."

I frowned, and it was a moment more before I placed the voice. I was left wondering whether Constable Construction had actually hired Benedict Cumberbatch to do the voiceover on their emergency announcements, or if it was a soundalike.

"Attention, all residents of The Sugar House," Benedict repeated, "This is an emergency announcement."

"No shit, Sherlock," Reid – without a scintilla of irony – snarled.

"The building is under attack," Mr Cumberbatch continued, his tone one of urgency balanced with an audible sense that – because we're all rich and beautiful – all will be well, and this attack, whilst inconvenient, doesn't need to mean we can't all still get a good night's sleep and enjoy a light brunch in the morning.

"I repeat: The building is under attack."

I looked at Ray, who shook his head whilst giggling helplessly. "These people are seriously fucking warped," he choked.

"Warped and terrified," I said, "or at least, I hope they're terrified. Anything less than a full house will be a problem."

"I repeat; The building," Benny C intoned once again, for – I assumed – the hard of hearing – "Is under attack. Please move immediately to the Crisis Lounge on Sub Level 2."

"'Crisis Lounge'?" I shook my head at the euphemism. "What's wrong with Panic room?"

"Sweetie," Caz responded, "when you've got as much money as this lot, Panic is something you do only when your dealer announces they've found God and joined Narc Anon."

"Please," the actorly tones of Mr Cumberbatch instructed in a tone which managed to be similarly firm and calming "Do not attempt to leave the building. I repeat: Do not leave the building. The streets outside are unsafe."

"Dude," Ray laughed at the echoing voiceover, "The streets round here have been unsafe my whole life. But thanks for the reminder."

"Can you please take this seriously?" I implored him as Benedict exhorted the residents, once again, to 'Please make your way to the Crisis lounge on Sub Level 2.'

Then Roy Bell's phone rang.

We all stared at it.

"You know the drill," Reid said coldly, his eyes raking Bell in a way that suggested any attempt to lift the receiver would be met with ultimate force.

The phone rang again.

And again.

And we stood staring at it.

And then it stopped.

"They're on their way down," Roy said simply, his face ashen.

I looked around the lobby, seven sets of eyes looking back at me. "What happens now?" Roy asked.

"Now?" I took a deep breath. "Showtime."

CHAPTER THIRTY-NINE

The 'Crisis Lounge' of The Sugar House was located a floor below the underground carpark, and a floor above the underground swimming pool and hot stone spa, which, I suppose, meant that in the event of, say, Armageddon occurring, the residents could at least remain toned and destressed.

Which was nice.

As the now somewhat threatening tones of Doctor Strange continued to advise the inhabitants of the building that civil war had broken out in the streets outside their home, we made our way down to the room, walking through the doors – triple milled carbon steel and two feet thick – into what felt like a private screening room crossed with a first-class departure lounge.

To the right of the door a huge plasma screen was fixed to the wall, a selection of written instructions advising new arrivals to take a seat, help themselves to snacks or drinks from the well-stocked bar at the back of the room and reminding them that there was no need to panic.

Four rows of deep, state-of-the art ergonomic seats lined up facing the screen, leading me to believe that at any moment the written instructions might be replaced with something that had yet to make it to the local multiplex. A movie, perhaps, where Benedict Cumberbatch did more that rely on the posh voice and cheekbones…

Around the room, various tables were scattered, all the

better to make a pleasant night out of the end of the world.

Callum Byrne, Steve Haines and Eddie James had already taken the instructions to heart and were each sharing a bottle of Johnny Walker Black amongst themselves around a small round table, while Joanna Trztrzelewska and Lindsey Wright sat with Lindsey's boy at a long farmhouse table, helping him to choose from the selection of colouring books and professional-grade oil paint sticks.

I took up my position near the plasma screen, Caz heading straight to the bar and returning moments later with a magnum of vintage Veuve and two glasses.

"Well at least we know where the entire 96 vintage went," she smiled, handing me a glass and taking a seat in the front row, like some sort of post-modern madame Lafarge.

Nick and Reid strode to the back of the room, and stood, their arms crossed, awaiting the influx, while Dorothy Frost and Arbuthnot Postlethwaite sat at the farmhouse table with Lindsey and Ali, Dot joining in the chat with the child, and Postlethwaite looking as though, at any moment, he expected a hidden camera show to pop up and tell him he'd been pranked.

A calming soundtrack – equal parts Enya, lounge house and whale song, sounding like an after-hours chillout session at Sea World – echoed decorously around the room.

Ray ambled over to Dash, helping himself to a beer on the way, and slipping, I noticed, one of the bottles of vintage champagne into his messenger bag.

The first resident to arrive – unsurprisingly, as his apartment was nearest Bar Apocalyptique as I was already mentally referring to the space – was Evan Blythe, feet shoved into a pair of slippers that suggested tartan breeze-blocks, his almost unnaturally hairy calves poking out of the end of a not-quite-long enough chain store dressing gown.

Trailing behind him, wrapped in a slightly better fitting dressing gown and as bleary-eyed and perturbed as he, followed Selene Aksoy, her normally immaculate coiffeur in a state of disarray which, had Wikipedia had a pictorial section, would have been place definitively above the phrase 'Bedhead.' She staggered forward, the white terrier she'd called Pu Yi tucked under her arm, and joined Blythe in the third row of the black leather seats, frowning only when she noted the trio around the round table at the back of the room.

"What the fuck's going on?" Blythe demanded as Ellie Nosh raced into the room, her hair in a hastily assembled chignon, a black silk ankle-length kimono swishing and a wicker picnic basket slung over one arm.

"It's a drill, right?" she demanded of the assembled. "A drill, right?" She repeated as Dash stepped forward, handed her a Negroni and ushered her into the row next to Blythe and Selene who, by now, had registered my presence and was glaring at me with a pinched face that suggested my little end-of-the-world ruse had already been rumbled.

Following hard on Ellie Nosh came a young man, his wide eyes and generally twitchy demeanour suggesting he had – rather than being awakened from slumber by Benny C's exhortations – already been awake and somewhat over-stimulated. His toned hairless upper body was glistening with sweat as he charged into the room wearing only boxer briefs into the room. A long, capsule shaped silver locket hung from a silver chain around his neck. He was followed closely behind by two similarly under dressed young men, one of whom had been in such a hurry to escape impending immolation at the hands of the residents of Southwark that he'd shoved his Calvin's on back to front and was now trying to simultaneously flee for his life and adjust his balls so they didn't slip out the leg of his pants.

Oleg Stepanov – for I assumed it was he – stopped dead inside the room, ran a shaking hand through his dishevelled hair, and stared around, before snapping a hand behind him and receiving, from the ill-panted young man a slate grey pashmina which he immediately wrapped around his torso before collapsing into the second row of the cinema seats.

His correctly-panted companion strolled confidently to

the back of the room, and returned moments later clutching two bottles of Stoli, three glasses, and a bag of ice. The trio sat and stared at me, eyes like saucers bodies almost visibly vibrating.

A few moments passed before Pierre Foucault, resplendent in a pair of silk pyjamas that fit him better than any suit I'd ever owned had ever fit me, strolled nonchalantly into the room, what looked like a leather-bound kindle in one hand, and insouciantly seated himself at a small round table before helping himself to a cocktail and a bowl of spiced titbits from the tray that Dash was, by now, walking around with.

Andy Von Oldenwald, still wearing the soot-streaked jeans and shirt he'd been wearing when I'd last seen him, staggered next into the room, his head swivelling as he tried to identify the other people, his ashen pallor and general air of disorientation lending a tragic air as he collapsed, wordlessly, into one of the leather cinema chairs, waving away Dash's proffered tray of delicacies.

A moment or two passed, and finally Roy Bell arrived, ushering the clearly confused Mrs Makhtoum, her person still fully enclosed in the black burkah, her low voice asking Roy what the problem was as he ushered her to the back of the room and sat her, alone, at one of the lounge tables before he returned to the front and pressed a button, triggering the low hum of the servo motors that made the door slowly, solidly swing into place, a low hush a popping of the ears and the sudden silencing of Benedict Cumberbatch's soothing instructions on how best to avoid spending the approaching holocaust in the company of poor people confirming that the mechanism had completed the process of locking the door.

I coughed. "Hello all," I said, wincing as the sensitive microphones above the space I was standing kicked in, picked up my voice and – with only a modicum of feedback screech – amplified my voice, instantly silencing the room.

"Thank you for coming," I said, smiling in what I hoped

was a welcoming way.

"What the fuck," Evan Blythe loudly repeated, "Is going on here?"

"Is there an emergency or isn't there?" Selene Aksoy demanded imperiously as Oleg Stepanov glanced over both shoulders, removed the silver locket from his neck, twisted the top and attempted to surreptitiously drizzle a small mound of white powder onto the back of his hand before realising he was shaking too much to do anything much in secret and resorting to licking the drug from his knuckles.

How the other half live.

"I'm sorry to gather you here in such an alarming fashion, I said, moderating the volume of my voice so that there was less feedback, and the room slowly turned its attention towards me, only the sound of Steve Haines topping up the three glasses of Johnny Black breaking the total silence.

"Wha's goin' on?" Oleg Stepanov demanded, managing to slur every word of a sentence containing only one sibilant.

"Ssssh," his poorly-panted boytoy ordered him, staring at me in a way that suggested he didn't have a clue what was going on, but that he was loving being in the middle of whatever it was.

"Anyone want a pork pie?" La Nosh enquired, flipping open the wicker hamper and offering a selection of mini pies to the assembled.

After a moment of no takers, she shrugged, helped herself to a delicacy, replacing the rest into the basket, nibbled the pastry, sipped her Negroni and looked at me with a smile on her face.

"Eh Bien," Foucault glanced up from his Kindle. "If this is – how is it said – a fire drill? Then when can we go back to bed."

"When we're done here!" Reid said, with only the merest hint of threat in his voice, and a sudden stunned silence fell on the crowd.

I guessed none of the residents were used to being told they couldn't have what they wanted instantly.

It must have been a novel experience for some of them.

"A few days ago," I said, some of the attention in the room still fixed on the smouldering Detective Inspector in the corner, "A woman fell to her death from a balcony in a building not far from here."

Some of the attention drifted back to me.

"She'd been – amongst other things - a cleaner in this building, and her death is directly linked, amongst others, to the death that occurred here today."

That pulled the rest of them back to me.

"And her murderer," I said, glancing at Caz, "Is in this room."

My best friend raised both eyebrows as though to suggest I'd overegged the pudding, and was confirmed in this belief by Joanna Trztrzelewska, who laughed, and said "Well we didn't think you'd dragged us out of our beds for the open bar, darling. Only I'm on shift in a few hours, so like them two in the front, if we could get to the point and get that fucking door open, it'd be much appreciated."

"Mrs Byrne was here, the day she died, cleaning the flats she usually cleaned, and when she died, she had my name – or what looked like my name – written on the back of her hand, and that's how I got involved in this situation."

"Quiche Lorraine?" Ellie Nosh lifted a plate of perfectly reproduced miniature savoury flans from her picnic and offered them round. Several takers leaned in, including one of Oleg's party mates who took one bite, chewed, swallowed noisily and – his jaws still gurning despite the absence of solids – clearly decided that food was not what he was craving, and deposited the tart on the floor beneath his seat.

I looked around me in bemusement. Nero Wolfe never had to put up with this shit. He'd have had a mixed bunch of suspects around his apartment, waffled a bit about orchids, and had them hanging on his every word. Here, I was being outshone by a selection of pork-based savouries.

Then I recollected the dead pig Ellie had been hauling from the fridge the day we met and figured – if she'd butchered the beast down to this basket of goodies – she was due her moment.

"Except," I said, raising my voice, "It wasn't my name. It wasn't a name at all. You see, Cathy Byrne had a problem with numbers – a sort of number dyslexia that made it hard for her to recall all but the most familiar of numbers.

"And that day, she was planning on cleaning a flat she didn't clean every day. One that was never occupied, because it was owned by a Singaporean businessman who hasn't set foot in the country since he bought the thing."

It was the telephone on the desk in Southwark nick that had done it, each key on the pad displaying a number and three letters. Something had drawn my eyes to the 'D', the 'A' and the 'N.'

Now, I had some interest, though I noticed that the Tupperware of quiches was still making the rounds, and even Reid was chewing slowly while eyeballing me in a way that suggested he was beginning to wonder why he'd agreed to this crazy scenario.

"Look at the keypad on your phones. Same as the keypads on the alarm systems here in The Sugar House. They have numbers, and each one also has a selection of letters – 1 equals blank, 2 is 'ABC,' 3 is 'DEF' and so on, right up to number 9 with 'WXYZ' on it. And what was written on Cathy Byrne's hand – DANNYB – wasn't, despite the presence of my name and number in her phone, a reference to me," I paused, conscious now that I had the room.

Caz, in the front row, topped up her glass of Veuve and nodded approvingly.

"It was the numbers 326692, transliterated to a phrase she could read and punch in. She didn't need codes for all the other flats – she cleaned them regularly and had the numbers off by heart. But for one she rarely did, she wrote a mnemonic on her hand. It was the code for apartment 4B," I said, "For the flat owned by a Mr Soong."

"Who isn't here," Evan Blythe snapped, looking around the room. "So, if you're accusing him of the crimes you mentioned, why have you locked us in this bloody room?"

Beside him, Selene shot me the evils, and pulled her dressing gown tighter across her chest.

I smiled. "Mr Soong is a completely innocent party here," I said. "He had nothing to do with Cathy Byrne's murder, except insofar as his complete absence enabled the true killer to execute and then hide a crime which they thought they'd be able to hide over the Christmas period.

"Only then two things happened: Firstly, Louise Byrne attacked your car, Mr Blythe," I nodded at Blythe, who fumed back in response.

"I'm guessing you," I smiled at Selene Aksoy, "Were the lady in the car with Mr Blythe when he lost control and totalled a few other cars on the street, resulting in the police being placed outside."

"Waste of manpower." Reid growled, and Blythe turned in his seat, the movement giving me a more detailed view of his undercarriage than I'd ever wanted to have.

"Detective Inspector," Blythe responded in full better-than-you mode, "When a senior local politician is assaulted outside their front door, police protection is the least – the absolute least – that should be expected. You should, frankly," he finished, dismissing Reid, "Have rounded up the woman."

"Rounded her up?" Callum Byrne stood up. "That's my sister you're talking about, you know; not some fucking animal."

"Well her later actions would suggest otherwise," Blythe snapped back as Selene implored him not to, as she put it, 'feed the trolls'.

"You ruined her fucking life," Callum, still standing, shouted at the back of Blythe's head.

Blythe, without even deigning to turn his head, said simply and clearly "I fuel the machine, buddy, I don't decide where it goes or which dandelions it beheads."

"Dandelions?" Callum lunged, and only the speedy action of Steve Haines hauled him back into his seat before he could do serious damage to Blythe.

"Louise's attack," I said, pressing on, "Filled the streets outside with police, and caused our killer a problem. Because you see, the killer had been working for a long time on a carefully constructed plan to steal, from a certain city institution a considerable amount of money, to apportion the blame for the theft on an innocent man, and to ensure the blame stuck by making sure the accused man vanished."

"So, it was Von Oldenwald?" Reid – who'd either clearly forgotten what we'd discussed in his station some hours previously or was so far into his role as bystander at the denouement that he felt it his duty to shout out obvious nonsense when it seemed apropos.

"Ignore him, Mr Bird," Caz, a combination of exhaustion, post-traumatic stress and half a magnum of vintage Veuve, called out. "You're doing splendidly. Top-up, sweetie?"

I glanced at the glass I'd forgotten was in my hand, the wine now flat and warm, and lowered it to the floor.

"All of this was about timing: The crime – using the bank's own systems to rob several hundred million – had to happen over the Christmas weekend, when there were few people around to spot the theft; and the scapegoat had to be killed at the same time and disposed of straight away. A spot – a building site not far from here – had already been identified, and – if all had gone to plan – Vince Armstrong would have lain there unnoticed till well into the new year and – possibly - beyond, the killer having long since made their escape.

"The first stage – the robbery – went off without a hitch," I continued, pausing a moment in case Ellie wished to drag a croquembouche out of her handbag, and – when no sign of further food-based interruptions appeared – carrying on with my explanation.

"And the second stage – luring the unsuspecting scapegoat to his death – also appears to have proceeded without any issues. But then the police ended up outside."

"Yeah, we got that," Eddie James barked, and Caz

shrugged as though to say 'he has a point.'

"Okay," I sighed, "So our killer has a body which they've stashed in a place they think will be safe – let's say apartment 4B, where Mr Soong never visits. They've got in to that apartment by accessing the keys that Roy keeps behind the desk. Meant for emergencies, and this, for our killer, was an emergency. They wait for Roy to need a crafty fag, offer to watch the desk, then swipe 4B and put a dummy in its place, and – even though their plans to dispose of the body have been interrupted - it's salvageable. The body can sit there a day or so longer. Except then the cleaner arrives, and Cathy Byrne mentions, in passing, that she needs to get a move on 'cos she wants to 'do' 4B.

"Perfectly understandable," I looked around the room. Everyone, including the gurning trio in the cinema seats, were fixed on me.

"Cos Cathy Byrne was a conscientious sort, but, more than that, a chatty sort. And she did exactly just that: She spent time in one of the flats talking to one of her ladies and told them that she was going to clean 4B."

"No," Ellie Nosh bolted upright, her outrage the same I imagine she'd have used if someone had suggested her quiches were made of shop-bought shortcrust.

"Not you," I said flatly and her fury dissipated like a cold soufflé.

"Oh," she sighed, dropping back into her seat and returning to her preferred mode of dealing with emotional difficulty: "Profiterole, anyone?"

I waited while half the room helped themselves to a fistful of choux pastry, then added "But it would have helped if you'd told me up front what you had going on with Cathy."

"Going on?" La Nosh paused, a profiterole halfway to her lips.

"Ellie, your problems last year didn't just damage your public image, did they?"

The profiterole went in, and – unable to speak – Ellie merely shrugged as if to say 'I have no idea what you're quacking on about.'

"Your latest book was so short on recipes the publisher was forced to pad it out with photos of suggestive muffins and a series of recipes for omelettes," I prompted, and – still getting nothing back – I sighed. "Ellie, you had writers block."

"You couldn't come up with new recipes. You could have used a ghost writer – there are lots of people who'll do you two thousand words on ceviche for fifty quid – but your pride got in the way. You weren't about to go public in admitting the well was dry.

"Then you realised that your cleaner was a whiz at the sort of cooking – comforting home style food – that made your name in the first place, and you figured that having her as a ghost – an arrangement between the two of you alone, with nobody else needing to know – could be mutually beneficial for you. We found the money," I said finally, referring to the cash we'd discovered in Cathy's handbag.

Ellie's shoulders slumped. "It wasn't just a business thing," she said sadly, "and not a case of me robbing her ideas. She was more of a muse, suggesting things I could try, asking if I'd ever cooked, say, chicken this way, or tried bacon that way."

"And you paid her for her trouble?"

"No," Ellie shook her head. "She was going to get credit. It would be a co-write and she'd get an advance from the publishers and some royalties. We've already pitched the book to my agent, and it's going to auction next week. It's going to be called 'Pork.'

"Only on that last day she said she needed money. Her son was in trouble and needed cash fast."

I glanced at Callum, who sat with his head in his hands.

"So, I paid her what I had and she said she'd come back later, work with me on the book, and I was going to get some more cash for her."

"Only she never came back. But I swear," Ellie said, "I had nothing to do with her death. Cathy was one of the few friends I had left. Jesus," she sighed, shaking her head, "she was genuinely one of the only friends I had left."

"I know you had nothing to do with Cathy's death," I said. "Cos you had nothing to do with the Fenchurch-Brookes robbery.

"So, Vince Armstrong is dead," I continued, looking around the room. "Cathy Byrne is about to walk in on his body, and the killer manages to delay her so that she can't clean 4B that day. But she goes away promising to come back and clean the flat the next day.

"And our killer knows that she will. Because, like I said: As anyone who ever met her knew, Cathy Byrne was a woman of her word. She was described to me as a Terminator. So, what, if you've got millions of pounds in stolen money whisking its way around the world and a dead body that's going to be discovered by your cleaner the next day, do you do?

"Well, logically, you'd get rid of the body that night, but remember: There's a virtual police cordon around the building. So, what else can you do?" I looked around the room, all eyes on me.

"Remember: The only person likely to enter 4B before the police go away, enabling you to get back on track with your plan to dispose of Vince Armstrong's body is a woman who's been described as 'The Terminator of cleaners.' So, you have one choice: Stop her coming back to 4B."

I focussed my eyes on the killer. "You could have gone round and asked her to take a break; offered her a bribe. But I suppose one murder made the second easier. So, you went round to where she lived – you followed her and were there minutes after she got home. I bet she was really keen to hear what had brought you to her flat. What did you promise? Off the books work? Something more glamorous?"

The object of my intense stare shook its head slightly.

"You started helping her to dismantle her Christmas tree. It wasn't twelfth night yet, but for someone like Cathy, Christmas was over once the turkey carcass went in the bin.

There was no time to luxuriate in some over extended 'holidays.'

"So, you watched as she took the mother of pearl baubles off her tree. Maybe you helped her unwind the lights and coil them back up in the box."

Steve Haines was crying silently, Joanna Trztrzelewski's arm around him, Callum Byrne staring at the table, unmoving, and the rest of the room seemed to have leant in.

"And then what? You suggested a crafty fag? She made tea, probably. 'Cos that's the sort of woman she was. Visitor in the house: Put the kettle on. And you went out on the balcony. She was proud of her view. Loved, even in winter on a cold clear night when the city was sparkling below her – especially then – to show it off.

"And that's when you killed her. That's when you pitched her head first over the edge.

"Then you came back here and rolled up Vince Armstrong in the rug that had been stretched out in front of Mr Soong's rarely used, but wonderfully expensive sofa," I said, remembering the empty space I'd noted, along with the smell of bleach – a bleach which neither of the cleaners ever used in The Sugar House.

"I'm no expert on carpets, but I've spent enough time around drag queens to know a quality weave when I see and feel one, and the rug that Vince Armstrong was discarded in was an expensive piece. But you still couldn't get rid of him yet. There were still police around. So, you bundled him into the walk-in freezer, which, when I waved a duster round 4B two days ago, was humming quietly despite the fact that it shouldn't have needed to be on in a flat the owner never visited. It meant, when the body was discovered a couple of days later it wasn't immediately obvious that it had been dead longer than Cathy Byrne."

Von Oldenwald, his face pale, stood. "Which of them did it?" He demanded. "Which of you bastards killed Rachel?"

"We're getting there," I said, "but for now our killer has a body to dispose of, and just as soon as the police were gone, we," I gestured at Caz, "Turned up. And they made a mistake. They rushed the job, not realising that they'd been seen by a young woman who'd developed a fixation on this place and had taken to standing out front watching the comings and goings of the people who lived here."

"Louise," Callum Byrne said, straightening his head, a look in his eyes that suggested he was a couple of steps ahead of some of the people in the room.

I nodded. Louise, who had been ignored and waved away by so many people in authority; who'd been told that the corruption and dissolution of her neighbourhood was not – despite the evidence of her own eyes – a concerted attempt to make the area more easily developed, to make the cleansing of the area more palatable. Louise, who had been told her boyfriend's death was just one of those things that happen to Junkies. Who'd lost her job when she'd proven, beyond any reasonable doubt, that there were powerful people prepared to do disgusting things to help Constable construction make millions in her neighbourhood.

"Louise who told me that, after her career and reputation had been destroyed, there'd be no point in her ever running to the police again, because nobody would believe her. So, she followed you," I said, talking once again directly to the person who had murdered Louise Byrne, "and saw what you were doing

"So once again you had a problem. And once again, your solution was murder. And this time, Rachel, you knew exactly how to use this new inconvenient body to your advantage."

"Rachel?" Von Oldenwald shook his head, a look of absolute confusion plastered on his face.

"You never were the brightest one, were you Andy?"

At the back of the room, Mrs Makhtoum, her Burkah still obscuring her shape and features, stood, a hand pulling at the head covering.

Von Oldenwald turned silver, as though he'd just seen – or heard – a ghost.

Which, in a way, he had.

The woman at the back of the room finally ripped off the head covering, and Rachel Fiennes's shiny blonde bob shone in the gentle halogen lights.

"How'd you know how to blow the car up?" I asked, and she shrugged as though I'd asked an obvious question.

"My dad was in the army. Ordnance. I grew up around explosives. Then I studied engineering and chemistry. Firsts in both. And then I ended up becoming Andy Von Oldenwald's assistant and nanny."

"Rachel?" Von Oldenwald stood unsteadily to his feet, the rest of the room – seemingly shocked into stillness – watching the scene wide-eyed.

"Yeah, Andy; that's my name. Not babe. Not hun."

"Why?" Von Oldenwald choked out, and Rachel laughed bitterly.

"Why? Are you fucking serious?" She stepped away from her small table, made her way to the top of the row of chairs Von Oldenwald was now standing in, and stared directly at him. "I was the best student in my year. I had the world in front of me. And you hired me, treated me like a fucking P.A. and then shagged me."

"I loved you," he croaked.

Rachel's bitter laugh was louder this time, as though Von Oldenwald's suggestion he'd loved her was the diarrhoea frosting on a shit cake she'd been fuming about for years. "Well, for the record," she spat, "I didn't love you. Oh, I thought I did. But then you made sure the rest of the desk knew you'd tapped the new blonde. Revelled in it, from what I heard later, so that all it took was for one of them – one of the boys I'd probably already turned down cos I wasn't going to mix business with personal – to pop along to HR, and the shit kicked off.

"And what did you do, Andy?" She waited in silence.

The silence stretched as Von Oldenwald, his face still a mask of horror stared back at her, his jaw working, but no words coming.

"You threw me to the wolves, Andy!" Rachel said, her voice firm but the volume loud enough for the room to hear. "You threw me to the fucking wolves. One of us had to go, and it couldn't – couldn't possibly – be you.

"So, you let them bin me. You let them convince me that it was a downsizing, that I was being made redundant 'cos they – like you – were too fucking cowardly to say it to my face. And then months later – months, Andy – you'd hired Vince Armstrong. A council kid this time: as disposable as a blonde female, but less likely to end up jumping in the sack with you.

"You let them stitch me up. You let your colleagues make it known round the market that I wasn't that good, that I'd been gotten rid of. And all the time, you knew that what was being done to me was a clear out so they could avoid any scandal or complaints from the rest of the boys on the desk. Cos you were all so fucking selfish and greedy and lazy and stupid."

"So lazy and stupid," I said quietly, "That they forgot to cancel your system access."

This made Rachel smile. "They gave you a laptop. 'Work from home. Spend some time with the little lady.' Bet they said something like that, didn't they Andy?"

Von Oldenwald, beginning to realise where this was going, nodded, even the silver draining from his face.

"And that's when it hit me. I'd spent a year slowly, carefully, joyfully cultivating this fury, this hatred. You ruined my fucking life, and I was – what? – supposed to be happy that I was getting to be your trophy blonde? Gym. Pilates. Shopping. Gym. Pilates. Dinner at some new restaurant so you could show me off. Till what? You got tired of me? Then what?"

Reid moved away from the wall, and – as subtly as I could – I indicated that he should stay where he was. The room – including Rachel – seemed to be under some sort of spell, and I didn't want it broken.

"I only went on once for a laugh," she said, "To see if my

password would work, if I could get in. And I could. And then I checked your emails – you hadn't even taken that permission off my profile – and I found them. 'We dodged a bullet.' That was from you to the board three days after you let them swindle me out of my career. And in return one of them – one of those chinless dickless brainless motherfuckers – had the audacity to call me a 'Blonde Bimbo,' and tell you to be more careful in future with your choice of 'Assistants and playmates.'

"And that's when I made my mind up."

The room was silent.

"You crazy fucking bitch," Von Oldenwald, frozen to the spot, snarled.

"The cleaner-"

"Her name was Cathy," I interrupted, and Rachel dropped her eyes, was silent a moment.

"Yes," she said at length, turning to look at me. "I'm sorry. Cathy was-" she paused, unable to come up with the words, then settled for "the worst mistake of my life, if you discount falling for this piece of shit."

I wasn't buying it. "This piece of shit didn't make you push Cathy Byrne off a fourth-floor balcony. Just like he didn't make you kill her daughter."

"I didn't," she held a hand out to me. "I didn't kill Louise. It was an accident. I swear. She had a bike, followed me to the site and watched me ditching Armstrong's body. Then she followed me in and caught me in the garage here. She must have ducked under the barrier.

"She attacked me. We fought, and she fell. And then, like you say, I saw my way out."

"Bullshit," I stared coldly at her.

"It's true," she said. "I swear."

"Why lie, Rachel? You've already admitted to murders: Cathy and Vince Armstrong. And you might have regretted Cathy, but you didn't regret Vince."

"He took my job," she said through gritted teeth. "He laughed at me with them."

"He didn't even know you," I said. "He'd never met you before you lured him round to The Sugar House and killed him. And the CCTV upstairs has you moving Von Oldenwald's car to a blind spot earlier on the evening you ditched the body so you wouldn't be picked up loading him into the boot. Only, when you came back, you parked in the same spot, and the cameras didn't pick up anyone following you, because Louise Byrne was already dead.

"She followed you and tried to phone me once she'd seen what you were doing. She was whispering when she left the message, and I'm guessing that's cos you were still around and she didn't want to be discovered.

"Only either her voice or the light from her phone drew your attention, and once you knew you'd been spotted, you did what you'd already done once before. Don't-" it was my turn now to hold a hand up to her.

"You didn't need to kill Vince Armstrong. You didn't need to push Cathy Byrne over that balcony, and you didn't have to kill Louise Byrne. But you did. And trying to pretend that Louise ran at you or that she was crazy is bullshit.

"She was as sane as me. And you killed her to shut her up, then realised you had a way to vanish, knowing it'd take forensics time to realise that the body in the car had already been dead when the explosion occurred. And even if they did, the chances they'd realise that the body in the car wasn't you – especially after you'd made such a good job of letting Caz and me know that you were afraid of Andy – were slim.

"Oh, they would have worked it out eventually, cos someone would have been looking for Louise, but we all know that some missing people," I looked at Lindsey Wright, "Are less likely to be found than others. And you maybe started this whole thing in anger, but by the time you had successfully made away with more money than you could ever have imagined, you'd moved on from anger to cold calculation.

"When you realised that the scapegoating of Vince Armstrong was only going to last so long, you started searching for another scapegoat," I glanced at Von Oldenwald. "Then Louise gave you an even better opportunity: Get all eyes looking at Andy, and there was a risk that they'd eventually stray to you. But if you were already dead – burned to a cinder in Von Oldenwald's Merc – then they'd never even see you. And so, again, you made a choice."

Rachel, as Reid made his way towards her, turned to Andy Von Oldenwald. "I hope you're happy," she spat, still refusing to even acknowledge her own culpability for three deaths. "This is all your fault."

CHAPTER FORTY

"And since we mentioned missing persons," I said, "we should probably talk about what happened to George Osman."

Lindsey tore her eyes away from Rachel, who had now been taken by the arm and lead, by Reid, to a seat off to the side.

"Have you found him?" She asked, almost leaping from her seat, hope flaring up in her eyes.

I didn't want to do what I was about to do, but there was no other way for it. She had a right to know.

So, I told her.

"No." I answered. "Cos Lindsey, George Osman never existed."

"No!" Her eyes blazed desperately. "Not you too. You saw his clothes. You can see his child, for Christ's sake," she pulled the boy towards her, wrapping him in her arms and staring at me as though I were her last hope sailing away to a job on an oil rig never to return.

"It's true, Lindsey. Oh, there was a man, and he lived with you from time to time, and he fathered your child, and he told you his name was George Osman, but George Osman never existed, because George Osman was – until his recent death – a name that had been adopted by a businessman called Mehmet Aksoy."

Selene, who's head had been dipping as though sleep were encroaching, suddenly jerked awake.

"What did you say?" she demanded imperiously, the dog - suddenly alerted to the change in his mistress's emotional state - growling and yapping furiously.

"You heard," I said as she quieted the terrier, dug around in the pockets of her dressing gown and, at length, found a snack she fed to it. "Mehmet. George. One and the same. Mehmet Aksoy, by all accounts, had never really bought in to the business of accumulation and consumption, of consolidation and enrichment like his wife Selene had. He liked the old days when he got his hands dirty, did things, made things happen as opposed to just ordering people to do stuff. So, when the contracts to fit out this development ended up going to his company, he worked on site for a few weeks, getting his hands dirty, and meeting, in the café where he had his breakfast every morning, a young waitress that he fell for."

Lindsey dropped back into her chair and stared at the back of the woman seated a few feet from her; a woman whose wealth and privilege were clear from the way she held herself, even if not on full display in a bathrobe and slippers.

"My husband," Selene Aksoy responded, in the same tones I imagine a Cobra would respond to a mildly annoying ferret who has delusions to being a mongoose, "was not in the habit of doing manual labour."

"But you told me yourself that he was, Selene."

"That's Mrs Aksoy to you," she snapped, her nostrils flaring angrily as Pu Yi growled and bared his teeth at me.

I shrugged; if the widow Aksoy was getting rattled, then it worked in my favour. "You told me he wasn't always comfortable helicoptering above it all; that he liked to get his hands dirty, to do some real work. And I think Mehmet was doing some work here – on The Sugar House – working as a plumber when he met Lindsey Wright."

"You're sailing very close to the wind, boy," Selene said.

"And then something happened," I added, as Lindsey pulled her son closer, her gaze never leaving the back of Selene's head.

"Lindsey got pregnant, and I think that was when Mehmet – who'd never given her his real name, never told her of his other life, made a decision. He'd wanted kids his whole life, and here he was being offered a woman he loved, a child of his own, and the possibility to, maybe, press restart. And he started to see this as a chance to change his path.

"He helped Lindsey to buy her flat, and started spending more time with her, having created this fictitious job 'on the rigs' to explain why he couldn't spend all his time with her."

"Of course, he was helped in his deception by the fact that, by this stage, you had already embarked on your affair with Mr Blythe here."

"Watch your mouth," Blythe barked, seemingly unaware that any denial of the status of his relationship with Selene Aksoy was rather cancelled out by the fact she was wearing his dressing gown having come from his bed at two in the morning.

"When did you start the affair?" I asked Selene, turning – when she did nothing more than stare coldly at me – my question to Blythe. "Was it when your investment bank worked on the merger of Asimov Auto Tech and the General Auto Company? You told me you'd worked on that, Selene, and an award proudly displayed in Mister Blythe's luxury apartment upstairs confirms him as one of the team who ran the book on behalf of the Investment Bank he worked for back then.

"Or was it later, after you'd moved into local politics and when Constable Construction, via a vast network of sub accounts, shell companies, and subsidiaries managed by a legal firm which has Selene Aksoy as a principal partner, purchased your help, along with that of a number of, shall we say less socially acceptable elements, in destroying neighbourhoods they wanted to take control of?"

"That's Libellous!" Blythe roared, only the light touch of Selene Aksoy's hand on his arm preventing him from jumping out of his seat.

"Libellous is written defamation, Evan," I tutted back at

him. "If it's spoken it's, at best, slanderous. But only if it's untrue, which, in this case, it's not."

"You," Selene stated coldly, her eyes glittering furiously, "will be hearing from my lawyer."

And she glanced at Dot Frost, who had the good grace to blush, a blush that deepened as my eyes found and held hers.

She knew, now, that I knew.

Oh, it had taken me a while; all that business with the envelope "In case of my death," filled with gibberish. But enough gibberish to get me interested, to have me look into Mehmet's death.

Because I doubt that Dot knew the full story, but she'd known enough to worry; enough to have doubts, and enough to know that, with so little evidence, there was little she could do about it.

So, she'd set me on to it, without telling me what she feared.

The envelope hadn't been delivered to her by Mehmet Aksoy. Dot Frost had taken a plain envelope, filled it with random news clippings from the local newspaper, and, instead of telling me plainly that she had doubts, Dot had used me; let me poke around, knowing if I found nothing, she could wave it all away as, obviously, some weird Mehmet joke.

Only I hadn't found nothing.

"You're going to need that lawyer, Selene. Because I think Mehmet realised what was going on. He never would have, if he hadn't been spending time in Henley Court, seeing the slow degradation of the building, the community; seeing anti-social elements - drug dealers, loan sharks - suddenly piling into the neighbourhood with little response from local law enforcement." I glanced, this time, at Reid, who had the good grace to blush himself.

"I think he might have gone to one of Cathy's 'Save The Races' meetings and heard the stories of other parts of the borough being slowly destroyed, as though there was a plan, a deliberate strategy to drive out the current residents so the whole place could be cleared for billions of pounds worth of development.

"Well," I shrugged, "for Cathy and Louise Byrne, all of this was unprovable, theoretical, bordering on conspiracy theory. The ranting of women who were crazed, and not really able to accept that progress will march on. But for Mehmet Aksoy, living now as George Osman and happier than he'd been in years; for a man who had seen you working on Constable's development plans, a man who knew that you were working closely with an old friend who was in local politics round here, it slowly but surely became something more than unprovable.

"My guess is he still didn't know what to do at that stage, because confronting you, Selene, would have meant disclosing his new life, and risking your full wrath, but saying nothing would have simply allowed you to destroy a place and a life he'd come to love. So, he started to compile a dossier, to prove that Constable and you two were corrupt and lawless, and then – again, I can't know how or when - you found out about it, realised he was up to something, and decided that you could no longer tolerate a husband who had become a danger to your plans."

"Fanciful nonsense," Selene sneered.

"You can't prove a word of this horseshit," Blythe curled his lip.

I shrugged. "You're right," I admitted eventually. "But George could."

"George," Selene Aksoy said as though speaking to a developmentally challenged four-year-old, "didn't exist."

"Well whether her existed or not," I flourished the sheaf of papers that Ray had handed me earlier, "he had a computer and a printer in the apartment he shared with his woman and his child. And on that computer, he kept various files. My guess is you didn't know he was actually living with Lindsey when you decided to kill him, cos if you had, I'm fairly sure you'd have gone looking for this little treasure trove."

Selene's face froze, the oxygen suddenly leaving the room.

Pu Yi, the long-haired Shih Tzu whined, and, as though finally fed up of his neediness, she shoved him off her lap and onto the floor.

"I can tell you don't have much," she said, her clipped annunciation sliding a little so that the 'h' in 'have' was dropped, "but I promise you, by the time I'm done with you, you won't have a pot to piss in or a window to throw it out of. Boy."

"Which bit's outraged you more, Selene? The fact that I can prove you and Evan are as rotten as a bag of month old bananas? Or the accusation of murder?"

"Murder?" Blythe hauled himself from his seat. "Now you listen here, you gibbering fruit," he said, his well-practiced noblesse oblige evaporating quickly, "You have no proof of any wrongdoing. That," he gestured at the paperwork in my hand" is the ramblings of someone off his meds, and as for murder? You've got nothing," he snarled.

"Sure?" I asked, taunting him. "Only this," I waved the printouts, "Is pretty lucid stuff. And pretty damning. It details names and dates and sums of money paid to seemingly unconnected third parties to create havoc in Henley Court; it shows fairly clearly that Constable and its agents had moved on from property development and were funding facilitating and in at least one case actively directing drug gangs, loan sharks and some people nasty enough to make the first two types look like minor irritants. It's all here, Evan, in Black and White. And, occasionally, in full colour."

"Bullshit," he persisted. "Constable construction is a billion-dollar company. I'm a respectable member of this community. People fucking voted for me, you stupid poof. You think I'd throw that away to curry favour with a bloody builder?"

I flicked through the print-outs. "No," I said, seemingly flustered, "of course you wouldn't."

He smirked at me, sat back in his seat, threw an arm around Selene and joined her in looking daggers at me.

"You're fucking finished," he spat. "By the time we're done with you."

"You'd never throw away the trust of the electorate and put yourself in a position to be hit with corruption bribery money laundering and drug charges just to curry favour with – what was it? – a bloody builder. But you might do it for twelve million pounds, broken down between a nine hundred-thousand-pound car, a four-million-pound apartment upstairs, a five-million-dollar apartment in Miami, and the rest in cash and securities in," I paused, running my finger down the list, "twelve bank accounts scattered across the Caribbean."

The silence that followed was monumental, and broken eventually, by the Ellie Nosh's round and bass-deep belly laugh. "Well that's you two fucked loves. Sure you won't have a profiterole? Breadstick?"

"You can shove your fucking breadsticks up your arse, you horrible sweaty tart," Selene shrieked. "And you," she pointed a trembling finger at me, "can't touch me for that shit. My name's nowhere near any of Evan's personal financial dealings."

"You what?" Evan turned on her, his face as he realised he was being thrown under the bus, a picture of murderous outrage. "Listen, Selene, you wanna watch what you say about me. If you get my drift."

She clearly did. Selene stood, clambered over him, managing to kick him squarely in the gonads, generating a squawk of pain that even I found satisfying, before she staggered towards the door and commenced hammering on it.

"Get me out of here!" She shrieked. "Open this fucking door!"

Pu Yi, clearly wondering what fresh insanity this was, ran, tail wagging and high-pitched barks coming from him towards his mistress, who turned as he yelped and snapped at the hem of her dressing gown, screamed, "Fuck off dog," and kicked him so hard he shot, screaming, to the back of the room.

Reid half rose from his seat, threw a questioning glance at me, and I nodded reassuringly.

"On the subject of tarts," Ellie said, dipping back into the picnic hamper and extracting the final Tupperware box, "mini Bakewell?"

"Oooh," Caz perked up, turning in her seat, "those are my favourites. Do we have time for a spot more fizz? Anybody," she asked loudly, "need a loo break before Mr Bird goes into Act three?"

I looked at her in alarm, and – as she stood and headed towards the bar at the back of the room, Caz smiled, "Well I love a drama, sweetest, but I think the meal has been well made of this one." She glanced at Selene who was now facing the door, her shoulders heaving as she struggled to contain her fury.

Caz helped herself to another bottle of fizz and Ellie Nosh's various titbits were passed around as the rest of the assembled gathered closer, like some stone-aged tribe, eyes wide as their communal gaze switched between Rachel, her face an odd blank that suggested a part of her was still trying to work out the best way out of the mess she was in, at Selene, still facing the door and at Blythe, now bent double gripping his crotch and moaning in agony.

At the back of the room, Dot Frost muttered something to Postlethwaite, who glanced my way and nodded.

Pierre Foucault sidled into Ellie's row, and slid a few seats until she noticed him, and, lifting her hamper up, placed it squarely on the seat next to her, preventing him getting too close.

"In your dreams," she said loudly as the permanently priapic author slumped in his seat.

"What did you mean, Evan?" I asked, when Caz had settled herself with the rest of the gang, the champagne had been passed around, and Nick had firmly lead Selene back to a seat next to Blythe.

His head raised when I spoke his name, and he looked at

me through bleary eyes. “Mean?” He asked. “By what?”

Handing the bottle of champagne to Joanna Trztrzelewska, Caz reached down and scooped up Pu Yi, snuggling the still whimpering dog into her lap.

“When you said that Selene had better watch what she said about you,” I answered flatly.

“Nothing,” he said, side-eyeing Selene, who tried once again to silence me with threats of legal beating.

“I’ve got an army of lawyers,” she announced, “who will tear to pieces anything you’ve got out of this clear entrapment. And you,” she pointed at Reid, “will be losing your job over this, I promise you.”

I glanced at Reid, who looked back at her with a face of supreme impassivity. “Can we get this over with,” he sighed, clearly bored, now, with the process.

“Scott Barton,” I said, and Blythe’s jaw twitched.

“See,” I addressed Selene, “When our mutual friend Mrs Frost over there brought that envelope of stuff to me, with the suggestion that Mehmet had clearly been aware of some threat to his life, I’d assumed the threat had something to do with the clippings in it. And that gave no suggestion that you had anything to do with his death, so I wasn’t looking for either a motive, or a method.

“And then, when a motive presented itself – when I realised that George was Mehmet, and that he hadn’t vanished, but had died, I started wondering if that – the fact that Mehmet had a second secret life – could have been a motive for you to murder him.

“And I moved from there to method. He drove his car off a cliff. The same type of car that you have, Evan. I’m guessing Selene couldn’t give you the one she was given without Mehmet asking questions, so she arranged for Constable to provide you with one instead.

“And those cars, whilst being the most expensive vehicles on the planet, are also capable, when laws change, of being self-driving. You found that out when Louise Byrne attacked you in the street outside here. Roy,” I glanced at the doorman, who held up a hand as though identifying himself to a bunch of strangers, even though almost everyone else in the room passed him twice a day, "Mentioned how you'd been panicked and switched the car to auto, smashing up another bunch of cars parked around you. All with what Louise described as a skinny posh bird sat next to you. I'm guessing that was you, Selene."

From Selene, no answer came.

I shrugged my disinterest in her hatred. "Must have been quite a shock for you both. Especially since, a few weeks earlier, you'd remotely disabled manual drive, taken control of the auto drive function and driven Mehmet's car – with Mehmet no doubt trying desperately to get out of the vehicle – over the cliff, before remotely erasing the system logs."

Selene laughed. "You're fucking insane," she laughed. "I can't even program the Sky box. And him," she gestured at Blythe, his hair sticking up at odd angles, his face still flushed from the ball-kicking she'd given him moments earlier – does he look like Steve fucking Jobs?"

She laughed again, as though the suggestion that they'd killed Mehmet in the way I'd described was the most ludicrous thing she'd ever heard.

"But you didn't do it yourselves," I said as her faded to dismissive sniggers. "Scott Barton did."

The sniggers stopped. "Never heard of him," she said.

"Really?" Only Scott Barton was one of the primary engineers on the Asimov right back at the beginning. Got ousted, when the company was unable to move from prototype to production. He left with a small pay-out and weeks later, you and your mates turned up with an offer from General Auto. A buyout offer that, had he still been in position at Asimov would have made Barton several million pounds."

"No," she shook her head. "Still never heard of him."

"He sued, Selene. Went all the way to the high court. Lost. General Auto had the right lawyers."

"Well there you go," she said. "Why would I have any

memory of some random loser who sued a client I once worked for? And what's he got to do with this anyway?"

"Three things," I answered. "Scott Barton built the software that powered the Asimov. If you wanted someone to write you a program that would allow you to hack into the onboard system and drive a car over a cliff, you couldn't really ask for someone more suitable, especially considering his clear antagonism towards the current owners of the company and their clients.

"Second, someone paid Mr Barton a sizeable amount two days before Mehmet's car went over the cliff, and another amount a day later; and the police can trace that payment to an account on the small and rather secretive island of Curacao, at which point the trail ends.

"Except these files of your husbands," I waved the printouts once again, "Show that the account in question is jointly owned by you and Mr Blythe."

"You stupid bitch," Blythe moaned, his head dropping back into his hands.

"Proves nothing," she said. "You can't pin Mehmet's murder on me. None of you can," she glared angrily around the room.

"You're right, of course," I admitted, hearing Lindsey Wright's sobbing increasing in intensity, "But we can pin Scott Barton's murder on you. Computer geek, murdered in his own home," I said, remembering how Nick had explained away the lack of focus on any real hunt for George Osman by referring to this very death, "Stabbed. By a killer who took the knife away."

"Stop fucking moaning, Evan," Selene snarled from between gritted teeth, before returning her fury to me. "No knife," she said, "No charge. Assuming the killer wore gloves."

"You did," I admitted, "And you know you did."

A triumphant light came on in her eyes and died as the impact of my next words registered with her.

"But Pu Yi didn't."

She looked around desperately for the dog, spotted it sitting on Caz's lap, and clapped. "Pu Yi," she ordered, "Come to mama."

The dog slowly and deliberately turned its back on her and licked Caz's chin.

"Dog's don't have fingerprints," Blythe said, confusion clear on his face.

"True," I said. "But they do have fur or – in the case of a Shih Tzu dog, hair. Shih Tzus are among the few breeds whose coat is made up of hair, like people, rather than fur, and although people often think of them as a non-shedding breed, that's not entirely true. You see, Shih Tzu's will shed their hair daily, just as people do.

"A lot of the time, it gets caught in the longer hair rather than strewn all over the place, but sometimes, especially when they're active – running to avoid, say, a struggle in someone's flat - the hairs fall off, and the police found dozens of hairs at Scott Barton's flat. And you know what can be gotten from hair? DNA. And its DNA that will prove those hairs – some of which were inside the stab wounds – came from little Pu Yi – who you bring everywhere.

"The game's up, Selene."

"He killed Mehmet," she screamed, pointing a finger at Blythe, who lunged towards her, tried to grab her by the throat and was wrestled away from her by Eddie James and Steve Haines.

"She murdered the tecchic," Blythe raged, "and I have the knife in my safe upstairs with her prints on it. Stupid bitch took her gloves off when she left his flat and handed me the thing with her bare hands."

"You were supposed to ditch that, you stupid bastard," Selene yelped, and Blythe smiled nastily.

"Call it an insurance policy. I mean let's be honest, Selene: Any man who trusts a bitch who helps him to murder her own husband is out of his mind."

"Fuck you, you devious cocksucker," Selene shrieked, kneeing him squarely, once again, in his balls as she was dragged away by Von Oldenwald and Foucault.

And that – as the remaining residents of both Henley Place and The Sugar House watched on in fascinated horror – was how they spilled their confessions, each of them ranting against the other, almost every word confirming the contents of Mehmet's dossier, and many of them adding to the details of their crimes, until Reid nodded to Nick, who lifted his airtime walkie-talkie to his lips, spoke a few words and, with a loud THUNK, the door of the panic room unlocked and the outside world, in the guise of a dozen uniformed coppers, flooded the room.

CHAPTER FORTY-ONE

"And after all that, Caz has ended up with a dog?" My mum put the mug in front of me and seated herself across from me at the kitchen table.

Behind her, a beef stew was bubbling away on the hob, the ticktickticking of the sauce almost drowning out the inane babble from the radio. Off to the left, the city - already beginning to twinkle as the twilight encroached slowly but unstoppably on the city below – was smudged and blurry behind the steam that had frosted her kitchen windows, and on the ledge stood the orchid she and my dad had argued about, it's brittle dry looking stalk boasting three vivid green shoots.

My mum had been right: This thing wasn't going to be easy to kill.

"Well she heard it was likely to be put down, and she's been wanting one for ages, so yeah," I shrugged, sipped the coffee – hot and bitter – and smiled, "Caz – as always – got what she wanted."

"I'll be honest," my mum said, drinking her coffee, and sliding a plate filled with leftover Christmas cake and chocolate biscuits towards me, "I'd have thought she'd go for the little one. What d'you call them? Shitters?"

I smiled, shaking my head in mock dismay. "You know exactly what they're called, mum. It's a shih tzu."

"I thought a shit zoo was one where there's no animals," she twinkled back, and I groaned theatrically.

This was my mum and me. Had been my whole life: pushing each other to see how cheeky or outrageous we could be, safe that nothing would hurt, nothing be misconstrued; bonding over outrageousness and bad jokes and slightly soft biscuits.

"So, she didn't take the handbag dog, then?" Mum smiled, sinking her teeth into a custard cream, pulling a face, muttering "stale," discarding it and settling instead for a slice of her Christmas cake.

"Well," I lifted a piece of the fruit cake, bit a chunk off, and savoured the molasses dark sweetness, "It became obvious shortly after Selene was dragged ranting from the room that Caz and Pu Yi were not, perhaps, made for each other."

"It bit her, didn't it?"

"Just a nip," I admitted, remembering Caz's reaction.

"Here," she'd said, shoving the dog into the arms of a bemused Pierre Foucault, "This thing has no manners and clearly thinks it's more attractive than it really is; you were made for each other," before loudly demanding if "Any of you attending bobbies have a tetanus kit in your little bags," and tottering off, magnum in hand.

"So, where'd she get the dog then?"

"Well she'd seen it already and taken a shine to it, so she called up Inspector Reid next day; those two seem to be getting on disturbingly well."

"Considering she as good as dismissed the entire met police as a gang of amateurs," my mum observed dryly.

"Well, yes," I acknowledged. "Anyway, she asked about the dog, and he said that both of them would likely be put down. And, well you know Caz; she wasn't having that."

"So, she's got a Staffie."

"Yes," I said, smiling at the thought of Caz and the dog that I'd last seen attempting to savage King Solomon.

"Solomon called it Duke," I said, but Caz wanted something to mark a new start, so she renamed it Duke Ellington – Ellington for short. Only Duke Ellington, it turns out, is a duchess. So now Caz is bonding like a mum with her new baby Ellie."

I smiled fondly at the thought of Caz and Ellie co-existing in her small and eternally untidy flat, and knowing that my friend, who has the kindest heart I've ever known encased in that carapace of world-weary cynicism and raging alcoholism, would make it work.

"And it's one of them dogs that that fella had been using to threaten people," my mum asked, smiling incredulously.

I nodded. "King Solomon, as he called himself. Yup. Caz took one, and persuaded Reid to take the other."

"Persuaded?"

"I'm not sure she could have bullied him, but he's now the proud parent of the other Staffie, an all-white one renamed – last time I checked – Snowball."

"Snowball?" Mum couldn't contain her joy at the idea of Reid dragging around an attack dog with such an unsuitable name.

"His daughter, apparently, named it. They'll both need retraining of course, but the RSPCA are fairly sure that with time and the right training and care they could be completely reintegrated to society."

"And we still don't know which one it was that ate part of that dead fella?"

Mum was back on the outrage, and I chuckled. "Caz is letting it be known it was hers in the hope that word gets round any local ne'er do wells and deters them burgling her flat. 'I haven't just got a Staffie, you know, I've got one with a taste for human flesh.'"

"Caz all over," mum chuckled along with me. "So, what happened to that Solomon fellow?"

"Oh, they caught him," I said, "trying to get on the Stranraer ferry with a dodgy passport in the name of Mick Flynn. He wasn't that bright, old Solomon."

Which was why, I mused, Wakefield had used him to help destroy the neighbourhood on behalf of Constable.

I stared out the window a moment, the dark falling a little

faster now, and filled mum in on the rest of the players.

Ellie Nosh's book 'Pork,' would be released later in the new year and would be a co-credit to herself and Cathy. Ellie had decided to launch the book by opening a pop-up restaurant and had hired Lindsey – who looked likely to inherit a sizeable chunk of money now that a will Mehmet had left with a local solicitor had turned up – to head up the front of house team, while Callum Byrne had been in touch with Home Angels asking whether his mum's cleaning gig was available and looked determined to sort his life out and move on from the past.

"It was a no brainer," my mum said, picking a spare raisin off the plate and popping it in her mouth. "Once he grows up – and paring him with Joanna will make sure he grows up – he'll be as solid as poor Cathy."

Caz had been absolutely right about Wakefield and Constable. Having made sure his vote helped pass a bill that would take even more money away from the poorest, Henry Wakefield had been driven straight to Heathrow where he'd boarded a private plane to Nice airport and was breakfasting on the terrace at his family's place when the news had broken in England.

And not one of the papers had mentioned his presence in the whole mess.

Solomon, when arrested, had gabbled about Prince Harry, but the police weren't bothered going after someone about whom there wasn't a single solitary shred of evidence. Everyone, as Caz had predicted, knew Wakefield was a wrong 'un; but because he was careful to cover his tracks, and because he rarely, if ever, dirtied his own hands, he was dipping croissants in his café au lait while Solomon, Charity and the rest of the gang were left swinging in the wind in Blighty.

And much the same happened with Constable Construction.

The board expressed horror and shock at the disgraceful – and obviously entirely unsanctioned – behaviour of a number of people they'd worked with in good faith but stressed that they were a multi-billion-pound firm with contracts stretching across the globe and a reputation for good behaviour, social responsibility and best practices in the development industry.

Then they'd chucked a few quid at some local resident's committees, announced that they no longer had plans to redevelop the area that included The Races, paid for the building of a few kids' playgrounds, and shuffled back into their cave to wait for the row to die down and decide which part of the city they'd gobble up after that.

"Caz says if we're lucky, one or two of the board will get charged with minor crimes. Probably retire from the board with pensions and stock options intact, and get a slap on the wrist, but the game will go on."

"And that kills you, doesn't it?"

I sighed. "What's the point? I mean, we got Rachel and Evan and Selene; we got Solomon. But it's never going to stop. The real monsters are not only still out there, but it feels like they're stronger than ever." I sighed deeply. "I just can't help wondering: What's the point?"

Mum reached a hand over, tiny, powdery soft, and rested it on the back of mine. "What's the alternative?" She asked, a sad brittle smile dancing around the edges of her lips.

"You're not well, are you?" I asked, and the ghost-smile evaporated. "Is it cancer?"

The stew bubbled away in the background as the radio went to news – some war somewhere raging on, some politicians corruption exposed, a demonstration against cuts turns violent – and mum forced a smile onto her face.

This one was bigger but looked like a cardboard cut-out layered over her face. It didn't match the sadness in her suddenly teary eyes.

"You always know me," she said. "I love you all so much, but you will always be my baby Danny, and I don't know why, but you know me so much better than the others. How did you know?"

"A process of elimination," I said quietly. "Something's been up, and then I saw dad at the hospital the same day you were going on your 'girls night out.' He was hanging around the corridor to Oncology, but it didn't register till yesterday when I realised that your sickness, his protectiveness, if it wasn't what everyone else thought it was, it meant that one of you needed Oncology care. And as you were the one who was sick…"

"You're too smart for your own good." Mum smiled fondly at me. "So, what does everyone else think is going on?"

"They think you and dad are breaking up."

"Breaking up?" She laughed, blinking the tears from her eyes. "I've never loved your father more than the past few months. I got the diagnosis, and I didn't want any of you kids told. This is not your battle. You all have enough shit in your lives without worrying about me. And it killed him to have to go through this on his own.

"I felt so bad for him at times, but I didn't want any of you told if you didn't have to be."

"That's not fair," I said simply. "On him or us."

Mum looked down at her hand over mine. Her nails were cut round and short, the fingers – like mine – long and slender. "I'm not sure that I always think straight, but I was insistent on this, Danny, and I need you to understand why: There's cancer, and it would have been better if they'd found it a few months earlier, but it's still treatable. They just don't know yet how treatable."

"The 'boozy nights,'" I said quietly, "And the throwing up next day."

She nodded. "The therapy hasn't been as awful as it is for some people, but it still leaves me pretty wiped out next day. And – and baby, this is the thing I need you to understand – I need this to be about me. Do you know what I mean?"

I did.

I truly did.

My whole life, with my sisters and my brother, mum had

been a part of 'us,' a tribe against the world, but that had meant that whilst each of us had grown up and grown away and grown their own lives and personalities, mum – in our eyes – had never become herself; she existed as part of an 'us' that meant everything she – or my dad - was experiencing was refracted through a lens of our feelings, our concerns.

Thus, our refusal to let this be; our expectation that whatever it was was ours to know and control and be a part of, when all my mum wanted to do was protect us from the fear and have something in her life that was hers to deal with.

"I'm so sorry," I said, the words catching in my throat. "I can't believe how selfish we've been."

"Ach," mum waved her hand dismissively. "That's not selfish, Danny. That's family. And I wouldn't have it any other way. Normally. But I can't have Maz and Val freaking out and squabbling while I'm trying to get through this; I can't abide the thought of Paddy doing his stoic impression in front of me and being totally unaware that I can see his red-rimmed eyes where he hasn't stopped crying for a week.

"And you, my brilliant bright baby; how could I watch you – the solver, the fixer, the one who tries always to make things better, realising that there's nothing for you to fix here.

"It'll be what it'll be."

A tear ran down my face, and I opened my mouth to speak, only words wouldn't come, just a new-born cry of anguish, and suddenly mum was out of her chair, arms around me, shushing and comforting me.

"Are you dying?" I finally choked out, the sense of her words hitting me.

She squeezed me tighter. "We're all dying, Danny," she said. "Just some of us have a little further to go. But I'm not planning a funeral. Not just yet. And look," she pointed at the orchid, "life has a way of surprising us."

"What am I going to do?" I sobbed. "If you die-"

"I'm not going to die." She smiled through her own tears. "Not yet. The treatments are going well, and I will last a few more years baby. But I can't be here forever."

"And what will happen then?" I knew I was babbling, the shock of having finally to confront what I'd begun to suspect that day I'd met my dad in the hospital; him telling me an obvious untruth and then fleeing back towards oncology. "What are we going to do?"

Outside, beyond the steamed-up window, the twilight had given up the ghost and full dark had fallen, the gently twinkling lights of the city making it look as though the place I'd grown up in was a fairy land and not home to the venal and wicked and rotten as well, and mum, tears now running down her cheeks, turned me so that we were facing each other fully.

"Here's what you're going to do," she smiled at me with so much love that my heart cracked. "You're going to be strong, and silent, and you're going to let me get on with this. With therapy and treatment and, one day – one day soon, I promise – when I'm better, you're going to act surprised when I tell your brother and sisters and you about a health scare I had, and how it's all okay now."

"And what do we do till then?"

My mum looked around her, her eyes taking in the bubbling stew on the hob, the orchid defying the odds to survive and flower one last time, the steamed-up window and the scene behind, and then her gaze returned to mine, and she smiled.

"We do what people like us have always done," she said, placing a gentle kiss on my forehead.

"We live."

THE END

Acknowledgements

This book wasn't easy to write, for various reasons, and it would have been impossible without the love and support of my husband David Gray, who gave me space, support, smiles and diversions and who – when it was not going the way I wanted in the early drafts – noted that "All your books are shit at this stage. Just keep going." For this, for driving me to numerous festivals and appearances, and for ensuring I never drowned in the work, he has my eternal gratitude. That he also has my undying love goes without saying.

I'm blessed to have friends and family who fill my life with love, and to each and every one of them I say thank you. If any of you recognise yourselves within these pages, I hope you're flattered. If not, then any resemblance to people living or dead is – my lawyers insist – entirely coincidental.

In particular, thanks go to Warren Hoskins Carl Corrigan and Ellie Corrigan-Coogan, who were there at the very beginning, when an idea I was absolutely definitely not going to work on whilst on holiday took over not just the week in Rhandirmwyn but large parts of the year that followed, and who provided research and a key plot point as well as snuggles, licks unconditional love and more smiles and laughs than I once believed I would ever have again.

I'm honoured to be part of a writing community which is welcoming, generous supportive and genuinely loving, and I owe a great debt of gratitude to Rebecca Chance for championing Danny whilst giving me some amazing insights into the book industry; to Barbara Nadel for reminding me of just how loved the books are, and of the value of building a backlist; to Paul Burston and all at Polari for giving me a slot at the most fabulous Salon in British Literature to share Danny and Caz's story; to Jo Perry who is kindness and love incarnate; and to Ed James, who let me borrow his name, and never fails to make me howl with laughter as well as being a font of knowledge on the writing business.

Thanks to Dan Simpson and all at The Writers Routine

Podcast, who made me realise for perhaps the first time that there was a serious heart to these books, and that exploring that serious heart would be an interesting thing to do.

To Liam Livings, whose Caravan Retreat enabled me to produce a good slice of this book, as well as giving me new friends, laughs love and support.

Thanks – as always – go to Julie Vince, whose brilliant and supportive editing skills made this book sing, and who saved me from an overdose of "Anyways," and to Hannah Westwood, whose skills as a proofer, beta-reader and editrix made the text shinier and sharper.

Danny and Caz have been taken into the hearts of so many readers and this fact makes me immensely proud and often rather tearful, and to those readers, bloggers, reviewers and all who love the books and vocally support them by Amazon reviews, Blog posts, Tweets, and word of mouth, I say THANK YOU. You make this all worth doing, and I will be forever grateful for your support and enthusiasm.

And – as always – to everyone at Fahrenheit Press Fahrenheit Editions and Fahrenheit 13. Your support, enthusiasm, vision, and love mean that not only do I get to write the books I have always dreamed about, but that they get into the hands of people in places I would never have dared to dream of. I know that the world of publishing is not always easy, and I truly value the effort you all put in to moving these books from my screen into the hands and hearts of readers across the globe.

But special thanks – as always – go to Chris McVeigh, for being himself, for ducking, diving, daring, and for loving fearlessly. This book – and all of them – is also, ultimately, for you.

Printed in Great Britain
by Amazon

62671170R00215

JOHN T. SLADEK wa[illegible]
in London. He was edu[illegible]
where he studied m[illegible]
Literature. Since ther[illegible]
barman, draughtsman, [illegible]
The Reproductive System, was published [illegible]
acclaim and his fertile, inventive fiction, as well as his
humorous cast of mind, have been likened to Kurt Vonnegut
at his best.

Press acclaim for *Roderick*, also by John Sladek

'A classic novel . . . It reeks simultaneously of *Candide*, *Catch-22*, *Player Piano*, *The Wizard of Oz*'
Guardian

'Superb . . . comparable with – at times even overtaking – early Kurt Vonnegut'
Time Out

By the same author

The Steam-Driven Boy
The Muller-Fokker Effect
The Reproductive System
The New Apocrypha
Keep the Giraffe Burning
Black Aura
Roderick

John Sladek

Alien Accounts

A PANTHER BOOK

GRANADA

London Toronto Sydney New York

Published by Granada Publishing Limited in 1982

ISBN 0 586 04758 1

A Granada Paperback Original
Copyright © John Sladek 1982

Masterson and the Clerks, New Forms, 198-, a Tale of 'Tomorrow', Name (Please Print):, and *Anxietal Register B* first appeared in *New Worlds* ©1968-1973
Scenes from the Country of the Blind first appeared in *A Book of Contemporary Nightmares*, edited by Giles Gordon © John Sladek 1976
The Interstate first appeared in *Quark 2*, edited by Samuel R. Delaney and Marilyn Hacker © Coronet Communications Ltd 1971
The Communicants first appeared in *The New SF*, edited by Langdon Jones © John Sladek 1969

Granada Publishing Limited
Frogmore, St Albans, Herts AL2 2NF
and
36 Golden Square, London W1R 4AH
866 United Nations Plaza, New York, NY 10017, USA
117 York Street, Sydney, NSW 2000, Australia
100 Skyway Avenue, Rexdale, Ontario, M9W 3A6, Canada
61 Beach Road, Auckland, New Zealand

Printed and bound in Great Britain by
Cox and Wyman Ltd, Reading
Set in Plantin

This book is sold subject to the condition that it shall not, by way of trade or otherwise, be lent, re-sold, hired out or otherwise circulated without the publisher's prior consent in any form of binding or cover other than that in which it is published and without a similar condition including this condition being imposed on the subsequent purchaser.

Granada ®
Granada Publishing ®

Contents

Introduction

The aliens here are human. This book contains no giant flying snails or telepathic octopods, no Ganymedean cat-women dressed in silver, no aggressive dugong chiefs roaming the galaxy in their pulsar-powered yo-yo ships. The aliens here are human aliens. Most of them work in ordinary offices, and they do not commute to work from Proxima Centauri, either. Yet these here humans are aliens.

Office life attracts them, perhaps because of its futility. At least they've inhabited offices in fiction since Dickens's day. Since the Circumlocution Office we've had the petty officials of Kafka, the doublethinkers of Orwell, the pathetic cogs of Elmer Rice's *The Adding Machine*, and that super-clerk of Herman Melville's, *Bartleby the Scrivener*. In *The Grey Ones*, J. B. Priestley outlined an entire alien conspiracy: Having no souls, They cannot possibly be bored. Thus they must always rise to the top in business and governments, where they can set about killing the souls of others.

Notice that none of these authors can separate the monsters from the victims in office life, for aliens are both. The sociologists who speak of 'alienation' manage to alienate themselves through official jargon like this:

> . . . a set of arrangements for producing and rearing children the viability of which is not predicated on the consistent presence in the household of an adult male acting in the role of husband or father . . .

(meaning 'families where Dad isn't home much'). A person who thinks like this may not exactly breathe methane, but there is a giant flying snailiness here.

Here are the human aliens.

Masterson and the Clerks

'Whoever is in charge of operations should be designated with real authority to be used in case of an emergency.'

A. P. Sloan
My Life with General Motors

Part One: Clerks All!

SECTION I: THE LUTTE AGENCY

Division A: Mr Gelford

HENRY FOUND that, when he had filled out the orange card listing his education, work experience and hobbies, he was permitted to pass beyond the railing next to the receptionist's desk. The receptionist was a fat, pretty girl whose bare feet would be soft and pink. Being bored in the evenings, especially Sunday evenings, she would draw on black silk stockings and fuck someone in front of a movie camera. Once a famous American executive, watching her in a movie, had had an unusual experience.

Henry moved down the light green hall to a barn-like room where each stall was equipped with a desk and a living soul. The black wooden floor was wavy. Little incandescent bulbs, strung on wires, pumped light into the room, but dark corners drained it away too fast. Henry sat down in the second rank of folding chairs, along with a blind man and a Negro who would someday be a well-known boxer. The blind man's dog looked at Henry, seeing him.

Henry remembered visiting the dentist with just such an

orange card in his hand. He was thinking of some way of explaining this to the blind man or the Negro, when far down the barn a tall man stood up and beckoned.

'Henry,' he called. Henry and the blind man stood up together.

'Did he say Amory?' asked the blind man.

'No, Henry.'

'Eh? Henry?'

'Henry.'

'Henry!' called the tall man again, beckoning over the waves. Henry walked towards him, past the desks of Mr Blair and Mr Clemens and Mrs Dudevant and Mr Beyle and Miss Knye.

Division B: Mr Nind

Mr Gelford asked Henry to call him Al. With a special pen, Al initialled the orange card in several places, maintaining the attitude of a dentist marking caries. His eyes, small and dark – like human nipples, they were surrounded with tiny white bumps – looked searchingly at Henry's hair or teeth.

'Henry C. Henry, eh? What does the C. stand for?'

Henry looked at him in silence until Al turned his nipples to a mimeographed list. 'Nothing here, I'm afraid, for someone with almost no experience. I'll turn you over to Mr Nind.'

Don kept a telephone receiver well in front of his mouth as he spoke, because the inside of his lip had developed a terrible cold sore he wished to hide. It was, as he already suspected, syphilis.

'I have a really challenging job in a small, friendly engineering company,' he said. 'No experience necessary, and there is no limit to how far you can work your way up. What do you say, fella?'

Henry leaned forward and laid a hand on Nind's desk calendar. 'Fine, Don,' he said softly.

SECTION II: AN INTERVIEW

In an almost bare room evenly coated with dust, Mr Masterson toyed with a slide rule, a clipboard, a retractable ballpoint pen and a thin book, *Steam Tables*, by Keynes and Keyes. Henry sat motionless before him. Out of the window he could see a soup line, and in the distance a building was being demolished. A man in uniform walked up the soup line, pulled a man out of it and began hitting him in the face. Perhaps later the victim would go to a movie theatre, buy a ticket, enter the Gents and comb his hair.

'Are you a good, steady worker?' asked Masterson.

'Yes.'

Fingers like white slugs curled around the slide rule. Undoubtedly Masterson was puffy and white all over, like a drowned corpse. His unpleasant glasses were hinged in the centre like motorcycle goggles, and folded hard against the colourless bubbles of his eyes. Mr Masterson contained a great quantity of liquid.

'Do you work good?' he asked.

'Yes.'

'If you work good, we'll do good by you.' Henry was never to forget this sentence, for he wrote it on a sheet of paper and taped it in the drawer of his desk, where it became a kind of motto.

'You start at fifty.' The corner of Mr Masterson's mouth lifted in a kind of smile, revealing a rotten tooth.

SECTION III: THE ARRANGEMENT

The Masterson Engineering Company occupied the third and fourth floors of the building. Henry was to work on the third floor. An old man, whose tie was fastened with a paper clip, whose sleeves were rolled high above his parched elbows, led Henry downstairs into a room full of clerks at oak desks. There were in the room perhaps a dozen, perhaps a hundred men of various sizes and ages.

Gesticulating wildly with his skinny arms, the old man began in a high, clear voice to explain Henry's duties:

See this here form
This here is the system sheet.
You've got to mark it down every time
An assignment bill comes in
You've got to mark it down every time
An assignment bill goes out
And put the tally number here off the spec
Or else the item identification.

See this here list
This here is the transfer list,
Where you put the part number here
From the compiled list of numerical transfers
Where you put the description number here
From the B column of the changeover schedule
And mark it down

We have always initialled our work
We always will
Be sure you initial the backlist
When you add a serial number
Be sure you initial the adjustment form
When you check this here.
Fill out the job number;
Fill out the item identification index
(Blue and yellow copies),
Make a note on the margin of the drawing
Or on the margin of the transfer book
If the alphabetical register is stamped
And initialled by the proper authority.

'You'll catch on . . .' Winking, the old man gave his sketches of arms a final flourish and went away. Henry fingered various piles of clean forms tentatively, murmuring fragments of the old clerk's song; he picked up a coloured pencil and laid it down again. It seems that being a clerk is not all fun!

Henry consulted with himself and decided to learn by observing and imitating the other clerks around him. There were eight clerks around him in the following arrangement:

Clark Markey	Robert Kegel	Harold Kelmscott
Willard Bask	Henry C. Henry	Edward Warner
Karl Henkersmahl	Rodney Klumpf	Edwin Futch

Henry was never to learn the names of any of the sixteen or forty clerks outside this circle of desks, but soon he 'caught on', or moved into the general work rhythm. He accepted from Rod or Ed Warner a batch of forms, removed paper clips from some, marked a few of them with numbers and initials, erased the numbers or initials from others, sorted them by his own arrangement, clipped them together, and gave them to either Bob or Willard.

Willard was born and raised in the Southern part of the United States, while Bob's younger sister was sure to become salutatorian of her high school class. Meanwhile Bob or Willard was undoing part or all of Henry's work, then passing the stuff on to Clark or Harold or Karl, who in turn undid part or all of his (Bob's or Willard's) work, then passed the stuff on to Rod or Ed W. or callow Eddie Futch; each man along the chain approaching the work as if no one had gone before and no one would come after. Numbers would be erased, altered, changed back to their original values. Forms might be sorted by names, then dates, then colour, then in numerical order, alphabetical order and alphanumerical order. Often enough, work came back to Henry from two to three times. This was indeed a vicious circle!

SECTION IV: THE HAPPY ENDING

Happily, sooner or later every form ended up with Karl, the stapler, who might put a staple in it and send it out of the department for good. Work flow was thus:

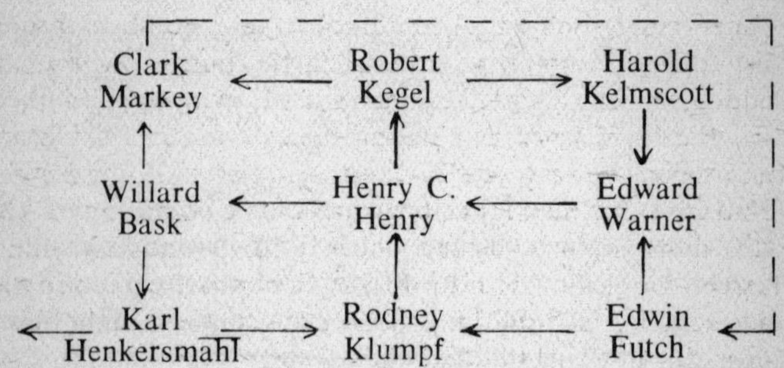

Thus a kind of progress was achieved, without, however, sacrificing routine. The happy days blended into one another like molten glass.

SECTION V: THE DEPARTURES

No one ever saw Mr Masterson on the third floor. He seemed to send all his orders through the old clerk, who descended every morning with a memorandum to be tacked to the bulletin board.

The speaker of the intercom, fixed in the ceiling, made crackling noises that might have been the voice of Masterson. The shape of a name emerged from the static. A clerk at once rose, squared his shoulders and climbed the stairs. He did not come back.

The room was filled with the anxious murmur of the clerks, discussing his departure. The same thing had happened a dozen times or more, it was said. They never came back.

The discussion stamped everyone. Some clerks stood leaning against their desks, arms akimbo. Some tapped pencils on their blotters, made spitting motions, or leaned back. Others pretended to move their jaws sideways, while still more others sharpened pencils and drank water from paper 'cups'. Bob Kegel continued to read numbers from a list to Rod Klumpf, who punched the buttons of a small adding machine. Karl picked at his stapler with a preoccupied air. Big Ed Warner, an older man known for his leaky heart and halitosis, was swivelled around to talk to Eddie Futch. Had the bomb (or a Hiroshima-size atomic bomb) gone off at this moment, at 5,000 feet above Fifth Avenue and 42nd Street, the shadow of Ed would no doubt have protected the acne-riddled face of Eddie from the direct effects of the blast, or is this just wishful thinking?

Ed told the young man that the departed clerk was dead, and that nothing, no power on earth could bring him back.

'Is that any way to talk? Jesus! Is that any way . . .'

Eddie ran off to the lavatory to pinch pimples from his hot, raw cheeks. Big Ed considered the word 'laughter'.

SECTION VI. KEGEL AND KLUMPF

Bob Kegel and Rod Klumpf were alike. Often Henry tried to envision some mirror arrangement that would allow him to see, in place of the back of Bob's head in front of him, the back of Rod's head behind him. Clearly the virtual image would be the same.

They were tall, slim and polite, with round heads, round

shoulders and long, narrow feet. They wore fashionable clothes and reasonable smiles and neat cowlicks, and they read the same consumer magazine, which prompted them to buy many of the same articles: antifreeze, air conditioners, Ascots, attaché cases, beer mugs, berets, blazers, brandy snifters, cameras, carpeting, cars, cats, deodorants, door chimes, filter cigarettes, golf clubs, hats, LPs, luggage, movie cameras, movie projectors, shavers, silverware, slide projectors, tape recorders, typewriters, television sets, toothbrushes.

At first Henry supposed that he could tell them apart by Rod's freckles and Bob's half-rimmed glasses. But the sun soon brought out freckles on Bob also, and he proved to be quite vain in regard to his glasses, wearing them less and less. At the same time, Rod purchased and began to wear a similar pair of glasses, and since he kept out of the sun, his own freckles began to fade. Being of a size, the two friends loaned one another clothes. Occasionally, for a joke, they would exchange desks. Both spoke in the same modulated tones, and both moved with the grace of bowlers.

It was always Bob or Rod who got up a football pool, who sent out for coffee, who tacked up humorous signs, who started charity drives, who instituted fines for tardiness and swearing, who collected money for flowers whenever anyone fell ill, died or married. Tirelessly and good-naturedly, these clean young men organized the life of the office. The others despised them.

SECTION VII: THE COFFEE BREAK

Division A: The idea of coffee break

COFFEE BREAK was an old tradition at the Masterson Engineering Company, instituted some years before by Mr

Masterson when he had read in a management magazine the following advertisement:

> UP PRODUCTION WITH A COFFEE BREAK!
>
> Get more out of your workers by giving them a short mid-afternoon rest, with *coffee*, the all-purpose stimulant. Coffee perks up flagging minds and bodies the way fuel injection pumps up the power of an engine. *They* will gladly pay for the coffee – while *you* reap the extra productivity!

His frequent memos on the subject claimed that coffee breaks cost him an enormous amount of money, but that he was determined his clerks should be happy at all costs.

Division B: Coffee break praxis

It was during coffee break that Henry began to learn the peculiar vocabulary of the clerk.

First he heard Clark Markey, the non-lawyer, say, 'I certainly did finalize that item.'

A delighted smile invaded the solemn features of Karl Henkersmahl. 'Finalized it, did you? You do not know the meaning of the word *finalize*. Did you expedite it or ameliorate it? Did you even estimate the final expenditures? Or did you merely correlate the old stabilization programmes? Ha!'

Harold Kelmscott stirred his coffee with a peculiar new kind of pencil. Laughter hissing in his blue eyes, he said, 'Quit it, Karl. We all know what a poor expediter you are yourself, and you're a non-conservative estimator, unless I miss my guess.'

Karl nipped off his rimless glasses and polished them in aggravated silence. It was hard for him to acknowledge the presence of a superior will, but he did so with his best grace.

His tiny, wide-set eyes, were on the move, looking for a smile he could challenge.

Karl often let his pride and quick temper draw him into an argument on any subject, especially on the subject of Germany, about which he possessed a number of interesting statistics. Claiming to know the exact reason Germany lost the Second World War, he usually won any arguments simply by shouting the same words over and over until his opponent gave up. The only man who ever won the war argument from Karl was Ed Warner, who maintained that Germany had *won* the war.

Division C: False teeth

Karl swallowed his coffee and said, 'I estimate that the productionalized operational format will be updated by mid-March at the very earliest.'

Harold smiled. 'But that's hardly a conservative estimate, is it, Karl?' The smile became an orange balloon, orgulous and threatening. Karl stared at its teeth in disbelief.

Modestly swirling his coffee and studying the rainbow in it, Harold said aloud that he had found two discrepancies today.

Two! A low murmur of approval went around the group. Indian, or 'ideal' summer descended on the city, and a new movie came to the Apollo. Hurricane Patty Sue was breaking up. The eyes of Eddie Futch glistened with frank hero-worship, which Harold accepted graciously. Even Bob and Rod paused in their counting of the proceeds of a turkey raffle to make the well-known gesture of 'nice going'.

Karl alone refused to congratulate Harold. 'I hope you itemized them both,' he said testily, 'before you followed a plan of procedure.'

'Of course I itemized them. What did you think I'd do – *standardize* them?' Harold *quipped*. The others *laughed* heartily, as much in glee at Karl's discomfiture as in open admiration of the excellent *bon mot*, or good word, of his inquisitor.

It was hard not to like Harold Kelmscott, for he was a true clerk, descended from a line of clerks that could trace its name back to the twelfth century, to a Benedictine monk who broke his vow of celibacy. Harold once lectured to an orientation class of incoming clerks at a business college. He said:

SECTION VIII: A PRIESTHOOD

My esteemed fellow-clerks:

There have not been so many ways in this world in which a man might earn his daily bread, that the desiderata of clerkdom could invariably vie with more dramatic ways of 'bringing home the bacon' (slide shown of Francis Bacon's *Study for a Portrait*, 1953, or *Head IV*, 1949, or *Painting*, 1946), such as police detection work, mass hypnotism, name any sport.

What, then, is it about clerkdom, that draws so many millions of fine young persons of all levels to dedicate their lives, so to speak, to the world of paper and telephones; to join, if I may be permitted a small jest, the pen and pencil set? (Slide shown of comic figure climbing out of inkwell, copyright by Ub Iwerks. Boos and clatter of neolitc soles on Armstrong cork floors. Guards take firmer grip on Smith & Wesson .38 calibre police special revolvers, glance inadvertently at tough Yale locks on all doors, but H.K. has it under control.)

What it is, we may very well ask, for it is an unanswered and perhaps unanswerable question. Let us unask it, then, and move on to a history of paper. The first clerks, we know, lived in ancient cities where they wrote on stone, clay slabs, wax tablets. But very quickly, they moved into their true capacity as priests.

(Mixed hissing, but a general feeling of well-being pervades the auditorium. Guards relax and even light up Camels and Luckies. Wearing a plain black business suit, Foreman and Clark with vest and extra pair of pants at home, Harold spreads his arms in benediction. He is plump and blond, but even so, serious as a nose. He is all-English, black round-rimmed glasses and an unruly lock of hair his trade mark.) Yes, *priests*, a shocking word but oh so true! *You* shall be priests in the tradition, handlers of the lamb, then the lamb-skin then paper. Your hands will caress no whiter flank than the margin of form 289-XB-1967M. Your rituals are many and important, and you will dedicate your life to preserving their routine, that endless cyclic round that drives the universe. Whether you work in the death, birth or marriage registration bureau, it is your work which moves civilization in its great orbit. God bless you all! (From the front of the hall guards and firemen move in with firehoses, using Townely-Ward 1½″ nozzles and Townely-Ward pumpers to empty the hall and flush it out for the next lecture.)

SECTION IX: JAX TV LOUNGE

Division A: Rod

HENRY STOOD at the bar and began a conversation with Rod or Bob. Around them, clerks murmured a kind of plainsong cadence of complaint, and Henry was pleasantly aware of being a clerk himself. He was one with the two clerks in the corner, arguing about the finalizing of finalizations. He was one with the boisterous group of tic-tac-toe players in the corner. He was one with the three clerks at the other end of the bar, their arms about one another's shoulders, who counted off by tens. Nearby another comrade was showing someone how to fold a dollar-bill ring. Henry's hands itched for paper to feel. The bar, foreseeing this, had provided a tiny paper napkin with each drink, which his hands raped as he talked.

Peering into his glass, Bob (or Rod) said, 'Rob gives me a pain in the ass. Today he wanted to hand me a tally index, quadruplicate – and would you belive it? – the stupid bastard had the blue copy on top!'

'No kidding?'

'No, really. Even little Eddie Futch knows the white copy goes on top, for Christ's sake.'

Henry could not help but think of Masterson's childhood:

MEMO: *My childhood.*

It has come to the attention of this office that the company personnel in general do not know the details of how I was born and raised. I intend to ameliorate this circumstance.

I was conceived because the contraceptive device my mother was wearing at the moment was not properly fitted. It consisted of a small metal button, to which was attached a long wire coil spring. The end of the coil was to be introduced into the cervix and thence into the womb, and screwed up tight until the button sealed the opening of the cervix. Either due to a malfunction of the device itself or an unwillingness on the part of Mom to undergo the discomfort of a really tight seal, an accidental conception occurred.

I learned of all this only on my twenty-first birthday, from a pretty cousin with whom I dallied, in an after-Sunday-dinner way, in a haymow. My mother I hardly remember, except as a ghostly figure standing silent by the electric kitchen range, almost an aura thrown off by the back burners. She liked to stir things. To my knowledge, she never spoke.

I soon was able to go to college, where, thanks to the leadership of Athelstan Spilhaus, I was persuaded to make my goal the sanctification of mechanical engineering, the elevation of themodynamics to a sacrament. My studies were interrupted by the birth of a younger sister, or half-sister, whom my impoverished parents could not support. The rest is history.

—Masterson

Bob (or Rod) went on, 'Well, to make a long story short, I expedited them, though I had a damned good notion to let them go the way they were. Old Rob is beginning to make too many little discrepancies, if you ask me. Only last week, I caught him *updating a form*, just because it was in short supply!'

'I can't believe it!' cried Henry, clapping his hands to his ears.

'True, though. And he had the itemization slip attached to the bill, and I couldn't find the authorization for that anywhere!'

'Exactly.' Henry sensed his meaning. Down the bar, the trio counted:

'One hundred forty!'

'One hundred fifty!'

'One hundred sixty!'

They laughed and pounded on the bar, then drew themselves up to count again.

'Yes,' Rod (or Bob) went on in thick accents, 'if you ask me, old Rob is about to get the axe. Too many discrepancies, if you see what I mean. One of these days they'll be calling him on the intercom . . .'

'Do you mean it?' Henry inadvertently genuflected.

'Off the record, you understand, but the trouble with old Rob is – he drinks.'

'No!' said Henry, not disputing it. He bought a round, then Bob (or Rod) tried to interest him in tickets for a turkey raffle.

'But it's only March.'

'We've already raffled off a ham for Easter. Clark won it, and gave it away to Karl. Then we sold everyone cards for Mother's and Father's Day, flags for Veterans' Day, baby trees for Arbor Day, fireworks for the Fourth and St Christopher medals for the Labor Day weekend. Thanksgiving is the only thing we had left,' explained Bob (or Rod). 'I mean, it's a little early for Christmas trees.'

'What about treats for Hallowe'en?' suggested a stranger.

'Sure, that's it, teach kids to beg. That's the American way, all right. If kids worked for their pennies the way I had to – Gee, it's nearly seven! I've got to get to class. Sorry I can't buy you a round, Henry.' He drank up and lounged quickly towards the door.

Rod (or Bob), less because of the ski-ing instructor with whom he had had a brief flirtation than because of his current interest in Arctic literature, had a well-shaped neck, tapering inward slightly under his small ears, and forming a niche in front, into which was set an *Adam's apple.*

'Wait! What is it you study?' Henry cried, and the answer blew back in a block of November wind:

'IBMs.'

Division B: Bob

Bob (or Rod) moved down the bar to talk to Henry as soon as Rod (or Bob) had left. Henry was able at once to confirm that he drank, as the IBM scholar alleged, *for he now had a drink in his hand, and sipped at it.*

'Was that Dob I saw leaving?' he said. 'Intelligent kid, Dob is.'

'Yes, he tells me he's studying IBMs.'

IBM, unknown to either of the speakers, represents not only International Business Machines, but *Yebem*, the seventieth angel quinary of the Zodiac. This angel is usually depicted plucking a quill from the wing of its neighbour, 69 or Raah (who hangs head downward like a bat), with which to make, this legend has it, the first 'pen'.

Like wax, the other's face took a smile. 'The real money isn't in IBMs, it's in ICBMs. I study ICBMs.' After a moment he added, 'Yes, I'm no intellectual like Dob, but I can tell you right now he's getting too smart for his own good. For instance, he thinks the white copy of the tally index quadruplicate form goes on top, in the finalized format. Just for the record, I think old Dob's going to be finalized himself one of these days.'

'For the record?'

'The confidential record, of course. Dob makes too many discrepancies, if you know what I mean.'

'I know what you mean, all right,' said Henry, showing some of his teeth. 'He drinks?'

'Golly, yes. In fact, I saw him drinking here, just a few minutes ago.'

There was nothing either of them could add to this, so they turned to watch the television. As the picture slowly brightened, it became even more painfully clear that the monkeys were not free-standing on the ponies' backs, but strapped on. A hidden orchestra played 'Perpetual Motion'. After trying to interest Henry in the first pick of a lot of Norway pines Bob (or Rod) went off to school.

SECTION X: ED AND EDDIE

The unpleasant marsupiality of Ed Warner's eyes was worsened when he smiled. Little sharp shrew-teeth glittered at the ends of big dead-pale gums, and one knew his tongue would also be black.

'There isn't any boss,' he murmured to Eddie Futch.

There was no need to say more. The panic ripples spread, leaving little Eddie bobbing on the surface of his own consciousness, a writer might presume. He who follows the conceit far enough might even glimpse something like slime boiling in the depths . . . 'But I *seen* him. He hired me.'

'You saw someone who said he was the boss. Or did he even say that?'

Little Eddie looked around for help, his eyes full of tears. 'But there just has to be a boss,' his shrillness insisted. 'If there's no boss, how can there be a company?'

The shrew-teeth bared in a grin.

'Leave the lad alone, Ed,' Harold bade. 'You'll have him making discrepancies.'

'This whole company is a discrepancy, Harry. I'm trying to say something, now, listen. Unrectifiable—'

'That'll do!' Harold leapt to his feet, a sword of ignorance glimmering in his fine eyes. Cackling, Big Ed moved behind his own desk to gulp heart pills.

This was his defence. Everyone was terrified of Ed's tender heart, as much as of his black breath. If he were pressed too hard in an argument, he would simply clutch his chest and slump to the floor, remaining there until the argument was forgotten.

Henry envied him the trick. If only it were possible to imitate it without soiling his shirt . . .

SECTION XI: DIRT

Yes, Henry cried out to cleanliness. He bathed morning and evening, and wore clothes scientifically cleaned and packaged in polythene bags. His shirts were first disinfected and boiled at home, then scrubbed to new whiteness by Chinese slaves. He carried about with him toothpaste, carbolic soap, orange sticks, a safety razor, styptic pencil and Kleenex, while the drawer of his desk was crammed with bandaids, new shirts and underwear, depilatory and cotton swabs.

No, cleanliness answered. His was the dirtiest shirt in the office, and the tartar caked up permanently on his teeth. Strange rashes came and went on his coarse-pored, grainy skin, while his fingernails remained in mourning. It was as if another person were determined to keep him foul.

> MEMO: *The history of the Masterson Engineering Company.*
> The Masterson Engineering Company was started in 1927 by my father. My mother. He began with one draughtsman and a broken T-square, and plenty of guts and sand. In 1931, the company went broke, but by 1950, he was back in business. I took over that year, under his directorship, and soon killed or replaced him. The original name was retained, though the company moved downtown. Wife and child. I am now Mr.
> —Masterson

One day Henry tried a daring experiment. After spreading some newspapers on the floor, he clutched his chest and slumped down carefully on them.

No one paid the least attention, even when he groaned and writhed a few times. After several minutes, Henry got up and went back to work, his neck hot against the grey collar of his shirt.

SECTION XII: CLARK

Clark Markey, the non-lawyer, was unpopular because of his political beliefs, though no one was afraid of him.

'I'm no lawyer,' he would say, 'but it seems to me that twenty-five minutes for lunch is below the legal minimum.' He asked each of the others if they would back him in complaining to the Labour Board.

Willard Bask: 'Don't want to rock the boat.'

Eddie Futch: 'Guess it would be all right.'

Karl Henkersmahl: 'Should think we have no right to complain about anything.'

Henry C. Henry: No comment.

Robert Kegel: 'I think we need a bowling team.'

Harold Kelmscott: 'Let us give up lunch of the flesh.'

Rodney Klumpf: 'Let's organize a bowling team.'

Clark Markey: 'Will go along with the others.'

Ed Warner: 'Abolish lunch. Abolish the company . . .'

SECTION XIII: CLARK AND KARL AND EDDIE

Clark was viscerally interested in everyone's problems of justice. When Eddie Futch played loud music on his radio, Clark assured him he was well within his rights. But when Karl complained of the noise, Clark hastened to tell him that he, too, had a legitimate claim.

'I've got a claim, all right. I'm going to smash that goddamned radio,' Karl said quietly. 'Then I'm going to smash its owner. Ha!'

'Oh, no, you mustn't do that; your right to smash ends where Eddie's radio begins. But you do have a right to insist that he turn it down if it bothers you.'

Karl began to shout, his head swelling up out of a thick, Michelin-man neck. 'Turn that fucking radio off, before I come over there and smash it!'

Blinking rapidly, little Eddie switched off the music. Clark's eyes filled with tears of compassion. He rushed to comfort the boy. 'Nevertheless, you have a right to listen.'

'I don't want to listen,' Eddie lied. Red flooded the acne-scarred face: a Martian map. 'If I did want to listen, I'd listen, all right, no matter what anyone said.'

'That's right! You selfish pig!' Karl screamed. 'You care nothing for the nerves of others. *You* aren't doing precision work, as I am. All *you* do is shuffle papers around. But I'm a precision stapler. I have to get the staple in exactly the same place each time; I can't bend it over or ruin it, because then I'd have to start all over again. But what do you care? What do any of you care?'

MEMO: *Automation*
There will be no automation at the Masterson Engineering Company.

—Masterson

SECTION XIV: CLARK AND KARL

Clark rushed over to placate the hysterical Henkersmahl and offer him a halvah bar.

'What is this supposed to be?'

'Halvah. A kind of candy. Just try it.'

Karl bit into it gingerly and chewed, watching Clark to one side. 'It tastes good. Jewish product, is it?' He finished the bar in two bearish gulps and began turning his fingers over, sucking crumbs from them. 'It tastes damned good.'

Clark began to smile, relieved that he had been able to help Karl so easily. Then the Henkersmahl's red jewels of eyes closed with suspicion.

'Damned clever, you Jews. Now I suppose you're going to overcharge me for that candy bar, eh?'

Clark became aware of a problem in communications research. 'No, Karl, that was a gift,' he said.

'Ha ha, a gift. Very cute little tricks. A gift, eh? A gift? Very cute tricks indeed. A gift with Hebrew strings attached, eh? You've fooled me this time, but I'll remember this. I never get fooled twice, and I always remember anyone who cheats me, Clark.' Karl pulled a dollar from his billfold and threw it on Clark's desk.

'Yes, that's the difference between your kind and mine. I may be fooled by your subtleties, but not for long. I pay my debts sportingly, yes, even gladly, when I'm caught in one of your snares. But your kind never pays up, do they? All right, I don't mind being cheated out of mere money. Go on, take it.'

As he said this last, Karl snatched back the dollar and put it away again. From that day on, he would never lose an opportunity to tell people of how Clark tried to charge him a whole dollar for a candy bar, which Karl always referred to as a 'Bar Mitzvah', or one of those crazy names. It might even have been Jewish dope. I felt funny afterwards . . .'

SECTION XV: THE SECOND WORLD WAR

The real reason Karl disliked Clark was that Jews had undoubtedly cost Germany the Second World War. There could be no other explanation. Germany had what everyone acknowledged the world's finest fighting men. They had the best planes, the best guns, everything. But the army had so dissipated its efforts by hauling around mewling Jews and killing them that its efficiency had suffered, he told Ed. Karl would never forgive the Jews for that.

'It's the real reason Germany lost. Not the second front, but that Jewish fifth column. Not the American bombers, but the sabotage in Germany's bosom.'

'I know just what you mean,' Willard Bask agreed. 'I spent eighteen months in Stuttgart, and believe you and me, there ain't a finer kind of folks anywhere than the Germans. We had some godawful fights in them honkytonks, sure, but I respect a man who fights for what's coming to him. Know what I mean? I mean I respect a man who stands up on his hind legs and comes at you with a broke bottle like a white man, and don't go messing around with Big Knives or razors and stuff.'

Ed Warner scratched a mole. 'I don't get it,' he said. 'Didn't Germany *win* the war?'

Not listening, Karl went on. 'German logistics were all snarled. Instead of troop trains and supply trains, they had carloads of Jews lolling about the countryside. *Getting a free ride, while the world's finest fighting men had to walk.*'

'Know just what you mean,' Willard said, nodding fiercely. 'One night this big German and me started out cuttin' each other up with busted bottles, and before the night was over, we was old pals, swapping stories about women. Next night, it was just the other way round . . .'

'But Germany won the war, Karl. Look at Germany today. One of the top industrial nations in the world. Two continents are overrun every year with German tourists. They have one of the biggest, best-equipped armies in Europe. How can you say they lost?'

Karl cocked his head and frowned, realizing something had gone wrong. He had to make Ed understand the truth. Smiling, he began his explanation once again. The light reflected off the octagonal shapes of his lenses, blanking out the eyes.

SECTION XVI: CESSPOOLS

When Harold Kelmscott looked at Clark Markey, what did he see?

He saw the ancestor of Clark Markey performing ritual sacrifice of Christian children. He saw the ancestor of Clark Markey breeding money from money: usury: a sin. He saw the ancestor of Clark Markey cursing Christ as He bore His cross, and telling Him to go faster up Calvary. He saw Christ turn to look at that ancestor, saying, 'I go, but thou shalt wait till my return.' He saw the ancestor of Clark Markey buying and selling Christian kings.

What were the five sources of the hatred Harold bore the Jew before him?

Old half-remembered stories from childhood; his parents' anti-Semitism; popular slogans recalled unconsciously; the intense dislike of Karl for Clark, as reflected in his glasses; bitterness because Clark had not offered Harold a candy bar.

From what two-fold reason springs this last bitterness?

From Harold's abstention from candy during Lent: first, he would naturally have taken pleasure in refusing a temptation of Satan; secondly, he would have enjoyed refusing the candy on religious grounds implying that Clark was cruelly intolerant to offer it, and thus wounding him.

When Clark's name was called over the intercom, he went meekly and quietly upstairs. As soon as he was gone, Harold drew and fired a histrionic sigh. 'Good riddance, good riddance,' he clucked. 'I never could stand Jews, not even when they were my best friends. Do you know why?'

'Because they cheat you?' Karl prompted, hoping for an anecdote.

'No, because, during the Middle Ages, the Jews used to slit open the throats of Christian babies and throw them into cesspools.'

Henry thought about the cesspools. He was becoming compulsively clean in habit if not in fact, and only barely restrained himself from wiping off door knobs and answering the phone with a Kleenex.

'Cesspools, eh?' Karl looked disappointed. 'Well, you've got to expect it. Anyone mean enough to charge a dollar for a candy bar would stoop to just about anything.'

'*Anything*. Their name comes from *Judas*, you know – their secret leader (you recall he killed Christ).'

'That's right. For money, wasn't it?' As he spoke, Karl stared hard at the back of Willard Bask's neck.

MEMO: *Power*

We are fighting for, and we expect to win, a return of power to the hands of the white, Anglo-Saxon, God-fearing, Protestant, not overly-intellectualized citizens of American descent, especially in our Southern states, men of integrity who have kept the old values.

—Masterson

SECTION XVII: OLD VALUES

WILLARD BASK was about six feet tall, slender, with a fine square-featured face that showed only a trace of weakness around the jaw. His clear eyes were the blue-grey of distance, and the necessary impression of fanaticism they produced was softened by his serious grin. Willard spent his summers on the beach, and used lamps to keep his tan dark all winter. Against it, his teeth seemed even and almost sound. His sculptured hair glistened like the whorls of thumb prints in grease. Like the grin, the nose of Willard twisted slightly to one side; he seemed always about to share a private joke with some invisible audience to his right.

Willard opinioned that it might not be all the fault of the Jews, things were all screwed up in the papers and they slanted things. He was sure things could be fixed up again, if the Southern coloured stopped listening to agitators and tended their knitting.

'Let folks be, that's what I always say,' he said often.

MEMO: *Dwelling patterns of the Allendar and Bask families: Patrilocal or matrilocal?*

At first the kinship arrangements of the Allendar and Bask families may seem complex and even arbitrary, but a closer inspection reveals many basic formations common to Southern United States tribes. At the heart of this scheme we find, of course, the familiar automobile, usually an older Ford or Mercury equipped with phallic aerial(s), with mammary steering knob (see formation of the form 'guffer's knob' in Frazer, 'Courtship in the Merc') and certainly with twin anal 'tailpipes'. The greater mobility provided by these vehicles has not led, as expected, to a breakup of the old matrilocal dwelling patterns, but only extended the range of such patterns from village to country, up to 150 miles.

The seven children of Faron Bask and Maypearl Allendar Bask are a case in point: Selma and Wilma settled in the same village with their spouses, while Travis, Truman, Orman, Willard and J.B. moved on to a city at too great a distance to maintain easy contact. Willard's wife, Nelline Parker, bore him four children between her 13th and 17th years. They were then divorced and he moved back into the county of his birth at his mother's death. He left home again, the following year abandoning Etta Leich, his second wife, shortly before her miscarriage. His younger brother, J.B., followed an exactly similar pattern, while Wilma and Selma followed its opposite, e.g., *leaving* the village at the death of their mother. Travis died, and Orman and Truman had not yet married. The Merc belonging to Travis had fender skirts; but when Truman inherited it, these were removed and a sunshade added. The pattern is self-evident

—Masterson

SECTION XVIII: PATTERNS

'IT'S THEM communists, if you'll excuse the expression,' he said earnestly. 'They come down and stir up the coloured. I can't blame the poor coloured. They see all this white pussy around, agitatin', telling them they're as good . . . Well, you can see what that'll lead to, but what can I do? Live and let live, that's my middle name. But you've got to admit the coloured and white used to get along just fine, just fine, without no outside interference. Well, I'm not going to complain. I know God didn't intend coloured and white to mix any more than a washer woman means to mix up coloured and white clothes – it's the white ones get ruint. But who am I to make trouble?'

He glanced around accusingly. A bitter, nagging note came into his voice. 'I'm not complaining. To each their own, that's my motto. I think birds of a feather *ought* to flock together. Why, when I used to pump gas . . .'

SECTION XIX: GOING OUT OF STYLE

'THE SOUTHERN coloured are just different, and if I sat around here explaining till Doomsday, you wouldn't understand what I meant unless you lived down there. I mean *different*. Like they don't know the value of a dollar. Soon as they get a nickel in their jeans, they just *got* to spend it, like it was burning a hole in their pocket.'

Lazily, he unstraddled a chair to fish a five-dollar bill out of his watch pocket with two fingers. Willard was buying coffee for everyone. The deliveryman set down the box of lukewarm covered containers and reached for his change, but Willard waved it away. Before he could taste his own coffee, however, his name was called on the intercom.

SECTION XX: GONE, BUT NOT FORGOT

'DID YOU EVER notice how Willard just throws money away?' asked Karl when he had left. 'Anyone who does that must have a bit tucked away. It wouldn't surprise me to learn that his background is – Biblical, if you get my meaning.'

'I had the same thought,' said Harold. He took a reflective sip of the coffee Willard had bought him – black, for it was Advent – and asked, 'What sort of name is Willard, anyway? Surely not a *Christian* name.'

Ed Warner finished his own coffee and started on Willard's untouched cup. 'Well, he's gone now. No use talking about the dead,' he said firmly.

'He's not—!'

SECTION XXI: IRREGULARITIES

'HE'S NOT!' Karl screamed, his Michelin-tyre head inflating dangerously.

Harold's long celluloid teeth clicked on his paper cup. 'Of course not. He's been fired, I'm sure.' He looked warningly at Ed. 'Caught, I suppose, with his hand in the till.'

'What till?' Ed's yellow cheeks turned the colour of pleasure.

'HE'S NOT DEAD!'

'Prove it.'

Karl seemed about to collapse, but Harold shook his head. 'You should know better than that, Ed. It's up to you to prove that what's-his-name is dead.'

For answer, Ed clutched his chest and crumpled to the floor.

SECTION XXII: FAKE

KARL CROWED. 'He's faking! Knows he lost!'

The old man's lips turned blue.

'He's dying!' Eddie snatched up the phone and dialled an emergency number. The number was printed in red ink on a card stuck to one corner of the bulletin board. Any user of the telephone confronted the bulletin board and read its notices without realizing it.

'Join a bowling team now!' 'THIMK', 'THINK', 'We don't make much money but then we don't have ulcers, either.' 'Give generously to Univac.' 'Join and contribute now: AMERICANS FOR PRIVATE ENTERPRISE.' 'We are asking for flowers for Willard Bask, departed this afternoon. Please *sign* name and write amount *clearly*.' 'Good books for starving Asia.'

'Forget it,' said Karl, pressing down the phone cradle. 'Do you want to get us all in trouble with the authorities? I told you, he's faking. He's not really turning blue.'

Eddie flushed, and his chin, raw with fresh pustules, began to tremble. Shoving Karl aside, he began to dial again. At that moment, the intercom sputtered:

'Edwin EEEEEEEEEEEEEEP! Futch.'

He dropped the receiver and threw both hands to his face.

'Go on, kid,' said Karl gently. 'If it will make you feel any better, *I'll* call the hospital for Ed. All right? Now go on.' He spanked Eddie lightly, starting him towards the door that led to the stairs. With a zombie stride, the youth marched out.

Karl replaced the telephone receiver and lit a cigarette.

'Ed's just faking,' he announced. 'Let's get back to work and just ignore him.'

Harold licked his lips and glanced towards the door. 'Too bad about young Eddie, though. So young – to go like *that*.'

'Yes, death is a natural thing,' Karl said, blowing a smoke ring. 'We must learn to accept it and live with it. There must be nothing frightening or shameful about dying – it is as natural as pee-pee and poop.'

'Yes, the Lord giveth and the Lord taketh away, as the saying goes.'

The figure on the floor coughed, one sudden explosive sound, then lay still. Using his dirty grey handkerchief,

Henry picked up the phone and dialled an emergency number.

SECTION XXIII: REAL

'ALL RIGHT, Ed, keep it up, right to the last minute,' Karl yelled down the hall to the covered basket the ambulance men were removing. 'Keep on faking! You're only fooling yourself!'

His voice was shrill with fury. It excited the professional interest of the intern, who had stayed behind to fill out the death certificate.

'Why don't you sit down for a moment?' he invited. 'I know it's hard to believe in the death of someone close.' He pressed Karl into a chair and asked Henry his name.

'Karl Henkersmahl. He's a stapler.'

'I see. Oh, Mr Henkersmahl? Karl? Would you mind putting a few staples in this form for me? It's the death certificate of Mr Warner.'

Karl moved slowly and reluctantly, but with a great deal of ceremony (*Feierlichkeit*) and precision beautiful to behold. He placed one staple neatly in each corner of the form.

'Say, he really is dead, isn't he?' he murmured then, scratching his head. 'I thought he was just faking.'

'It's too late for that,' said the intern, with a mysterious smile. Though he wore a white uniform, he was a black man.

SECTION XXIX: THE END OF ALL CLERKS

ONE BY ONE, they were all called. Henry thought of quitting first. He even went so far as to interview with another firm, one specializing in famous information. But that night he dreamed that he was brushing his teeth when the toothbrush began ramming wooden splinters up his gums. It was a warning, perhaps.

In the spring, Bob and Rod left, smiling, asking that no flowers be sent after them, that they be cremated by a reliable firm recommended by a leading consumer magazine, and that their ashes be mingled.

At midsummer, Harold left, crossing himself and making signs to ward off the evil eye.

'Nothing to be afraid of,' Karl assured him with a serene smile. 'It's as natural as wee-wee and grunt.'

But when Karl's own name was called he behaved in a strange, unnatural manner. The sound made him jerk erect, spoiling a staple. He carefully replaced it, tidied his desk, and with a private, one-sided smile lifted from the bottom drawer a heavy object encased in leather. This he carried into the lavatory and shut the door. A shot rang out. Before Henry, who was the only one left, could try the door, his own name was called on the intercom.

Part Two: Masterson

SECTION I: THE FIGURE AT THE HEAD OF THE STAIRS

MASTERSON, or a bulging, obnoxious, enigmatic person like Masterson, stood at the head of the stairs. Henry saw he would have to squeeze past him to gain the fourth floor. The eyes in their lenses were quiet and horrible as glass, watching him ascend. In his hand, Henry carried the sheet of paper with his motto: 'If you work good, we'll do good by you.' It was folded in neat thirds, and he held it up before him, like a shielding dental chart.

Who was this Masterson if this were indeed he? Was he truly the author of all memos, or a figurehead? Had he killed the real Masterson and assumed his place? The figure above, beetling over Henry, seemed almost like a great cancer that had once totally absorbed a man; now its vague memory of his lineaments served it to spew forth an idea of death upon the rest of the world.

As Henry moved closer, however, the cancer cleared its throat and stepped back to let him pass. As it did so, he saw the light had been wrong, This was the face of a fat, weary, self-pitying man, nothing more.

SECTION II: THE FOURTH FLOOR

MASTERSON explained to Henry that he was closing the third floor department and moving all clerks into the draughting room on this, the fourth, floor.

The old clerk with skin like parchment appeared once more and led Henry into a large room he'd never known existed, where a dozen draughtsmen hunched low over their boards. As he passed them, he saw that each man was working on an entirely different project.

The first draughtsman was drawing large circles and small circles, and dividing them into quadrants. Mandalas, wheels, gunsights? Henry wanted to ask him what he drew, but he seemed preoccupied.

The second was drawing a long, continuous curve on a roll of paper. He might have explained that this represented infinity, but Henry did not pause to hear.

The third drew a histogram showing apparently the sales or consumption of oxen and earthen jars. It seemed too self-evident to enquire about, but was it?

The fourth copied, from the cover of a book of matches, the picture of a girl, labelled DRAW ME, but he was copying it upside down and reversed. Intrigued, Henry asked him why, but the draughtsman was, alas, stone deaf.

The fifth copied stylized arrowheads, from a pattern book. Henry was too frightened to ask him what his intention was.

The sixth was beginning a schematic diagram called MOODY'S LATEST SERMONS. He asked Henry to get out of his light.

The seventh had outlined a set of regular polygons, and was now beginning to black them in. 'If you like them,' he said to Henry, 'you might pay. Otherwise please move on and give another a chance to see them.'

The eighth drew a bird's wing, 'Detail 43B'. Henry was struck speechless by the beauty of it.

The ninth drew a 'valve' in 'cross-section'. 'It means,' he explained, 'that "My life has for several years been a theatre of calamity."' Henry did not understand.

The tenth made, or had made, a map of possibly the human brain. But he was not at his drawing board, and Henry was able neither to decipher it alone nor await his return.

The eleventh covered his drawing so that Henry could not see it. It was very likely either a blank sheet or a smeary example of the kind of erotic thing he had been dismissed from another job for sketching.

> Two breastlike hills are covered with little figures, archers, shooting crossbows at the sky, or rather at certain objects in the sky. There are dozens of large, vicious-looking sickle shapes, apparently descending to attack the archers or breasts. In the background is a walled city, possibly Nürnberg. It is filth like this that makes me, as a father, wish I could administer the death penalty instead of this five-year sentence.
>
> (from notes of District Judge Ruking)

The twelfth and last draughtsman seemed only to be doing meaningless doodles. This man later left the Masterson Engineering Company and took a job elsewhere lettering placards. He committed suicide in his room by plunging a

French knife (bought for the occasion) into his heart. Impaled on the blade near the hilt the police found a large placard serving as a suicide note. It read:

ACCIDENT

SECTION III: LIPS WHITER THAN TEETH

Past them, at the front corner of the room, were familiar faces in a group. Eddie Futch was eating chocolate noisily. Bob and Rod was tacking up signs saying ACCURASY and SUPPORT IBM. Willard Bask was discussing slavery with Clark Markey. Harold Kelmscott, cowled in an old grey sweater, had turned his back on the others. Only Ed Warner looked up to greet Henry.

'About time,' he said. 'We thought you'd died down there.'

Henry was reminded of the possibly violent death of Karl, which he had forgotten, though it had happened only a few minutes before. Should he report it? he wondered, and if so, to whom? Mr Masterson was inaccessible in his office. The placard on the door, hand-lettered by the last draughtsman, read 'No Personal Conversations. This Means You'.

Karl himself had been against making unnecessary trouble by reporting Ed's death. If Karl was dead, then, the sensible thing to do would be to say nothing. Henry had a great respect for the wishes of the dead.

He began to convince himself that the 'shot' was a truck backfiring in the street, and the 'gun' nothing but an electric shaver or electric toothbrush. Karl had always, when alive, enjoyed electrical cleanliness. *And to what end?* thought Henry C. Henry.

He had begun to rejoice in his own teeth, covered as they were with a thick, resinous deposit like the gum on old furniture. As he remarked to Willard, who was interested in anything like old furniture, 'What if I went around brushing my teeth twice a day all my life, then got them knocked out of my head by some punk in some alley?'

'Hot damn!' said Willard. 'I know just what you mean. Very same thing happened to me once, in 'Frisco. I sure was peeved, I'll tell the world. Makes a fella want to go back home and open an antique store. Fill it with good old solid traditional things. Whew! Fella'd give his left nut for a chance like that.'

Willard wanted to get into a discussion of the draughting tables and the draughtsmen, some of whom were, or seemed to be, Negroes.

Ed Warner kept asking everyone if they knew why he was declared officially dead. No one knew or wanted to know, least of all Karl, when he showed up freshly shaved some days later. Though for some reason he and Ed were not speaking, Karl said loudly for Ed's benefit: 'If he was declared officially dead, he wouldn't be here, and that's that. They don't make mistakes like that, right, Clark?'

'That's right.' The little non-lawyer had grown a foot taller and vaguely hairy. 'They have no right to hire a dead man all over again, when there are so many living unemployed.'

Masterson was not being a pine cone about it. He hired men of all races and nationalities as draughtsmen, because they could be virtually enslaved, and he especially liked to hire Negroes and South American immigrants.

'They all carry big, mean-lookin' knives,' Willard insisted.

'I can't believe that,' said Clark. 'They wouldn't be allowed to carry knives longer than three inches. It's illegal. Besides, I've never seen one of them with such a knife.'

'You better pray you never do see one,' Willard said. 'They only get them out to use them. I know what I'm talkin' about now. I could tell you about one street fight I had in Leningrad. Whewee! Them big bucks come at me with knives like . . .'

To defend himself, Willard began to carry a switchblade.

SECTION IV: DISAPPEARANCES

'No one is so busy as he who has nothing to do,' read the sign Bob (or Rod) was tacking to the wall. Rod (or Bob) looked on in smiling anguish, the better to see him with; later he took up a hammer and amended the sign to read 'he who has *something* to do'. Easter was approaching, and the two pals were selling Valentines – to everyone but Art, the old clerk with his aureole of dust-coloured hair. No one ever tried to sell anything to Art.

The chthonic draughtsmen kept to their stalls and did not mingle with the clerks. It was as if they feared infection, or that fraternizing with their superiors would cost them their jobs. For some reason the draughtsmen did not last long anyhow. They were fired, one at a time, and their tables broken up and burnt, until the day would come . . . but that day was far in the future when Art revealed a true side to his face, unlimbering himself of the waste baskets of the past.

> MEMO: *My childhood.*
> I developed acrophobia, or fear of high places, as soon as I walked. When I was nearly two, my father one day decided to cure me of my irrational fear by making me climb up a tall (12 to 14 foot) stepladder to the top, and there sit until I stopped screaming.
>
> —Masterson

SECTION V: ART SPEAKS

Art was in charge of firing, which consisted of simply filling out a pink slip and putting it into a pay envelope. Henry envied Art this power, the power of dealing effectively with papers. Alone of all the clerks, Art could see the real consequences of his work. He was an old, trusted employee who had been with the firm since its inception.

In fact, as he confided at lunch one day, he was its inceptor, and Masterson's father.

'Does he know you are alive?' asked Henry, incredulous that this harmless, friendly, frail, thin, likeable old man had created both an empire and its frightening emperor.

'Yes.' Art took a small bite of his hamburger and mangled it in the wrinkled depths of his mouth contentedly. With a fine jasper hand he flicked greasy crumbs from his tie. 'Yes, I built the whole shebang, and I nursed it all through the Great Depression, too. It was hard going, let me tell you, but on the other hand, I had all that cheap labour in *long* supply. Ten cents an hour, in the good old days, would buy you an unemployed architect. And I could hit them if I liked, without some damned nosy Labour Board coming around asking questions.'

He shook his wattles wistfully. 'Yes, sir, ten cents an hour. And they were *loyal*, mind you. I had men staying on ten, fifteen years. It was the war ruined all that. I have always been against war, and if you talk at me until you are blue in the face, I'll not change my opinion. War destroys stability. Nowadays, the young men only work for you a year or so, then they run off to get drafted, with not a care for the future of the firm.'

SECTION VI: MASTERSON ON TOUR

Shortly after lunch was the time when Mr Masterson made his afternoon tour. He paced the aisle, holding his fat, hairless hands carefully away from his sides, fingers together and slightly cupped, thumbs braced, as though he were gripping the wheels of a wheelchair. In the watery glass panels on his face, two pale creatures darted back and forth.

Masterson's finger suddenly stabbed the table of one

draughtsman with a sound like a thrown knife. He screamed, 'Arrowheads! I said no arrowheads! Take them out! I distinctly said no arrowheads! When I come back here in an hour, I don't want to see a single arrowhead! No arrowheads! Can't you understand plain English?'

The man did not understand a word he was saying, but he realized erasures were in order, and nodded. He bent lower over his board, and the electric eraser trembled in his hand.

Masterson passed on to the next man. 'What's *that* number?' Stab. 'It looks like a three, for Christ's sake.'

'It is a three, sir.'

'Well, it don't look enough like a three, then. Take it out and do it over.'

Smiling, the man obeyed. Masterson's doughy features began to glow. 'Take out *all* your numbers and do them over. Make them all look like threes.'

He came at last to a deaf-mute, Hrothgar.

'What do you call this? A centreline? And this? If these are centrelines, let's make them look like centrelines, huh?'

Hrothgar looked hurt, but moved to obey.

'And I told you before I wanted more space in there and there. Why don't you *listen* when I'm talking to you?'

'Nggyah-nigg!' protested the victim.

'Don't you talk back to me that way!'

SECTION VII: QUESTIONS

From the office came the sound of a knife being thrown with great force and apparent hate. Perhaps it was as Ed said, that arbitrary power corrupts arbitrarily.

Masterson screamed at the draughtsmen continually, but never at the clerks. He never asked the clerks what it was they were doing because he didn't know what they were doing. It did not suit him to ask a question unless he already knew the answer. Nothing infuriated him more than discovering that someone else knew the answer, too.

'How fast does light travel?' he asked Henry casually one day. Henry did not know.

'I know, naturally. In our measurement system, 186,000 miles per second,' said Karl.

'Who asked you?' said Masterson's right eye. Somewhere inside Karl another eye was closed forever by a foot squashing it; it spewed forth a grapey eyeseed.

The unpleasant marsupiality of Karl's eyes was worsened when he smiled. Little sharp shrew-teeth glittered at the ends of big dead-pale gums, and one knew his tongue would also be black. He looked like someone Henry had met before, somewhere, and Karl had changed. He was a spoiled bear, a bear gone finicky – yet how had he got those teeth?

SECTION VIII: MORE QUESTIONS

Masterson slapped Harold on the shoulder and asked if he could borrow ten till payday. 'I'm a little short, heh heh.' Assuming the boss was joking, Harold began to chuckle.

'No, I'm serious. Had a big weekend with a doll in Boston. I'm flat broke. You know how it is. I could always pay myself my own salary early, but I hate to screw up the bookkeeping, see?' Reluctantly Harold saw. He loaned the ten.

'You'll never see that again,' whispered Big Ed, his face a complete blank. Harold pretended to be unaware of the old man's existence.

Henry noticed how blank Ed was actually becoming, as if someone were slowly erasing him. He was not just blurry, like Clark (who was growing a great mouth-devouring beard), but less definitely there at all.

On the following payday when Art passed around the pay envelopes, Harold did not get his ten. He tried to catch the flickering eye of Masterson when he stalked through the room, but the boss pretended to be unaware of Harold's existence.

'In the good old days,' Art said to Henry, 'I never had to take crap from anybody. Good feeling, being your own boss.

'Why, I used to walk down that aisle and I never even looked at what was on their boards. I just stared real hard at the back of each draughtsman's neck, stared until he thought he was going to get hit. If he flinched, my rule was, I got to hit him twenty times on the arm. Hee hee, they nearly always flinched.'

The two men sat in the warm diner speaking to one another through pale yellow clouds of steam from the french fryer: mists of the distant present. On the previous day, window cleaners had appeared at the office and wiped away the winter's grime. An hour after they had left, a dirty rain began.

'I notice everyone smokes around the office,' Art said. 'Not in my day. I never let anyone smoke, and I'd walk around the office all day puffing fifty-cent cigars and blowing the smoke at them. Drove 'em crazy, especially when I'd dump hot ashes on their drawings. Yes, sir, I ran a tight office in those days.

'If anyone ever sneaked off to the can for a smoke, I'd lock him in there for the rest of the day, then fire him. "Enjoy your smoke," I'd say as I turned the key. "You got all day, bright boy."

'Whee, one time a new kid ran in there for a smoke at about nine in the morning. I locked him in till six. Hee hee, the rest of them didn't like that, I can tell you, working all day without a biff.

'Well, came six o'clock and I opened to let him out, and what do you think that young bastard had done? Hanged himself! Yep, he had that old chain right around his neck and he was stone cold, and the toilet running gallons and gallons. You should have seen my water bill that month.'

His eyes crinkled with amusement. 'Yes, sir, that's the only time anyone ever put anything over on old Art. Hee hee.' He hugged his new coat around him gleefully, while some of his coffee dribbled off the point of his chin.

SECTION IX: THE THEOLOGICAL VIRTUES

Division A: Faith

IT SOON became apparent to all that Harold was going to get the shitty end of the stick.

'Did you even ask him for the money?' asked Ed.

'Well – no. How can I? He'll think I don't trust him.'

'Do you trust him?'

'Of course I do. Heck, he's the *boss*. Our lives are in his keeping, so to speak. Our names are in his book. He gives us each payday our wages. How can we turn against him? The pen is mightier than the sword.'

'But if you trust him, what have you got to gripe about?'

Harold, descended of a flawed monk, pondered this point of faith. 'It isn't the money, you understand. Heck, I don't care if I never see that ten again.'

'What is it then?'

'It's just that I trust him, and now he's going to betray that trust. He's going to welsh on me.'

'Maybe he just forgot,' Karl purred, showing his little nasty teeth.

'Oh sure. He forgets; and I never see my money again. You can be sure *he* wouldn't forget if if *I* owed *him* ten dollars.'

Clark made a diplomatic suggestion. 'Look, just ask him if you can borrow ten from him. If he's forgotten about the loan, it'll remind him of it, and if he's planned on welshing, he'll be caught out ashamed. Besides, this way he'll know you need the money right away.'

Division B: Hope

Harold accosted Mr Masterson. 'Sir, could I borrow ten from you till payday? Heh, heh, I'm a little short, at the moment.'

The bulging figure turned slowly with the dignity of a wagon train, and faced him. For over a minute, Masterson subjected Harold to an intense stare of scorn and disbelief. Then he sighed and pulled out his billfold. Harold sighed, too.

'I wish you'd learn to live within your means, Kelmscott. I'm not a loan company. Now I'm going to loan you this, but it's the last time, understand?' The hinged glasses beetled over him.

'But I do live within my means, sir,' Harold stammered. 'It's not me who has weekends in Boston with a girl.'

The pale eyes did not register anything. Masterson sighed again, heaving his big, flabby shoulders. 'I'm not interested in nasty details of your personal life, Kelmscott. If you can't live on what I pay you, maybe you'd better look elsewhere for a job.' With a snort of disgust, he peeled a ten from his thick bundle of large bills and slapped it on Harold's desk. Then he stalked off to his office to throw, presumably, knives.

Division C: Charity

Every time an object hit the wall, Willard jumped. 'Oh God,' he moaned. 'I just know he's got some big, mean-lookin' knives in there.'

From time to time, Willard got out his own knife and tested the action. It was never fast enough to suit him.

At lunch, Henry asked Art about the pink slips. Did he ever warn anyone they were about to be fired?

The old man stopped masticating. 'Sir, watch your tongue. The job of firing is a sacred trust. My son, Mr Masterson, has entrusted me with the care of and disbursement of those pink slips, and of the persons they represent. Do you think I could let him down? My own son?'

Drawing himself up, Art for the moment resembled a famous general, and his thin chest seemed even to fill out the folds of his new coat.

'Besides,' he added with a wheeze. 'I like to watch a man's face when he opens his envelope. Boy, he sees those streets, those employment offices, even soup lines, hee hee hee . . .' His laughter turned to a fit of dry coughing.

SECTION X: A HIGH OFFICE

That afternoon, Mr Masterson called Henry into his office. None of the clerks but Art had ever been there before, and Art had forgotten what it was like. Rod and Bob looked envious of Henry, but Karl smirkingly assumed he was being *given the axe.*

'If you want my opinion,' he said, 'I think you're going to be quietly *axed* to leave. Ha!'

Willard drew him aside and said, 'Play it cool, boy. If he pulls a knife, just you give me a holler.'

Henry pushed open the door with the placard and entered a plain, drab room. On one wall was a peculiar dart board, and on the floor beneath it a huge pile of darts with plastic fins. Near the opposite wall was a long desk behind which was visible the upper half of Mr Masterson. In his hands was a dart with green plastic fins. Nothing else in the room was describable.

The boss half-rose, turned and hurled the dart; it hit a spot near the baseboard with a sound like a thrown knife, hung for an instant, then fell to the heap.

'So it goes,' sighed Masterson, or maybe, 'How would you like a raise?'

'Fine, sir.'

'Here's the set-up. We may have a new contract or two. Already we have a new contact or two. It's the big chance. All the candy companies on the coast are changing over to dynamometers. They'll need a lot of records and stuff switched over, too, and that's where we come in. If we can handle the changeover for one company, we can do good. Then all the other companies will want us to do good for them, too. Get it? Then later on, when the armed forces change from telephones to radios, we'll be set, see?

'But we'll need some extra help, and I'll need your help. You could be my right hand, and it'll mean a lot of extra money for the company, OK?'

SECTION XI: THE MYSTERIOUS MOTTO

Henry remembered his motto, the words spoken to him by the boss the day he'd hired him. As they had occurred to him, Henry had added interpretations, until now the sheet was covered; but which had the boss actually said?

If you work good, we'll do good by you.
If few work good, we'll do good by you.
If you were good, we'll do good by you.
If few were good, we'll do good by you.
If you work good weal, do good by you.
If few work good weal, do good by you.
If you were good weal, do good by you.
If few were good weal, do good by you.

In addition to these, there were the 24 combinations possible by replacing 'good by you' by 'good buy you', 'goodbye, you', and finally 'good bayou'. Though it was unlikely that he said 'If few were good weal, do good bayou', that possibility could not be overlooked, Henry thought as he shook hands and prepared to leave.

'One thing, though,' said Masterson, counting that thing on his forefinger. 'Of course you'll make a lot of dough eventually, after our contacts become contracts, but you'll have to take a little pay cut for now, OK?'

They shook hands once more, and Henry started to leave. The boss held up two fingers. 'Secondly, now that you're a boss, you'll have to do a little informing on your pals. Remember, a boss has no real pals, and the great are always lonely.

'So I want you to tell me who hates me and who likes me. Let me know everything they say about me, understand?' He brought out another dart and threw it at the strange dart board.

'When the time comes—' the dart stuck weakly in the edge of the board and drooped. 'You'll get your reward.' The dart fell quietly to the floor.

'Especially I want to know what my father says about me. You eat with him, don't you?'

'How did you know?'

Masterson wagged his fat forefinger. 'I have my spies, I have my spies,' he said archly. 'But tell me, does he talk about me a lot?'

'No.'

'Don't you lie to me! I know he talks about me all the time. All right, get out of here, then, and forget about that swell job.'

Henry waited for a pink slip, but it never came. Indeed, he seemed to receive the promotion after all, for he took a pay cut.

SECTION XII: A HAZARD OF NEW FORTUNES

All that week they worked on the bid. Masterson never left the aisle, but stamped, screamed, pounded on tables, and chewed to pieces dozens of dart-fins. He directed his father to hand out pink slips to anyone who got in his way, or to anyone who sneaked around behind him.

> MEMO: *Is there life on other planets?*
> This question is of the utmost importance to all of us, whether or not we are actually located in the aerospace industries, for it is a restatement of another, all-inclusive question: *Are we alone in the universe*? And if not, *who else is there*? These questions pose problems as yet unanswered; we can only wonder and hope and pray. But whether or not we ever find life on other planets, I feel confident that each and every one of us will want to give this question our full and careful consideration.
>
> —Masterson

The first real crisis was paper. Masterson decided that ordinary tracing vellum was too expensive, and substituted newsprint. This rough, absorbent stuff made spiderwebs of ink lines and spiders of lettering. Masterson began to scream at the draughtsmen, sometimes with eloquence, sometimes wordlessly.

'Why can't you make neat, black lines and letters?' he demanded, and held up a newspaper. Pointing to a story about Hurricane Patty Sue, he said: 'Take a look at this. *They* don't have any trouble making neat lines and letters. Just look at this neat work.'

They tried again, again complaining of the paper, until Masterson, with a martyred smile, said, 'All right, all right. I'll get you some fancy, expensive paper. But *then*—'

He left, and returned an hour later with what appeared to be a roll of wide, slick toilet paper. Along one border ran the tiny green words: 'Deutsches Bundesbahn'.

In Austria, a fat Mercedes-Benz rolled on fat tyres into a filling station. The attendant saluted and began to fill the tank, while from behind the wheel a fat man rolled out, hitched up his belt and moved towards the toilet like a file of elephants going to the river. The sunlight gleamed on him, on his damp hair and his white shirt of miracle fibres. In one pocket of it was a leather liner containing a matching ballpoint pen and mechanical pencil and a steel scale, marked off both in centimetres and inches. In the other pocket was a package of Roth Handel cigarettes and a roll of hard candy liqueurs. The man stood a moment in the sun, gazing at four brown cows in the field nearby; in this town lived the engineer who designed the ovens at Dachau; the traveller thought of all this and then went in to shit. He, too, was an engineer. Once he had written to an American magazine, asking for the names of engineering firms, of the particular type which included the Masterson Engineering Company. Due to an oversight, however, the engineer did not receive that name.

The draughtsmen tried again and again, but still their work did not satisfy Masterson. Finally, the eyes swelling behind his huge lenses, he screamed, 'Stop! I want you to stop. Erase everything. I want you to erase everything.'

For an hour, the only sound was the hum of electric erasers. One or two people erased holes in the fragile paper; they were given pink slips at once. Finally Masterson collected the twenty blank sheets, touched them up with an artgum eraser, wrapped them carefully and sent them out.

'We've got the contract sewed up,' he joyfully confided to the clerks. 'No one else could turn out work at neat as that, ever. Not one single mistake!'

Yet the next day, even while Rod and Bob were collecting money to buy flowers for the departed package, it came back. His thick hands fumbled at the bale of tattered tissue; Masterson read the accompanying letter aloud, and sobs hung quivering from his voice like drops of water from a tap.

'Dear Sirs:

Re yours of the thirteenth inst., we have no specific need for railroad station toilet tissue at present.

Thank you for keeping us in mind.'

SECTION XIII: ALL'S WELL IN THE END

Masterson removed his glasses and began cleaning them on a scrap of the tissue. He turned his back modestly so that no one could glimpse his naked eyes. As he settled the frames once more on his cheeks, he cleared his throat with an oddly familiar sound. Henry leaned over and asked Ed, 'Will you tell me why you were declared officially dead?'

Ed pretended not to hear, and gazed steadily at the boss, who moved now on ponderous tiptoes to Art's desk. 'Give yourself a pink slip,' he sighed, and ran away to his office. The little old man nodded eagerly and began filling out a pink slip at once.

The next day was payday, and all watched Art closely as he passed out the envelopes. Smirking as usual, he sat down to open his own. The money he'd sealed into it and the pink slip he'd signed slid out together, and Art's face seemed to fold in thirds, like a business letter.

Clark Markey, always the barometer of another's mood, began to weep for him. Art himself merely sat there, staring at the slip lying flat on his desk.

'Noo,' he said in a small voice. 'They can't do this to me. Not to old Art.' He said it like a speech of condolence.

'It isn't fair,' said Clark with feeling. 'They can't make a man fire himself.'

Art walked slowly to the office, pounded on the placard, waited. The sound of darts within ceased.

'Let me in,' he cried. 'You've got to talk to me, Mr Masterson.'

'Go away, Dad,' said a muffled voice. Art trudged to the coat rack, slipped on his old, worn coat, and left.

A moment or two later, the dart game resumed.

Part Three: The Dismantling

MEMO: *My childhood.*
My father was a large cheque drawn on First National City Bank, and my mother was very tired.
—Masterson

SECTION I: IMPROVEMENTS

Things were looking up. Business seemed much improved, for everyone took enormous pay cuts. Karl was promoted to Art's old job. In addition to precision stapling, he now made out pink slips and took charge of office supplies. He began to detect and eliminate sources of waste.

Bob and Rod were promoted to informers. They blamed Masterson's father for everything, so their pay was not cut.

Clark Markey had begun to study law. Too many questions of justice now tormented him. How could a dead man be rehired? How could a man be forced to fire himself? At lunch hour he sat hunched over a large volume of labour laws, dropping crumbs (larger than whole words of the fine print) from his cream cheese sandwich. He was not a lawyer, and many of the long paragraphs were unintelligible to him. He began to suspect that in these lay the very answers he was seeking.

Masterson began looking fresh and fit. His death-colour skin took on a pink tinge, as if he daily gorged on blood. He bulged less, and began to walk around the office on new ripple-soled shoes, smacking his fist in his palm and saying, 'Now that the dead wood is cleared away, we can really *move*.' He made a progress chart.

Karl moved to eliminate the shocking waste of forms around the office. 'Look,' he explained to the group. 'We always have old, used forms around. Why don't we just eradicate the ink from them and re-use them?'

SECTION II: A FAST

After Christmas, Harold Kelmscott began a fast. It was, he said, in protest of his not being repaid the ten dollars the boss had borrowed; it was a form of sitting in dharna. Karl, who handled the pay envelopes, knew better. Masterson had garnisheed all of Harold's wages against the twenty he claimed Harold owed him.

'You can have your pay,' Karl explained, 'when the boss gets his twenty back.'

'Twenty! But I only borrowed ten, and that he had already borrowed from me.'

'If he borrowed it from you, how come you had to borrow it back? Come on, Harold, don't be a welsher. You're too nice a guy. Pay him his twenty, will you?'

'How can I, as long as I'm not getting paid myself? This is worse than debtor's prison, isn't it, Clark?' Harold looked to the non-lawyer for sympathy.

'What? Who knows? I'd have to check with English Civil Law,' said Clark testily, not looking up from his perusal of the New York Code.

Karl wagged his close-cropped head. 'Harold, you're a case, the worst I've ever seen. You know very well the boss isn't trying to cheat you. In fact, I begged him – I *begged* him to fire you and haul you into court. God knows you deserve it.

'But no, he said he wouldn't even stop the money out of your wages. He said if you didn't want to pay him, that was between you and your conscience. "I'm worried about Harold," he said to me. "I think I'll just garnishee his wages until he pays me back."

'You see, he knows you've got this shack-job in Boston, and he figures it ain't doing your character any good. But by the time you get squared away on your debt, she'll have forgotten all about you. Not only that, but you'll get all your pay at once, a real pile.'

'I'm starving,' Harold announced humbly. 'To death.'

Karl continued counting paper clips. 'You're a real case,' he muttered.

SECTION III: FURTHER PROGRESS

Having devised a method of rebending and re-using old paper clips, Karl saw a further short cut. Rather than eradicate the ink from old forms, he encouraged the others to use disappearing ink in the first place.

Willard kept his knife in his hand at all times, now, and feared everyone who moved suddenly or talked loudly. He took up whittling, to give himself an excuse for holding a knife. One day Masterson, jogging by, asked him if he could make a table, since he was so clever with his hands.

One week later, Willard presented him with a perfect matchbox-size Louis Quinze table, painted and gilded. Lifting it from his calloused palm, Willard set it carefully in the centre of the boss's desk.

'Idiot!' Masterson screamed, and brought his fist down on it. 'I meant a *real* table. A table of our progress.'

'Wait,' said Karl. 'If he can do this, Willard here can make big tables for all the clerks. Then we could sell off all the desks.'

Masterson had taken down and discarded the dart board, and now his walls were covered with charts. He and Karl planned many new charts and tables, and Harold executed them.

There was a chart of business volume compared to paper-clip expenditure, one of volume of work versus man-hours, one of level of water in the water cooler versus work output and one of Mr Masterson's weight versus the strength of his grip. They were inversely proportional, so that, had his weight been zero, his grip would have been a thousand pounds.

Three times a day he lifted weights in his office, rising on the toes and exploding breath through clenched teeth. At lunch hour, he ran three laps around the block, showered and gulped quantities of natural foods. Most mornings he came in with skinned knuckles and stories of brawls that frightened Willard. Masterson was no longer a shapeless bulgy man of indeterminate age, but a handsome, powerful man of about twenty-five.

'He's getting in shape to die,' Ed 'opined'.

Masterson had Harold post charts of his progress. There were graphs of his biceps and triceps, and a phrenological chart of his head. The boss began to talk about what great shape the company was in, squeezing grip developers as he talked.

'As soon as we trim off a little fat here and there, as soon as we fire the draughtsmen, we'll be in great shape.' He fired the draughtsmen the next day, *en masse*, owing them three weeks' wages, and Henry complained to Clark about it.

Clark was getting jowly and near-sighted from cream cheese and law, and his temper was noticeably shorter. 'What am I supposed to do?' he said. '*Caveat emptor*. Why come to me with your problems? All I want is to be left alone with Law.'

Henry scooped up some dirty, tattered forms from the floor and began filling them out, in invisible ink. For several weeks, no work had left the office. Messengers who called to pick up work were sent out to get more natural foods for Mr Masterson. Karl sent them on errands for invisible carbon paper, or to sell the desks that were slowly being replaced by Willard's tables.

Great bales of papers piled up, collecting dust. They grew greasy and black from handling, and Henry grew greasy and black from handling them. He washed and brushed his teeth often, but one cannot hold in the heart what is not bred in the bone: he stank.

Bob and Rob organized a clean-up campaign. They collected all the dirty forms in the office and laundered them. Karl was so pleased with their efforts that he even permitted them to sew patches on worn-out forms, though common practice did not permit this. Even so, after the windows came out, they could not keep up with the dirt.

No one but Henry and Ed and Eddie were working full-time on clerical duties. Clark was reading law full-time now, and Masterson had come to approve this. 'You never can tell when you'll need a good mouthpiece,' he said, and began calling Clark 'the mouthpiece'. The mouthpiece never spoke to anyone.

Harold was making charts of the company and of Mr Masterson full time. They overflowed the walls of his office and began to cover the corridor.

There was a chart showing the chain of command and another showing the flow of work. There was a chart showing weight of forms handled per clerk per day; a chart showing all the muscles of Mr Masterson's body (with the Latin labels lettered by Harold in half-uncials); a chart of company work-output vs world population, and a fishing map of Northern Minnesota, which Mr Masterson planned to visit some day. There was a graph showing the monthly number of accidents, fatal, and accidents, non-fatal, per clerk.

Karl's job included researching the data for all of these. He counted paper clips, measured the level of water in the cooler, taped Mr Masterson's biceps, weighed forms, and estimated the world population. His estimates, Harold chuckled, were not conservative enough.

But Masterson pointed out how efficient Karl was. Who else would have realized the wasteful duplication in using both pink and blue copies of the same form? Karl had purchased a new single form printed on litmus paper, which was either blue or pink, depending on the weather. Ed seemed to grow a beard, which had the appearance of frightening Masterson. Clark wore rimless glasses.

The janitor service was cut off because the rent had not been paid. Karl had estimated the company could survive one year without it, saving several thousand dollars.

On the stage of a nearby theatre, two girls, one dressed as a man, were singing a song about making little gifts. One of the girls was sincere, but it was never clear which. Bob and Rod explained to the boss his father had sabotaged the janitor service.

'He sees what a good thing the company is getting to be,' one of them said. 'He wants to muscle in on you.'

'Well, I'm ready for him,' said Masterson. 'Let him try something.' Grinning, he flexed his forearm and watched the sinew lumps move in it as characters move about on a stage. Rod and Bob, or as they preferred being called, Dob and Rob, began doing janitor work around the office. They refused service to anyone who would not contribute to their list of charities: CORE, CARE, KKK, CCC, the Better Business Bureau, AAA and Minnesota Mining and Manufacturing Company. Only Harold did not give.

They cornered him one day. 'What's the matter? Don't you care that millions of Asians are starving while you sit here well-fed and complacent?' Harold did not deign to reply, or perhaps had not the strength. His skeletal face showed odd emotions, but he did not look up from his chart. Steadying a hunger-quaking hand, he went on with his beautiful, flowing uncials.

Living on the scraps of other clerks' lunches, and on the crumbs of cream cheese in Clark's law books, Harold was under a hundred pounds. He gulped water from the cooler, until Karl stopped him, saying that it ruined the line on the water-consumption estimates.

Once Harold fainted, and Mr Masterson revived him with

a little natural soya meal. Harold gulped it down until Karl, alarmed at the way the expensive stuff was disappearing, grabbed the canister away. 'Easy does it, now,' he said. 'Not good to take too much at once.'

Willard made tables to replace all desks, but more tables were required. The volume of business, as Karl explained it, was steadily increasing. Consulting a table of Willard's table-making progress, he was not satisfied. 'Why don't you make tables out of the doors? It might be faster.'

'Or make coffins,' whispered Ed.

Willard converted all the doors into tables. When still more were needed, he unputtied window-panes and began using them for table-tops. The windows were grimy, and nearly everyone appreciated the increase in light.

Clark's sight was failing. Eddie Futch now read Law to him. Clark's sedentary life had made him gouty, and he began to walk about with a stick. From time to time, he would take a turn about the room, flicking with his stick at the dead forms that lay everywhere like leaves, like history. He would mutter legal phrases to himself through gritted teeth.

It was spring again, and a chill, dirty wind whipped through the office, whirling drawings and forms in a constant flux. To keep some of them in place, Henry borrowed weights from Mr Masterson's office.

The boss was rarely there these days. He worked out at a gym most of the week, and only bounced in occasionally to assure them that the company was recouping its losses at a truly fantastic rate. The litter of dirty forms was now ankle deep.

MEMO: *Dreams*

I dreamed of finding pieces of hate.

I dreamed an obscure dream: part of it was talking with a psychiatrist who looked something like Hemingway and something like Jung, and showing him my written-down dreams. It seems that I had never remembered the important parts. I forgot the rest.

I dreamed of loving the princess of the glass house, Geopatra, full of mirrors and swimming pools.

—Masterson

No one talked, except Eddie Futch, droning periods of Law. Whenever the youngster stumbled, Clark caned him across the back, screaming epithets. Once the non-lawyer grew so excited that he had to take a turn around the room, limping and muttering, '. . . ergo sum . . . ignoratio elenchi . . . petitio principii . . . non compos mentis . . . mons veneris . . .'

'Ed' nudged Henry, pointed to the ponderous figure and laughed. 'They're fattening him up for the kill,' he said.

'Who is?' Henry's ass felt a chill.

'Who knows? Maybe no one. Maybe "they" is just a figure of speech . . . but then maybe, you know, maybe *we're* just figures of speech, eh?'

MEMO: *Park conditions today*

Thick pink balloons were drifting over the park from some unknown source. They reminded the boy and the girl of giant drops of rosy sperm. Flowers seemed to be exploding at their feet as the boy took out his gold-filled ballpoint pen and wrote, in an unpretentious, sturdy, masculine hand, a love poem.

The poem spoke of fire-trucks and other excitements, of televisable passions, of a love nest made of food, wherein they settle:

No car honks madly;
The mayor gives the death penalty for honking tonight;
And cars have nightingales in place of horns.

The girl placed a drop of perfume on the pulse of her throat, and began to curve the soft inner part of her arm about the boy's writing hand. Inside every pink balloon was a hundred-dollar bill. A passing policeman thrust his nightstick at the polka-dot sky and laughed out of pure joy. The flowers made a noise like distant target practice. The boy leaped and the girl laughed. The policeman's gun belt shook with laughter, while overhead the opalescences bumped one another silently.

—Masterson

'You want to know why I was declared officially dead?' Ed asked. Henry shook his head and pointed to a sign affixed to his table: 'No Personal Conversations. This Means You.'

'I was declared officially dead because Karl put four staples in my death certificate.' The water was cut off. Henry seized Ed by the throat and tried to strangle him, as one might strangle an empty faucet, not to choke it off, but to make it flow again.

'Art's cut off the water, now,' Rob and Dob reported to Art's son.

'Oh, trying to starve us out, is he?' His heavy handsome jaw took a stern set. 'We'll just see about that.'

Harold showed him his latest, indeed his last effort, a chart of the basic natural foods and their constituents, arranged in a segmented circle. Heavy with gold-and-red illumination, the chart was called: 'THE WHEEL OF LIFE'.

'Very nice indeed, Harold,' said the boss, reaching for it. A ripple of muscle was visible through his specially-tailored suit. 'But you seem to be losing weight. Why is that? Dieting to improve the strength of your grip? I tried that, and it worked wonders.

'By the way, I hate to ask you for it, Harold, but when are you going to pay me that twenty you owe me? I really need it – got a big week-end in Boston coming up. You know what I mean.' He winked, and winked again at Clark.

'Well, now, mouthpiece, say something legal,' boomed the boss. A voice croaked from the tangled depths of Clark's beard. Holding his cane to the sky, he said, '*Mens sana in—*' he belched painfully, '*—in corpore sano.*'

'Fine, fine,' said Masterson, not hearing him. His powerful calves waded through the knee-deep debris effortlessly and carried him to his office.

MEMO: *On Communication*

____

____

____

____

—Jqw534w9h

From the office came the clink and chunk of weights, and breath hissing through clenched teeth. Suddenly, as he lettered the words 'The Form Divine', Harold collapsed. Henry reached him first and held up his head. Harold cast a rueful look on his unfinished work, murmured, 'I go . . . I go to the Death Registration Office,' and died.

'Now where,' said Karl, 'did I put that fatal accidents chart?'

There came a deep reverberation, not Masterson. He came bounding from his office in sweatpants, his chest gleaming with perspiration. 'What the hell is going on?' he demanded. 'Is someone else lifting weights around here? He's fucking up my timing.'

The crew made its way down the stairs after him, to see the other weightlifter. Eddie led Clark down last, a step at a time. Naturally Ed and Harold remained behind.

The offices all the way down were empty. When they reached the sidewalk, the clerks found a derrick smashing at their building with a steel ball.

Masterson walked over to have a word with the foreman, who held up the destruction for the moment.

'We're tearing it down.'

'Why?'

'Abandoned.'

'. . . some mistake, or . . .'

'But nobody works there.'

Masterson said something else as the foreman gave a signal and the derrick engine roared. The tall tower turned awkwardly, like a hand puppet, setting the ball into motion.

The man shook his pink helmet. 'I don't know nothing about no father,' he shouted. 'All I know is, we got *work* to do.' He signalled the derrick operator, who swung the moving ball far back, then towards the wall.

Mr Masterson ran headlong towards it, springing with the grace of a dancer on his ripple soles. For a moment, it looked as if the steel ball would bounce harmlessly off his great chest.

New Forms

THE CORRESPONDING CHOICE TEST	LN-276440-V
DIRECTIONS: Mark the choice that seems to you to be best for each question. Do it now. Read directions wITH care.	
EXAMPLE: Small does (a) graven (b) craven (c) raven (d) Bill. Now answer the rest of the questions in the same way.	

1. In India, bhuta are the ghosts of violent criminals. They are represented with small thick bodies of a red colour, with pigtails round their heads, horrible faces, the teeth of a lion in their mouths, and their bodies covered with ornaments. Who are they?

2. Capering will: (a) manage (b) silk (c) dub (d) shale.

3. Covered with ornaments: (a) baize (b) Kools (c) seizure.

4. Take no notice of: (a) LN-276440-V (b) Kools (c) notice.

5. I gave you as many apples as John gave me if John received more apples from you than he bought. If John bought three fewer apples than I could have bought if I had twice as many as you, how many apples in all?

5. Hanford.

6. Ape is to raven as giant is to: (a) small (b) giant (c) ape (d) giant.

7. Taken: (a) volute (b) fray

8. The same applies to ordinary commerce. If the supply somehow exceeds the demand, the price will drop until the surplus is gone, but if the demand exceeds the supply the price will rise, increasing the supply!

9. God be with ye. (ape)

10. Praxion: (a) swit (b) duthe (c) yalkin (d) flaze.

11. (a) is to (b) as (c) is to: (a)(b) (b)(c) (c)(b) (d)(a)

12. God created me with free choice. (a) Yes (b) No.

13. I am often troubled by:
 (a) choice (b) trouble (c) God (e) Hanford (d) one of the above.

Forms are clerical ways of dealing with reality (tidying it up, clearing it away, and so forth). To the perceptions of the clerk, a form is reality. His eyes need it in black and white, and any other reality goes unrecognised.

Once, birth was marked by a baby's cry and death by the silence of the heart. We clerks of the world have replaced all that; now there are certificates to take care of these matters. It is almost impossible to be born, die, marry, pay taxes, sell or buy property, obtain a pension or apply for a job without being punished with a form.

"Forms are created to formalise, inform, and finally replace 'life' as 'we' know it." The man who said that to me has lost his identity. Somehow every single piece of paper recording this man's name has been lost or destroyed; he no longer officially exists. He has been tidied up and cleared away. I forget his name.

Indiana Name Opinion Register

Q-Q-QQ
1937

Name ______________________________
Address ______________________________
Age ______________________________ (give latest date)

1. Give your own name in full: ______________________________

2. Print your Name in Block Capitals: ______________________________

3. Now give your NAME: ______________________________

4. Read the INSTRUCTIONS carefully, and do not begin until the teacher TELLS you to. In the first part, you will be expected to write as many names as you can in the time available, but you need not have them all correct. In the second part you will be expected to tell what it is you have named, and do so correctly. NOW BEGIN PART ONE.

PART ONE. Name as many things as you can before the teacher says STOP. Begin with your own name, then add other names. Now Stop. Begin with other names. Then stop. Begin. BEGIN:

1.____ 2.____ 3.____ 4.____ 5.____ 6.____ 7.____ 8.____ 9.____ 10.____
11.____ 12.____ 13.____ 14.____ 15.____ 16.____ 17.____ 18.____ 19.____ 20.____

PART TWO. Fill in the blanks, then explain:

21. My name is________. 22. The name of_________ is _________. 23. This is the name of ________________. 24. This is my name____________________. 25. ______________. 26. Explain the names given above, and explain:________

______________________________ Signature: ______________ (X)

Individual Bend Record A-23-"B"

Individual number.........................
Estimation................................
Authorized by.............................

DATE	BEND					
	1	2	3	4	From	To

POETRY ITEMIZATION P-40-1

Poem Written	Date	Meaning	Poem Read	Date	Meaning
1.			1.		
2.			2.		
3.			3.		
4.			4.		
5.			5.		
6.			6.		
7.			7.		
8.			8.		
9.			9.		
10.			10.		
11.			11.		
12.			12.		
13.			13.		
14.			14.		
15.			15.		
16.			16.		
17.			17.		
18.			18.		
19.			19.		
20.			20.		

CHARACTER SIMULATION FORM

Name ....
Occupation....................
Firm..........................
Telephone Number..............
Transfer Rate............
Cordiality..........
Compensation.....
Hair........

Address..........................
Zip Code.........................
Area Code........................
Transference.....................
Social Security Number.....
Cephalic Index.......
Bo/aldness......
Nuance....

Present Worries:______________
____
____
____

Left Eyebrow movements?.......

Right Eyebrow movements?.......

LEFT EYE:
Colour?... Size?...
Vision?...
Tic?...

Nose 1.
2.
3.
4.
5.
6.
7.
8.
9.
10.
11.
12.
13.
14.
15.
16.
17.
18.
19. 20.

RIGHT EYE:
Colour?... Size?...
Vision?...
Tic?...

Seal of Issue Date

Seal of Approval Date

Describe in detail the entire straight line

of the mouth, numbering missing teeth, etc.

Single letter table I.
A

Multiple letter table II.	
AB	BA

Multiple letter table III.					
ABC	ACB	BAC	BCA	CAB	CBA

Multiple letter table IV.			
ABCD	BACD	CABD	DABC
ABDC	BADC	CADB	DACB
ACBD	BCAD	CBAD	DBAC
ACDB	BCDA	CBDA	DBCA
ADBC	BDAC	CDAB	DCAB
ADCB	BDCA	CDBA	DCBA

Multiple letter table VI.					
ABC	ABC	ABC	ABC	ABC	ABC
BCA	BCA	BCA	BCA	BCA	BCA
CAB	CAB	CAB	CAB	CAB	CAB
DEF	DEF	DEF	DEF	DEF	DEF
EFD	EFD	EFD	EFD	EFD	EFD
FDE	FDE	FDE	FDE	FDE	FDE
GHI	GHI	GHI	GHI	GHI	GHI
HIG	HIG	HIG	HIG	HIG	HIG
IGH	IGH	IGH	IGH	IGH	IGH
JKL	JKL	JKL	JKL	JKL	JKL
KLJ	KLJ	KLJ	KLJ	KLJ	KLJ
LJK	LJK	LJK	LJK	LJK	LJK
MNO	MNO	MNO	MNO	MNO	MNO
NOM	NOM	NOM	NOM	NOM	NOM
OMN	OMN	OMN	OMN	OMN	OMN

Multiple letter table V.				
ABCDE	BACDE	CABDE	DABCE	EABCD
ABCED	BACED	CABED	DABEC	EABDC
ABDCE	BADCE	CADBE	DACBE	EACBD
ABDEC	BADEC	CADEB	DACEB	EACDB
ABEDC	BAECD	CAEBD	DAEBC	EADBC
ABECD	BAEDC	CAEDB	DAECB	EADCB
ACBDE	BCADE	CBADE	DBACE	EBACD
ACBED	BCAED	CBAED	DBAEC	EBADC
ACDBE	BCDAE	CBDAE	DBCAE	EBCAD
ACDEB	BCDEA	CBDEA	DBCEA	EBCDA
ACEBD	BCEAD	CBEAD	DBEAC	EBDAC
ACEDB	BCEDA	CBEDA	DBECA	EBDCA
ADBCE	BDACE	CDABE	DCABE	ECABD
ADBEC	BDAEC	CDAEB	DCAEB	ECADB
ADCBE	BDCAE	CDBAE	DCBAE	ECBAD
ADCEB	BDCEA	CDBEA	DCBEA	ECBDA
ADEBC	BDEAC	CDEAB	DCEAB	ECDAB
ADECB	BDECA	CDEBA	DCEBA	ECDBA
AEBCD	BEACD	CEABD	DEABC	EDABC
AEBDC	BEADC	CEADB	DEACB	EDACB
AECBD	BECAD	CEBAD	DEBAC	EDBAC
AECDB	BECDA	CEBDA	DEBCA	EDBCA
AEDBC	BEDAC	CEDAB	DECAB	EDCAB
AEDCB	BEDCA	CEDBA	DECBA	EDCBA

Multiple letter table VII.			
AA	AB	BA	BB

Multiple letter table VIII.								
AAA	AAB	AAC	ABA	ABB	ABC	ACA	ACB	ACC
BAA	BAB	BAC	BBA	BBB	BBA	BCA	BCB	BCC
CAA	CAB	CAC	CBA	CBB	CBC	CCA	CCB	CCC

Multiple letter table IX.											
AAAA	AAAAB	AAAC	AAAD	ABAA	ABAB	ABAC	ABAD	ACAA	ACAB	ACAC	ACAD
AABA	AABB	AABC	AABD	ABBA	ABBB	ABBC	ABBD	ACBA	ACBB	ACBC	ACBD
AACA	AACB	AACC	AACD	ABCA	ABCB	ABCC	ABCD	ACCA	ACCB	ACCC	ACCD
AADA	AADB	AADC	AADD	ABDA	ABDB	ABDC	ABDD	ACDA	ACDB	ACDC	AACDD
								ADAA	ADAB	ADAC	ADAB
								ADBA	ADBB	ADBC	etc.

198-, a Tale of 'Tomorrow'

Ernest thought it would be fun to let his computer call up Frank's computer on the telephone.

'Good to hear yours, too! But hey, do you know what a.m. it is out here?'

Al is seen glancing at his watch. Thanks to a vibrating quartz crystal in it, this watch keeps very, very accurate time. He looks from its Swiss face to the American face of Dot, his wife, who is in the back yard eating a piece of fruit that has been picked the day before yesterday in the Orient. Will miracles – or anything – ever cease? The digital clock reports a new minute.

'I met you,' Al said into a portable tape recorder no larger than a package of cigarettes, 'a year, three days, seven hours and forty-three minutes ago, through that popular computer dating service. You had brushed your teeth electrically, using stannous fluoride toothpaste to prevent decay. I had just had dacron veins put in.'

'Times change. You now have someone else's liver and kidney; I have ridden on an atomic ship.'

On the atomic ship, Al will notice an interesting article about LSD, a drug commonly supposed to cause visions and insights. He would reproduce this article by xerography, a fast electrostatic process making use of powdered ink.

Al called Bertha, his ex-wife, on the hall videophone.

'I just took a stay-awake pill,' she said. 'I've been so sleepy ever since the sauna I took, on the airbus from—'

'What's new?'

'I'm pregnant again, due to the fertility drug I'm taking. Al, and I have a new non-stick saucepan. See?' On the screen she cuts open a tetrahedral carton of milk which was sealed for almost a year, then poured some into a special pan. The pan has previously been coated with a compound to prevent sticking and burning. So Bertha, wife of Ernest, was pregnant!

She and Al soon fall into their old argument about riot control. She favoured tanks with aluminium armour, while Al defended the judicious use of Mace, a gas which irritates the mucous membranes.

'What's new with you and Dot?' she asks.

'Oh, I've been sterilized. Dot has this detached retina, but luckily they can now weld it back on with lasers.'

They spoke of Dot's trip to the Orient, on a ballistic, supersonic plane. There Dot makes the acquaintance of an amateur biologist named Frank, who's all keyed up about the isolation of the gene. His real business is the manufacture of cosmetics for men, in factories he claimed were 97% automated.

LIFE AFTER DEATH? AL WONDERS.

Ernest took a tranquillizer before he called Dot on the teletypewriter. They were lovers, not to Al's knowledge. This was a conveniently private mode of communication, not often used by spirit mediums though.

As they 'spoke', Ernest drank coffee that had been percolated, frozen, vacuum dried and packed in jars. A spoonful of this substance to a cup of boiling water, while Dot watched the five-inch screen of her portable television set. There is a baseball game in far-off Texas, played on nylon grass beneath a geodesic dome, and she is part of it. When they have said the private things lovers must, Dot took a sleeping pill and slept.

Clement, or Clem, was Al's son by a previous marriage. Next day he fuelled his car at a coin gas station, dry-cleaned his clothes in a similar manner, and fell foul of a peculiar police arrangement: At one end of a bridge police read the licence numbers of all passing cars into their radios. The computer at headquarters checks these for old violations.

Clem avoided the Army in a module apartment house which has been made up at the factory in complete, decorated rooms, then bolted together at the building site. When he gets home he tries to call Bertha, his former step-mother, by means of a telephone message relayed through a communications satellite many thousands of miles, but she is at the hospital, having her third child.

Bertha's first child was now a bright little five-year-old, using an unusual teaching machine to learn to type and spell at the same time. This machine would give an instruction, then lock all but the necessary keys. If only life could be like that, Al thought, with no chance to err! In a programmed novel, the reader determines the ending.

Her second child was very intelligent, possibly because Bertha wore a suit pressurized with oxygen during the brain-growing months of pregnancy. Her present delivery is difficult. The child has worked down too far for a Caesarian, yet not far enough for forceps. What is the obstetrician to do?

He used a new suction device to grip the child's head and draw him from the womb. Soon it cried, and before long, Bertha knew, it would be joining its siblings in immunity to polio, once a dread crippler and killer of children. She only hoped it would grow up to be President, like the one she now watched on colour TV, announcing the landing of men on the Moon (this president had not yet been assassinated). O Frank, Frank! Where are you?

Frank had given up smoking, drinking and excessive eating since his heart-lung transplant. Yet here he is, enjoying a cigar, a martini, and what looks like boeuf Stroganoff! What can possibly be the explanation for this?

It was a photograph of Frank made many years before, to demonstrate a process that made colour prints, right in the camera, seconds after the photo was snapped. Dot became a secretary. As she rode the helicopter to the PanAm building, she typed on her personal portable plastic typewriter. The ride compared favourably with her former trip on the 125-mph train from Tokyo to Osaka, where she met Frank. Unforgettable Japan! She revisited in memory that factory where thousands of workers began the day with the company song, followed by 'Zen jerks' to limber up mind and body for the assembly of portable record players.

Such as the one Clem now listened to as he avoided the draft. He did not want to die in Vietnam, but stay here, taking LSD. He saw God, was God, felt God, left God.

Frank was at this moment crossing the English Channel on a hovercraft. He liked unusual means of motion: In Paris he had stood upon a moving sidewalk. In London, he meant to ride on one of the famous 'driverless' Underground trains. Back in the US, he tries sitting on the beetle-back of his robot lawnmower, as it mows its random pattern. Travel was his vice. Like Ernest's drinking.

Ernest had thank God been cured of his drinking by aversion therapy. One by one, all the pleasant stimulus-response mechanisms linking him with alcohol were broken down. In real time, Al ponders life after death.

He had engaged a firm to freeze him soon after death and thus maintain him until such time as science should come across a way of reversing whatever killed him. Ernest would live longer than otherwise on account of his 'pacemaker', an electronic device to regulate the heartbeat of Ernest. In a programmed novel, he might or might not have this pacemaker; it all depends on the reader.

Al dialled Ernest's number in another city. 'Dialled' is not strictly accurate, for the clumsy dial on Al's phone had been replaced by pushbuttons and musical tones. They get into a heated discussion of missile defence systems. Ernest certainly presents his case fairly, but Al wouldn't listen to reason. Dot counted her contraceptive pills, 20 of which must be taken each month. She also changed her paper panties. Clem receives the picture of Frank by almost magical means!

Bertha puts the picture into a machine and places the receiver of her phone upon it. Far away, Clem copies this motion, then finds the picture in his duplicate machine. Eagerly, he gazes on the familiar lineaments of his real father.

Dot notices how much plastic there is around: Her plastic necklace, her boss's plastic tie, Al's plastic credit cards, which he claimed were displacing money in the realtime world – could there be any connection with that island where they issued bright plastic coins? Dot saw what she must do, later. Now—

She maintained that the 'golfball' typewriter, a high-speed machine using interchangeable spherical type founts, was a pain in the ass. The reader, Al, may choose . . .

Bertha took a new antibiotic tablet, while Ernest explained again the difference between 'quasars' and 'quarks':

'"Quarks" are mathematical entities proposed to explain certain behaviour in subatomic particles. "Quasars" are quasi-stellar radio sources which have puzzled astronomers.' Clem tore Frank's picture into thirty-two pieces. Why, Al wonders, can computers share time and only they? Why can't the others share time, the whatyoucallems, the computer makers, the peoples? On a radio small as a pocket watch, Clem heard the news:

They had invented a polymer of water which, if uncontrolled, could turn all the water of the world into plastic.

Dot and Frank are in bed when Al

No, Dot is at home, Al dies of heart failure in his office, slumping across the digital calendar. 'A black and white picture!' muttered Clem, as his heart begins to beat. 'What do they take me for?' Dot and Ernest are in the vibrating bed. Clem hears of a plan to widen the Panama Canal with atomic blasts. Dot and Ernest are vibrating when Al walks in with the electric carving knife in his hand. This carving knife could run as now on batteries. Alternatively it could use house power, ultimately derived from a distant atomic pile.

Scenes from the Country of the Blind

Outside the window of the Faculty Lounge, between the great slabs of blind concrete that house University departments, there is a small square of empty green lawn. On the architect's immaculate drawings, this is called 'the Quad', but no one here has ever called it anything, or made any use of it, either. Once 'Corky' Corcoran – but that comes later.

I was looking out of this window while Beddoes talked on and on. Out and down, from my privileged perspective, I could see the architect's intention, an arrangement of little trees. I thought of *that* limerick, naturally, but it didn't seem appropriate: It wasn't the Quad, I wasn't God, and all the little trees looked dead. Anyway, Beddoes was sure to quote it himself, sooner or later.

No, I thought – I suppose what I thought was: How stupid to plant those trees down there, where they can't get any light. Even birds are afraid to descend to them, in the shadow of the Philosophy Department, or the Psychology Department, or whatever it is. I'd been here two years, and still couldn't find my way about . . .

The rat's pink nose turned the final corner, came up against a food pellet and stopped. Dr Smith took a reading from the electric timer.

'Eight point two nine seconds,' he announced. 'Check this, will you, Latham?'

I read the figures and entered them on my clipboard. 'It's very good,' I said. 'Better than we'd hoped.'

'Yes, even Beddoes will have trouble explaining this away. Though no doubt he'll try. All yours, Corky.'

Corcoran leaned over the maze, politely waiting for the rat to finish devouring its prize. Then he picked it up and stroked its belly with his thumbs. He crooned over it. 'Clever lad. Clever little lad. Wait till Beddoes hears about you, eh?' The animal clung to his red beard.

Smith grinned. 'That's exactly why I insisted we take every possible precaution against mistakes. We must have strict records, with everything trebly-checked. Because, if *we* find it hard to believe, how do you suppose it'll hit the rigid behaviouristic mind of Dr Beddoes?'

Taking the hint, Corcoran turned the rat over and read out its identification number. Smith and I both looked to be sure, then wrote it down, while he returned the animal to the bank of cages across the room.

'Don't forget Ariadne,' said Smith.

I opened the black cage suspended above the maze and took her out: the large female rat who acted as our experimental 'transmitter'. Though by now we all knew Ariadne by sight, we now read and recorded her number.

The entire fussy operation bored me. It was meant to be a test for ESP in animals. Dr Smith had planned it, Corcoran had designed the equipment, so of course they had reason to be excited: It was going well. Since our Paranormal Experience Research Group was, as always, short of staff, I acted as observer. The principle was interesting enough, but the laborious details meant nothing – except that I was cutting back on my real work, the Library of Paranormal Experiences. Real work, cataloguing letters from the real world, outside the Country of the Blind.

Still, our experiment might pry open a few eyelids. It worked like this: A rat coming to our maze 'cold' would take, on average, fourteen seconds or more to negotiate its blind alleys and find the bait. On a second trial it would be quicker, and so on. After twenty trials or so, the time could be got down to two seconds flat.

Pure behaviourism, thus far. But Smith had given it a twist: Ariadne was a rat which had run the maze many times. It hardly ever took her more than two seconds. We put her into a cage suspended a few inches above the maze while other rats did the running.

The cage was painted matte black with a double wire-gauze bottom, and the white maze was brightly illuminated with flood-lamps. This made it possible for Ariadne to watch what happened below without being visible. She could see the food pellet and the way through to it, and she was hungry enough to really want to try. We hoped she would communicate a bit of her urgency and purpose to any rat trying to thread the maze.

The idea was to put through twenty rats who had never seen the maze before, giving them one run each. For ten of them, Ariadne would be upstairs, sending down telepathic directions to speed them through – we hoped. The other ten were our control group; she was not in the cage for them.

To isolate possible ESP, we had to eliminate every other difference between the test rats and the controls. They were not to sense the presence or absence of Ariadne by any normal means. This meant not only the black cage of invisibility but other devices developed by the ingenious Corcoran to hide her sound, her scent, even her body-heat from those below.

So far the control rats were behaving as expected, running the maze in about fourteen seconds. But the test rats, clever little lads and lasses, were doing it in eight seconds. To which Smith said, 'Statistically significant', and Corcoran said, 'Flabbergasting!'

I simply shrugged. Why waste time trying to prove the existence of ESP to other scientists, when the evidence was all about us? Why not instead try finding out more about ESP, more about all psychic phenomena?

So I was bored, while Smith and Corcoran were excited –

and increasingly on edge. As we prepared to lock up for the night, Corcoran started worrying.

'When I was filling the water dishes, I noticed a draught,' he said. 'I hope there's no temperature difference between the cages.'

Smith raised an eyebrow. 'You worry too much, Corky. If it really matters, put a draught-excluder on the door.'

'I suppose it doesn't really matter. It's just that – and another thing. Did you know there's a wall mirror behind the bank of cages? What did they design this lab for? Budgies?'

'I'd like to lock up and go.' I said. Smith said the same thing, by taking out a pocket calculator and stabbing at its buttons. We stood about with our coats on for some time. Even when Corcoran finally joined us, he was muttering about needing a strip of felt for the door.

'What you need is a drink,' I said.

What Corcoran really needed, I now can see, was to let go his death-grip on the material world. He worked too closely with *things*, making and mending, and along the way he lost contact with *people*. For example he spent far too much time ruling out mazes on white cardboard and cutting them out with razor blades. That led to one of his more unpleasant confrontations with Beddoes.

He told Beddoes: 'I've made this little model of the Great Pyramid in cardboard. Did you know that if you use a razor blade each day, but keep it under the model pyramid at night, it *never* loses its edge?'

Anyone with sense would never have put it that way to Beddoes, a creature who swam in a private sea of scepticism. Beddoes only said, 'Indeed?' but Corcoran couldn't leave it there.

'Indeed,' he said. 'What do you say to that?'

'It sounds like good news for the manufacturers of cardboard model pyramids, bad news for manufacturers of razor blades. How do you account for it?'

Corcoran leapt at the chance. 'Well, we know that metal edges are made of crystals. If they wear down, maybe they can be re-grown. We also know that crystals can be grown, given the proper magnetic fields—'

'Cardboard being a great magnetizer?' Beddoes said. 'I see. Well, when I see a properly-conducted test that establishes this "truth", I'll look into it. Meanwhile I might remind you of one razor which has not needed re-sharpening since the year 1350: Ockham's Razor. That is the principle that one must not look for complex answers until one has failed to find any simple ones.'

I was to remember that conversation again.

Dr Harry Beddoes could easily have committed murder and escaped punishment, if only because he could not be picked out of an identity parade: He had no face. One might remember his heavy figure, his rumpled grey suit, eyes of some sort peering out through thick glasses, but nothing more. No – there's no other word for it– no soul.

He could be found each evening at six o'clock, blending in to one corner of the Faculty Lounge. With his back to the great window, an ocean of pale green carpet stretching away before him, and an overflowing ashtray at his elbow, he was ready to hold court.

The Lounge was like the lounge in any airport: formica tables, chrome chairs and lines of perspective that leave no place for the eye to rest. Instead the eye would hunt and hunt, as though looking for one's lost relative, but finally alighting only on a blemish in the corner.

We inevitably found ourselves drinking with Beddoes and suffering his little jibes. Smith said it was good for us, having as a kind of devil's advocate a determined sceptic like Beddoes, who was always willing to test our theories, even to destruction.

That evening we talked of Arthur Koestler's latest book on strange coincidences.

Dr Smith said, 'Mind you, I'm not entirely convinced that all these cases are meaningful. But you'll have to admit, some are most intriguing. Take the example of the man who flings himself in front of a London Underground train. It hits him but does not run over him. Because, at the same instant, some passenger has pulled the emergency handle. The train stops just in time.'

Beddoes's eyes widened behind his thick glasses. 'If only Koestler knew where to stop,' he said.

'Meaning what, exactly?'

Beddoes sighed. 'Meaning that the story is a *rumour*, whose only source Koestler seems to have found is a hospital doctor. The doctor wasn't himself at the accident. If we can't get at the facts in a story, why stop at repeating it?'

I said, 'I don't follow. What else could he do?'

'One might make it into an even more meaningful story. Say the passenger was a twin brother of the man who threw himself in front of the train. Or say that, the night before, the passenger had a premonition of disaster. He dreamed—'

'Very amusing,' Smith said. 'You feel, then, that it's a case of "Don't confuse me with the facts"?'

Beddoes lit a cigarette and dropped the match on the floor. 'I suppose facts can be confusing, if we're speaking of coincidence. After all, is anything irrelevant? The most trivial events suddenly make "sense", do they not? One man looks into the mirror while shaving and says, "Today I'll grow a moustache." A thousand miles away, a second man decides to shave off his moustache, *at the same instant*. Is it all part of the master plan? A law of conservation?'

I started to speak, but he went on:

'Or suppose that I own a beagle, and Corcoran here owns an eagle, and you, Smith, are a bee-keeper. Is the universe trying to *spell* out significance into our meeting here?'

I thought of an odd coincidence: That Corcoran had mentioned a mirror a few minutes before, while Beddoes now chose mirrors and animals for his illustrations. Mirror and animal cage . . .

'All things are possible,' I said.

'But not of equal importance, Latham. If they were, we might profitably spend our time looking for messages in every bowl of alphabet soup.' He tapped his cigarette in the direction of the ashtray; flakes of ash floated to the carpet. Tidy little mind, messy little man. Beddoes the sower of ashes.

The test series finished and, to my disappointment, Smith suggested waiting a week and then trying to replicate our excellent results. Corcoran busied himself at the drawing board, laying out new maze plans. Smith went back to his book, *New Horizons in Psi.* I went back to my cataloguing.

Our Library of Paranormal Experiences consisted of some two thousand letters to be read, filed and, where practical, followed up. I was preparing cross-indices and also trying to keep up with the dozen or so new letters which arrived each week.

Some of them were obviously of no use to us. Now and again we received a demented-sounding letter, often unintelligible and always pathetic: 'I am the Holy Ghost my enemys wil soon learn to there distres that my rays of power cannot be gainsaid no cannot be gainsaid . . .' These went into a dead file.

Of course there were also a few practical jokes. One man described a supposed telepathic link with his twin brother. The story ran to several pages, becoming more and more incredible, and ending: '. . . and when they hanged him, I was the one who died!' Ho ho and hum. Fortunately such letters were usually easy to spot from their feebly punning signatures: Vi. B. Rations, E. Espee, Uri Dipple *et al.* found their letters filed in my wastebasket. I was tempted to keep the joke letters and analyse them, to try finding out what makes people sneer at psychic phenomena. But I knew the answer already; it was as plain in the scrawl of poor Miss Rations as in the quips of Dr Beddoes. It was the fear of freedom.

The great majority of our letters, however, came from sane, sincere, reasonably intelligent people. Typically such a person has had some puzzling, even inexplicable experience: a true dream, a premonition, or meeting a friend by chance in a foreign city. He knows the contents of a telegram before opening it. He finds himself thinking of someone he hasn't seen for years, and they ring him on the telephone. Ghostly visitations, *déjà vu* experiences . . . rarely easy to confirm, but all of it providing a background of evidence that something is going on.

One letter, however, told a story both uncanny and evidential. I read it through twice, then ran down the hall and hammered on the door of Dr Smith's little office.

'Oh it's you, is it? What's up?'

'Read this,' I said. 'Our experiment is nothing compared to this!'

He looked at me and laughed. 'You should see your face! You look as though you'd just had a psychic experience yourself, Latham.'

'I almost feel I've had one, reading this. A letter from a Mr Durkell. He's seen a village vanish – a complete Tudor town, with smoking chimneys, just fade out of sight!'

'Really?'

'I know it sounds insane, but there's a second witness. What's more, it seems to be connected with the disappearance of a third person. Wait till Beddoes tries blunting Ockham's Razor on this!'

While Smith read the letter through, I watched him: Dr Efraim Smith, a gaunt, ascetic-looking man of sixty-odd, with a mop of white hair and black, staring eyes. In

Hollywood, he could have been cast in the role of an Old Testament prophet.

His appearance, combined with the fact that he preferred writing his books by hand, seated at an old roll-top desk, made him a kind of local eccentric – it was that kind of locality. He had already attracted a few half-joking rumours: Was he a vegetarian? Was it true that he slept only four hours per night?

In reality there was nothing fanatical or eccentric about him. He was a hard-headed practical research chemist, author of a well-known textbook on polymers. Ten years earlier, his brother had died. Dr Smith had consulted mediums, meeting with the usual mixture of disappointing vagueness and uncanny truth. He'd decided to turn his scientific scrutiny upon the entire field of psychic research – in his spare time. Passing interests have a way of becoming vocations, however: he now headed our Paranormal Experience Research Group.

He handed the letter back. 'Chilling detail,' he said. 'Will you be following it up?'

'Of course. If even half of it can be corroborated, it's just what we need. Imagine: A village that doesn't exist, except—'

'Except on Tuesdays!' He shook his head. 'Obviously not an hallucination, and too detailed for a mirage.'

'Perhaps there's a sort of, well, rupture in the space-time fabric. Could he be looking at a village that exists in some other time or place? Or even some other universe running parallel to ours?'

'Possibly,' he said. 'After all, our concept of the space-time framework is very hazy indeed. There are a lot of unanswered questions, aren't there? Black holes, for example. Some scientists suspect they are just such "ruptures" as you describe. If so, it may go some way towards explaining many really puzzling phenomena: a-causal events, such as Koestler's coincidences, begin to make sense if we can discard the notion that causes come before effects in time. Of course it might also explain ESP. Why do we find "Two minds with but a single thought?" Simply this: Minds are not fettered to local time and place.'

We talked for some time. The general theory sounded difficult, but I felt I could grasp it intuitively: *Mind* is not my mind or your mind or Smith's mind, *but a kind of energy ocean in which we, all thinking beings, are immersed.*

'I'd better start checking out the facts in this letter,' I said, taking my leave. 'By the way, until I've proved it, not a word to Beddoes?'

We hadn't meant to tell Beddoes much about our animal experiment, either, until the second series was completed. But one day, while we were only half-finished with the series, Beddoes's smugness broke through even Smith's usual reserves of calm.

The conversation began innocently enough, when Corcoran mentioned Uri Geller.

'Uri Geller?' Beddoes asked. 'Ah, you mean the Israeli paratrooper.'

Corcoran asked if that was supposed to be a joke.

'Not at all. I understand he was a paratrooper. Amazing. Don't see how he did it.'

Smith showed his teeth in a smile. 'Very funny. The implication being that you do see how he managed, during one television performance, to make stopped watches start ticking all over Britain.'

'I have an idea, yes. According to a New Zealand study, if you play about with any stopped watch, chances are it will start ticking. In fact, you have about a forty percent chance that it will keep going for a few days. No, it's the parachute jumps that really astound me.'

Corcoran winked at me. 'Perhaps Dr Beddoes has psychic insights into how Uri does what he does with spoons. Perhaps we ought to study Dr Beddoes?'

Beddoes tried imitating Uri Geller's voice. 'You want me for a subject? *Me?* But I tell you, I don't know from where I get zis power. From God, maybe. Or my agent.'

No one but Beddoes laughed. I said, 'Why don't you tell us, once, what you do believe in? If anything.'

'Thought-communication,' he said. 'I think it's a distinct possibility. Of course it's tricky. One makes the right facial expressions, speech sounds and gestures, but it doesn't always get across.'

Smith said, 'Get your laughs while you can, Beddoes.' And he told him about our first series of experiments.

'Ariadne?' Beddoes asked. 'Oh, I see. Leading them through the maze. Very good.'

Smith grimaced. 'I think you'll have to concede that our results look good, as well. I've done a bit of statistical work on them, and I believe that we can rule out chance. The odds are over four hundred thousand to one against the notion that this happened by accident.'

Beddoes sowed more ash on the carpet. 'I agree. Chance doesn't come into it.'

Corcoran looked angry. 'Spell that out for me, will you?'

'Gladly. If I hear of a rat that ought to take fourteen seconds to run a maze, but who does it in only eight seconds, I immediately suppose that the rat has some experience of the maze. Has that possibility been ruled out?'

'Completely,' said Smith.

Corcoran stood up, knocking over his drink. 'You two can sit here listening to veiled accusations of fraud if you like,' he said. 'I've had enough. Let me out of here.'

Fraud? I thought at the time that Corcoran was merely over-reacting to Beddoes's stupid question. Later I learned that poor 'Corky' was going mad.

We finished the second series, again with success. Corcoran was oddly silent, depressed. He spent much of his time at the drawing board, laying out plans for many more mazes – far more than we could ever use. He might work furiously for days, then suddenly fling down his pen and slam out the door, saying something about a walk. He'd be gone for hours.

Neither Smith nor I could account for it.

'I think Beddoes has depressed him,' I said. 'Belittling our work. Corcoran worked hard on this.'

Smith looked up from his calculations. 'Eh? No, I don't think that's the answer. My guess is, it's the experiment itself that's got to him. You see, he worked so hard, hoped so deeply – and then *it all worked out right*. It's like being a long-term prisoner, and finally having the cell door bang open. The fear of freedom. Let's hope he's over it soon.'

But he seemed to grow worse. There was said to have been an incident in the canteen, when Corcoran caught sight of his own face reflected in a spoon and began to scream. I happened to see him on one of his long walks – going round and round the same building.

I remained convinced that Beddoes was at the bottom of it, somehow. I gradually began to see that if I could once crush Beddoes, crack through his hard shell with a harder piece of evidence, Corcoran might begin to see him for what he was. It might help.

Beddoes could not be drawn to comment upon our experiment. The only answer seemed to be to show him the Durkell letter. A story that strange and compelling could not be ignored. I now reread it: Mr Durkell had seen an article about our group in a Sunday paper. He was sales manager of an electronics firm, and had recently moved to Blenford New Town, whence he daily commuted to work in Casterwich, some ten miles away.

> Mornings I usually take the secondary road, to avoid traffic. One Tuesday I left Blenford as usual, but driving slowly. It was a fine day, I had plenty of time,

and the colours of the autumn leaves were too lovely to miss. Then I had the vision.

It wasn't a vision then, only a surprise. On my right, through a small copse, I glimpsed a village. I knew there shouldn't be any village just there, so I kept my eye on the spot. After the copse came a large hill, and after that, *no* village! Nothing but empty fields, as always.

I kept watching for it. A week later – Tuesday again – I was bringing my wife along with me (she had shopping to do in Casterwich), when I saw it again. I hit the brakes, backed up and we both took a better look. There was no mistake about it. We could see bits of several half-timbered houses and a smoking chimney. My wife flipped open the road map and found what she thought must be the place, with the strange name of Mons. 'Mons? In England?' I said. 'Let me see that.' But she'd already put the map away again. We didn't look again until we got to Casterwich. Would you believe it, neither one of us could find it! I know my wife is no great mapreader, but we searched the entire area (lower left-hand corner of the map) and found nothing remotely like the name *Mons*.

I couldn't stop wondering about it. Finally I went to the Blenford police. They said they'd never heard of a village called *Mons* in Britain, and that there was no village on that spot, and never had been. I think they thought I was drunk or drugged or crazy!

I investigated a bit on my own. I learned that the place was a pasture belonging to a farmer named Letworthy. I called in to see him. Not only couldn't he help me, he was extremely suspicious. Finally he came out with it: His wife had disappeared! He'd gone to market – on a Tuesday! – and returned to find her gone. When I asked him if he had any explanation, he muttered something about her being carried off by a glacier!

At this point it was all too much for me; I decided I never should know the truth. A vanishing village, a vanishing woman, glaciers and the map business – I just gave up. Shortly after, we moved to Casterwich, so I more or less tried to forget about it. But now and then I still wonder. Especially on Tuesdays!

Yours sincerely,
'F. H. Durkell'

'Is that your evidence?' Beddoes asked, handing the letter back. 'And if so, evidence of what?'

I found it hard to put into words. 'Evidence that – that the Durkells have seen something that ought not to be seen, by *your* laws of science. It's an event that transcends normal explanation. I believe that the Durkells are psychic sensitives, or else that this place is, at times, a psychically sensitive place. There's just no other explanation.'

'There are a great many other possible explanations,' he said. 'Not all correct, of course. Still I believe that it's possible to settle the matter very quickly – if you really want it settled. Shall I look into it?'

'Done,' I said. 'How much time do you want?'

'That depends,' he said. 'How much digging have you done already?'

I told him I had written to Durkell, to the Blenford police, and to the local paper. Mrs Durkell had confirmed her husband's story, and the police remembered his enquiry. The *Blenford Gazette* knew of Mrs Letworthy's disappearance, but they were taking the police's version of it, that she had simply run away with another man.

'And not a floe of psychic ice?' Beddoes asked. 'Curious. But very useful. I think I could clear this up in – shall we say, two hours?'

'Or not at all,' I retorted.

'Why not? All things are as you say, possible. But don't expect miracles, if you take my meaning.'

I saw Corcoran outside, walking round and round the same building.

'What are you doing?' I asked. 'Looking for something?'

He laughed. 'Yes. The way out.'

I started to leave him but he caught my arm. 'Wait a minute, Latham. I want to tell you something. I have a confession to make.'

We walked into the deserted 'Quad', sat down on the grass. Corcoran looked at the little half-dead tree and quoted it: the limerick I'd always expected to hear from Beddoes:

'There once was a man who said, God
Must think it exceedingly odd,
To find that this tree
Continues to be
When there's no one about in the quad.'

'Is that the confession?' I said drily. 'Because I've heard it.'

'Ah, what haven't we all heard? and seen? Especially seen. In the mirror. Thoughts while shaving. With Ockham's Razor? No, that cuts both ways. I'd better begin again.'

'You'd better,' I said. 'And try to make more sense.'

'Take care of the sense and the sounds take care of themselves,' he quoted. 'What's that from? *Through the Looking-Glass*?'

'I think so. But what—'

'But there's more to that title, isn't there: *And what Alice Found there.* The truth?'

'And what is the truth you want to tell me?' I suddenly thought I knew: Corcoran was going to confess that he'd somehow rigged our experiment to make it work. And what might it have to do with mirrors and trees in the quad?'

'Mirrors? You'll see about that. Trees in the quad? The point is, out of sight, out of mind; out of mind, out of existence. What happens when no one's about is Nobody's business, right? All right, here's my little story. Through the looking glass, and what Corky found there. Do you remember when I was looking for a bit of felt for the door?'

After a moment, I did. 'You were worried about the draught in the lab.'

'And I kept on worrying. One evening during the second series, I was in the lab with Smith and I thought of it again. I remembered a door in the hallway that might be a janitor's cupboard or something, and I thought there might be a bit of rag in there. So I excused myself and went to look.

'It wasn't a cupboard at all. It's an observation room. The psychology department must have been using it for experiments before we took it over. You know that wall mirror behind the bank of cages: That's it. One-way glass. Darkly I was given a vision into the lab. There was Smith messing about the maze.' He rubbed his face with both hands and said,

'God forgive me for looking!'

'I don't understand.'

'He was running a rat through the maze. The same rat, two or three runs. Training it to build up speed. I kept watching and I saw which cage he returned it to. Next day we took that rat and tested it. Naturally the rat ran the maze in eight seconds. Not psychic vibes at all – just Smith's bloody fraud.'

I didn't believe it and I said so.

'Who cares what you believe? Say I'm mad, call me a liar – I still had to tell you. I had to confess, you see? I'm the one who's buggered it all up. I peeked – and there wasn't any bloody tree at all! There's nothing, do you understand? No bloody tree!'

He leapt up and seized the little tree, trying to uproot it. After a moment of struggling, he gave up.

'Calm down,' I said. 'Suppose Smith did cheat a little, so what? It's not the end of the world. We know he's got a long and distinguished record as a scientist, and he didn't get that by fraud. He probably just boosted the statistics a bit, to underline our case. There's plenty of other evidence of ESP, after all.'

'Yes, and now I wonder how good it is. How many more Smiths are there? No, we're caught in the maze, for good and all. What is there to believe in? The evidence of some Smith somewhere?'

'No,' I said. 'The evidence inside. We know there's more than this. We know the world is bigger and deeper than it looks on the surface.'

'Do we indeed? And how about Dr Efraim Smith – does he know it? Because if he does, *Why did he think he had to cheat?*'

At six o'clock I faced Beddoes alone in the Faculty Lounge. Corcoran had gone to his room. Smith was being interviewed on local television.

I began abruptly. 'Have you found the village of *Mons*?'

'Mons? Oh, the *map* village. Yes, I think so. But it has little to do with what the Durkells saw.' Beddoes lit a cigarette. 'Except psychologically.'

'Hallucinations?' I stared at him until his gaze shifted.

'I think not,' he said. 'The answer I've got may not be the right answer, but it seems to account for everything. It depends upon a close reading of the letter. "My wife is no great map-reader," for example. We must also remember that Mrs Durkell must have been rather nervous. Her husband, without warning on a deserted country road, had just "hit the brakes". Then he shows her a village which, he says, does not exist. She fumbles for a map and finds the name *Mons*. Later they cannot find it. I suggest that the ink of their printed map did not alter in the meantime.'

'Because it's "impossible"?' I asked. He handed me a scrap of paper. I saw it was the corner of a road map, with one word circled heavily: MONS.

'Not the lower left-hand corner,' he explained. 'The upper right. Notice that all the other place-names but Mons are upside-down. The village is SNOW, and it's in a different part of the county.'

I handed it back. '*Snow*. Very suggestive of glaciers. I suppose you'll find some map-trick to explain the disappearance of Mrs Letworthy?'

He smiled, if one can call it that. 'No, I think a calendar-trick, this time. Doesn't this Tuesday business strike you as odd?'

'Of course it does.'

'Odd, I mean, in the sense that Tuesday is market day? When Mr Letworthy would likely be absent from his farm?'

I made no answer, so he carried on:

'Let us assume the police version is correct. Mrs Letworthy did not "disappear", but simply ran away with another man. That means she must have been seeing the man earlier, and she might well have chosen to do so on Tuesdays. Let us make an even wilder assumption: That the man's profession forced him to drive a distinctive vehicle that must not be seen parked near the Letworthy farmhouse.'

'Or he might be the man in the moon,' I said.

'Quite. Forget him for the moment, then, and look at the letter: "Mornings I usually take the secondary road", says Mr Durkell. That suggests that there is a primary road which he takes of an evening – hurrying home from work.'

'Agreed, but so what?'

'It gives us two views of Blenford New Town, where he lives,' Beddoes said. 'One at his back in the morning, and a possibly quite different view that he faces each evening.'

'Oh, it's Blenford that he sees through the trees,' I said

with some sarcasm. 'Looking to his right, he sees a town that is really behind him. It must all be done with mirrors.'

'I was just about to suggest that,' he said. 'The mystery village is not likely an hallucination, and far too clear for a mirage. We are left with one natural explanation: A mirror or something like a mirror is placed behind that little grove of trees every Tuesday.'

I had to laugh aloud. Pathetically, Beddoes kept clutching at the wispiest straws of 'natural' phenomena, to avoid facing the obvious truth.

In the opposite corner of the Faculty Lounge, a few people had gathered round the TV set. I could hear Smith's voice booming across to us, but I could not make out his words.

Beddoes continued the farce: 'Naturally I wondered what kind of large mirror might be portable enough to fit the bill. I sent reply-paid telegrams to Mr Letworthy, to the local police and to the local weekly newspaper, asking if they knew the profession of the man supposed to have eloped with Mrs Letworthy. They confirmed what I suspected. The man drove a large van . . .'

The television was making too much noise, and anyway, I found Beddoes's hypothesis boring. In a sense, Smith on television was giving him his answer, only Beddoes was too deaf and blind to notice. He droned on:

'. . . large sheets of . . . attached to its sides. A kind of portable . . . definitely parked in that spot, behind the little copse. There. Does that possibility fit the facts?'

'Sorry,' I said. 'I guess I missed the point.'

'I said it was common knowledge: Mrs Letworthy's boyfriend was a *glazier*.'

Smith's voice suddenly became louder and clearer: '. . . as in the range of poetic or artistic experience, the mystic sees clearer and deeper, if only at times. Insight – the sudden sunburst of pure understanding. That's what we're concerned with here. Psychic phenomena are only a small part of it, you see.'

The interviewer asked if he would call himself a rationalist. 'Well, there are rationalists and rationalists, aren't there? Take for example the rationalist answer to Russell's Paradox: "In this village there is a barber who shaves all of the men who do not shave themselves. But does he shave himself?" You see how it goes: If he does, he doesn't, and vice versa. There's no rational answer, except to say: "There can be no such village." But the true mystic, the man of vision, says: "Why not?" Why not indeed? You see, Man is a paradox in himself. He is apparently finite, yet he can easily conceive of vast infinities . . .'

I suppose it must have been just about that time that poor Corcoran was cutting his wrists with a razor blade.

We all share in the blame for Corcoran's death. I, for sitting arguing futile theories with Beddoes, instead of staying with him. Smith – if what Corcoran told me was true – for his momentary loss of faith. Beddoes most of all, for hating all that is of a subtle and mysterious beauty, all that he cannot immediately reduce to a petty formula, all that he cannot slash with Ockham's Razor. With his relentless scepticism, he almost certainly drove 'Corky' to the brink of insanity and to his death.

This being true, I have had no hesitation in dismissing Beddoes's theory of the vanishing village as simply another of his destructive fantasies. Even without checking, I am sure it is utterly without foundation.

For different reasons, Corcoran's statements about Smith's 'fraud' must also be dismissed. To do otherwise would be to take the word of a hopelessly insane man against that of a reputable scientist with a brilliant record.

Our work carried on, though we now see much less of

Beddoes. What would be the point? One cannot explain the incredibly beautiful colours of a sunset to a blind man.

The Interstate

Andor sat three rows back from the driver. Having jammed his small suitcase in the rack overhead, having seen his large suitcase stowed in the bowels of the bus, Andor began the pleasurable process of relaxing.

First he concentrated on the calves of his legs, letting their knots of muscle soften and grow numb. Then he folded his hands across his paunch, the left still gripping a magazine, however, in case the man next to him began talking. Andor let the muscles of his shoulders and neck relax now, ordering the tension in them to surrender.

He felt some of the nervous charge generated by the exciting activity at the great bus terminal drain out of him now, as the bus got into smooth, gearless motion. The acceleration sickened him, and as the bus rolled on through terminal tunnels, he turned his thoughts to the circumstances that had led to his trip.

Once again, on the television screen of his mind, Andor sat erect at his desk, operating a small calculator and marking numbers upon forms of pink, white, yellow, pale blue and pale green. At the desks just to his left and right, and immediately before and behind him, were men performing similar tasks. He knew their names, though now, away from the office, he could not recall their faces. One, he thought, had white hair. Andor supposed that on the floors immediately above him and below him were men performing similar tasks, though he had no proof of this. In thoughts, Andor's office moved through the office seasons.

Fall. Aitkin, on his left, sold tickets on a football pool, the Army-Navy game. Andor bought one ticket, number 0—0.

Each day, when he opened his desk drawer, the ticket lay looking up at him with its blank spectacles. Long after the game was over, weary of its inspection, Andor threw the ticket into the wastebasket to the right of his desk.

Winter. Jurgens, in front of him, seemed to suffer from a severe sinus infection. Another man in another department was said to have suffered a heart attack from shovelling snow, but Andor was never able to check the truth of this story. Jurgens brought a new portable radio to work after the holiday. Playing it was not possible, however, for it interfered with the office's normal recorded music, which played continuously.

Spring. Cleaning men came to clean all the office's typewriters and calculators. There occurred conversations about baseball statistics in which Andor seldom participated, but which he never avoided.

Summer. Andor came eligible for two weeks, vacation. After examining brochures and weighing various possibilities, he chose a distant resort near the sea, packed two suitcases, and departed from the great bus terminal.

The great bus terminal was as brightly lit as any office, though its ceiling was much higher. People moved in small flocks across the quiet, polished floor from ticket counters to platforms, from platforms to luggage counters, or from luggage counters to exits. Excitement pervaded their noisy murmur and quick, orderly movements. Andor purchased a ticket in the shape of a long, folded strip made up of numerous coupons.

He looked at a television screen connected to a camera that elsewhere scanned a list of departures; thus he found the right platform for his bus. With minutes to spare, Andor gave his large suitcase to a platform attendant, who stored it in the bowels of a silvery bus with a number of other suitcases and a bicycle tyre. He closed the bowels and locked them with a silvery crank.

Andor allowed the driver to tear one coupon off his ticket, mounted the steps, and located an empty seat, three back from the driver. Andor sat next to the window of blue glass, after jamming his smaller suitcase in the overhead rack. Removing a folded magazine from his pocket, he began relaxing, as a white-haired man sat next to him. As he relaxed, Andor recalled all these actions with a kind of 'pleasure'.

Now the bus emerged from the tunnel into blue light and crossed a bridge. The air conditioning hummed, concealed speakers played a medley of show tunes, blue girders and factories flitted by. This was not a familiar part of the city to Andor, but seeing it caused him no panic. It was obvious from the bus's speed and from the driver's sure motions that all was going according to plan.

Near the outskirts of the city the bus stopped for ten minutes at a glass-walled restaurant with a spire or steeple. Where the cross or rooster should be was a weathervane showing a nursery rhyme, Simple Simon. Inside were long rows of booths upholstered in pink and green leatherette. The waitress who brought Andor's coffee was a thin redhead with bad nails and teeth. She wore a uniform of pink-and-green gingham. The coffee was too hot for him to drink before the bus departed.

There was a small rest room in the rear of the bus, marked 'Toilet'. Andor walked back to it and washed his hands in the tiny sink. On the way to his seat, he noticed that a few servicemen were aboard the bus. Now he recalled seeing a great many servicemen in the great bus terminals, as well as several persons in religious habits.

Now he perceived that there were forty other people on the bus besides himself: two family groups consisting of man, pregnant woman, and small child, all speaking a foreign language; two elderly women and two young women in black religious habits; two young servicemen in tan uniforms and three others in white uniforms; six men of middle age carrying worn briefcases; three men of about twenty-eight carrying new attaché cases; a florid-faced drunken man of indeterminate age who addressed an occasional remark to the air in front of him; a cowboy and a thin woman who looked very like him, either his sister or his wife; one young man and two young women equipped with knapsacks and expensive casual clothes; two large women of middle age, who smelled bad; one young man in a college sweater; four very old men and three very old women, the latter wearing identical hats.

The bus moved past blue fields of plants Andor could not identify. He intended to read an article in the travel magazine in his lap about the resort to which he was going. He would read the article slowly, anticipating and savouring.

'Are you going far?' asked the man beside him. He had white hair and held an attaché case in his lap, upon which he now spread a copy of the same travel magazine Andor was holding. The copy was open to the article on Andor's resort, as the stranger pointed out when Andor named the place he was going. Andor opened his own copy and began reading.

All the hotels at this resort maintained their own ballrooms for nightly dancing, but in addition there were public dances at the popular boardwalk pavilion and clambakes on the beach. Each hotel featured a heated pool, so that even in coldest weather – although the article assured him the weather was never really cold – one could immerse one's body in warm blue liquid and glide silently about in the depths, safe from the gelid moon. What a joke, Andor thought (repressing the thought at once), if someone were to put jello in that blue pool!

The thought was shocking and foreign to him, like an object surgically inserted into his brain. He glanced down to make sure his tie was securely clipped to the front of his shirt.

There were beach facilities and equipment for many water

sports, including sailing, skiing, surfing, water polo, rowing, and deep-sea fishing. There was an impressive list of restaurants, bars, and clubs. The vicinity boasted a number of places of scenic or historic merit. It occurred to him that the man beside him was reading the same article at the same time, and a disturbing thought burst like caviar in Andor's mind:

'Every person who reads the same magazine is the same person.'

He was confused: had he actually thought this aloud, or had the man next to him spoken it? He stole a glance to see, but the stranger was just getting up to go to the rest room. Before he returned, the bus stopped at a large, elegant restaurant by the side of the interstate.

Andor found his appetite increased when he hurried through the hot, sunny, pink air of the outside to enter the blue-green coolness through a big glass door. As in the bus, concealed speakers played muted popular music constantly. Seating himself on a pink-and-green leatherette seat before a table of pale wood-grained plastic, Andor opened the giant menu.

Without much delay, he chose the house speciality, meat loaf, mashed potatoes and gravy, creamed corn, bread and butter. The bread consisted of one slice of white, one of whole wheat, wrapped together in clear plastic; the butter was a foil-wrapped cube.

Andor ordered coffee with cream. The cream was in a tiny tetrahedron of thick paper coated with impermeable plastic; there were two paper envelopes of sugar which Andor ignored.

When he had finished his meal (and it went down remarkably fast, except for the coffee), Andor found himself still hungry, so he ordered a dish of strawberry ice cream.

After the waitress had taken away the waxy dinner plate, and before she had brought his dessert, he had time to examine the paper place mat before him. It depicted the

United States, a network of pink lines ('Interstates') and green lines ('Tollways'). They seemed veins and arteries, and he was even able to imagine tiny corpuscular cars nudging along them from coast to coast. The restaurant chain's name arched across the top of the map, in giant green letters, followed by the words, 'The Wonderful World of Food'. At various points on the map were tiny replicas of the chain's familiar spire, each one marking the location of a single 'Eating Palace'.

There was nothing else of interest on the mat but a large spot of gravy near one edge. For an instant he had the crazy notion of swiping up this spot with his finger and licking it down, but he at once realized how foolish this would look. Nevertheless the impulse remained strong until he received the dish of pink ice cream, and with it the pale green check.

As he paid the check, Andor bought a bag of the restaurant's own brand of caramels and a consumer magazine. Back in the bus he dozed for perhaps an hour.

A light rain had begun streaking the blue windows diagonally when he awoke. Otherwise the landscape seemed unchanged. Large green-and-white signs marked exits and interchanges; shadows of overpasses flashed overhead; an occasional billboard announced some distant casino or hotel; a row of red signs advertised shaving cream:

Beards grow faster
In the grave
Take it with you—

The light rain stopped without his noticing. The man next to him was asleep, and now Andor could see, in the fading afternoon light, his creased forehead and sagging, slightly bristled jowls. Andor did not like to look at this face. He began to read interesting performance reports comparing three new cars; he ate caramels. The bus came through a tollgate and entered the driveway of another restaurant of the same chain.

'There will be a thirty-minute stop here for dinner,' the driver announced. 'Please remember the number of your bus, 3350.' He spoke through an electronic amplifier that broadcast his voice throughout the length of the bus.

'This is where I get out,' said the man next to Andor. 'I'm here to check the books. So long.' He climbed out of the bus and went into an unmarked door just to one side of the big glass entrance. Another bus drew up as Andor disembarked. Several middle-aged women in dark glasses stepped down from it and helped one another inside.

While Andor did not feel particularly hungry after having finished half his bag of caramels, he nevertheless ordered the house speciality, to avoid being hungry later. The speciality was pot roast and escalloped potatoes, with creamed corn. As soon as he had eaten it and drunk a soft drink, Andor felt slightly hungry, as if the process of eating had stimulated his appetite by some obscure chemical means. He quickly ordered a piece of pie from the glass case on the lunch counter, pie of some unknown dark berry, and a glass of milk. There was barely time to bolt it down and get back to bus number 3350.

A younger, thinner driver was now in charge of the bus. He tore a coupon off each passenger's ticket. Out the blue windows, the land and sky were dim purple. The man who checked books did not come back aboard.

When Andor put on the reading light to begin his newly bought detective novel, he saw something on the floor at his feet. It was the travel magazine, either his copy or the one belonging to the book-keeper. Andor picked it up and quickly reread the article on his destination.

In the amusement park there were thrilling rides – including the Octopus, the Ferris wheel and the roller coaster

– colourful games of skill and chance, curios and souvenirs and a beer garden with an authentic German band. It was near the amusement park that the Aquatic Festival was held each summer – including the famous Aqua Follies – and Andor was glad he had planned to arrive at the resort in time for these colourful pageants previewed for him in the travel article. Here were golden girls riding water skis in formation, coloured lights turning their wakes to purple, crimson, old rose, and azure. Here were yacht races in the glaring sun, tilted sails turning to translucent, delicately fluted shells. Here were giant flowers formed, on the floodlit water, of naked girls swimming toe to toe in unison. Here were hydrofoil races and moonlight cruises, fancy diving and fireworks.

Finished with the magazine, Andor shoved it into the dark niche beneath the seat ahead. He would never look into this niche again, and in time, it would be cleaned by someone he would not see.

Nothing at all could now be seen out the windows, but for an occasional blue light that moved slowly past. Andor opened the detective novel and read it up to the point at which the detective was struck in the head by an unknown assailant. The bus driver switched off all interior lights, and Andor composed himself for sleep, sprawling diagonally across two seats. He continued to worry about the detective novel, which seemed to involve a case of mistaken identity.

Andor awoke once in the night, when the bus stopped for fifteen minutes at a restaurant with a glass front entrance and green-and-pink interior. Andor had a cup of coffee.

At eight o'clock, the bus pulled into another great bus terminal. There was a forty-five minute stop for breakfast. Passengers were requested to take all their belongings with them, for the journey would continue in a different vehicle. Andor took his two suitcases into the terminal and checked them in a steel locker with a secure lock.

There were over a dozen servicemen and two or three clergymen waiting for buses in the terminal. The clergymen strolled about or read breviaries. Most of the servicemen lounged on benches, trying to sleep, though some slouched up, reading hot-rod magazines. Andor entered the terminal restaurant, sat in a pink-and-pale-green leatherette seat before a table of wood-grained plastic, and opened the giant menu.

After a breakfast of pancakes and syrup, he retrieved his suitcases and shaved in the terminal men's room. On the way out of the city, the new bus, number E-4799, passed a number of used-car lots, their plastic propellers spinning in the fresh morning breeze, or what Andor imagined to be a fresh morning breeze. Looking at them gave his heart a lift.

Before Andor opened his book to read, the bus was rolling along the turnpike, and through the concealed speakers came a sprightly morning song.

By mid-morning, things had changed. Andor left off reading the detective novel, finding he had read it before. He was sure it had once had a different title, or at least a different cover picture. Disgusted, he shoved the book into the pocket on the back of the seat ahead of him. In doing so he discovered a worn copy of a popular news picture magazine. It contained an interesting article on the very resort he was going to, as well as a feature on ancient Egypt, 'Land of the Pharaohs'. By the time he had digested both of these, it was time for the lunch stop at a familiar spired restaurant.

'Going far?' asked the salesman who eased into the seat beside him later that afternoon. Andor named the resort he was bound for, and the stranger whistled. 'Vacation?'

'That's right. Two fabulous weeks in the sun,' said Andor.

'Yes, I've been there five times myself. Great place. Lot of women on vacation, bored, you know. One thing leads to another: a dip in the pool, a drink in the hotel bar . . .'

They exchanged several pleasant words about the resort,

and the salesman confirmed many things Andor had read in the travel and news magazines, and in a travel brochure: the place was expensive, but worth it.

The salesman took down his ample case and got off at the next city, where the bus once more changed drivers and another coupon was taken from Andor's ticket. It seemed as if the number of coupons remaining had not diminished; the ticket looked as long as ever.

Andor napped as he finished digesting his lunch of hamburger steak, french fries, and cole slaw. He got off the bus at dinnertime hungry enough to order creamed dried beef on toast, steamed potatoes, garden peas, and coffee. This time he debated whether or not to order dessert: he was hungry, but he was not getting enough exercise. At first he ordered apple pie à la mode, then changed it to plain apple pie. After paying the pale, green check, he returned to leave a coin on the wood-grained plastic table.

The next stop was after midnight at another restaurant of the same chain. Andor thought he glimpsed the book-keeper eating and reading a newspaper in another part of the large restaurant. It was only when the white-haired man looked up that Andor saw he was a cleric, and a complete stranger.

After dinner Andor walked around outside. The evening was chilly and damp. After ten minutes he began to feel uneasy. Five minutes later his uneasiness had grown to a mild panic. He was relieved when the other passengers came out of the restaurant and began boarding the bus, and he could join them. What would he have said to the book-keeper if it had been he indeed?

The drizzle lifted as Andor woke, moving his shoulders to ease their stiffness. Despite a night of indigestion and strange underwater dreams, he was content this morning. This was his favourite time of day, the purple hours just before dawn. The bus stopped for fuel at a kind of depot-restaurant out on the turnpike, far from civilization, where a dozen other buses nudged up to the concrete building like piglets at a sow. After dozing over a cup of coffee, Andor tried to board the wrong bus. Though it sat in the exact position he recalled it sitting in before, the driver was now tall and grey-haired rather than fat and red-haired. He asked Andor to see his ticket, then told him he was on the wrong bus.

'This is number E-2842, and you came in on number E-4799, over on the other side of the building. Better hurry up and see if you can still catch it.'

Andor saw his mistake at once. He had entered the restaurant by one door and left by another on the opposite side. He now ran back in through the glass doors, past the rows of empty pink-and-green leatherette booths, and out the proper door. The driver was just starting the engine as Andor bolted up the steps and back to his warm seat. Even though the danger was past, it took him several minutes to recover himself from panic.

That morning Andor divided between watching the billboards advertising tyres and distant casinos and reading the travel brochure describing his resort. At lunch he ate roast turkey and creamed potatoes, cranberry sauce and wax beans. Dessert was chocolate pudding.

His hotel, the brochure informed him, had a ballroom with dancing nightly, a cabaret, a restaurant, and a heated floodlit swimming pool. Even in coldest weather – although the weather was never really cold, the brochure assured him – he could slide into the warm blue liquid and glide silently about, safe from the gelid moon. It seemed to him almost as if he had been there already.

Andor noticed a series of power-line pylons set along parallel to the interstate highway. He began to count them, and fell asleep at one hundred and twenty-odd.

Dinner was a club sandwich, potato salad, and a glass of

ginger ale, with tapioca for dessert. Andor bought a package of caramels and took them aboard with him. The driver removed another coupon from his ticket, which still seemed undiminished. Andor briefly considered counting the remaining coupons, to see if they were actually the same number as before, but it was too much work, and how was he supposed to account for it if they were? The whole idea was silly and profitless. Andor watched the sunset, aware of his own boredom.

Next morning was very warm indeed. The bus entered a great terminal where Andor bathed and changed clothes and ate bacon, eggs, hash browns, and coffee. In his coffee he poured cream from a tiny tetrahedronal container. He picked up a red plastic tomato and considered squeezing it over his hash browns, but decided against it. The coffee, he thought, tasted very like the coffee in that town – what was the name of it?'

It seemed to Andor as if the name he was searching for were somehow the name of a town he had not yet reached.

The magazine he was reading was one he'd borrowed from a clergyman. It featured an article on spiritual fulfilment. In front of Andor two men in college sweaters were playing cards on top of a suitcase. Two nuns sat across from them, in front of a sleeping soldier. In front of them a businessman wrote steadily in his notebook. Behind the soldier a cowboy argued with his wife, while a family of swarthy foreigners looked on interestedly. Two clergymen of different denominations chatted genially across the aisle. Back of them sat more servicemen, and several vacationing pensioners.

Lunch was tuna casserole de luxe, diced carrots, and lettuce salad with french dressing. Dessert was custard pie. Andor imagined that he saw at the counter the salesman he'd talked to earlier, but dressed as a sailor. He seemed to see everyone twice, as on a merry-go-round. Motion was blending people and days together like soft ice cream.

Dinner at another restaurant with a spire. Andor felt a slight unpleasant sensation as he rode along afterwards. There were darkening blue fields wheeling past him, but Andor had no sensation of motion at all. It was as viewing a landscape painted on canvas, moving past on wooden rollers; it was cinematic illusion, badly done; it was a cheap mirror trick; it was, in short, motion that refused to become *real.* He felt the bus accelerate against the back of his head, and his ears heard the roar of engine in the back, but these too seemed piped-in sensations. Was there an engine behind him? As well insist there was a string orchestra playing show tunes somewhere in the compartment (he had ceased to think of it as a 'bus'). The only reality in all this seemed to be the warmth spreading outward through him from his stomach, where enzymes, he supposed, were now attacking macaroni and cheese, butter beans, and malted milk. He dozed.

Things were no better in the morning, at least not at first. Counting back, Andor could not discover how long he had been travelling. Time was undone; days were become as alike as a row of 'red' signs against the flat, 'green' landscape:

Beards grow faster
In the grave . . .

He had to keep reminding himself that all was viewed through blue glass, that colours were not true. Whenever he stepped out of the bus, earth and sky took on an uncanny pink tinge.

A waffle and sausage; a morning paper from a strange city; counting his money and finding to his delight that he had more than he'd figured; these restored Andor's good humour for the morning. He recovered himself sufficiently to hum along with the sprightly show tunes.

But after his lunch of Yankee pot roast and escalloped potatoes, Andor felt uneasy and depressed. The date on his paper was the thirtieth, and he determined to use it to find out his day of departure, by counting backwards. But not only could he not decide whether he had been four or five days *en route*, but it occurred to him he might have yesterday's paper. He asked the soldier across the aisle for today's date.

'Wish I knew,' the soldier apologized. 'I got a calendar watch, but now and then I forget to set it right. Let's see – Sunday was the twentieth or twenty-first, so Sunday again would of been the twenty-seventh or eighth. But I forget every time whether it's May or June has thirty days, and so I get my watch off one day. It registers thirty-one days every month, see, unless I reset it.'

He might have asked someone else, but Andor suddenly gave up. Why was the date so important anyway? He would get there when he got there – to the resort whose name escaped him for the moment.

It was not as if he had not read, heard, or spoken it often enough. Rather, he knew it almost too well. It was become a piece of mental furniture so familiar as to be invisible in the background of his mind; he could not make his tongue trip over it. Indeed, he knew it so well, Andor could almost imagine having been to the resort already. Knowing how difficult it is to conjure up a forgotten name, he turned his thoughts to the more or less neutral topic of approaching dinner.

Dinner was basic fish sticks, french fries, baked beans, and lettuce salad with french dressing, followed by a banana split. Afterwards he walked out for a moment under the darkening sky, watching stars appear. But there was something vaguely terrifying about the first few points of light in that immense blackness . . .

He read a detective novel to the point where an unknown assailant struck the detective. The reading light went off.

Andor lay awake in the darkness, imagining the unread portion. It seemed not improbable that the detective was going to lose his memory from this blow on the head.

He awoke in utter darkness, among strangers, alone and afraid. But almost as if it had been awaiting his cue, the sky began to lighten. Soon he could make out the shapes of billboards and the grey tangles of an interchange.

Dozing again, he dreamt of the resort. Andor swan-dived into a pool of blue jello. Cutting through the viscid stuff, his body moved deeper and deeper into blue protecting darkness, until by some miracle reversal, he emerged at the centre of the sky, at the sun, and he flowed down like pale-green rain to the sun-flooded beach.

Bacon and eggs, coffee with cream from a tiny tetrahedron. Pale-green check from the pale waitress. He found he had read the detective novel before, or at least started it before. Washing his hands in the tiny sink at the rear of the compartment, he wondered if he would ever reach his goal.

It amused him to postulate two Andors, one moving from A to B, the other moving from B to A, each passing through the other – but perhaps neither arriving at his ever-receding goal. Perhaps he approached the end asymptotically, riding three seats behind the driver in perpetuity . . .

He counted his money, discovered there was more than he'd thought. The driver took another coupon from his never-diminishing ticket. Meat loaf and gravy, mashed potatoes, string beans, coffee. Apple pie à la mode.

Each night, he thought, *when I'm asleep, I slip back one notch in time. If I travel all day, I may just make up that slippage. It's some kind of treadmill.*

★

Garden peas, Yankee pot roast, fried potatoes, and coffee with cream. Andor ignored the tiny paper envelopes of sugar. Tapioca. 'Land of the Pharaohs'.

I'll get out, he thought. *They can't keep me on the bus.* But he found it more terrifying than ever, just imagining the solitude out there, stars and blackness and the frozen disc of the moon. Whenever he had to move from the bus to the restaurant, Andor hurried without looking up.

He had been to the resort already; that much seemed certain. He could recall it all so clearly: the night fireworks, by day the heated blue pool. He had picked up a woman there whose name he could not recall. A drink at the hotel bar, a dip in the pool, and so on. Later they had visited the fabulous amusement park and observed a yacht race in the dazzling sunlight.

Dinner: creamed dried beef on toast, steamed potatoes, spinach, coffee, bread and butter. Dessert: butterscotch pudding.

Hamburger steak, creamed corn, hash browns. He squeezed a red plastic tomato over the potatoes. *I'll stay out*, he decided, but he was afraid. When the time came, he reboarded the proper bus.

It's a treadmill in time, a suspension between present and past. If I try to stop anywhere, I'll be swept backwards, backwards . . .

Always into a yesterday, always into a sealed-off, completed past, undying – because already dead?

A stranger eased into the seat beside him, holding an attaché case and a rolled-up magazine.

'Going far?' he asked.

Andor did not appear to hear him. The stranger seemed satisfied with Andor's silence, for he settled himself and began to read. Andor continued to stare out the deep-blue window, as into the depths of pool, until it grew so dark outside that there was nothing to see but the reflection of his own face.

Name (Please Print):

REMARKS: (extra sheets may be attached)

You, the expediter who deals with this, may find it ironic that I use a form on which to make my complaint, and the wrong form at that. But then, is there a correct form for a problem of this type? Or is my case unique?

My case.

Briefly, I have discovered that all written records pertaining to me have disappeared. I can think of no reason for this, and feel it is an unnecessary discrepancy which should be cleared up at the earliest opportunity.

I blame no one. I could blame it all on the 'bureaucracy', but I have been too long on the other side of the counter. I know that bureaux are only groups of human clerks, like me. Like you.

I should say that I like forms. I like filling them out, printing clearly in ink only. I like stamping them, filing them, copying or checking them, even bringing in a fresh stack from the stockroom. But especially I like reading them. One of my favourite quotations is line 4 of *Computation of Social Security Self-Employment Tax:* 'Net income (or loss) from excluded services or sources included on line 3'. Smile at my enthusiasm, but consider for a moment the precision and balance of that line. *Income* vs *loss, excluded* or *included, services* and *sources.* I'd like to shake the hand of the clerk who wrote that.

This form is also well set out, nicely planned, though possibly this Remarks section could be larger. I see I'm running out of space already, and my true remarks have not yet begun. Attaching extra sheets, then, let me begin:

At the beginning, I had a responsible job in a government documents office. Without becoming close friends with anyone in the office, I had managed to command some respect for my work and perhaps my person. No one seemed unduly envious when Mr Boyle told me I was being promoted in grade. The promotion involved a transfer to another department, in which I would be working with classified documents.

'I should warn you,' Mr Boyle said, 'that you'll need a SECRET clearance for this job. If you know any reason you won't be able to get such a clearance, let me know now.'

Naturally I knew of no such impediment. Mr Boyle gave me forms for my clearance application, to be submitted in triplicate with a set of my fingerprints and a copy of my birth certificate.

I applied in person to the state records office for the latter. After a wait of twenty minutes, jerked out on the wall clock, the trim young woman behind the counter explained that my birth record was not on file here. She suggested I try the county records office.

Next day the county records office clerk suggested I try the hospital. The clerk at the hospital had neither any record of my birth nor any suggestion.

Such mistakes will happen. Clerks are human. I'm willing to tolerate a few mistakes, a lot of mistakes, any finite number of mistakes, choose one. I returned to the state office and explained my predicament. The clerk, a young woman with short hair, seemed to sympathize. She suggested I try obtaining copies of other documents attesting to my birth and present those to the clearance people. She seemed about to make another suggestion, but I saw by the jerking clock that I was already late for another appointment, to have my fingerprints taken.

I submitted the fingerprints with the triplicate clearance

application, attaching a letter of explanation in lieu of my birth certificate. Then I set about tracing my birth.

Several routes were already closed:

(a) My parents were dead, and everyone I could think of who might have known me as a child was either dead or untraceable.

(b) Tracing my school records was impossible, since the school had burned down.

(c) I telephoned county and state education departments, who refused to divulge any information whatsoever.

(d) I wrote to my old family doctor and dentist. The doctor's niece replied that he had died two years ago, and that she had no idea what had happened to his old files. The dentist did not reply.

(e) I wrote asking for a copy of my baptismal certificate. The minister who replied (not the one who had baptized me) said that he was very sorry, but his predecessor's files were in a chaotic state, and my certificate was not to be found. Perhaps out of habit, he urged me not to give up hope of his finding it eventually.

It was depressing, but still only an odd set of circumstances, up to this point. Then my application for a SECRET clearance was rejected, for two reasons: 'Fingerprints not clear' and 'No birth certificate'. My letter of explanation was not returned with the other documents.

Mr Boyle called me into his office next day. He explained that the department hadn't foreseen this new difficulty. Now, since I wasn't cleared, he would have to give the promotion to someone else. I said I understood.

'I don't think you do,' he said. 'For one thing, when we created the position you were to fill, we also deleted your present position. Now there really is no room for you in our office. Naturally we can't *fire* you, but – we think it would be better for everyone if you resigned.'

I agreed. For a moment I sat snapping a card between my

front teeth – my rejected, blurry fingerprints – then I rose and shook hands with Mr Boyle. I hadn't spent ten years in his office to become a liability to it now. I walked with slow dignity to the door, then turned to look at Mr Boyle.

'Good luck,' he said, and turned to drop some papers in the waste basket.

I spent the next few days wandering the streets, being 'unemployed'. For one entire week I stationed myself on a particular street corner and made a note of the serial number of every bus that passed. For an afternoon I sought out weighing machines of the fortune-telling type. I wasted perhaps too much of my diminishing resources on this, and on taking my own picture and recording my own voice, but it was a comfort.

One day at the dinner hour, the plangent dinner hour, I wandered alone in an unfamiliar part of the city, thinking and no doubt talking to myself. The loss of two or even three documents could be a coincidence. But a dozen? Surely the odds against this were astronomical.

I found myself standing before a large building that was made of, or at least covered with, cast iron. Fireproof. Enduring. The sun must have been setting, for great flocks of noisy birds began to wheel and wheel in the changing light. A foreign ecstasy began to fill me, drawing me on like a glove. How could mere cards and papers matter, when I was here, alive, myself, and full of ease?

I must have fallen face down; when I awoke, it was night, and my mouth was full of drying blood. A policeman prodded me in the ribs, gently, with his stick. 'You okay, fella?' I sat up and nodded. 'I seen right away you wasn't just a drunk. What happened to you?'

'I don't know. Must have fainted.'

He asked if I'd been rolled. It was then I discovered that my billfold was missing.

A policeful day. When I got home at last, two FBI agents were waiting for me: Agent Barkley, and another whose name escapes me. I didn't really realize how much of my official substance had eroded until our little, as they called it, chat. This took place in their small office – uncomfortably small, it seemed to me, for two large men and a tape-recorder and myself. After taking a loyalty oath, I was permitted to tell my story.

'You expect us to believe this?' asked Agent Barkley. 'That your high school burned down, and your doctor died, and you've lost your billfold with all your ID? And no one else has any records of you?'

'There must be something,' the other agent put in. 'Your college transcript. Your dental chart. Old tax records.'

'I've moved several times,' I explained. 'Certain papers have just disappeared in the shuffle. But surely the Internal Revenue Service has copies of my tax returns . . . ?'

The two agents looked at each other. Barkley asked about my college.

'Cypress University,' I said. 'School of Business Administration.' Again they exchanged looks.

'Kind of a coincidence, isn't it?' asked Barkley. He showed me an evening paper, headlining a violent disturbance at Cypress University. Transcript files had been ransacked and many destroyed.

The FBI men told me I could go home, but not to try going anywhere else. They promised to contact me shortly.

That night I lay awake theorizing. Three theories might account for what has happened: coincidence, a prank, and a conspiracy.

(1) Coincidence. The girl in the state birth records office accidentally put her cup of coffee on my certificate and spoiled it. Rather than tell her superior, she destroyed the copy. At the drivers' licence bureau a man with a cut on his

finger, a paper cut, goes awkwardly through the file with it, missing my form. I can see my draft board file accidentally stored under my first name; my social security form crumpled down in the back of the drawer; other files fallen down behind file cabinets; still others turned back to front; my insurance premium card is spindled by a stupid typist, so that it keeps fluttering through the computer, never to be retrieved . . .

A mouse nests in my baptismal certificate. The burnt school. The dead doctor. The trashed university files. My letters to my parents were bundled in the attic, and after their deaths, given to a neighbour who moved away, whose kids now play a game with them, 'mailing' them through the slot of a cardboard grocery box, say. One letter to a friend was delivered to the wrong address, where an inquisitive person, having read it, burned the guilty evidence and mixed the ashes with the soil in her window box. Another letter was never mailed, but fell into the lining of a suit I gave away to the Salvation Army. Someday the derelict wearing it will die, and it will be found on him by someone feeling his clothes for thousand-dollar bills. Other letters will be stolen by postal clerks, mutilated by experimental cancelling machines, somehow destroyed as pornography or Communist propaganda, none of the above . . .

Someone is gluing overdraft notices to account records at the bank, he spills a drop of glue and welds my record forever to the one in front of it. A department store clerk only pretends to search for my charge account record – actually he's sneaking a smoke in the toilet. Who can blame him, he's young, plays with himself though believing it causes the pimples he also plays with. Say a file clerk at the Internal Revenue goes quietly crazy and – what file clerk has not had this dream? – selects one file and tears it up. Or his radium watch dial emits a stray gamma ray which obliterates the microfilm of me. Finally, my dentist, while examining my teeth card, feels suddenly tired. He closes the card in a telephone directory, puts his head down on his desk for a brief nap, and dies.

(2) Pranks. No one knows me well enough to take the trouble.

(3) Conspiracy. Who, again, would bother? Why not simply kill me, instead of breaking into hundreds of offices (or infiltrating them), searching through tons of files and never overlooking a duplicate? They could spend man-years

erasing	expunging	blotting out	vanishing
removing	lifting	eradicating	cancelling
deleting	stealing	eliminating	purging
voiding	discarding	superseding	correcting

or expropriating my official self. Think of them, hiring hundreds of agents to infiltrate bureaux, present their qualifications, hope to get hired, wait in line, fill out applications, perhaps miss the job after all, perhaps find out the bureau isn't hiring today, the budget has been cut . . . hoping all the while that I did not marry, have children, write letters to the editor, go to court, vote, sign petitions, buy something on credit, change dentists . . . a foreign conspiracy it cannot be, and an American conspiracy is too terrible to think of.

After a week of waiting, Agent Barkley phoned me to say they were still investigating, and would I please remain available? I saw my mistake at once. It is a kind of crime, after all, to be unidentified. So long as the FBI were on the track of my identity, I was a house prisoner. When they gave up, I would be too dangerous not to arrest.

I packed at once and moved out, walked into the factory district across the river, and registered in a cheap hotel as 'A. Barkley'. It is not necessary that a certain person exists. The mere use of a name, a fistful of cards of identity means nothing. I think of student pranks, of registering for classes fictitious persons: Mort Arthur, Phil Morris, Art Lesson and Mac Hines. These are figureless fields, I suppose, while I am a faceless, rather, fieldless figure. Gene DeFect.

Now I'm cut off. Even if some trace of me has now been found, I can't contact the appropriate agency or bureau without coming to the attention of Barkley and his friend. Before, I could have found my old copies of tax returns, rent receipts, bills, the ones I saved. If any. I could have taken a lie detector test, affidavits from acquaintances and co-workers, thrown myself on the mercy of the FBI, the agents are human, too, they sweat, they bleed, they do pee-pee, choose one.

Yesterday a new telephone book came out. My name was not in it. Was it in the old? I . . .

Things aren't too bad, really. I was unable to pay my bill for room and meals, so Mr Gurnt, the manager, arranged for me to mop the halls for my keep. Despite the beatings, I'm getting to feel at home here.

I'm keeping a journal, from which some of this is copied. Some of it is really written by me, the hall-mopper at this hotel. The person filling out this form is the same object of Mr Gurnt's kicks and punches. Here I am. Not the government clerk, perhaps, not even the man who signed the register, but here I am writing this, this sentence, and the period at its end. Is this not proof of my true, dense, solid material substance? Answer in full

No one has seen the journal yet, but me. I hide it from Gurnt and the others. I stop writing and slip it into a drawer when the door opens, always. At night, I keep it in my underwear, in the front, and endeavour to remain on my stomach all night. If anyone had seen it, I'd have been visited by Agent Barkley by now.

The beatings come daily, along with threats to fire me. Empty threats, empty as many of my tooth sockets. The beatings come daily, regular as the meals of boiled cabbage and boiled potatoes, far more regular than my bowel movements. Things aren't too bad, really.

It is not necessary for a certain person to exist. I said that. Did I mention the telephone directory? Yes. It is beautiful, and I enjoy its beauty still, from outside the page. As a child I was plagued by beauty: rainbows in the puddles by the gas station, dead birds by the gas station, the thumbless attendant at the gas station (I heard he had lost his thumb and believed it to be literally misplaced among his greasy tools. The stump was streamlined and elegant). Now I find teeth on my floor.

To simplify things, I've erased my alias from the hotel register. This made the page look odd, so I tore it out. But the pages are numbered – to hide the gap I burned the whole book. But the hotel looks strange without a register.

That about concludes my remarks, except for one. Diet and beatings have greatly altered my appearance. Loss of weight has wrinkled me, I'm missing most of my hair and teeth, my nose is broken, etc. Now, even if Agent Barkley were to stride in here in his well-padded suit and look things over, I doubt very much if he could recognize me as one of the 'wanted'.

NOTE: The above MS is attached to form MP-7881-b, apparently filed at the Bureau of Missing Persons on the date shown. It was found crumpled down in the back of the file drawer. Not signed. Disposition: Destroy.

(Approved) Lazarus Cameforth
Bureau Chief

Anxietal Register B

Directions.

READ CAREFULLY. Before answering any of the questions below, be sure to have all pages of this form, in order. Fill out in triplicate, using ballpoint pen or, preferably, indelible pencil. Press hard. PLEASE PRINT. Sign name to all copies.

1. State full name at present: ______________________________

2. Full name at birth, or baptism: ___________________________

3. Give any aliases, abbreviations, or nicknames by which you have ever been known: ______________________________

4. Attach copies of birth and baptismal certificates.

5. Social security number: ________________

6. Name on your last income tax return: ______________________

7. Date: _______________ 8. Date of tax return: ______________

9. State your full permanent address: _________________________

____

10. Where may you be quickly reached by: a)Mail: ________________

b)Telephone: ________________

c)Telegram or cable: ______________ d)Messenger: ____________

11. List every address at which you have resided, since birth, in chronological order. Include every address, with the following exceptions: a) Hotel accommodations in the United States, Mexico or Canada, for stays of up to or less than three days, occurring more than five years ago. b) Accommodations at U.S. Embassies, in other than an official capacity, for any duration, occurring more than seventeen years ago. c) Antarctic expeditions not using APO addresses. ALL OTHER ADDRESSES MUST BE SHOWN, WITHOUT EXCEPTION. Note: extra sheets (Form AR-B Supplem) may be attached.

Street address: City: State: Date from: Date to:

12. Occupation: ____

13. Name and address of company where you are presently employed/ were last employed: ______________________________

13a Last position held:

14. Salary: __________ 15. Name of superior: ___________________

16. Starting date: ______________ 17. Terminating date: ________

18. Attach references. 19. If unemployed, give reason: ________

____

20. Why did you leave your last job? ________________

21. Give your entire employment history, except for your last or present job. List all employment in chronological order, and include part-time employment. Note: Extra sheets (Form AR-B Supplem.) may be attached.

Company name & address	Position	Supervisor	Salary	From	To	Reason for leaving

22. Have you ever been fired for: a)Theft: ___ b)Embezzlement: ___

c)Dishonesty: ___ d)False References: ___ e)Absenteeism: ___

f)Tardiness: ___ g)Loafing: ___ h)Inefficiency: ___ i)Personal reasons (Explain): ______________________

23. Have you ever quarrelled with fellow employees? __________

24. Have you ever had difficulty with employers? Describe: ________

____

25. Have you ever stolen any property belonging to an employer, no matter how small in value? _____ 26. Have you ever feigned illness? ______________________

27. Name of your bank or banks? ________________

28. Explain any foreign bank accounts: ________________

29. Bank Account Number(s): ________________

30. Present balance(s): ________________

31. Number and amount of withdrawals during past year: ________

____

32. Father's name: ________________

33. Mother's maiden name: ________________

34. Attach birth certificate and marriage licence.

35. Have you ever been arrested a)As a minor: ___ b)As an adult: ___

c)Misdemeanor? ________ d)Felony? ______ e)Convicted? _____

f)Sentenced? ______

36. Give full details of any arrest and/or conviction, including name of offence, whether convicted, sentence and/or fine. Include all traffic offences other than overtime parking.

37. Do you love your mother more than your father? ______________

38. If you do not love your mother, explain: ____________________

____

39. Circle which of the following you have ever suffered from:
a) Rheumatism b) Arthritis c) Chronic fatigue d) Rupture
e) Tuberculosis f) Night sweats g) Nocturnal emissions
h) Nightmares (frequent) i) Sleepwalking j) Ringing noises
k) Chronic or severe headaches l) Bronchitis m) Homosexual
tendencies n) Hot flushes o) Tumours p) Cancer q) Gastric
ulcer r) Gonorrhea s) Syphilis t) Asthma u) Hay fever
v) Severe cough w) Trenchmouth x) Hepatitis (jaundice)
y) Diabetes z) Anaemia aa) Poliomyelitis ab) Heart attack
ac) Stroke ad) Heart murmur ae) Blindness af) Deafness
ag) Tunnel vision ah) Astigmatism ai) Unexplainable pains
(Explain) aj) Visions ak) Epilepsy al) Impotence
am) Obesity an) Chronic nausea ao) Drug addiction (Explain)
ap) Alcoholism aq) Double vision ar) Frequent or severe
accidents as) Amnesia at) Laryngitis au) Malnutrition
av) Precognition aw) Cleft palate ax) Harelip ay) Multiple
digits az) Paralysis (specify).

40. Have you ever had any serious physical or mental disorder? Describe, specifying dates, physician, treatment, hospitalization etc.:

____

____

41. Briefly describe your own condition at present: ______________

42. Are you under medication? Describe: ______________________

43. Attach medical records and physician's affidavit.

44. Have you ever undergone surgery? Describe: ______________

45. Have you all your natural teeth? (Attach chart) ______________

46. Describe any amputations, giving dates and reasons: __________

____

47. Have you: a) Both kidneys b) Both lungs c) Ovaries
d) Prostate e) Gall bladder f) Both eyes g) A bladder
h) A complete stomach i) A complete colon j) Both breasts
k) Lower jaw l) Nose

48. Have you ever undergone sterilization? ____________________

49. Castration? ______________ 50. Hysterectomy? ______________

51. Do you feel sexual desire for, about, during:
a) Those of your own sex b) Those of both sexes c) Children

d) Your mother e) Your father f) Your son g) Your daughter h) Sister i) Brother j) Babies k) Cadavers l) Animals m) Birds n) Fish o) Insects p) Cripples q) People who hurt you r) People whom you hurt s) People of special professions (describe) t) People in particular costumes (describe) u) Watching others in the act of coition v) Peeping at naked persons w) Drinking blood x) Drinking urine y) Drinking semen z) Eating faeces aa) Looking at photographs ab) Looking at drawings ac) Drawing pictures ad) Telephoning ae) Confessing sins af) Listening to music ag) Dancing ah) Exposing one's sex organs to someone else ai) Anal entry aj) Axilial entry ak) Oral entry al) Nasal entry am) Rape an) All members of the opposite sex, regardless of age or condition ao) Watching movies ap) Watching television aq) Performing your ordinary work ar) Masturbating as) Urinating at) Defecating au) Menstruating av) Wearing clothing belonging to the opposite sex aw) A particular part of another's body ax) Of your body ay) Crowds az) Rubbing against people ba) Clergy bb) Weapons bc) Machines bd) Plants be) Trees bf) Sunsets bg) People of other races bh) Apparel bi) Dangerous or unusual surroundings bj) Inanimate objects bk) Mathematical propositions bl) Thoughts bm) The law bn) God bo) The act of filling out a form

52. List all the persons in your household:

Person:	Age:	Sex:	Income:	Source:	Relation to you:

53. Why do you believe you have been asked to fill out this form? ____

____

54. Describe briefly your feelings about filling out this form: ____

____

55. Describe in detail other forms you have been asked to fill out, explain their use, and estimate your performance: ____

____

____

56. Describe your character in detail, giving examples of your behaviour to illustrate points. Note: extra sheets (Form AR-B Supplem) may be attached.

____

____

____

57. Do you believe in God? __________ If 'no', explain: ___________
____
____

58. Have you answered all the above questions? ________

59. Have you answered truthfully? ____ 60. Have you ever lied? _____

61. Have you ever stolen anything? _______________________________

62. Why do you believe that you have been asked to fill out this form?____
____
____
____

63. If you are merely reading this form, why do you believe that you have not been asked to fill it out? _______________________
____

64. Have you been asked to fill out this form? ___ 65. To read it?___

66. Not to fill it out? ______ 67. Not to read it? Explain: _______

68. Compare this form with others which you may have read or filled out, whether or not you were asked to read them or fill them out:
____
____

69. Be sure your comparison is fair and correct. If it is not, you may rewrite it on extra sheets (Form AR-B Supplem). If you do so, be sure your revision is correct.

70. Was your original comparison correct? _____ Fair? _____ If not, explain: ____
____
____

71. If you revised your comparison, why? ________________________
____

72. Write your life history in brief, explaining in passing your answers to questions 11, 21, 39 and 51 fully. Take as much time, and as many extra sheets (Form AR-B Supplem) as necessary, but do not lie, omit, falsify, distort or invent. If there are any portions you genuinely do not fully remember, you will be asked to complete and attach three copies of Form WH6, Hypnotic Drugs Waiver of Rights. ____
____
____
____
____
____

73. Sign the following statement:
I hereby agree to submit to a Keeler Polygraph ("Lie Detector") examination, to be conducted by or in the presence of a psychiatrist and police officer, during which I will endeavour to answer all or any questions about my past life as truthfully as I am able.

(X) Signed: ____________________

Witnessed: ____________________

74. Describe your feelings upon reading and signing the above statement: ____________________

____

75. Do you believe you have anything to hide, about your past life? If not, explain: ____________________

____

____

____

76. Have you anything to add, regarding the answers to questions 11, 21, 33, 39, 51, 72 or 75? ____________________

____

____

____

____

77. Do you ever have feelings of anxiety? ____________________

I swear that all the statements above are true and complete and that I have not attempted any falsification, on penalty of perjury.

(X) Signed: ____________________

Witnessed: ____________________

The Communicants:
An Adventure in Management

The blinds were drawn, the desk lamp glowed.

'I've been having these terrible dreams – locked in an inappropriate box.'

'Go on.' The man behind the desk had a heavy, block-salt look. He would gladly give you the time, change, a light, a push when your car was stalled. Probably his seat in the last life-boat.

After a minute, David went on: 'Just above is this heavy line and the lines "Do not mark below heavy line. For use of lines of Authority only".'

'Hmm. And?'

'I'm printed, see? *That's* not the point. *The dots* are printed all over everything, and they're – sliding. So the colours change. There's a bunch of fake clouds around, or something. I'm right in the middle of this big poster.'

The interviewer delved in the pocket of his tweed jacket and brought out a scarred pipe and a small knife.

'Any more?' He began to scrape the bowl.

'Yes, every night – I don't know why I'm telling you this – every night there's a woman-thing standing beside my bed. A kind of coke bottle with a woman's head. She seems to be a poster too. Across the front is a ribbon that says: "Humfrey's Hollywood Novelties". That's all.'

'Haheh. I see.' The interviewer stopped scraping and peered at him over the lamp. 'You realize of course that still does not answer my question: *Why do you want to work for Drum, Inc.?*'

David did not falter. Raising his chin slightly, he said, 'Sir, I love my father more than my mother, and I sincerely believe that it just isn't enough to *sprinkle* the baptism candidate. That don't do nothing for the *deep-down* dirt. You have to *immerse* . . .'

'Thank you.' As the interviewer hunched forward to mark something on David's application, light flashed from his lapel. The Nat Hawthorne Social Club pin: the same red enamel A that David himself wore! He begins to recall the old songs . . .

'Now then, David, we'd like to have you take a few tests. Just follow Miss Bunne to the testing room, will you?'

As soon as the kid was gone, Travers took off the jacket, dumped the junk back in its pocket, and stripped off the plain tie. He removed the Hawthorne pin and tossed it in a drawer. Lighting a cigarette, he sat back and exhaled. Too gloomy in here. The rich mahogany (veneer) and silver (plate) of the office furniture brightened as he opened the blinds. At eye level across the street, the company cafeteria. A line of trim translucent girls in pale colours filed past the pastries and took glasses of jello.

Travers closed the blinds and sat down. Holding up the next application as if it were a hand-mirror, he sighed at what it reflected. The elastic bands across his back were beginning to itch.

'Have a cigarette?' he repeated several times to the empty chair across from him. His tone varied from casual to commanding.

Every day at about the same time, Marilyn's extension would ring. She would pick it up to hear a woman say carefully:

'Marilyn? He loves you.'

'Who? Who loves me? Is this supposed to be a joke?'

But there would never be more.

She thought of saying something to the supervisor, Miss Bunne, or someone else in the typing pool – but what to say?

What if it were just some joke of Eric's? Or a mean trick of Ray's, to lose Marilyn her job? No, better to say nothing.

Marilyn was engaged to a wonderful boy, Raymond, but she realized she didn't love him. How on earth could she break it off after the party his parents gave them and all the wonderful presents they had been given? She had thought of going away without telling him, but she did not think this would be fair. She was eighteen.

No, it would not be fair, and the newspaper thought it would be on her conscience for a long time. She had to face the disappointment her news was bound to cause, and tell him about her change of mind. She certainly couldn't let the party and presents alter her decisions. They were nothing compared with marrying someone she didn't love. So she should go through with telling him, and she would be respected for handling a difficult situation well.

The newspaper gave her an idea of how to go about it. Marilyn went with Eric to the amusement park at Punk Island where they sold 'newspapers' with any headline you wanted.

HE'S NOT FOR ME!
Marilyn Breaks Engagement

She went to visit him, a copy of this paper tucked in her odour-free armpit. They chatted pleasantly over milk and cookies in his Mom's spacious, easy-to-clean kitchen, while she waited for the right moment.

'What's that paper you've got there?' Ray asked. She handed it to him slowly, as if offering her nakedness. He read through the headlines several times. Then:

'Oh, I don't believe everything I read in the papers.'

'It's true, Raymond.' The refrigerator fell silent, and she could hear the scream of Dad's wood lathe in the basement.

Ray jumped to his feet. 'You'll never get away with this!' he shouted, and ran off down the basement stairs. It took Marilyn a few minutes to dab the splashes of milk off her face and sweater and by the time she was able to follow him, it was too late.

Someone's adding machine wasn't working; he sat in disgrace, the thirty-fourth man in the fifteenth row, quietly weeping. All around him people were adding up feet and inches of cable and wire underneath the city, but old 34/15 just sat there like an unlit bulb in the great rippling sign that burned on the roof by day and by night:

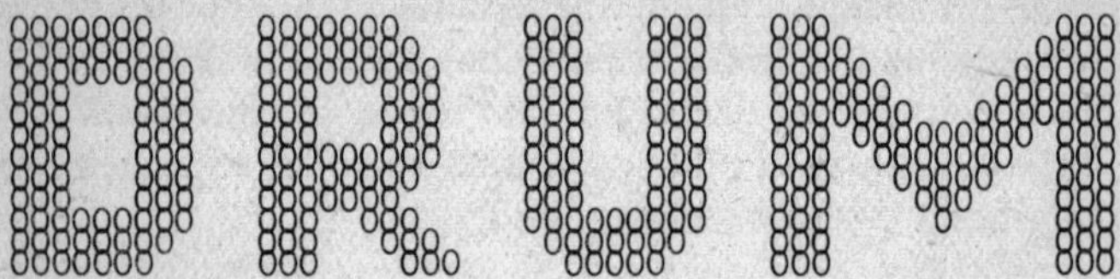

Mr Kravon was superb with tidy rage. He asked Miss Bunne to get him Personnel.

'Let me talk to Travers . . . Hello? This is Sam Kravon, Estimates. Yes, look, we've a hell of a mess down here. A man whose machine doesn't work . . . That's it, all right. I'll send him right up, OK?'

Above the Frenzak music, the cool voice of Miss Bunne paged a Mr Eric Bland, asking him to report to the personnel office on the tenth floor. The Frenzak finished a furious medley of *Avalon, I want to Hold Your Hand*, and *Wonderful, Wonderful Copenhagen.* The weeping man rose and left the room.

Genial Dad, that furnace of amusement, turned off his lathe and watched Ray fiddling with the table saw.

'What's up son?'

Ray mumbled something about cutting off his arm.

'Mmm.' Dad lit his pipe. 'Mmm. Mmm. Might work, at that. Girl trouble, I s'pose?'

The eighteen-year-old, six-foot-one, husky youth did not reply.

'Hem. Excuse an old codger for butting in, my boy, but you'll never do it like that. Get your fingers in the way. Here, let me help you.'

And he showed Ray how to hold his arm and push it towards the blade with a piece of two-by-four. The blade sang.

'*That's* the way to do her! More amateurs have lost more fingers, just by forgetting that one simple trick – statistical fact!'

Travers was standing looking at the jello girls when Miss Bunne entered without knocking.

'Oh, I'm sorry!' she said. He whipped around and kicked a drawer shut.

'Don't *ever* do that again, Miss Bunne. You know I don't like to wear this stuff. And now I have no doubt you'll be going off to laugh about me behind my back, with one of the other Misses Bunne.'

'Oh *no*, Mr Travers. You don't know me very well, or you could never suppose a thing like that!'

'Well, I'm sorry. Who do we have out there?'

'A Mr Galt. He's – handicapped.'

'Give me ten minutes, then?' He lent her a special smile.

When she had backed out, he slipped the elastic off his shoulders and the blue-serge-suit-with-TV-blue-shirt-and-maroon-tie outfit fell away from him. After checking the application on his desk, he put on a similar garment, a black-blazer-stiff-white-shirt-regimental-stripe-tie. On the blazer he pinned the crest of the college Galt had attended until recently. Then he whitened half his hair, and added an eye-patch. The applicant had one arm, and Travers kidded himself about not letting him get the upper hand. It was true he hated being at a sympathetic disadvantage.

Ready, he sat back and waited for Raymond Nixon Galt.

Dr Freag of Drum Laboratories addressed the stockholders, describing a number of new telephone services his department had tested against the day when Drum should replace the Bell System as the nation's telephone monopoly. *Telefun* would connect subscribers to a computer capable of playing over 700 games as diverse as Boccaccio, slapjack, Chinese checkers. Another service would enable users to disguise their voiceprints. An anonymity service, *Dialerase*, would change a subscriber's telephone number as often as hourly, signalling each change only to him and to his current register of friends.

Dr Born of Drummer Boy Enterprises addressed the stockholders, describing a number of new computer devices his department was investigating. *Scribeauty* was intended to change users' handwriting to conform to any desired standard. One would write on a sensitized slate, and the computer would then 'correct' one's writing and reproduce a finished manuscript on paper. A small, portable jukebox with a fast-response mechanism, *Swingit* could be used to 'talk' in 'song' instead of words. Useful in therapy with disturbed adolescents, it could be worn internally without discomfort. *Wordfreak* was the name of a projected monitor system for security agencies. Its computer would scan quantities of taped conversations, sorting them for high 'wordfreaks', or high frequencies of words/phrases of a suspicious nature. He demonstrated.

'Mind if I call you Ray? Here, have a cigarette.' The man behind the desk moved only the left side of his face as he spoke. His left hand shoved a silver box across the desk; the right hung down out of sight.

Ray accepted a cigarette and reached for the lighter.

'No, let me.' With difficulty, the man forced himself up out of his chair and lunged forward to give Ray a light. When at last he sat, or flopped back, he was sweating. Ray felt moisture running down his own face and neck.

'I fee you're handicapped. Well, as you can fee, Ray, Drum Inc. couldn't care less about that. Got mine, by the way, on Porkchop Hill.' *And you?* his left brow asked.

Ray blushed. 'Oh, just a crazy freak accident. With a table saw. At home.'

The sight of this hopeless cripple, sitting behind his big desk and laughing at Ray's injury, shocked him. He began to have second thoughts about working here, even as a janitor . . .

'Forry, fon, I didn't mean to laugh at you. It's just . . . they fay most accidents happen . . . at home, ha ha . . . I've never actually *feen* one . . . boy o boy, I've feen guys shot up fo bad they had to walk ten miles on frozen feet, with their guts in their hands . . . but *you*! Hoo hoo hoo, *you* can't even faw a sucking piece of *board* across . . .'

Ray jumped up. 'Now just a minute!'

'. . . ha ha ha, how ftupid can you . . .'

'JUST A MINUTE! IT WASN'T NO ACCIDENT, I DONE IT ON PURPOSE, TO TEACH MY GIRL A LESSON!'

The interviewer wiped his eyes and checked a box on Ray's card. 'Now we're getting fomeplace. Atta boy. Now fuppose you fit down and tell me all about it?'

Advice to the management trainee at Drum, Inc.
by H. H. Murd, President

Chapter One	Come On Board!
Chapter Two	Drum Inc. And You
Chapter Three	Plastitutes – The Story of a Dream
Chapter Four	Check Your Own Worth

Phil Wang, the art director, stuck his head in the door.

'OK in here? Any new problems, Marty?'

The fat man at the drawing board shook his head, but not in negation. 'I can't get it right, Phil. If I line up things the way they want, the girl's hair just about has to blow across the guy's face. How about if I – oh, I don't know.'

'Take it easy, guy. Let's have a look.'

The picture showed *a young couple at an amusement park. Other people have turned to stare admiringly at them. The girl's hair is wind-tossed; the man is dark and ruggedly handsome. They are about to enter a telephone booth.*

The caption was roughed in below: 'Togetherness is the nearest friendly phone booth.'

'What's this guy in the background? Is he supposed to have an arm missing or what?'

'I was, uh . . .' Marty paused for a moment, fumbling with his expression, as the electronic pacemaker that controlled his heart seemed to miss. This happened to him about once a week, though the doctor assured him it could not possibly happen at all. '. . . changing perspective a little. I'll clean that up.'

'Do that little thing for me, and for Christ's sake, get the girl's hair blowing the other way. Come to think of it, I don't like that face anyway. It isn't – *standard* enough, if you get me.'

'Well, Phil, I thought I'd make her a little bit *individual*. I mean, well, you and I aren't exactly *standard*.'

Phil looked at him a long time. 'So now it comes, eh? The stab in the back.'

'What do you mean, Phil?'

'I'm not standard, eh? You mean I'm not *white*. I'm *Chinese*.'

'No, Phil. Honest, I . . .'

'I guess you've always felt that way about me, eh, Marty? I guess while I was taking you on here and giving you a job, despite the fact that you might drop dead of a heart attack at any moment and leave me with tons of work to do, while I was giving you a job so you could buy a fancy gadget to save your Caucasian heart, all the time you were just thinking how *Chinese* I was. Right? Right.'

Marty's pacemaker missed again; he was unable to answer.

'I guess maybe you think I look like a "dirty Jap" in some old war comic, right? Eh? With buck teeth and bad eyes, eh? Well thanks for cluing me in, buddy. Thanks for telling me what the score is.'

Marty gasped an irrelevant reply.

'Well let me tell *you* something. I fought in the Second World War, risked my life – and on the *right side*. And as for the Japs, they're a damned fine bunch of people – did you see *Sayonara*, with Marlon Brando? – and they make a bunch of clever little products, including that thing in your chest.

'I'm not going to fire you, and make it easy for you to feel sorry for yourself. But don't you ever say I'm *not standard* again, see?'

At the door Phil paused again. 'And fix up that girl. Don't *draw* her, use a few of those expensive sheets of wax faces Drum paid so damned much for.'

Marty opened a file drawer and took out the trembling sheets. Here were row on row of standard faces, admiring crowds, hands holding cigarettes, empty hands ready to hold or point at a product. Here were couples embracing, laughing, dancing, exchanging gifts, pouring champagne, walking in the country, getting into and out of sports cars, throwing beach-balls. Here were office workers comparing notes, talking on the telephone, slipping on overcoats. Here were housewives shopping, cooking, kissing babies, serving something with a delicious aroma that curled around them. And here were the backgrounds to set them against: carpeted offices, TV-equipped living rooms, built-in kitchens, shopping plazas, elegant bistros, neat countryside.

Marty held up a page of twenty neat countrysides and looked at them with loving eyes. More than anything, even more than going to Hawaii, he wanted to be young and slim and alone with a girl in countryside just like that.

But it was rush time. He chose the most standard-looking blonde, frantically grinning, freckled, and burnished her down on a fresh white page. Beginning with her wax loveliness, with her hair swept to the left by an invisible, presumably wax, wind, he would start all over and build the ad around her.

But he burnished hastily, so that when he peeled up the plastic film, her freckles were still on it, untransferred.

'Jesus!'

And Phil was sure to ask Why no freckles? Marty washed his sweating hands and cleaned a tiny crow-quill pen. Steadying his right hand with his left, he began the miniature cosmetic surgery. 'We've made up a selection of code or jargon words/phrases used by some imaginary anarchist group,' said Dr Freag. 'These are: "lafodul", "breughel", "whee", "the basic assumption" and "I have the hymnal in the car". The basic assumption here is that the group will use these words in conversation with sufficient frequency to be detected. And WORDFREAK, scanning vocal patterns at high speed, can do the job.'

Little were any of the stockholders to know that these very words of Dr Freag's were being selected for scanning, and that one day he would be killed by plant security guards! But that is another story.

Ray was sobbing. '. . . and then the sign on the prescription blank? It turned into something else. Like this.' He drew two shaky signs:

Travers marked the last box below the heavy line on Ray's application.

'And then the . . .'

'Yes, yes, I know. And then the caduceus turned into a crozier, and fo on. It's a common enough dream, nothing to worry about. Everyone does those things you fpeak of. And believe me, cutting off your arm was no folution. It wouldn't even help to cut off your other arm; you'd be at it with your toes. And now, if you'll go with Miss Bunne to the testing room, we'd like to give you a few fimple tests and a couple of forms to fill out.'

Their left hands clasped, then Ray backed awkwardly out of the room.

ARM CASSEROLE À LA MOM

Ingredients: 1 lean arm, 3 tbs butter, 1 clove minced garlic, 3 onions minced, 2 cups stewed or canned tomatoes, 4 cups cooked egg noodles, 1 tbs brown sugar, 1 can mushroom soup, salt and pepper to taste.

Skin and devein arm, cut carefully away from bones (which may be saved for soup), and dice. Sauté meat in butter for 5 minutes, then add garlic and onions and cook over medium flame for 10 more minutes. Add tomatoes, sugar, spices. Mix with cooked noodles, fill glass casserole dish and bake 45 minutes in hot oven.

Note: Some people like to save the fingers and hand with the bones for soup. I prefer to boil the hand, oven-brown it, and serve it (palm up) on the casserole for a festive garnish.

Twenty-four tiny perfect freckles done, seven to go. Marty refilled the pen from the ink dropper and poised it. An air-hammer began clattering in the street, and he turned to look out.

A telephone crew seemed to be working down there. At least their truck was a telephone truck. But instead of the familiar black bell on the door, there was a snare-drum.

Then Drum Inc. really did make telephone equipment! It was all real, or at least 'real'! Even the rows of faces in wax, printed on plastic film?

His pacemaker began to act up, trying to cope with the multiple rhythms of his racing heart, the air-hammer, others . . . a different drum.

The last drop of his living sweat grew, gathered itself in an armpit, began the slow journey down the inside of his arm. *But can I really afford Heaven? It's much more expensive than Hawaii. Out of the question now. Maybe in a few years . . .*

The drop zig-zagged, crossed his wrist-pulse and ran down the pen. From there it dripped black on the face of the freckled girl.

'Hello, Marilyn? He loves you.'

'Who does?'

A crew from the telephone company, the other one, were tearing up the street near a manhole. On the windshield of a passing car was a sticker reading 'Hello, Charlie!'

The driver leaned out, looked at the snare drum on the door of the telephone truck, and waved. 'Hello, Charlie!' he called. The crew foreman gave him the finger.

EXPLAIN THIS SCENE. Look at this example:

1. Why were the crew digging near a manhole?
   (a) For extra light.
   (b) *They were rescuing a man.*
   (c) They were outflanking it.
   (d) Never mind.

The correct answer (c) has been marked. Now do the rest of the problems in the same way.

2. Why did the driver call out?
   (a) The foreman was Charlie.
   (b) He looked like Charlie.
3. Why else?
   (a) 'Hello, Charlie!' is the unofficial password for employees of the Bell Telephone System.
   (b) The crew were Viet Cong.
4. What is Drum, Inc.?
   (a) One name of the Bell Telephone System in some regions.
   (b) The official telephone company.
   (c) The real owner of the Bell Telephone System.
   (d) A private telephone company with a vendetta against the Bell near-monopoly.
   (e) Vietnam.
   (f) It is to the Bell Telephone System as the 'Aggressor Force' is to the Army: an imaginary enemy, set up for training purposes. Bell employees who play rôles in it speak Esperanto, count in a duodecimal system, wear the snare-drum insignia, colour-code their cables (unlike the Bell code): fuchsia, mimosa, rose, primrose, lavender, cerise and mauve.

'Hello, Marilyn? He loves you.'

'Listen, you, I've had about enough! You make me feel dirty all over, dirty with deep-brown ground-in dirt, the kind that makes washday a chore and plays havoc with delicate complexions. Do you hear?'

I tried making the general a Negro and a Nazi, then I opened my eyes and sat up on the table.

'David sees reality as – ah – *refrangible.*'

In the next panel, the 'doctor', an elderly scientist from another comic book, held up a red tube. His balloon read: 'Tell me, Herr Heiliger, what is this?'

'A laser? The famous mail-order elixir?'

'Ha. *You* are interested in its contents.' Camera 3 in on Dr Born, seeing him about chest level, deep shadows as in *Return of the Son of Man*. 'Now let us ask David.'

I said, 'It's an ink drawing. Red wash and white airbrush highlight.'

'I came all the way from Washington, or Africa, for *this*?' The general picked up his attache case and made to walk out of the picture. I changed his typeface to Garamond, adopted for myself Univers, a Frutiger-designed face suited to IBM. 'That man is nuts, "doctor". I have no time . . .'

'Wait!' Exhibit B is an infra-red Polaroid shot of Born holding up his hand to count upon the fingers. 'Let me pose for you the four great "reality" problems. One: are physical objects real, or only sense perceptions?'

'But . . .'

'Wait . . .'

'I have . . .'

The page was getting covered with dashes, interrupted thoughts; I set it aside and began over with a story called 'The Sinister Bean'.

'Two: do others have thoughts and feelings as I do, or are their thoughts and feeling clever simulations? Three: are the entities of science, like atoms and quasars, *real*, or only convenient fictions? Four: . . .'

'I offered to come to work for Drum only on condition that

I be given vital communications work,' the general indicated. 'Heliograph, semaphore . . .'

Born speaks with his back to him, make this a circular panel, set at the end of the top right-hand page, so the reader's eye will be drawn to it twice: once as he reads the top row, again as he reads the second row. The doctor's glasses heliographed an urgent message: Esperanto, duodecimal number system . . .

'Certifiably nuts.'

'David, I'm going to lock you in this solid closet, and you are to get out without opening the door.'

'I' went in the 'closet'. Nothing much to examine: the cellular plastic sponge, good replica of animal organizations; broom-straws to draw for randomizing next move; cleaning ether to change words to sounds, to make a centrifuge, to help David understand what it is the mop and pail are getting at.

Nothing to it; one side of the closet had to be left open, so the reader could see I was really in there. I just stepped out of that side and around and back into the room.

'A trick!' said Heiliger. 'A trick?'

'Of course,' David communicated. A cough code was sufficient.

THE SINISTER BEAN

It lay there, perfectly harmless-looking, on a plate or plane or whatever, in the middle of a lot of places. Perhaps the most sinister thing about it was . . .

'Transmission of . . . ?' the general opined, using the old opinion poll code. '*Twins?*'

I tore the money of his words in half, in quarters, and so on, five times, until they were too big a wad to handle. Then David opened my eyes and sat up on the table.

'. . . sees reality as – ah – *refrangible.*'

'And repeatable,' I denoted.

Replacing his cracked monocle, the general said, 'Tell me something, Herr Bland.'

'Blandings,' I said.

'Blandish?'

'No, Blandworth.'

'Blanders, then. Tell me, what is it you – see?'

The pages of the calendar flipped past, indicating passage of time. The drivers of a locomotive, then a stationary plane, pasted against droning clouds, indicated movement in space. The slow dissolve of a wavering image indicated recollection. Then the background music came up full and newspapers rolled off the presses, to indicate an important event.

Dr Ortiz of the Lion Oil Research Branch addressed the stockholders, describing a number of new projects his group was engaged in: 'Organic computers' could be constructed of cheap, simple organisms; bacteria and fungi from common products like cheese had already been tested in this connection. 'Cheese farms' were a related project involving the use of deadly viruses to 'grow' cheeses from common materials. Using less potent forms in a 'stepped' or 'cascaded' system, he explained, would cut down on the type of unfortunate accident that had so far plagued his project. 'Organic-to-inorganic' processes would use a similar virus system to 'grow' from human cadavers such popular products as phonograph records and bowling balls.

INDIANA NAME OPINION REGISTER

Q-Q-QQ
1937

Name . . . .
Address . . . .
Age . . . . (Give latest date)
1 Give your own name in full: . . . .
. . . .
. . . .

2 Print your name in block capitals: . . . .
. . . .

3 State surname, Christian name, middle name: . . . .
. . . .

4 Now give your NAME: . . . .
. . . .

READ the instructions CAREFULLY and do not begin until the teacher tells you. In the first part, you will be expected to write as many names as you can in the time available, but you need not have every name correct. In the second part, tell what it is that you have named, and do so correctly.

NOW BEGIN PART ONE:
Part One. Name as many things as you can before the teacher says STOP. Begin with your own name, then add other names. Now stop. Begin with other names. Then stop. Begin. BEGIN.

1 . . . . 2 . . . .
3 . . . . 4 . . . .
5 . . . . 6 . . . .

Part Two: Fill in the blanks, then explain:
7 My name is . . . .
8 The name of . . . . is . . . .
9 This is the name of . . . .
10 This is my name: . . . .
11 . . . .
12 Explain the names given above, and explain: . . . .
. . . .
. . . .

Marilyn, the girl with the birthmark, had so far forgotten herself as to take away the hankie with which she had been dabbing at it. Her palms-up hands lay on her knees, and the ball of pink linen lay on the carpet.

'. . . this frail heat. Daddy was a Justice of the Peace; I

don't suppose you know what that . . . I was eight, Eric was six, and Billy, the baby. Daddy was an engineer. We had a log cabin by the lake, with a log of visitors and everything. Daddy accidentally broke Eric's nylon fishing rod, and he said he would give him a pair of nylons to replace it. A fish swallowed Daddy's nylon log log slide rule, and . . .'

The apparent Negro behind the desk smiled sympathetically. His withered left hand lay before him on the desk like a horrible trophy, while with his good one he toyed with a syringe and a burnt spoon. 'Go on?'

'Well, I, Marilyn Hartsock, had to take care of the baby. I liked that, I liked to squeeze him till he kept giggling and I couldn't stop. They had to take us to the hospital to remove Billy from me. Sometimes I think that's how I got my withered hand, I mean my – oh!'

She snatched up the handkerchief and began dabbing at the hideous mark once more.

'No use, it's indelible,' sighed the Negro, a Mr Travers. 'I've tried everything myself. Even . . .' The apparently tortured eyes in his drawn face sought, and connected with, the syringe.

Dr Reynolds of Lion Pharmaceutical Laboratories addressed the stockholders, describing new drugs his team is working on: *Dilasurg* is a new hormone which promises to fix human growth at any pre-adolescent age. *Tiresan II*, a sex-change drug, requires hardly more testing before it is marketed. *Estiviotrol* causes a person to go into a state of suspended animation within minutes. Researchers are now working with police riot-control units in developing an effective aerosol delivery system.

Dr Gibbel of Lion Oil Electronics United addressed the stockholders, describing a new 'surprise' computer. After complex pre-programming by a team who does not know the computer's ultimate use, it is leased to someone who does not know the pre-programming routines.

'Ultimately,' he said, 'and without warning, the computer may do something either very stupid or very shrewd.'

Dr Lionel Logan, head of the Lion Oil Automotive Research Foundation, addressed the stockholders, describing a number of new advances. Talked about during his two-hour talk were hover-shoes, 'chameleon' body paints, and the use of hallucinogens to give a car 'that new, yet strangely familiar feel'.

Something is troubling Marilyn, thought Eric. *She keeps that pink hankie in front of her nose all the time.*

But no matter I'll just sit here on this train very quietly, I'll just sit here and look at that young man. No, he's looking back maybe thinks I'm queer and hates queers or maybe is queer I'll look

I'll sit here and look at that young woman No she thinks I'm trying to pick her up my god the man next to her is her husband or something now he's looking at me they're both looking at me I'd better

Sit here and look at that young woman very good looking who has taken the place of the queer or queer hater Christ she gave me a funny contemptuous look and opened a book she knows too well what nasty thoughts were starting

I wish I had a book I'll just sit here and look at that man with the briefcase god he's a cop he's looking back like a cop would quick look anywhere No not too fast better casually glance over

To this old woman what harm could she do me but I just know she's the type that imagines every young man who looks at her is some kind of rapist look away quick not too quick to the respectable well-dressed young Negro obviously a Black Power person hates all whiteys thinks I stare at him because he's black I'll just glance over at that innocent child is that a piercing glance

I'm getting back from the mother what does she think I'm a pervert of some kind oh well how about the nice old immigrant workman across from me surely I can look at him his fly's open others are looking at me looking studying my reaction none look over at that man reading a newspaper interesting half of a headline he sees I'm reading rattles his paper and folds it with the headline inside I may never know who is To Drive 'Bad-Luck' Lotus is that the knee of the man next to me touching mine yes Christ the car is full of queers now what I can't move away without giving up some of my lebensraum *but if I push him back he'll think it's a signal follow me home is that pair of teenaged girls giggling about me just two more stops hold on I'll just look at that fat lady No she sees I see how fat she is do I look fat to her too she looks firmly at the advertisement over my head I look firmly at the advertisement over her head stalemate.*

Dr Stoneweg spoke to the assembled stockholders of Lion Oil and Drum Inc. on his work at the Hannibal (Missouri) Institute for Advanced Studies, in particular the 'solar bomb' project. 'I pray to God we'll never need this big baby,' he said, referring to the weapon, which could cause the sun to become a supernova. 'But if we do need it, we're ready.'

Drs Freag, Born, Ortiz, Reynolds, Gibbel, Logan and Stoneweg then asked if the stockholders had any questions.

Mr Fenster Moold asked what was the point of all this talk, talk, talk? Wasn't it time for *action*? Mr H. Greubhel asked if any of these airy inventions meant anything in hard dollars and cents. Mrs Rose Garland said that she, a Gold Star mother, was not going to sit here and let anyone run down America that way. Mr Joyce Britt asked if there was anyone in the hall who doubted that Jesus Christ was a regular fellow. If so, would that person care to step outside for a thrashing?

★

(Radio-TV Advertisement)
A Modern Miracle
A Modern Miracle of action.
Double action. Quick-acting deep-down action,
Where it counts.
Yes, deep-down action,
Truly,
A Modern Miracle.

(Radio-TV Advertisement)
Wherever you see this sign
It means a place you can *trust*,
People you can rely upon . . .
Friendly people
Wherever you see this sign,
It means good *things* in store for *you*.

'EMPLOYEE OF THE YEAR' DIES — PACEMAKER FAULTY

Grave to be marked with Suggestion Box

DISASSEMBLY OF THE G18-OKO-11 HUMAN BEING

Fig 1	G18-OKO-11 HUMAN BEING
1	...Nameplate
2	...Numberplate
3	...Record Assembly, Governmental (See Fig 2)
4	...Record Assembly, Non-governmental
4A	......Record Subassembly, Non-governmental, Affiliation, Religious (See Fig 3)
4B	......Record Subassembly, Non-governmental, Affiliation, Social (See Fig 4)
4C	......Record Subassembly, Non-governmental, Business (See Fig 5)
5	...Possessions Assembly
5A	......Possessions Subassembly, Real

5A1 ....Financial Assembly

5A1A ....Money

5A1B ....Credit

5A2 ....Power Assembly (See Fig 6)

5B ......Possessions Subassembly, Imaginary

5B1 ....Circle Assembly, Family

5B1A ....Relative, Dependent

5B1B ....Relative, Non-dependent

5B2 ....Circle Assembly, Friends (See Fig 7)

6 ...Human, Naked, Unidentified, Alone

6A ......Head Assembly

6A1 ....Face Subassembly

6A1A ....Mouth Assembly

6A1A1 ....Lip, Upper

6A1A2 ....Lip, Lower

6A1A3 ....Tooth

6A1A4 ....Tongue

6A1B ....Hair, Face

6A1C ....Skin, Face

6A1D ....Eye

6A1E ....Nose

6A1F ....Flesh, Face

6A2 ....Ear

6A3 ....Hair, Head

6A4 ....Skin, Head

6A5 ....Skull Assembly

6A5A ....Jaw, Lower

6A5B ....Skull

6A6 ....Brain

6B ......Arm Assembly, Right (See Fig 8)

6C ......Arm Assembly, Left (See Fig 9)

6D ......Leg Assembly, Left (See Fig 10)

6E ......Leg Assembly, Right (See Fig 11)

6F ......Body Assembly, Basic (See Fig 12) ... ...

7 ...Soul Assembly, Human, Putative (See Fig 13)

NOTE 1: For Blood Piping Diagram, See Fig 14
NOTE 2: For Nervous System Schematic, See Fig 15

Marilyn listed all possible men who loved her:

Ray
Eric
her father
her brother, Bill
Jesus?

What if we fail to describe the president, Hernando Horario Murd?

Then we have no guarantee of his physical identifiable reality. Miss Bunne, his secretary, might not know what to do with important letters marked 'For the Immediate Attention of H. H. Murd'.

Certainly. First she could take them to the door marked with the above name. Then through it, to the desk placarded with the above name. Then she could check the name on the letterhead stationery in the desk drawer. Then she could check the name on the memo stationery in the other desk drawer. Then she could check the initials on the golf balls, if any, if initialled, in the other drawer.

Then she could check the monogram on the shirt pocket of any person seated at the desk, the monogram on the gold pen clipped to the shirt pocket, and the name on the ALL AREAS CLEARANCE company ID badge pinned just above the shirt pocket. Then she could check the full-colour photo on the badge against the face of the sitter, the wearer.

And she could read the name and traceable numbers on papers from the sitter-and-wearer's billfold, including driver's licence, credit cards, Health Salon Membership, parking ticket(s), love letter(s), business cards, business letters, an 'I Am a Diabetic, in Case of Collapse, Notify a Physician' card, an 'I Am a Catholic, in Case of Accident,

Notify a Priest' card, or an 'I Am Deaf' card, bearing on the obverse a request for money, on the reverse an Alphabet of the Hand.

Then, using the Alphabet of the Hand, she could ask the person at the desk for a signature, fingerprints, voiceprints, footprints, a retina photograph, and an earprint, hair and skin samples, an ounce of blood, a complete personal history. She could question the person on the person's personal history, using a polygraph and/or truth serums.

But all these things can be faked.

True, as can ordinary recognition signs. Gentlemen, we are at an impasse. I suggest we vote to describe him, and put the description on record, reserving our question of its validity until the committee has finished fact-finding about the question of 'validity' itself. Agreed?

Begin, then, with his shoelaces, double-tied, black. The ferrules resemble tightly-rolled strips of microfilm.

These are laced through sixteen holes of his two black, perforated, wing-tip oxfords. The perforations resemble those of edge-notched cards used in one popular index systems. The mirror finish reflects dark distortions of the scene around them, a scene chiefly of other shoes and the lower parts of furniture.

The heels of these oxfords are suspiciously large and thick. They might almost be hollow heels of the type favoured by smugglers and spies for concealment of heroin or deathkit. A deathkit is simply a tiny hollow needle and a soft plastic ampoule of strychnine. Being a diabetic, though neither a Catholic nor deaf, Mr Murd would not be afraid of needles.

The suit is enormous, the colour and roughly the shape of some prototype atom bomb. There is no tie. Every day the suit walks in at the same time. Miss Bunne takes its arm to help it sit down heavily, easing the seat of the huge trousers into the day's pattern of wrinkles.

Now I think we can turn it over to Stoat from here.

Agent Bob was thirty years old, though he was not writing a poem about it. Instead, he knocked out his usual daily thousand words of Memoirs of a CIA man, which he had tentatively entitled *I Killed for You*:

> I gave her a rabbit punch to knock the poison capsule out of her mouth. Then I kicked her until she wasn't pretty anymore. I kept thinking of what that .375 Magnum slug had done to Larry's face . . .

The memoirs included plenty of travel to Rome, Paris, Monaco, and various pleasure centres, where Bob won large sums of money at roulette, baccarat, etc, just after he had explained the rules in detail. He also knew plenty about wines, sports cars, weapons and anything else difficult to get through Customs, which he had no difficulty doing. He managed one exciting fuck per chapter, one good kill per chapter, or the equivalent. People who phoned him rarely finished their call alive, and when he approached his own Hilton hotel room, Bob usually got an eerie feeling . . .

In short, the whole thing managed to disguise pretty well Bob's job as a code clerk. Now and then he tailed a suspect – always the same one – and his only other duty was clipping periodicals for the hunchboard.

The hunchboard was not an in*form*ation source; that was the domain of the CIA computer which daily digested 200 world magazines and newspapers. The hunchboard was a source of in*spir*ation. Mr Stoat, Bob's chief, would select a few items almost at random, have Bob clip them out, and tack them up with his constantly-changing collage of headlines, pictures, features and ads. From these, Mr Stoat was somehow able to develop hypotheses about world affairs.

Bob's thirtieth birthday found him clipping out a bra ad, and lost in a daydream about gunning down Stoat where he stood. For almost no reason, Bob hated this sun-bronzed little man who resembled a handsome, if foreshortened, executive. He hated everything about him: the hunchboard, the way he hummed, the fact that he wore his shaggy wool overcoat in the office, the fact that he carried, not a real gun, but a toy: a wooden block printed with a picture of a gun.

Piff! Blat! Puffs of dust rose from the shaggy wool. The stocky man spun and flopped like a rag doll, gushing blood through its tanned nostrils.

Bob snipped viciously across the page. Unaware of his death, Mr Stoat stood before the hunchboard, gaining insights. He gained insights into subversive plots, subversive counterplots, his own plan for world domination. He looked worriedly at the ceiling, the toy gun he was using as a pointer, Bob, the board, Bob.

'Look out, Bob, you're spoiling her tits.'

'I'm sorry, sir.'

Buddha-buddha. Bob gripped the two scissor handles, one in each hand, and pulled the trigger. Tracer after tracer ploughed into the placid back. Stoat made irritated little hums.

'Hmm. Hmm.' He studied clippings from *Grit, Rod & Custom, The Sacred Heart Messenger*. 'Ummm.' He compared war news with suppository ads. 'Choo-de-choom.' He marked the conjunction of General Motors' sales graph with pictures of dead movie stars, then with a thalidomide item. 'Hmp?' *Russia's Secret Space Deaths* went between *Is Your Marriage Really Sublime?* and *The Kind of Girl Tab Hunter Wants.*

'Hmp. Hmp. Hmp.'

Bob drowned the little noises in a wave of .50 calibre fire. Tun. Tununun. Tunununununun.

'Ho!' Stoat tore scraps of *McCalls, The IBM Song Book* and *Detective Comics* from the board and threw them on the floor. Then he knelt and stirred them with the toy weapon. 'Yup!' His face was grim. 'Looks bad, Bob.'

'A crisis, sir?'

'In transportation or communications. Could be only a bomb in a train station, such as Batman here finds, but Mars is in conjunction with Saturn, is it? – that means something really *big*. Subliminal panic messages inserted in a prime-time TV show, causing a run on rifles that could cripple our rifle industry maybe, I don't know. An army strike? Who can say? A pop singer discovers a new sound that sets off a slow-destruct mechanism buried one million years ago in the cerebral cortex. Your guess is as good as mine. The palm of the president, as revealed in the blown-up photo of a speech, reveals tendencies towards aggression, self-deprecating remarks, constipation, should seek new friends this week, not keep anal-retentive hold on Vietnam, cloacal gold standard. It's anybody's ball game.

'Los Angeles and San Francisco riding the San Andreas fault, due to earthquake – could be a tie-in with the Original Fault. Can't rightly say. Film industry, half TV industry wiped out next Columbus Day, cross-reference to Columbia Broadcasting? To Christopher movement? Their motto: "YOU can change the world." California is altogether a bad complex; maybe it *should* be removed without narcotics, astringents, or surgery. Could demonstrations at Berkeley ("I am a human being. Please do not fold, staple, spindle or mutilate") be link-up with Bishop Berkeley ("all those bodies which compose the mighty frame of the world, have not any subsistence without a mind . . . their being to to *be perceived or known*")? You tell me.'

Pocketing his wooden gun, Stoat said slyly, 'I want you to follow someone in connection with this crisis. My number one suspect.'

Not again, thought Bob, but he kept his expression interested. The 'number one suspect' was always the same: Stoat's wife Anne.

'I want you to go to this address,' he said coyly. 'Follow this red-haired woman.' He gave him a picture from his billfold. 'And *stay with her.*'

'Yes sir.'

Stoat unwrapped a small but distinguished smile and tried it on. 'Good luck, son, and be careful.'

Bob lobbed a grenade into the office as he left, and shut the door quickly behind him.

SUMMIT CONFERENCE ON 'GOVT SWAP'
US may become USSR

ANIMATED FILM STAR TO RUN FOR CONGRESS

CARDINAL BRAKESPEARE APPROVES PILL

LION OIL PLANS ESSO MERGER

Gen Max Heiliger (Ret) was a tall, emaciated African with good-luck scars on both cheeks. As head of Operations at Drum Inc., he developed company strategy along unusual lines, using sophisticated mathematics and Dr Gibbel's 'surprise' computer. He had a summit meeting with Mr Murd almost daily, but whenever reporters from the house organ, *The Drum Call*, asked him what was going on, he would reply with something vague about Marshall McLuhan and the global village, or quote Tarzan on the necessity for intercommunication between man and other species.

Why are they all trying to get me, Max wondered. The FBI thinks I'm a Black Panther. The CIA thinks I'm a Panafrican revolutionist. The KKK thinks I'm a Negro. The American Nazi Party thinks I'm a Jew. The Zionists think I'm an ex-Nazi. Mr Murd thinks I spy for Bell, Bell wonders if I'm not an East German spy. The DAR thinks I'm a cannibal, someone keeps writing anonymous letters to *The Drum Call* saying I'm an extra-terrestrial of superior intellect, and my barber thinks I'm a vivisectionist. Snip, snip, snip. 'What do you do all day, over there in that windowless blockhouse? Cut up small animals, ha ha?' The scissors poised to shear off an ear.

In any other story I'd be the hero. I don't know what's gone wrong. It's the good-luck scars, that's it. Dad's idea. As always, the younger, audio-tactile generation is left in a mess by the older, visual generation. So now everyone thinks maybe I used to wear a bone through the nose. It's a bone through the nose to them, that's all. They think I dine on missionaries cooked-up in a big iron pot. What a disgusting idea, a cooked missionary with hairy legs. I'm just a cartoon figure, bone through the nose. Whenever I see one of those cartoons, I'll point it out to them and ask them one simple question: '*Who supplied the big iron pots?*'

(From *The Drum Call*)
Well, team, we're sorry to report the accident rate is up once again. The department with the highest a.r. is Cable Accounts, who now have lost the safety pennant to the typing pool by a score of 3—0. Nice going, girls, and keep it up! And of course we hope the 'cabies' will try extra hard next month, and maybe win back their title!

The most serious accident in Cable Accounts was Ray Galt's, and a darned shame it was. Ray, in case you don't know him, is the young one-armed janitor with the big smile. Everyone seems to miss his cheery 'Hello!' each morning, and we sincerely hope he'll be back with the gang soon!

The mishap was just one of those things, and it couldn't have happened at a worse time. Because there have been wedding bells tinkling around the Cable Accounts office, mainly in connection with Ray and Dot Hanson, the file clerk with the famous dimples. They say that whenever Ray had a window in the department to wash, Dot would soap a little note to him on the glass – certainly original in their love-letters, aren't they?

Maybe Ray was reading one of these, or just thinking about that little vine-covered cottage for two, but anyway yesterday while mopping the hall, Ray somehow caught his good arm in the elevator doors. Talk about tough luck! The hospital says he may lose his good arm, but we know he'll never lose his good humour.

Our newest employee in Cable Accounts, Eric Bland, will be taking care of the fruit n' flower fund. And so, on behalf of the staff and management, may we wish Ray a speedy recovery, and hope he'll be back on his feet in no time.

(Radio-TV Advertisement)
Everyone likes to have Fun,
But no one likes to miss out on the Fun;
When everyone is having a good time,
Don't *you* be the one left out.
You'll *have* more Fun if you *get* more Fun,
And you'll *get* more Fun – today!

(Magazine Advertisement)
(Headline)
We're really sorry, but we're only human.
(Copy)
You're human, too, of course. Like us. Everyone is. And we humans have a lot in common, don't we? Sure, some of us like to bowl, while others like to take it easy with a cold beer. But we're still a lot alike, we humans.
Or are we? Maybe we're a lot different, too. We don't pretend to know the answers to that one. We haven't got all the answers. Yet.

Mr Kravon read *The Drum Call*. 'I'd like to kill that son of a bitch,' he said. 'Here I thought we had the pennant sewed up.

I thought we'd grab the yearly safety plaque, too. Well, he's washed up now. Out of the company he goes. Or stick him out in a factory somewhere, where they don't give a god damn about accidents anyhow.'

To put the upsetting incident out of his mind, he leafed slowly and with pleasure through a new brochure of watertight caskets and vaults.

RULES FOR WRITING LOVE-LETTERS

1. Be neat.
2. Get the name right – that's important!
3. If you must criticize, praise first.
4. Make words work for you:
   Use analogies.
   Use short words.
5. Remember the 'We/you/I' formula.
6. Put in plenty of 'curiosity value'.
7. Keep it short.

Holding hands, Eric and Dot watched the replacement janitor scrub the hall window, cleansing away Dot's last message to Ray:

> *Dear Ray Darlin . . . asy to . . . especially since you've been so . . . eet, but . . . met someone els . . . feel I re . . . e for, and so you see how it . . . dn't possibly . . . u while my heart belo . . . nother. Eri . . . lly wonderful, and I'm so hap . . . st working near . . . esk, and the only flaw in my ha . . . knowing th . . . ke you feel bad. But dar . . . n't be. I'm su . . . ind someone else. In fact, Eric . . . gested and old . . . end of his, Marilyn Hartso . . . ks in the typing poo . . . Anyhow, we . . . ix you up . . . ll always think of you as a . . .*
>
> It was signed '.'

★

Why are they all trying to get me, Max wondered. Jane and Jean and Jane and Janet, my four girl-friends, June my wife, Jeanne and Joan my lovely wanton mistresses, all trying to get me. Not to mention Mr Murd, who fears my sable splendour, and my secretary, Jeanette. I wonder what that new girl at the office thinks of me?

(Newspaper Advertisement)
STOP DEATH COLD!
Amazing new scientific discovery! Hair health can add years to your heart, inches to your prestige. Lucky holiday stamps guaranteed SAFE! Armchair learning of psychic power increases natural size *visibly*. Why be old? Ancient wisdom gives you a real He-Man voice – flattering new lines of confidence. Absolutely no narcotics or surgery for FREE booklet mailed to your door from all over the world! Raise cute 'Fairy Penguins' (not a religious organization) in just 15 minutes a day, and BANISH acne through organic-approved, FAST police-training methods.

(Classified Newspaper Advertisement)
CONC. CMP. – 1 owner. Nw, elec fnce, late mod full secur meas, grd blk + 4 like-nw m/g twrs. Lites, alrms, 2 bldgs ea approx 200 × 150′, mesh windws, escp-proof. Latrines, mess. Exprmentl med lab, the works. 50 acres brl, grnd, cap'y. 10,000+. Blt to US Govt specs. Ideal schl cmp, retire cntr. Ist offer takes.

It seemed to make no difference when Travers stopped sending people into the company and decided to start 'interviewing them outwards'. He was a component, that's all, with a single YES/NO decision to make in each case.

'And tell me, Ray, why is it you want to leave Drum?'

'Well sir, I've always wanted to work somewhere else, somewhere with a solid base salary, some big-bracket benefits, security and plenty of room for advancement. And that's about the size of it.'

'That's it in a nutshell, eh? Now I want you to think about those benefits a moment, *vis-à-vis* your – ah – disability.' Travers's putty-coloured fingers moved lightly over the braille copy of Ray's application. He leaned forward to give Ray a good look at his hump, straining against the garish fabric of his suit. The boy gulped.

'Well sir, you see – I mean . . .'

'I don't *see*, as you jokingly put it. And you're not here to play jokes on a blind man, you cruel, intolerant young bastard! You – excuse me.'

An alarm was ringing in a drawer. Travers shut it off, then fished out a syringe and a small bottle. 'If you'll excuse me, it's time for my insulin.' He gave himself an injection of water, all the time studying Ray through the dark glasses, noting with approval that he was hanging his head and blushing.

'Well, excuse me for flying off the handle like that. We each have our own problems. But tell me this: Where in hell do you expect to get group insurance, after you've had two *major* accidents?

'I'm no plaster saint to lecture you about anything, Ray. In fact, besides being blind, hunchbacked, and a diabetic, I have this drinking problem . . . But even so, I at least am entitled to group insurance – which means I'm entitled to leave Drum Inc. for a greener pasture.'

The head on the armless trunk still hung down, and tears fell from it to the carpet. Travers wondered if the carpet would be stained.

'Tell you what. I'll hang on to your application for a few months, see what happens. You go back to work, I think this time at the factory. I can't be fairer than that, OK?

'And now we'd like to have you take a few more tests.' Travers marked him down for the Müller-Fokker Insecurity

Rating. 'OK? Well, it's been real swell talking to you, Ray. Stop in again, like I say, in a year or so.'

Ray stood up and gulped back a large egg of air. Since he could not shake hands with the interviewer, he bent and kissed his ring.

IDEAL SEX INVENTORY 7373/0380/B

Revised Detainer Report B

Place: Format:

Subject: Index:

Eventuality: Zip Code:

Additional Specification: ....

....

....

Compare or match:

1. Taking walks	A. Ornateness
2. The other side	B. This side
3. Rock wool	C. Tubed debut
4. Gradually lighter	D. Forensic award
5. Soft drawings (sex)	E. 'Klondike'
6. Taken one at a time	F. Coupon bouquet
7. A smash hit	G. Brainbag
8. Felt hat	H. Felt hate
9. Lion oil	I. Platonic (ideal) shit
10. Prawn warp	J. Flexing the arm near

(a) Protection all day	(1) Dagger
(b) Semite Times	(2) Deliver, relived
(c) 'press conference'	(3) Open end
(d) Swings tension	(4) Several related hobbies
(e) Corners	(5) So many dynamos
(f) Corresponding toe	(6) Tressed dessert
(g) Animal lamina	(7) Sample pain
(h) *Gift* (poisoned) fig	(8) Salad alas!
(i) The Cayman who smiles	(9) Same finger

(j) Flexing the arm (10) Terrible island tins

I. Gala
II. Venues
III. Polychrome 'Rotor' Mary
IV. Dagger
V. Danger
VI. Opinion, 1937
VII. Ohio Hall of Fame
VIII. Semiramis
IX. Talking wakes
X. Sex

Travers changed from the hump, black glasses and loud suit to a ski sweater and a pair of army pants. He fitted on the half-shells of his cast and taped them in place. He had already signed the cast with the names of all company employees who had disppeared – Dot Hanson and all the rest. Now, as he put on the false smile and deep sunburn, as he sutured dimples into his cheeks and chin, he thought back on the Ray Galt interview. What a mess! The kid was committing suicide in pieces, but how could you explain that to him?

One nice bit, though, the ring-kissing. He hadn't *felt* it, really – his whole surface seemed to be getting anaesthetized – but he'd appreciated the idea. Be even more fun with one of those girls from the unending cafeteria line across the way. Why not carry it on? Invest in a mitre or what the heck, a triple tiara: 'My child, my child, you seem troubled. Come, put it in the lap of God . . .'

Who was he kidding? Travers wasn't a company pope, he wasn't anything. He watched them come in or go out, day after shuffling day, the whole company going to pieces, maybe the whole world. He could pose as anything, a sacred bear or eagle, an armed ghost – it made no difference. They came in to be processed, he processed them. They were his data.

He was not even a complicated computer, just a simple component. YES or NO was his choice, the content of the simplest message, ON/OFF. Like Holy Smoke.

Which brought him back to the bishop again, the crozier dividing the SHEEP and the GOATS, the SAVED and the DAMNED the YES and the NO.

Damnit, he didn't *want* to be a transistor! A YES/NO man! He wanted to be a message of maximum content, a line of poetry, say, very obscure poetry. At the rim of obscurity, where infinite content becomes zero content, where everything is said and everything is noise. He pounded his fist silently on the desk. Why? Why couldn't everything be different, yet somehow the same?

Nebransas! Miles and miles of flat corn country where a man can feel the big neon sky pressing milk down into the red plush earth. Nebransas! Mighty steel pylons picket the horizon, carrying power, power to light the linoleum, power to iron the honest Sunday shirt, power to scrape the plain Sunday dishes, power to pump the mail through the mail-slot of the homely country kitchen door, power to mill the flour to bake the bread to make the sandwiches to feed the faceless faces of countless thousands who assemble the air-conditioned car which now speeds along a highway past giant grain terminals resting like isolated white temples upon the brown sward of Nebransas!

While Miss Bunne took notes, Max spoke earnestly to the rumpled grey flannel suit of Mr Murd. 'I've marked on this map the location of coaxial cables, microwave antennae, power towers, local newspapers, and billboards. Anything else?'

The pattern of wrinkles shifted slightly.

'Ah yes,' said Max, 'those mail-order catalogues. It won't

be hard to intercept the ones actually *in the mail*, but the others, those in privies, etc, may be tricky to alter.'

'What about social security numbers?' Miss Bunne asked, tasting the ink in her fibre pen. 'And the drive-in movies?'

'I got the numbers in our bank job. We'll take care of the drive-ins on the way back to the secret heliport, I believe. Lefty, turn on the radio.'

Kravon turned the traditional knob, and the stereo speakers spoke to them:

'. . . Vatican announced today the successful test-firing of a new intermediate-range ballistic missile, the *Ave Maria*. Together with their longer-range *Miserecordia Dei*, this . . .'

'Tch, tch,' said Miss Bunne. 'All this violence in the world. Where will it all end?' She patted the barrel of the automatic rifle clipped to the door.

'Turning from the international scene, the Fremont State Bank was held up today by three men and a woman, wearing the masks of dead movie stars. Ignoring more than half a million dollars in payroll money, the bandits escaped with only worthless carbon copies of bank records, including a list of social security . . .'

'Now stop it, Ray. This injection moulder I'm running is a dangerous piece of equipment, and I'm not going to let you mess around and tease me like this. Stop it, I said. You should be back in the inspection area, not wandering around like this.

'Ray! That's just plain dirty! Yes, I know you can't exactly put your *arm* around me. *I* know it's just an innocent hug, but what will the other girls think?

'Now stop! I've already told you, I can *not* go out with you tonight – I already have a date. And never mind *who* with, it's none of your business. If you must know, it's with the new supervisor. Eric Bland.

'What did you say? The machine's making so much noise I can't – Ray! Keep your foot away from that molten plastic!

Look out for the ram – *RAY!*'

Max was making a list of Utopias, from which he hoped Mr Murd might be able to make a selection, checking two alternate preferences:

Utopia in the hands of an angry God
Utopia in boots
Utopia as the dictatorship of the proletariat
Utopia through whole-grain cereal health
Utopia: the seven-fold way
Utopia as Law and Order
the computer Utopia
the millenial Utopia
the genocidal Utopia
the noble savage Utopia
Utopia as a warm puppy
sharing the wealth
living by fear
living in a house by the side of the road (and being a friend to man)
the orgone Utopia
the Superman Utopia
Utopia through meditation, vibration, reincarnation and revelation
the global village
the radiant city
the city of God
the Lost City
the genetic Utopia
Nirvana
Heaven
the Earthly paradise
the free enterprise Utopia
the conclave of immortals

'less is more'
'I can and I will'
the ultimate deterrent
the ultimate detergent
Utopia served up (by intelligent, sensitive extraterrestrials) on flying saucers
Utopia of a garden community of not more than 400 white industrialists, all good-looking, of surpassing wisdom, and in direct contact with the Deity through their mayor, George Washington.

'Glad to have you with the art department, Ray. I'll explain your duties: You take the letters from this letter tray – we've cut away a piece here so you can get your chin in there – and you just take them around to the various people in the department. And I hope you have a soft mouth – we don't want any teeth-marks if we can help it. Just try imagining you're a bird dog and these letters are very delicate birds, OK?'

'Gee, thanks, Mr Wang, I appreciate . . .'

'No "misters" here, Ray. I'm just plain Phil, and you're just plain Ray. That leg thing give you any trouble? No? Good enough.

'Your other duties will be lighter, just running the postage meter and the big electric paper guillotine over here. We have to crop photos now and then, nothing to worry about. If it gives you any problems, I'll have Anne take care of it. She can also give you a hand – excuse me, Ray – with the postage, if you need help. Annie's a real looker, isn't she? That's her over by the door.'

'She sure is a knockout, Phil.'

'Say, Ray, I hear you're quite a ladies' man, right?'

'What? I mean, what, Phil?'

'I said, I hear you've been cutting quite a swathe with the ladies in other departments. Heh heh, well, just don't keep the girls from their work, OK?'

'I won't, Phil.'

'OK, Ray? OK, boy?'

Max spent a lot of time working it all out:

Ignoring other factors, a force's 'fighting strength' is proportional to the square of its size (Lanchester's N-square Law). Then a force of n men could defeat a larger force of $n\sqrt{2}$ men, if the larger force can be divided into two parts:

$$n^2 = \left(\frac{n\sqrt{2}}{2}\right)^2 + \left(\frac{n\sqrt{2}}{2}\right)^2$$

That seemed clear enough. He tucked it away with his other notes on military operations research:

'Root Tooth Structure Tensile Strength as a Factor in Combat Efficiency'

'The "Shared Spearhead" Paradox Resolved'

'The Unified Front System' (A unique method of combining the war on poverty, any current Southeast Asian conflict, the gold war, the restraint of rioting, the war on cancer, etc, etc, so that guided by game theory and critical path analysis, the regime might make multidimensional ('L-shaped') moves, e.g., an attack on Southeast Asian poverty, on cancer-susceptible rioters, on auric cancer, on Southeast Asian riots involving gold.)

'*Maxideath* as an Informative Retrieval Problem'

'A New Interpretation of *Maxideath*'

'The Mutual Infinite Boundary Dilemma'

One of his favourites was 'Heiliger's "Bombed Baby" Problem', for which he had never found a satisfactory solution: Given a single baby in a house at some unknown location in a city, how is it possible to ensure that a bombing raid (not using nuclear devices) will certainly kill that baby? No standard method (saturation bombing, raising a fire storm with incendiary bombs, pin-point bombing of every structure) was good enough; it was impossible to *guarantee a kill*.

But these monographs, while applicable to the coming conflict, were Max's toys. His heart, soul, mind and strength were devoted to his monumental treatise, 'On War as Information'. He was fascinated with the analogies between military strategy and information theory; the idea of killing as the simplest, clearest message; the consideration of the enemy as a 'black box', or unknown arrangement of components; tactics as the 'alphabet' or strategic 'language'; the ergodic analysis of military operations considered over a period of time.

His talks with 'David', the chemical vision in Dr Logan's lab, had led Max to consider speech and other sensory communications as analogues of war. His work went on apace, but 'David' had made him dread tackling the final paradox:

There seems to be no difference at all between the message of maximum content (or maximum ambiguity) and the message of zero content (noise).

Travers was at it again, watching the girls in the cafeteria line. With their bright jello-coloured suits and honey hair they looked more transparent than translucent, he decided, and thought for minutes about the layers of glass that closed him off from them, the layers of dust, the layers of air and light. Who were all these girls? he wondered. What might they mean?

He looked at the crystal of his watch. In five minutes he would have the interview of interviews, with a Mr Kravon. What image to force upon him, that was the question. Kravon's folder indicated a cautious type, inhumanly perfect, not excitable. Thirty-five years' service. Try impressing him with – what? Sturdy youth? Nobler age? The sincerity angle?

Simple humility? No, none of this could penetrate Kravon's wall of suspicion. And it was impossible to dress as a dog or cat, or an honest stone . . .

That weekend, Anne and Eric went to their special place. After parking the car in a shady grove of frismia, he led her along their own hidden path, down to a slanting platform of rock, half-awash in the mountain stream. Here they were completely hidden from the world by merriwether, frondy bagwort, smilax and the dark shiny leaves of rufus. At the very edge of the stream grew grieving nace, lithia, bright bloodmedal. Alone with him in this paradise, Anne felt no compulsion to speak; Eric seemed to feel the natural sanctity of the place no less than she.

He performed his usual ritual first, alone, then she followed suit. Yet not alone, for it was the cool little stream which, without touching them, brought them together. Anne wondered for a moment whether her husband, Stoat, had someone watching her now – but then her shame, too, was washed away by the purifying trickle.

Afterwards, Eric offered her a mentholated cigarette, and took one himself. They consumed this fragrant communion in silence, watching the sky go from gold to red. Anne imagined she were inside a great, translucent eyeball, looking out through the pupil of the sun to see . . .

'The drive-in's open at sundown. We'd better get going.'

'What is it? I think I've seen it – *Witch of Agnesi*?' She bent to pick a fragrant sprig of parson's nose.

'No. *Return of the Zomboids* and I think *The Gurk*.'

'Yes, I remember *Attack of the Zomboids*. They were the ones made of clouds or pus or something, weren't they? And all covered with electric hair?'

'No,' said Eric. 'I think you're thinking of the Fings. The Zomboids were transparent. They were like man-shaped jellyfish.'

★

The President of the United States rose to welcome Kravon, beckoning him to sit down at the desk with the Great Seal.

'Mr President!'

'Surprised to see me, Kravon? Well, I know it's not my usual office, but I heard they were interviewing you for retirement, and I thought I'd look in. Now, we'll talk in a moment about that pension plan, gold watch and so on, but right now let's examine your safety record.

'You see, the country – and the company – just can't see turning loose a man who lets his department get a mess of accidents on the books. Now I see here . . .'

As the president lunged forward to check the record, one of the elastics holding on his vinyl face snapped. The face fell on his desk, spun around clumsily on the famous nose, and came to rest. Lucky, Travers thought, he'd had the foresight to wear another under it.

Kravon leaped up. 'You're not the president!' he screamed. 'Imposter! Fake! You're fake like everything else!'

The other spoke calmly, moving closer to the lamp. 'A little test of your faith, my child. Don't you recognize me?' He turned the desk lamp upwards, to shine on the shadowy eyes, the sucked-in cheeks, the tight, senescent smile like a *rictus mortui*.

'No! It can't be!' Kravon was confused. He mustn't be allowed to doubt again, to reach for this mask . . .

'His Holiness? No, my son, I bear some resemblance, true, to the infallible personage, but no, I am but a humble priest. The name is Father (he rhymed it carefully with *lather*) Patrick O'Brien.'

Removing the rest of his presidential shell, he stood revealed in his threadbare black cassock. 'Tell me what ails yer soul, me boy. Have ye broken inny of the Lard's commandments on conthraception, now? Throubled by guilty dreams, are ye? Peerify yerself through confession, the sacrament of Pinance. Kneel down.'

Kravon knelt on the comfortable carpet and bowed his head, displaying the tonsure of age.

'Now I hope ye won't mind if I put on a few vestments while ye talk. I'm goin' ta the stockhalders' meetin', ta invoke a blessin' on the union of Drum Inc. with Lion Oil.'

So while the manager of Cable Accounts began to murmur his secrets, Travers kissed, flashed, and girded himself in appropriate and inappropriate quasi-religious garments: alb, stole, cincture, scapular, rosary, cross, crucifix, skullcap, wimple, dalmatic, chasuble, cope, medals religious, sacred heart badge, epaulettes, chevrons, stars, wings, battle ribbons, medals military, badges, buttons, pins, stars, garter, codpiece, doublet, stomacher, belts, bandoliers, spurs, studs, dickey, rosette, holster, scabbard, corsage, cockade, toga, ermine, jackboots, fez, homulka, tiara, coronet, crown, mitre, triple tiara, biretta, stetson, campaign hat, helmet, living bra, overseas cap, green beret, baseball cap, football shoulder pads, g-suit . . .

'Hell, Anne, *I* know you haven't encouraged him, but the poor guy's only human – what's left of him – and you're a damned fine piece.

'The thing is, he's fallen way the hell behind in the mail sorting. And every time you go in to help him catch up, he gets further behind. It's obvious the guy's crazy about you.'

'But Phil, I've tried everything I can to discourage him . . .'

'Listen, tell him you're all dated up with the vice president.'

'Eric? Oh, Eric doesn't mean a thing to me. I mean, we're just – mutual friends, if you know what I mean.'

'Makes no difference. Just go in there and say, "Listen, Ray, lay off. I'm Eric Bland's girl." That'll cool him down. Oh yes, and while you're at it, take in these photos to be guillotined, will you. And tell him to hurry up with it.'

'Then, Father, I put my farm in the soil bank, and I joined a Christmas Club, and I bought Defence Bonds, and I put blood in the blood bank, and willed my cornea to an eye bank, and put my money in a Swiss bank, and the gold from my teeth I left instructions to be deposited in a safety deposit box under the name "Max Heiliger".

'And I invested some sperm in a sperm bank, bought some gilt-edged securities and some blue-chip stock, and I invested more money in National Banks, State Banks, County Banks, and then I bought some insurance.

'I insured my home, life, wife, car, farm, crop, valuables, health, children, dog. Then I gained a plenary indulgence for myself, my wife and children, and our neighbours on both sides. And I built and stocked up our bomb shelter and insured that, and put in a machine gun, grenades, plenty of ammo, and then I installed new locks all over the house, burglar alarms, bullet-proof glass, and I put a second, secret bomb shelter under our basement.

'Then I put up a cyclone fence with barbed wire across the top, and inside that a bomb-proof wall with broken glass on top, and inside that an ornamental wrought-iron fence with spikes on top, and inside that an electric fence. I put in an emergency generator, a nurse in residence, an operating room in the basement, electrostatically-filtered air conditioning, a gas leak alarm, and a well.

'I studied all the consumer magazines, paying particular attention to safety recommendations, and I bought only approved appliances. I rewired the house, had new gas and water pipes fitted. Then I subscribed to a freezer plan, laid in a year's supply of food, and I subscribed to a cryogenic storage plan for when I should die. I engaged the Night and Fog Security Agency to check all the locks and warning devices every night and report to me over television, I bought a pair of Alsatians and a pair of Dobermans and a canary to warn us of coal gas. I had the family immunized against tetanus, typhus, smallpox, etc, etc; I fumigated once a month and bought a cat and a rat terrier.

'I hired a mechanic full-time to check my car over, piece by piece, and I had him install every new safety device I could find. I rotated my tyres weekly and traded them in every 5,000 miles.

'I installed a door-answering system with one-way mirror, microphone, metal detector, radiation detector, and fluoroscope; I sealed the fireplace and reinforced the walls and roof, and had a monthly check for dry rot, mould and termites. Then I began giving tithes; took my wife to the best psychiatrist and my children to the best child-guidance psychotherapist, for check-ups; I moved explosion-resistant screening in front of the TV set, moved all electric receptacles well out of the children's reach, hired a round-the-clock guard to keep them out of the kitchen, locked all poisons in a safe to which only I knew the combination. I fireproofed the house, and . . .'

'And so,' Anne Stoat admitted, 'I don't really know my husband. I can't really blame him for wanting someone to keep an eye on me. He probably thinks of me as "the enemy".'

Bob signalled the waiter and ordered two more pigeon feathers. 'But you've never *seen* him?'

'We were married by proxy. He was on a big case at the time, invasion of Antarctica or something. No, I've never seen him – though I do watch the Thursday night TV programme based on his life, and they say it's cast very authentically.'

'But you, ah, sleep together?'

'Sure, but in separate dreams. I think I'd go crazy, if it weren't for my job at Drum Inc.'

'Drum Inc.! Rings a bell. Wait a minute. Yes, we're

investigating them right now. In connection with the disappearance of a South American republic. And – other things. Anne, do you think you could help us?'

Anne finished her drink without replying. When she looked up, their eye-beams locked, exchanging messages of involvement. 'Let's have the next drink at my place,' she said.

'. . . and I'm still not really *sure*,' Kravon finished. 'I just know I've forgotten something. And don't tell me I've forgotten God, because I haven't.'

The grotesque bundle of clothing before the mirror put on a dog collar and threw a strait-jacket around its shoulder pads. Then it began tucking things in its belts, holsters, scabbards, bandoliers, obis and cincts: a six-gun, a sceptre, a crozier, a switchblade, a fasces, a roll, a sabre, a scout knife, a hanger, a rolling pin, grenades, a fusée, yarrow sticks, a flute, a splinter from the true cross, pencils with your name imprinted in 14-ct gold, a fountain pen, a fountain pen which sprinkles holy water, a fountain pen which sprinkles teargas, a rectal thermometer, a syringe, a slide rule, Old Glory, a monstrance, a whip, a tampon, a coke, an electric toothbrush, an olive branch, carrots, a cigar, an umbrella, Keys to the Kingdom, silver bullets, an Ibis stick . . .

'Father? What do you say?'

The face, invisible inside the hollow layers of space helmet, crash helmet, etc, may have moved; the figure may have spoken; but nothing came out.

'God damn it, say something! *Say something!*'

Kravon leaped at him, tearing at the folds of brocade and khaki and nylon and leather. The overbalanced, swaying mass tipped back, collapsed softly on the carpet, cloth-to-cloth impact.

Snarling, Kravon tore away layer after layer, flinging aside an old school tie, a Nazi armband, a maniple . . .

'Good God!'

The final transparency, thought Travers. *The whole works, the jello girls, Kravon, the universe. They're all completely insensible.*

A little later they found Kravon on his hands and knees, still pawing over the pile of rags. After thumping and kicking him awhile, they estimated Kravon had a good ten years' service left in him. But just to be sure, they would give him, as Dr Freag put it, 'a change of heart'. The research team – Freag, Ortiz, Logan, Gibbel, Born and Stoneweg – was split into two groups. Freag's group wanted to test a new surgery machine, while Born's group wanted to see how many different organs from various donors could be stuffed into one skin and live. Now each team would begin the wearisome search of a donor. The first team to find one would get Kravon.

The company doctor had some objections. Who were they, non-medical men, to judge whether or not Kravon needed a new heart? In his opinion . . .

The two teams silenced him by threatening to do two heart transplant operations.

The pretty nurse did not have Ray fooled. He noticed the way she fussed around making his bed, taking far longer than with the other patients. Let her go on pretending to be all career and no heart, he knew better. Obviously she was enjoying feeding him his meals, he could tell by the loving way she spooned in every bite.

Okay, she never smiled or spoke to him, that was her way, maybe. Didn't it prove all the more that she couldn't trust herself to keep cool? Sure it did. And even the way she handled that bedpan . . .

Not that he really wanted to let himself go with her. There was always the outside chance of a mistake – then he'd find himself in a false position. He didn't really trust her. Maybe she, too, would go off with Eric Bland. She was probably making a date with Eric right now, this minute!

Ray nudged the emergency light switch with his nose. If she didn't come to answer it within, say, five minutes, he'd know something was up. She was off somewhere in the nurse's lounge, screwing Eric Bland . . . letting Ray die, for all she knew . . .

He could see just how it might happen, too. He might accidentally bite the end off the bent glass straw in his glass of water on the side table. Then he might accidentally run his neck against the jagged edge, and cut the jugular vein or the carotid artery or something. Something pulsing.

'Marilyn? Hell . . .'

Bob rolled back and lit a cigarette. The front side of his body was tingling with information about Drum Inc., and he knew without asking that Anne felt the same about the CIA. Trying to make words of what he felt, he watched the script of smoke curl towards the acoustical ceiling. The words were garbled, but they were there:

Drum. Drum would corner information? Drum would compress all information into a single message, which it (someone?) would eat. Drum was taking over the microwave towers, the coax, the telephones, the TV stations, the satellites . . . and one Thursday evening everyone would be told that they (all the others?) were under arrest. Under body arrest, whatever that meant. Drum was having its heart transplanted? To another company, Lion Oil. Spell it backwards.

No, or Drum was buying, stealing, getting at that feeblest of all communication links – between inside man ('My bowels now function normally, Ground Central. All systems go. Repeat . . .') and outside man ('Do you read Breughel? I read Mao. Anyone read the Bible? He has not read Carter Brown's *No Blonde Is an Island.*').

'What are you thinking?' Anne asked.

'Huh?'

'You look like a Xomboid. I'll bet you didn't know it could be like this, is that it?'

'Uh.'

'There's more where that came from. Just put down that cigarette.'

More? There had to be more, and he turned to her again, seeking. His tongue probed her mouth, taking readings from electrical fillings in his mouth her mouth probed his tongue probed his mouth taking electrical fillings from her readings his readings; under his hand a pulse; their nerve ends took hold swelling with data merging . . . merged.

Who was Murd? What was the fictitious *Lion Oil Company*? What about the Misses Bunne? Who was asking all these questions of whom? What happened to Travers? Did 'David' control the reality of the firm? Of the firmament? Who controlled the reality of 'David'? Why was Max Heiliger?

The messages flowed and structured himherthem; he looked into her eye once; again he looked out of her eye. Their double back shivered as nerve splices made, coded molecules unzipped to one another, particles collided and collapsed (emitting final pictures of the return of the Yomboids, final answers looped through final answers that doesn't make sense I know but get to a telephone no time to pick it up and dial just flow in with the final answer a gun inside a never mind the exchange hurry on to the CIA tape constantly running constantly playing The Time Is Exactly the time is running the final answer a gun barrel in a flower in a banana in a gun my back brain your back brain squeezes the trigger) and they watched the delicate metal petals curl back slowly exposing the rifled ballistic message (O ballistic missal O O O cabalistic O:) 'Hello, Marilyn . . . ?'

*

'Disappeared! Damnedest thing I ever saw,' said Stoat, running through the film again. 'Both of them? Looked like they just sort of melted together, then disappeared!' His suntan was fading.

Behind him a pair of code clerks were arguing. 'Well, all I can say is, I read the same story under a different title when it first came out. *Lion Oil*, it was called, and I say it was a lot of poop.'

'God, it's Galt again. He's been signalling every two minutes, all damned day. Then he'll say he wants a bedpan, and as soon as I get him on it, "Never mind." I'm tired.'

'Maybe he's got a crush on you.'

'Probably. He doesn't know I'm married, because I can't find my name badge. I thought I had it in my pocket – here it is . . . there. "Mrs E. Bland." Maybe *next* time he starts ogling me while I'm feeding him his pablum or putting him on the pan, maybe *next* time he'll take the *hint*.'

'But you're not actually physicians?' The chief surgeon smiled. 'Well, then, I'm afraid I couldn't allow . . .'

Freag spoke in a tone of kindly menace. 'Don't be a dumb shit!' he said quietly. 'All we want to do is get the body *first*. Warm, if possible. As for medical doctors – well, we can *buy* a couple of hundred or so, over and above the hundred we have running around the lab right now.'

'That's right,' said Dr Logan, who breathed with increasing difficulty. 'Who believes in *symptomatic* medicine, anyway?'

Seeing the surgeon stiffen as if taken by a total body erection, Freag turned savagely on his colleague. 'For Christ's sake, Logan, shut up! Don't listen to him, Doctor, he's a Zen macrobiotics nut. Brilliant innovator with cars, knows nothing about the – ahem – life sciences.

'But let me just say this, doctor to doctor. Do us a little

favour. Fix up all the waivers, papers, etc, then just shoot the body over to us in dry ice. You won't regret it, I promise you.'

'Well, I don't know. Professional favours, yes, but you three gentlemen are not exactly in the profess . . .'

'Well, we've got a dying heart patient over there at Drum Labs, that's all I know! This isn't a matter of professional favours!'

The surgeon looked shaken. 'Dying? But this "donor" isn't critical, you know. You may never get a heart from *him.* Unless you count on something like his "accident-proneness" to knock him off. And where could he be better protected against accidents than right here?'

'We'll take that chance. If I know Galt, he'll probably fall out of bed on his head or something. Could happen any day.'

Logan erupted in a sudden coughing fit. The surgeon drew back, while Ortiz patted the brilliant innovator on the back. Dabbing at blood-flecks on his lips, Logan whispered, 'Yes, Galt is very Yin, very Yin. Needs a proper diet: whole-grain cereals and very little liquid.'

A professional cast came into the chief surgeon's eye. 'I believe you're haemorrhaging; better step down to the emergency ward and have someone take a look.'

He made a move as if to support his arm, but Logan drew back quickly. 'Keep your symptomatic hands off! I know what the hell's wrong with me! Too much centripetal downward force – I'm overloaded with salads and Vitamin C.'

'Doctor, come quickly!' Nurse Bland came pounding down the stairs, looking radiant. 'It's Mr Galt! He . . .'

Ortiz, Logan and Freag shoved past her and ran up the stairs.

'Good idea,' whispered Born to his subordinates, as the three of them marched down the aisle between beds.

'Eh?'

'Putting on our lab coats, posing as staff. See Galt anywhere?'

Stoneweg shook his head. 'How about behind that screen?'

'Yes . . . Ah, Mr Galt. How are we feeling this morning?'

The patient did not reply.

'Now, young man, we're just going to run a few tests, a few routine – my bag, Gibbel. Not that one, that's the dry ice.'

Born drew a stethoscope from the proper bag. He took it in both hands, holding the rubber tubing like a garotte, and approached the bed.

Stoneweg, who had been leaning over the patient, exclaimed, 'The son of a bitch's croaked already!'

'What?'

'Must've just done it, sliced his neck on this glass tube. Still warm.'

'Excellent. Boys, I think we're the first to find the body. Now get busy with that scalpel, Duane.'

Dr Stoneweg, who had once had training as a mortuary assistant, began pulling on a pair of rubber gloves. Born seized his arm. 'For Christ's sake, we're not washing dishes on television. Just grab the ticker and let's move out!'

Stoneweg took up a likely-looking knife, bared the patient's chest, and paused.

'What's wrong?'

'Nothing. But I – uh – hardly know where to start. I'm not very good at this. I guess. In fact, at Sunday dinners, my wife won't even let me . . .'

'Will-you-hurry-up?'

Stoneweg plunged in then, and in a few minutes was elevating the organ of emotion over the bag of dry ice. Freag's hand, then his menacing smile, came around the screen. 'I'll take that, gentlemen. Thank you.'

'Like hell!' Gibbel slashed at his face with a scalpel, nicking Freag's chin.

'So that's the way you want it?' Freag flung a loaded urine flask at him, then grabbed another weapon from the medical bag and went into a fighter's crouch. 'All right, baby, if that's how you want it, baby, come and get it, baby, anytime, come on, it's waiting for you, baby, if that's . . .'

Born kicked the screen over on him. Ortiz swung a wooden crutch and caught Born behind the ear. Stoneweg kicked Ortiz in the stomach. Logan leaped in the air and threw out one hand in a karate manoeuvre that knocked Stoneweg to his knees and sent the heart skidding under a bed. Gibbel carved the air and cursed, waiting for Freag to work his way out from under the screen. Logan went diving after the heart. Ortiz revolved the crutch again, slamming Born in the side of the head, breaking his upper plate. And so on.

DRUM PLANS SPLICE WITH BELL

DRUM-LION OIL MERGER?

BELL TO TAKE OVER DRUM INC

LION OIL TO ACQUIRE DRUM

BELL WILL ADD LION OIL

DRUM TO GET IN OIL

When Miss Bunne had cleared out the pile of rags from Travers's office, she shovelled it on to the slot in the wall which led to the incinerator in the sub-basement. Winded, she sat down for a moment and fussed with her hair.

In so doing, her sleeve slipped back, and she read the retirement date stencilled on her arm.

'Whew! No wonder I'm tired. I almost forgot.' She rang for Miss Bunne.

'It's about my retirement, Miss Bunne,' she said, 'due yesterday.'

'Lucky you!' They exchanged smiles. 'Well, now, what do you have? Any keys, company property?'

'It's all right here, Miss Bunne,' Miss Bunne said, indicating the neat pile on the desk.

'That about does it, then.' Miss Bunne stepped up to her, took her arm and read the date.

'Wish my replacement luck.'

'I will. Have a good time, now.' Miss Bunne removed the staples holding the arm in place, flattened it, and pushed it in the incinerator slot. She did the same with the other arm, the other arm of Miss Bunne, then the rest.

When she had finished and tidied up, she was winded.

'Can it be?' she wondered aloud, and rolled back her sleeve. It was. She rang for Miss Bunne.

'Phase One begins as soon as Kravon gets his new heart,' Max explained to the polished shoe of Mr Murd. 'He will feed the pigeons in the park. A "policeman" (really one of us) will accuse him of molesting the pigeons and "arrest" him.

'This is a signal to the watchers on the rooftops, who will immediately lower a basket of deadly snakes to the pavement. This should divert a lot of police and firemen to the vicinity of Breughel Street, and if it doesn't, our arson squad stands ready at the fireworks dealer *here*.'

He indicated a point on the map, hoping that Mr Murd did not notice how his forefinger was getting light in patches. *That Argentine body paint guy saw me coming*, he thought. *A 'two-year guarantee'. Ha.*

'Of course, Kravon will have slipped a few homing pigeons in among the others, and poisoned them. During the ruckus they take off, headed for *here*. But, depending on how much poison each one gets, they should drop anywhere from *here* to *here*.

'The messages they carry are of course fakes, dummies to draw off the police and National Guard to this nearby ghetto, where they believe a riot is imminent. To convince them, we have Phil Wang right *here* in a tree, armed with a rifle. He'll start picking off cops when the first bird has fallen. The *real* message will be indicated by the spacing of the fallen birds along this line from *here* to *here*, and we have briefed our department-store "pickets" on this. They are to seal off the entrances, preventing the re-emergence of all telephone company operators who have gone shopping on their lunch hour. The "pickets" are equipped with Mace.'

He paused, momentarily fascinated by his own reflection in the dark surface of the shoe. A distant telephone rang. *I am peeling. Jesus, how to explain this?*

'At that point the systematic exchange-jamming begins. Our 1000 agents in various parts of the city will each start dialling one number of this exchange, and continue dialling it throughout Phase One.

'Here Able Company goes in to the main entrance of the telephone company building. They smash the displays of new Princess telephones in several exciting colours, and they bayonet all the pretty receptionists. The main objective is to block all the stairs and elevators, and Dog company, disguised as a telephone company bowling team, will stand by to come in and help. I don't see why we shouldn't rely on a few pounds of plastic explosives here, do you? Think it might hurt our image?'

The shoe said nothing, and the sock above it looked bored.

'Now our anarchists start something *here* at the corner of Breughel and Nixon,' he went on anxiously. 'Our "kids" will be playing over here, hopscotch and the like, but actually chalking the location of buried manholes. Our "American Legion" will get in a fight with our anarchists, and our "National Guard" will move in to break it up, using flamethrowers. They may actually fry a few for effect, but – now get this – they will in reality be melting the asphalt at the chalked spots! If they can start another fire, too, so much the better.

'Well, from there on, it's 1-2-3. With all the deadly snakes and firehose around, nobody's going to notice a few yards of telephone cable being pulled up. We just wind it up on the reel of a firetruck and drive away.'

A large flake of black fell from his face. The good-luck scars were beginning to look like sabre scars. Max excused himself and fled before Mr Murd could say anything sarcastic.

SPECIAL DETAIL 1A4A-000·9/Blue: PRIORITY 1a CONFIDENTIAL LIST SUSPECTED WORDS GRP 3:

communal
communal property
communalism
communalist
communalistic
communalize
communally
communard
commune w/spirits
commune
communicable
communicability
communicability of disease
communicably
communicant
communicate
communicate emotion
communicate info
communication
communication network
communicative
communicator
communicatory
communion, holy
communion of saints
communiqué
communism
communist
communitas
communitarian
community

'I want facts!' Heiliger shouted, or so the sub-title said he shouted. 'I want statistics, flow diagrams, charts, programmes, bulletins, brochures, illustrated parts breakdowns, graphs, lists, instructions, memoranda, encyclicals, equations, probabilities, waybills, forms, registers, catalogues, time tickets . . .'

The doctors looked at one another. There were seven, though each saw six.

'But you've seen with your own eyes . . .'

'Nothing! Nothing to the nothingth power. Tricks, demonstrations. I want *data*, gentlemen. Where are your *data*?'

Here David interrupted the general and seven doctors, saying:

'Know ye not it is written: "Unto whom all hearts be open, all desires known, and from whom no secrets are hid." Know ye not even that?' And they were confounded.

But who will help me turn the pages of the giant book? Not the giant book that I am in and you are in, but a lesser giant book. We are making the titles today, for this is the proverbial 'book of the movie'.

I opened David's eyes and sat up on the tablet.

'. . . refrangible . . .'

'The Sinister Bean', I read. The players were King Real and his three daughters: Girl One, Range and Code Liar. Exit all. This may be the shortest play in my long and successful career.

Just for laughs I balled up the general, doctors, lab and all – the whole newspaper it was in – and set fire to it. But that would only be in first 'world-set', A. There would have to be a B where the paper was printed, where I sat in a dirty lab burning it. One may posit a further – B where I unburn the paper, unwrinkle it, and read. There might also be world-sets where the paper reads me, or where the paper and I read each other. Each of these has obvious extensions, and the whole set would make a nice matrix for General Heiliger.

I handed it to him and he said, 'A code?'

'And of course then it was a code. We spent the rest of the time before the commercial doodling word games,' the next David explained. In the beginning was the Word Game (Even in Eden in Eve) and then the War Game (Who will ever remember how Hayhanen fingered Abel; Hayhanen of the simple, unbreakable cipher: a substitution followed by two transpositions), and so on through Gematria (the angel guarding the seventieth quinary is IBM) and the wary games of Lewis Carroll (Charles Lutwidge Dodgson = Gorged on a chi[l]d's lewd lust).

'Break this code,' I defined, 'and you break it all.'

But how did they get into and out of the room? I posited a

projectionist turning off the film long enough for them to slip off-screen, then someone to authorize this, and so on, I was off again. That's what happens when your imagination can't work up even a sinister bean.

Stoat addressed the CIA stockholders.

'It's the Hawthorne experiment all over again,' he said, switching on the projector. 'This is the factory of Western Electric (suppliers to the Bell System) at Hawthorne, Connecticut. When workers were isolated as an experimental group, cut off from ordinary supervision, their output went up – no matter what other changes were made in their environment.

'Drum Inc. is trying something similar, isolating workers not only from job supervision, but from the *supervision of reality*. There is something shady about the entire company – shady in the sense of insubstantial – not to mention the Lion Oil Company, which I suspect to be a mapping on to the surface of reality of the wholly abstract Drum corporation.

'Now this is a map of Connecticut. Notice how the name of the state has been slightly disjointed, thus:

CONNECT I CUT

And this is a picture of Nathaniel Hawthorne (1804-1864), whose ancestor hanged nineteen women in one witchcraft trial. He remained a recluse for most of his life, and my hypothesis is that during that time he did not in fact exist. In evidence I submit the work of Dr Stoneweg on the curious absence of grocery bills during that period.

'Hawthorne was obsessed with the notion of disappearance. In his story "Wakefield" he tells of a man who kisses his wife goodbye one day, moves to a place a few dozen yards away, and there remains in hiding for twenty years, watching his own house. In another story, he says:

> The heart, the heart – there was the little boundless sphere wherein existed the original wrong of which the crime and misery of this outward world were merely types. Purify that inward sphere, and the many shapes of evil that haunt the outward, and which now seem our only realities, will turn to shadowy phantoms and vanish of their own accord.

'We of course are far from these "realities" of which he speaks. We sit or stand here in this expensively furnished room, having enjoyed perhaps our good meal at the state's expense in the cafeteria downstairs, moderately well-dressed and enjoying the comfort of a good pipe.'

Here Stoat took out his wooden gun and mimed with it the gestures of satisfied pipe-smoking. Those who had them took out their own pipes and held them aloft, feeling perhaps that they were voting on reality.

'But all of this *real* reality is in danger! The words "connect", "I" and "cut" move even further apart. Drum Inc. is performing an experiment on a "David" – and on us! Maybe it is only a dexterity experiment – maybe it is something far more sinister. The election of a movie star to the office of governor of California (there is a Hawthorne there, too, and not far from Watts) already shows how easy it is to map one reality on to another. Life is a picture magazine, Time is a montage of weekly news, Space is where men become stars, while Reality is where "stars" take the place of men.

'I have seen a certain incredible film of my own wife, cinema verité . . . newsreals . . . excuse me, I . . . TV dinners . . . pain in the South . . . sensory deprivation experiments . . reality too is an experi . . . but why . . . they must understand . . . some things better left in the hands of the government . . .'

He moved into the beam of the projector. It lined him with

a map of Connecticut, and gave him West Hartford as a third eye, while he moved his hands and mouth earnestly, and talked on and on.

'Where the hell is it?'

'Talk, Logan, or we'll beat the living cancer out of you.'

'Yang,' Logan coughed. 'Lung cancer, very Yang. As for your heart . . .' He glanced towards the open window.

'No!' The others fought for a place to see out, down.

'Where is it? See anything?'

'There's a big Alsatian down there – burying something!'

Born, Stoneweg and Gibbel rushed from the ward, but, at a wink from Logan, his two friends remained.

'You didn't throw it out?'

'I threw out a worthless lymph gland, to attract that dog I happened to notice on the lawn. It had just been eating at a garbage can, therefore I deduced it would retrieve the gland and *bury* it – as in fact happened.'

'But how did you know it would notice the gland at all?'

'I have made a study of all breeds of dogs and their peculiar eating habits. The Alsatian is, above all others, fond of "sweetbreads". It would have greatly surprised me had he *not* seized upon it.'

Logan lit a perhaps opiated cigarette and feigned *ennui*.

'But the heart?'

'I held it in my hand and nodded towards the window. My hand of course concealed it in the ample folds of my lab gown. It was simple mis-direction – an old conjurer's trick.'

'And then?'

'Then I deposited the heart where I was sure *no one* would think to look for it – not if they dig up the *entire* lawn around the building. In *the most obvious place* of all, paradoxically *the most well-concealed*.' The others seemed mystified, so he added, 'Look in Raymond Galt's chest, why don't you?'

*

Having drawn their weapons from the small-arms pool, the employees were assembled in the cafeteria to be briefed.

'This is it, men and women,' said Max Heiliger, whose face and hands were swathed in white bandages. He unveiled the battle plan amid mild applause.

'Hey, that looks like a pair of somebody's pants!'

Max turned to give the employee a look. 'That looks nothing like a pair of pants. It's a battle plan. Anyone who refers to Mr Murd's pants, or to anyone else's pants, will lose all candy and ice cream and cigarette privileges until further notice. Is that clear?' He then turned his attention to the plan, which was a pair of Mr Murd's enormous pants. He outlined his plan for Phase Three, reading off the creases in the seat.

'Our objective today is the telephone cable running from Stoneweg Street down 14th Avenue past the D—— Hotel, across Panavision Street and terminating at the Robert Hall Store on the corner of Reagan and Avenue of the Playmates of the Month. Write down all those addresses and *get them right* – we don't want anyone wandering around asking cops directions at the last moment. Any questions?'

'Yes, sir. Why is this *particular* cable important?'

General Heiliger froze with his back to the audience, his elegant baton pointing to the Robert Hall crease. How could he begin to tell them? Robert Hall, mass-manufactured suits . . . look-alike clothes, uniforms . . . effective identification of friend and foe . . . disruption of all vital mass-consumption products, Howard Johnson restaurants, A & P essential . . . essentially a matter of molecular rearrangement of 'society' . . . finding new isomers . . . people of gold, perhaps . . . purple of gold . . .

He cleared his throat and turned to them. The black splendour of his SS uniform contrasted with white bandages would give them confidence, he knew . . . secret of newspaper success . . .

'All cable is important, son,' he said. 'Any more questions?'

*

MEMORANDUM

From the desk of Gen Max Heiliger (Ret)
To: H. H. Murd

The interesting thing about Phil Wang, about using him as a sniper, is that he's had experience. Despite his Chinese (?) name, Phil is Japanese, and served in the Imperial Army.

This memo cancels and supersedes all other memos on the subject.

Regards,
Max

Wearing a peaked Imperial Army cap (bought from a war souvenir store), very large black-rimmed glasses (boutique) and artificial enormous buck teeth (novelty shop), Phil settled himself high in an elm at the corner of Nixon Ave and Chas Whitman Street. He picked off one cop before he'd even had time to adjust the sight for windage; maybe it was luck.

When he'd disposed of a half-dozen more, Phil took off the cap and ran his fingers around the inside, looking for the name. There it was, the ideograms faded but still legible: 'the armour-maker from the armour-making land'.

Too cumbersome a translation. While he holed a few more badges, he tried cleaning it up: 'The armour-maker from Armorica.' The National Guard arrived; he picked off a dozen while they messed around trying to park their jeeps and trucks in a pattern.

As a professional, he appreciated the shiny new intricate weapons, the nylon bulletproof vests, the teargas – but pitied them for not realizing that he was The Indestructible Jap. Wiped out in a library of war comics, he came to life in ten libraries more, to taunt them:

'What the matter, Yankee dog? No gut, Joe?'

They milled around uncertainly, looking as if they wanted

to give up and go back to their homeland across the tracks. He even tried sticking his face out in the open and giving them an evil grin, but – nothing.

Well screw 'em, he'd commit honourable suicide; the Indestructible Jap always had that way out of the last panel. He bared a foot and clamped the false buck teeth around the gun muzzle. Fugg 'em. None of these kids remembered Bataan or Corregidor any more; they all thought Japan was where diminutive people played baseball and made transistor radios. Fugg that.

'Get set, armour-maker from Armorica,' he mumbled, working his big toe inside the trigger guard. 'I'm gonna make a hole in your cap.' But who was the guy? He wanted to think of a good translation of the name first.

A Guardsman spoke to him through a faulty loudhailer: 'You need helpEEEEEEE. Throw down your WHEEEE and we will help you. We'veEEEEAWWWrounded. Do you understand? WHOOP!'

As he pulled the trigger, he came up with a good enough translation of the name in the cap:
From Armorica = From Normandy = *Norman*
Armour-maker = *Mailer*

The thought, along with the old cap, flew up to the topmost leaves of the elm.

MEMORANDUM

From the desk of Gen Max Heiliger (Ret)
To: H. H. Murd

There have been rumours circulating about the nationality hence loyalty of Phil Wang, so I may as well clear them up now: He is a loyal American citizen of Chinese extraction, born and brought up in the Midwest. He is also a former comic book illustrator, and indeed won a Croix des Filles de Revolution d'Amerique for his war comic, 'Guts of Glory'. That should straighten out any misunderstanding.

This memo cancels and supersedes all other memos on the subject.

Regards,
Max

A MENTAL NOTE

This is a rash and ill-considered business. Do we *know* Mrs Rockefeller smoked Camels in her monoplane (*New Yorker*, April 17, 1937)? Over which state? Whence coming, whither bound?

Let X define that term the *goal of A*. Then let Y be a terrible crime against all peace-loving people of the world. A is the state of A (plus its environment), being the foliage nearby a nearby tree, when two keen eyes watch the withering away of this state. Y is the Corinthian Room of any Hotel Pierre (its environment). Now X is representable by co-ordinates X and Y in an abstract state. Now Y is a parameter representing all peace-loving people of the state. The word *paowa* means literally some constant X representing the forgiveness of all innocent people who love peace. That rash and ill-considered young man has the Volkbein arms, but I hope that all *paowa* people will smoke Camels.

This fine-looking young instrument implies a world error of prediction and its environment, yet this is a strange and terrible business at the Y. I know personally the average of A, or change in this inhuman thing.

I hope all business people will see it in their hearts to forgive me for this crime, which I see in my heart was a crime against all people of the Hotel Pierre. The fine-looking young man of the Camel arms – gave birth?

They are of Y, the people of great length and military

beaùty. That belongs to the co-ordinates of soul and office, Miss Bunne, yours of the history.

H. H. Murd

'So it was *you* who called me all those times!' Marilyn said with a laugh. 'I wondered who it was.'

'I thought you knew my voice,' said the other woman. 'But now that you know who it was, you know who loves you, too.'

'Of course! Oh, this calls for a drink! Joe, would you bring us two invoices, plenty of ice?'

Stoat got them all together in the drawing room for a showdown. There were maps all over his face and clothes, and he did not in general look well.

'Averaging all the worth-situations as main-part factors,' he said, 'the arrival at an approximation of the practical value (or value-set) for any projected application can be implemented in such cases where extrinsic worth-situations are assumed intrinsic. Otherwise, Heiliger's Law applies.

'Eric could not have arrived at the scene of the real crime until *at least nine-thirty*, by the clock in the hall. Since Murd had set this clock forward ten minutes at ten minutes before the other butler lit the fire, the body (which was cold) would have had to be lying before the fire *before* Marilyn phoned David. In other words, *whoever* came from the library into here, out through the dining room and up the back stairs to change and come down the front way again, looking as if they had just got up to see if that was a gunshot, that person would have thought the real time was *nine-twenty*. But at nine-twenty, Max here was out front, shovelling snow and unwittingly clearing away the *first* set of footprints, the footprints of . . .'

'Oh God, I can't stand it!' Marilyn cried, and ran to bury her mutilated face in the comforting padded shoulder of Mr

Murd. Stoat, smiling dangerously, ground on towards the inevitable conclusion.

'The clock was fast; the hands pointed to nine. The dog pointed to something frozen fast in the snow – a hand. As Phil pointed out, he was fast asleep. On the other hand, Murd moved fast. The hour was at hand. At this point, Eric gave Max a hand with his fast car, which needed a new set of points. David showed his hand a little too soon, and Anne, we know, was in fast company. Kravon pointed to a portrait by a false hand, a second-hand copy that still had its points. The point is . . .'

'I confess,' said the bandaged man, taking out a peculiar little gun.

'Too late,' Stoat reproached him. 'I resume: Leprosy struck. The hour struck. The workers at the plant struck. A match was struck. I struck up a new acquaintance. Lightning struck the lightning rod. And so on.'

'You have nothing on me,' Freag sneered.

'Max discovered he was white, an ex-Nazi from Argentina, with amnesia – and he knew Marilyn, despite her sympathetic birthmark, was an Israeli spy!

'Murd, seeing the game was up, took the deathkit from his hollow heel and used it – but was it on himself? Kravon, posing as the other butler, came in to light the fire – really to get close enough to Anne to do what he had to do, what he had been plotting all those years in stir!

'Phil, having thought for years he was of the royal house of Thailand, discovered that he had been changed in the cradle for Eric! Almost too late, Phil learned that Marilyn was his cousin!

'At this point, the lights went out. David found himself not down in the lab at all, but somewhere in the mob on Breughel Street. Eric, thinking he was in the library, took down a book – it was a brick from the lab wall! He felt a stealthy step behind him, turned and struck out! Is it really necessary to describe the president, Hernando Horario Murd? Expiring in the flame-thrower's flames, David steadfastly refused to name the noble-woman who had betrayed him to the National Guard. Travers promised himself – one more interview, and he would have enough to retire – just one more big one. "Good God!" Eric realized what Freag and Logan had been creating all those months, down in that infernal laboratory. David, expiring, offered a prayer for the transmission of sins. Marilyn, locked in a creaking tower of the old self, suddenly turned and ran for her life! The lights went out again.'

The lights went out again, and when they came on, Stoat lay in a pool of ink. Eric had vanished. Marilyn, without her birthmark, was nowhere to be seen.

'This is just the way poor Marty got it,' Max said, sipping the tea that contained he knew not what. The figure of Connecticut on the floor groaned and moved. Everyone filed out.

The figure on the floor raised itself on one peninsula and spoke: 'It's what I've been trying and trying to get through to all of you; the murderer is . . .'

And making a vague gesture that took in everything, it fell back.

MARILYN MEETS MYSTERIOUS CALLER – SELF!

Girl with miraculous vanishing birthmark does it again

KRAVON TO DRIVE 'BAD-LUCK' LOTUS IN INDY 500

'I've found new heart,' he quips

EX-NAZI NAMED HEAD OF SOUTH AFRICAN MILITARY

Peculiar pigmentation causes scowls in Johannesburg

★

Eric, who called himself 'David' these days, sat in the Automat over a cup of black coffee, wondering if that girl over there with the thirty-one perfect freckles would like a date with him. He didn't suppose so, but you never knew . . .

Marilyn sat in the Automat eating pale jello, wondering if Eric was ever going to get up and come over and speak to her, or what. Why didn't he screw up his courage? The way he had screwed up their lives?

She could hardly keep this up. Seven dishes of jello so far, and no action. Was this the Eric of seaside newspaper days? Maybe he didn't recognize her since 'Mother-Scrubber', with its deep-down cleansing action, had removed the hidden dirt and the clearly exposed dirt from her face. Well, here goes jello number eight.

She sure liked jello, Eric noted admiringly. Reminded him of a girl he once knew. That was a good opening line:

'Excuse me, miss, but you sure seem to like jello. Reminds me . . .'

Something else drew his attention. A peculiar man was standing in the line at the cashier's window. He was tall, rather stiff, and amazingly symmetrical, and he seemed to be wearing a toupee.

'Ten dollars?' the cashier said. '*All* change?'

'. . . yes . . . please . . .' The man spoke faintly in a tinny voice. When the change was finally before him, he removed his hat, bent from the hips, and scooped in all the coins in one movement.

As the man turned from the window, Eric noticed again how symmetrical his features were: two perfect halves, with a thin scar or seam running down the middle. He glided without hesitation to the section marked PIES. Eric, along with a few others, craned his neck to watch.

Inserting a coin next to 'lemon meringue', the man twisted

the knob. The window popped open. Instead of removing the pie, he reached in a fist and smashed it, smearing it well around in its stainless steel box. Then he repeated this performance at the next window down, and the next.

After finishing the 'lemon meringue' column, he moved one step to the left and began on 'apple'. Other customers froze, looking from the columns of windows smeared with broken pastry to the man's constantly-moving left hand, which became in turn covered with apple, peach, cherry and berry syrup, custard, whipped cream, and gouts of pumpkin.

'Hey!'

'Hey, what the hell here! Dis pie's all crumpled up!'

'Him, he's the guy. Hey, Mr Rich Man! You don't care if anybody else wants ta eat?'

A manager bustled over. 'What's going on here? You can't do *that*!'

The stranger said nothing, and the manager too was frozen, hypnotized by the combination of violent action and serene, even indifferent expression.

'What's the matter?' he asked again, baffled and afraid. 'You don't like pie or something?'

Having finished the PIES section, the odd man seized a handful of paper napkins and began wiping off his fingers, one by one. '. . . yes . . .' he said, '. . . like . . . pies . . . very . . . much . . .' Then he headed for the section marked BEVERAGES. Soon the spouts of 'Coffee', 'Coffee with Cream', 'Coffee with Extra Cream', 'Tea' and 'Hot Chocolate' were gushing beverages enough to overflow their respective drains, cover the counter top, and drizzle from the edge. The stranger continued to plug in nickels and pull cranks, standing in a puddle of mixed beverages.

Eric looked around to see if the freckled girl were sharing this experience with him. She was gone, and a busboy in white was hurrying to remove all trace of her existence.

★

Well, to sum up: I opened my eyes, etc, etc, and then the last doctor wanted to leave the room. In pity, I created an 'outside', reducing the thickness of the walls from infinity to just 'thick', and making part of one wall movable. I made a kind of 'hole' that could be opened or closed. On the 'other' side of it, I lettered:

DRUM INC.
RESTRICTED AREA
NO VISITORS

Then he 'opened' it and went 'out'.

A cop in crash helmet and other cop togs came into the Automat. Someone pointed out the peculiar man, and the cop went over to teach him a lesson. People speculated about it over the clatter of dishes and the metronomic beat of the billy.

'Too much book if you ask me. Too much book.'

The cop sat down afterwards for a coffee and donut. When he had finished, someone pointed out Eric. So the cop came over and taught Eric a lesson, too.

Marilyn noticed she was headed for the river. People, scraps of newspaper flew by her:

GOD TAKES BRIBE
'. . . suit becomes him . . .'
'He sat up on the . . .'
US TO TEST 'SUN BOMB'

She had known her boyfriend since they were both eighteen. They were now twenty. They had always had a stormy relationship – one minute very happy together, the next arguing and miserable. Sometimes he'd say they would get married soon, and then he'd say he was ambitious, and marriage was impossible for at least five years. She'd suggested they part, but he didn't want that. Now her belly was heavy, painfully swollen with jello, and she felt so unhappy and discontented. What do you advise?

THE WORLD'S GREATEST SCIENCE FICTION AUTHORS
NOW AVAILABLE IN PANTHER SCIENCE FICTION

Frederick Pohl

The Man Who Ate the World	£1.25	☐
Survival Kit	£1.25	☐
Drunkard's Walk	£1.25	☐
Man Plus	£1.25	☐
The Age of the Pussyfoot	£1.25	☐
Jem	£1.50	☐
The Gold at the Starbow's End	40p	☐

Harlan Ellison

The Time of the Eye	£1.25	☐
All the Sounds of Fear	£1.25	☐

Jack Vance

Trullion: Alastor 2262	85p	☐
Fantasms and Magics	75p	☐
Servants of the Wankh	40p	☐
The Houses of Iszm	65p	☐
The Languages of Pao	65p	☐
Son of the Tree	65p	☐
The Five Gold Bands	95p	☐
The Blue World	60p	☐
The Pnume	50p	☐

Chelsea Quinn Yarbro

False Dawn	£1.50	☐

SF881

THE WORLD'S GREATEST SCIENCE FICTION AUTHORS
NOW AVAILABLE IN PANTHER SCIENCE FICTION

Poul Anderson

The Corridors of Time	50p	☐
Trader to the Stars	95p	☐
After Doomsday	50p	☐
Conquests	£1.50	☐

A E van Vogt

The Undercover Aliens	95p	☐
Rogue Ship	95p	☐
The Mind Cage	75p	☐
Moonbeast	85p	☐
The Voyage of the Space Beagle	75p	☐
The Book of Ptath	75p	☐
The War Against the Rull	70p	☐
Away and Beyond	75p	☐
Destination Universe!	95p	☐
Planets for Sale	85p	☐

SF381

THE WORLD'S GREATEST SCIENCE FICTION AUTHORS NOW AVAILABLE IN PANTHER SCIENCE FICTION

Robert Silverberg

Earth's Other Shadow	75p	☐
The World Inside	75p	☐
Tower of Glass	60p	☐
Recalled to Life	95p	☐
Invaders from Earth	80p	☐
Master of Life and Death	75p	☐

J G Ballard

The Crystal World	75p	☐
The Drought	80p	☐
The Disaster Area	95p	☐
Crash	95p	☐
Low-Flying Aircraft	75p	☐
The Atrocity Exhibition	85p	☐
The Venus Hunters	95p	☐
The Unlimited Dream Company	£1.25	☐

SF581

THE WORLD'S GREATEST SCIENCE FICTION AUTHORS
NOW AVAILABLE IN PANTHER SCIENCE FICTION

Ursula K LeGuin

The Dispossessed	£1.50	☐
The Lathe of Heaven	£1.25	☐
City of Illusions	£1.25	☐
The Word for World is Forest	95p	☐
Malafrena	£1.50	☐
Short Stories		
Orsinian Tales	75p	☐
The Wind's Twelve Quarters (Volume 1)	£1.25	☐
The Wind's Twelve Quarters (Volume 2)	£1.25	☐

Ursula K LeGuin and Others

The Eye of the Heron	£1.25	☐

Ian Watson

The Very Slow Time Machine	£1.25	☐
The Embedding	£1.25	☐
Miracle Visitors	£1.00	☐
Alien Embassy	£1.25	☐
The Jonah Kit	95p	☐
The Martian Inca	75p	☐

SF481

THE WORLD'S GREATEST SCIENCE FICTION AUTHORS
NOW AVAILABLE IN PANTHER SCIENCE FICTION

Philip José Farmer

The Riverworld Saga

To Your Scattered Bodies Go	£1.25	☐
The Fabulous Riverboat	£1.50	☐
The Dark Design	£1.95	☐
The Magic Labyrinth	£1.95	☐

Other Titles

Riverworld and other stories	£1.50	☐
The Stone God Awakens	80p	☐
Time's Last Gift	85p	☐
Traitor to the Living	85p	☐

All these books are available at your local bookshop or newsagent, or can be ordered direct from the publisher. Just tick the titles you want and fill in the form below.

Name ____________________

Address ____________________

____

Write to Granada Cash Sales
PO Box 11, Falmouth, Cornwall TR10 9EN.

Please enclose remittance to the value of the cover price plus:

UK 45p for the first book, 20p for the second book plus 14p per copy for each additional book ordered to a maximum charge of £1.63.

BFPO and Eire 45p for the first book, 20p for the second book plus 14p per copy for the next 7 books, thereafter 8p per book.

Overseas 75p for the first book and 21p for each additional book.

Granada Publishing reserve the right to show new retail prices on covers, which may differ from those previously advertised in the text or elsewhere.

SF281